# Bitcheye Commando

*To Scotty*
*From one Vet to another*
*Thank you,*

by

Steve Joyner

PublishAmerica
Baltimore

ISBN: 1-60703-164-7
PUBLISHED BY PUBLISHAMERICA, LLLP
www.publishamerica.com
Baltimore

Printed in the United States of America

# Dedication

This dedication goes to anyone out there who has decided not to give up in spite of overwhelming bleakness and hopelessness. That is the spirit of the Bitcheye Commando. While it is acceptable to abandon a cause or a project, you should never give up on yourself. Barry Manilow said it best when he said that it is okay to give in and it's okay to give out, but it is not okay to give up.

Specifically, I would like to dedicate this book to Sergei Kourdakov. He has been a role model that I wish I remembered more often. He is unknown to most people but I will never forget him.

He, without a doubt, was the strongest man that I have ever met. He was hard from the inside out. No man could ever do what he did. Though he never won any Mr. Olympia contests or ever received any recognition for his strength, he, along with his firm handshake, was perceived by me to have had what it took to take on Arnold Schwarzenegger. If ever they were to have made a movie of him, Arnold Schwarzenegger (at his peak) would have been the perfect person to play the part.

# Acknowledgments

There are several people who have made this work possible. Such people have inspired me to write a novel. There is no way that I could have accomplished the writing of this book without their encouragement.

I would like to thank COL Michael "Dupe" DuPerior (AKA Little Bird) for his encouragement. He stated that if this were to get published it would sell. By sell, he did not commit to how many it would sell, and qualified his statement by saying that he did not mean making the top ten of the *New York Times* bestsellers list.

COL William Renfroe (AKA Big Bird) demonstrated how catchy the term "Bitcheye Commando" could really be. He did offer a lot of encouragement while we were off duty. While I was gearing up for my departure without the presence of Bill, I should've cared less about mission accomplishment. However, I still cared up until the time that I left. I think that Bill would've wanted it that way. While he did have an impact on how missions were accomplished, he also influenced my motivation for completing this novel.

Another voice of encouragement came from COL Marc Hernandez who expressed approval of the introduction and articulated interest in the finished product. I wish that I could state that my support spanned beyond Air Force and Marine colonels and my son Cadet Sean Crossfield Joyner, but it didn't. However, this was enough to motivate me to put the story in print.

# Foreword

This story is fictitious; names have been changed to protect the writer from possible lawsuits for damages resulting from accusations of libel. In the age of political correctness, I am surprised that people continue to write non-fiction. I decided to write fiction for a number of reasons. The problem with non-fiction is that the onus of proving facts falls squarely onto the writer. Many facts are difficult to substantiate. Not only is the writer obligated to support all of his claims, he must also be convincing. This is an arduous task to perform with the availability of documented resources. It is impossible to support any claims that were either a direct experience or occurred off of the record. A lot of people involved would probably prefer to forget certain incidents. Many incident reports were deliberately buried. It is amazing how distorted recorded records really are. Many reports such as news items that proclaim to be factual have been sanitized to the point that they should be classified as fiction. I felt that I would not be able to meet my standards when it came to writing non-fiction. Besides, fiction sells better.

Intentional exaggerations are used to express points that subtle hints fail to deliver. This coupled with imaginary events will definitely qualify this novel as fictitious.

Since this story is based on fact and factual accounts that I lack the imagination of dreaming up, true and actual parallels will exist. This is a record of my accounts in Korea from my point of view. It is here and abruptly, that butter turned into gold. Second Lieutenant bars are gold in color, but they are often referred to as butter bars. In most cases they may as well be butter. There are circumstances when some would wish they were gold. Those days are gone, but may return again in isolated incidents without warning or notice of any kind. Korea was such an incident, one that violated typical standard textbook scenarios with amazing results.

There are two ways of learning: from experience and from the experiences of others. Very few are able to learn from others. For those few, this book is for you. Generally speaking, people are limited by their own experiences, and fail to recognize those of others.

The combat veteran doesn't talk about his experiences with everybody. That's because people just don't understand. They may want to hear about war without actually going there themselves, yet they fail to listen and comprehend that there are differences other than what they can imagine. In most cases, the audience will fail to understand or even listen.

My thesis is that the military is only as good as the people who are in it. How it is supported or not supported will reflect on how objectives are achieved or not achieved. Understand that we do not live in a perfect world and that unforeseen circumstances can catch even the most organized groups off guard. Comparatively speaking, the military is far more organized than other organizations. However, military organizations themselves vary greatly in quality and performance. Recognizing the shortcomings and downfalls is the beginning of correction and heading towards the direction of perfection. Yes, some organizations, military and civilian, have reached and operate on a perfection tempo. That doesn't mean that they are perfect, but when they fall short of perfection they still come very close. The direct path will not get you there, the indirect one will. While that may not sound logical, it is factual nevertheless. The philosophical remark that you can go broke by saving money is hardly understood unless you explore it a lot deeper. Many advertisers will encourage you to buy more products than you need because subsequent products will be offered at a discount. Also they will provide limited offers that must be acted upon without hesitation to provide you with additional discounts. Many offers for saving you money depend upon you spending more of your money. Jumping at these offers will cause you to go broke. Logic doesn't always breed success.

The term Bitcheye Commando originated from summer ROTC (Reserve Officer Training Corps) Camp. It was the best term developed from our platoon. I respect what it stands for. Slogans seemed to be a very big part of the Army during my cadet days. ROTC cadets were always arguing about which slogans were best. We believed in the "Power of the Slogan." Our platoon slogan was, "Third leads the way," although "Third Platoon is good," was a close second. The group name, Bitcheye Commando, lost out to Millersville Liberator, but in my opinion it was too significant to discard. There was a conflict between the Millersville Liberators and the Bitcheye Commandos where the Bitcheyes were forced to stand up to a foe that consisted of the majority. The creed of the ROTC camp as well as the rest of the Army was, "I am woman, hear me roar!" Women's Lib was a strong pillar in the ROTC community. John Wayne and Audie Murphy were replaced by Richard Simmons and Andy Warhol. We also had Helen Reddy and Ralph the Mouth. The Fonz was just too cool for us and we knew it. Even Orville Redenbacher was starting to look like a man's man to us. It was a time of change and transition. For the dinosaurs who refused to die, it was Bitcheye Commando all the way.

I was not about to surrender to the forces of Women's Lib or the likes of Casper Milquetoast. Later on it would be homosexuality. Bitcheye Commando stood for something. It stood for standing your ground even if you had to stand it alone. It meant, seeking reality for what it actually was. It meant having the ability to see the obvious. It meant going against the grain when you were right. A wise man once said that to remain silent when we should protest makes pussies out of us all. Being a Bitcheye meant to continue seeking the answers while the ROTC cadre was doing a great disservice to the cadets. Out of the summer camp, came the one thing that I valued the most: Bitcheye Commando.

# Preface

While the story continuously goes off on tangents and detours, it remains focused. There was no way to include indirect information in a convenient manner. Putting background information tidbits at the end or by themselves in a separate isolated category was even worse than the way it was done. I have included anecdotes and events that may not have occurred in Korea or during the time frame in which the story takes place. A lot of the information is factual and has been included to inform the person who may not have had any previous military exposure. Definitions and information are provided throughout the book to ensure that the reader isn't permanently sidetracked. I have also included some definitions here for your edification.

**Bitcheye** \'bich- \ *n* (pronounced: bitch eye, as in a female dog's eye) **1:** a person who overcomes unfavorable odds in a crisis **2:** someone who goes against the grain The *bitcheye* really surprised everyone when he unexpectedly rescued the child from the burning building. **3:** nonconformity based on moral principle

**Bitcheye Commando** \'bich- ca-man-do\ *n* **1:** a person belonging to the Bitcheye open fraternity **2:** an organization of individuals who are sworn to accomplish a mission in spite of unfavorable odds **Note:** The mission in question may be either official, unofficial, approved, disapproved, unapproved, recognized, unrecognized, or a combination of the mentioned criterion **3:** a conspicuous Bitcheye who sticks to his principles in spite of opposition

**Cassandra** \ke-san dre\ *n* **1:** *Greek Mythology,* a daughter of Priam, the King of Troy, endowed with the gift of prophecy and the ability to accurately foresee the future, but fated by Apollo never to be believed **2:** One that utters unheeded prophecies

**schadenfreude** \shad'n-froi'duh\ *n* malicious delight derived from the misfortunes of others

### Derived from Bugle Notes '99
**lying:** to deliberately deceive another by stating an untruth or by any direct form of communication to include the telling of a partial truth or vague or ambiguous use of information or language with the intent to deceive or mislead

### The Three Rules of Thumb
These rules are intended to assist an individual in exceeding the minimum standards.

1. Does the action attempt to deceive anyone or allow anyone to be deceived?

2. Does this action gain or allow the gain of a privilege or advantage to which I or someone else would not otherwise be entitled?

3. Would I be satisfied by the outcome if I were on the receiving end of this action?

### GENERAL ORDERS
1. I will guard everything within the limits of my post and quit my post only when properly relieved.

2. I will obey my special orders and perform all of my duties in a military manner.

3. I will report all violations of my special orders, emergencies, and everything not covered in my instructions to the commander of my relief.

## EXCERPT FROM SCHOFIELD'S DEFINITION OF DISCIPLINE

He who feels the respect which is due to others cannot fail to inspire in them regard for himself, while he who feels, and hence manifests, disrespect towards others, especially his inferiors, cannot fail to inspire hatred against himself.

"The orient defies logic as it exists without rhyme or reason; one has to actually see it to believe it."—1LT Elwood Taquard

"The wise learn many things from their foes."—Chinese proverb

### The Oath taken upon being commissioned in the Army

"I, (your name), having been appointed an officer in the Army of the United States, as indicated above in the grade of second Lieutenant do solemnly swear (or affirm) that I will support and defend the Constitution of the United States against all enemies, foreign and domestic, that I will bear true faith and allegiance to the same: take this obligation freely, without any mental reservation or purpose of evasion; and that I will well and faithfully discharge the duties of the office which I am about to enter, SO HELP ME GOD."

# Introduction

A lot of acronyms and terminologies that are used throughout the book are militarily based or are the product of a local subculture. The book is written with the assumption that the reader is familiar with such vernacular, yet the assumption is recognized as an unrealistic assumption. I understand that many readers are not familiar with the unique terminologies or their nuances. Most military members today are not familiar with acronyms of events that I have experienced. For example, I ran into an Airborne Ranger who graduated from Ranger school in 1986 who emphatically stated that there was no such thing as a one-eyed alligator at the Ranger school (Florida Phase). I heard stories of Big John the one-eyed alligator while I was at Ranger school. There were different stories circulating about how he actually lost his eye. I heard one about how a private was assigned to a grass cutting detail. He was told to cut the grass, but misunderstood the instructions (very common in the Army) and began cutting the grass inside of the fenced in area. The alligator inside of the fence attacked the private. The private's immediate response was to raise and point the running mower at the charging alligator. When the alligator collided with the running lawn mower the private ran away and the alligator lost an eye. The other story that I heard was that, well actually, there was no other story, but in 1982 people were certain that the lawn mower incident was true. Today Big John is dead (I was told that he died in the year 2000) and has been reduced to nothing more than an urban legend.

I may as well add another urban legend into the fray while I'm at it. In 1982 I saw a white Corvette with a Texas license plate that said RANGER. This is a true story although I wouldn't expect anyone to believe it. In the 1990s my wife and son, who happen to like Corvettes very much and the color white in a car, spotted a white Corvette in Georgia. It had a Texas tag that said RANGER. In 2004 I drove down to Eglin Air Force Base with a Sergeant Major to buy a T-shirt with a one-eyed alligator on it. I didn't have $10 on me to buy one back in 1982. There was a white Corvette in the vicinity. I would have bet a month's pay that the tag on it was from Texas and said RANGER. Not only that, but the RIs vouched for the existence of Big John (although they didn't endorse the story about the lawn mower incident) and the store had T-shirts with his depiction on it. This was not enough to convince other Rangers that such an alligator ever existed. If the Rangers from the 1980s can't be convinced that such an alligator ever existed, then it would be impossible to convince anyone else of anything. I'll say one thing about Ranger school, once you've been through it you never run out of things to say. Most other Rangers agree. With most Rangers, the stories match spot on even if they weren't in the same class. Get two Rangers together and they have something to talk about. I will admit though, the Rangers who denied the possibility that a one-eyed alligator could ever exist didn't have anything to say. I've also met Rangers who said that it didn't get cold in Florida in the winter; they were probably summer students. This is one of the main reasons that I have decided to write in fiction. No amount of facts or proof will ever convince anyone in the Army that events that they weren't a part of ever occurred. Readers may include those who are or were in the Army. Nothing is more frustrating than to try to convince someone of something that is both true and uncommon. Once something is introduced as factual, I get caught up in the endless battle of trying to prove it. This takes forever and evidence is usually ignored. Trying to prove a point distracts from the main purpose. But in fiction, convincing people of anything is not necessary. There are also other advantages in writing in fiction.

When I introduce a place or concept to the reader I am assuming that the reader is not familiar with it. I am also assuming that he will not understand the story without any background knowledge. In most cases, acronyms are spelled out the first time that they are introduced. I am trying to put the reader in the same frame of mind that I was in when I was experiencing these adventures. For this reason I tend to provide background information and explanations. I feel that most of the background information that is provided is interesting, informative, and relevant to the story in some way. It appears that I am going off on a tangent, but don't worry, I'll get you back on track again.

# Author's Notes

This book was written for me. I understood that I would have to conform to the whims of many critics in order to gain any hopes of ever getting this published. I realized that it would be impossible to satisfy even one single critic, let alone a myriad of them. I wrote this book because I wanted to, not because I had to get it published. I wrote it for myself. Even with that in mind, I do hope that others will enjoy reading it as much as I enjoyed writing it.

While writing this book was a lot of fun, it also had its challenges. There were times when I pushed myself to write even when I didn't feel like writing. I didn't usually push myself too hard under those circumstances. I also went back and revised what I had written under the condition of writing when I didn't feel like it.

Once I finished writing the book, I went back and made additional inserts. While I eventually set a deadline for myself, I didn't do so at the expense of the book. The deadline was more of a goal than a landmark. It was flexible. Once I wrote about 200 pages I began to see light at the end of the tunnel.

I also enjoy reading a lot thanks to a book that I read that outlined Evelyn Wood's speed reading methods. The best advice that was offered was to read books about subjects that you enjoy. The books that I enjoy the most are non-fiction.

I am surprised by the amount of garbage that gets published today. It is hard to find interesting books these days, even in renowned and established name-brand book stores. I seriously wonder how some books ever got published in the first place and I never see anyone buy the books in question.

A lot of people aren't familiar with the term, ajossie. It is pronounced (a da she). It is a Korean word identifying a man. It is also a respectful word that has been bastardized by the Army; myself included, and refers to a Korean dirt bag or grease ball. In this book I refer to ajossie in the bastardized version. Orientals are very good at earning one's respect; they are also good at earning one's hate. While they can be extremely generous and kind they can also be the extreme opposite. While I would enjoy visiting the Orient, I would never want to live there again. It is true that American GIs typically bastardize the local vernacular and impose rhetoric when it is unwarranted. This is not only true in Korea but in every foreign country that they go to. This causes clashes to occur during joint operations as well.

While I was considering the writing of this book I consulted a lot of people and also received a lot of unsolicited criticism. Whenever you seek advice, be prepared to get criticism. Criticism is not always bad; some of it was downright helpful. Encouragement also came with criticism. The one thing that became evident to me was the fact that I had to get the book written. Once I started I could consider my work a draft and revise it later. As my good friend Colonel Ronnie Sketo used to say, "We're going to eat this elephant one bite at a time." This is good advice even though he was referring to another issue at the time that he said it.

One principle that has served me well has always been: If you don't have a dog in the fight, don't put a dog in the fight. I need to follow my own advice more often. This is one of the reasons for writing and including this gem in my book.

I have referred to *Wikipedia* very often to confirm dates and information about places. I found it to especially helpful in writing my first chapter: Slaying at Panmunjom. The automatic spell check software that my computer came with was more of a nuisance than a help especially when I utilized vocabulary that wasn't in English and when I wrote dialogues.

The Army claims that it's in the business of saving lives. This is a lie. The people in the Army are in the business of getting promoted even at the expense of others. People in the Army can't handle the truth.

# Chapter One

*Slaying at Panmunjom: Wednesday, 18 August 1976*

Complacency and overconfidence make us all vulnerable to surprise attacks. Although no one ever suspected it at the time, complacency and overconfidence were the main factors to the foundation of a tragedy that resulted in the brutal deaths of two soldiers whose mission was to simply prune a tree. All they had to do was to follow the usual monotonous routine of periodically trimming a tree. The signs of aggression were obvious but went unheeded. Maybe this was the result of performing such a boring task repeatedly in a routine manner. Or maybe it was the result of the Army's traditional state of denial. Either way, going into a Demilitarization Zone (DMZ) unarmed is just plain stupid.

The Army chose to ignore the blatant signals along the DMZ between North and South Korea at a time when hostilities were commonplace. Since hostilities weren't usually reported, everyone assumed that they didn't exist. Those who experienced hostilities first-hand were simply ignored or told to shut up. Those who didn't shut up were made to wish that they did. This was no conciliation for the two men who would suffer the blade of the axe.

The Democratic People's Republic of Korea [DPRK (North Korea)] and the Republic of Korea [ROK (South Korea)] were both created in 1948. The DMZ has been a breeding ground for incidents ever since. On the DMZ, the Joint Security Area (JSA) monitored an insignificant bridge known as the Bridge of No Return. About 100 feet from the bridge was a poplar tree, much like you would find in South Carolina. The tree disrupted the line of sight between a checkpoint (CP), CP 3, which was next to the Bridge of No Return and an Observation Post (OP), OP 5. The Korean People's Army (KPA) from North Korea had repeatedly made egregious attempts to kidnap as many people as they could from CP 3 and drag them across the bridge into North Korean territory. The location of CP 3 made it an obviously vulnerable target of opportunity and was nicknamed "The Loneliest Outpost in the World."

On 18 August 1976, five Koreans with security escorts including the Joint Security Force (JSF) Company Commander, Captain (CPT) Arthur Bonifas, and his South Korean Army counterpart Captain Kim, platoon leader First Lieutenant (1LT) Mark Barrett, and American and South Korean enlisted men, went into the JSA to trim the tree. Both Captains were unarmed. The amount of weapons that the US brought to the DMZ was limited for fear of provoking an incident. The Americans staunchly adhered to this philosophy and insisted that their allies do the same. The logic was that if you went to a gunfight unarmed, the opponent would keep his weapon in check and engage in a harmonious relationship of civil dialogue. This Age of Aquarius logic works extremely well in both movies and cartoons alike. Apparently the North Koreans didn't subscribe to our way of reasoning. Perhaps they didn't watch our TV shows. Maybe somebody forgot to pay the cable bill. Either way, something got lost in translation. One should never assume that just because you do something a certain way or believe in something a certain way that everyone else will too.

After the trimming began, several KPA soldiers arrived on the scene under the command of Senior Lieutenant Pak Chul. He was known throughout the United Nations (UN) community for his lengthy record of instigating confrontations and was affectionately nicknamed "Lieutenant Bulldog." After Pak observed the tree trimming for a while he abruptly broke out in his usual confrontational manner and ordered the ceasing of the tree pruning. CPT Bonifas countered by ordering the detail to continue working. Bonifas then turned his back on Pak and ignored him.

One of Pak's men ran across the bridge followed by a truck loaded with twenty KPA soldiers who disembarked. Pak again demanded that the tree trimming stop. Again, CPT Bonifas turned his back. Pak removed his watch and carefully wrapped it in a handkerchief and placed it in it his pocket. This was a well-recognized gesture that was displayed in approximately the same manner by Ernest Borgnine in the movie *Bad Day at Black Rock* when he challenged Spencer Tracy to a fight. Although this universal preamble to a fight was well known, it was not recognized by CPT Bonifas. In Hangul, Pak shouted, "Kill them!" as he swung a karate chop to the back of CPT Bonifas' neck. The KPA used the axes dropped by the tree trimmers to kill CPT Bonifas and 1LT Barrett. Additionally, all but one member of the tree trimming detail was wounded.

Observers noted that about five members were being forcibly dragged by their heels across the bridge into North Korean territory by the KPA. Then they further observed KPA guards going into a depression for about two minutes, then coming out and handing his axe to another guard who would go down the ravine. A couple of minutes later the round robin process would have another trade off. This went on for about ninety minutes. Although observers could not see inside the depression, a subsequent search team discovered that it was the body of 1LT Barrett that they were mutilating.

President Ford was so upset by the incident that he responded by ordering that the tree that was initially scheduled for pruning would now be cut down completely. By golly, he meant business. He was determined to demonstrate his intolerance of such an intolerable incident. Total retribution would be achieved, and by gum, the president was not about to settle for anything less. The wrath of vengeance was wielded in Operation Paul Bunyan. The KPA watched as the execution of Operation Paul Bunyan was carried out, resulting in the felling of a tree that was initially scheduled for pruning. Operation Paul Bunyan resulted in no casualties and was declared a success.

One lesson that was learned by one person, who was too young to vote for Ford at the time he was defeated by Jimmy Carter, was to never go on the DMZ unarmed and to never turn your back on an armed North Korean who threatens you. It was decided right then and there, though unpredicted, that the only way to deal with the KPA or their supporters was to kill them. When in doubt, kill. Unless it is certain that you can do otherwise, kill. Instead of hesitating, kill. When arriving at the point of uncertainty, kill. When you meet a guy whose name might be Pak, yes, you guessed it, kill.

Instead of killing a tree, BG Taquard thought that they should kill at least three Koreans to even the score.

"Maybe we could show them that we really mean business by putting up a sign that says 'In your ear with a can of beer,'" the general sarcastically remarked.

"Or maybe we could tell them to go sit on it," Elwood added. "That's what the Fonz would do."

Although Taquard appreciated the situation that men are confronted with, he himself was not the type to think about joining the military. He never excelled in school nor emerged as a leader of any group or function. While other locals in his age group were engaged with hunting, fishing, and participating in the Future Farmers of America (FFA) and the Four H (Head, Heart, Hands, Health) Club, Taquard quietly engaged in artwork and collecting things that no one could care less about. Unlike the people of his community, he transferred from another state and was viewed as an outsider. As sad as the affairs of an underachiever may have been perceived, he preferred drawing cartoons and making mobiles to participating in pro-abortion rallies or hanging out at the feed store. Although the community didn't have a lot to offer, they definitely had an established social hierarchy.

There wasn't a lot of ambition on Taquard's part since fitting in was never a priority. And though he was never the type to put on a uniform he couldn't help but think how screwed up the situation on the DMZ was. The question that he pondered was, how do you respond to a situation like that when the country is satisfied with operations like Paul Bunyan? The Koreans didn't have to worry about BG Taquard. However, they would have to contend with Elwood.

# Chapter Two
## *Current Events: Wednesday, 1 September 1976*

Morton Madison conducted his class with an air of professionalism while setting the example of how courses should be managed. He was the latest recipient of the "Teacher of the Year" award at La Grange Parker High School while he was unanimously considered to be the ideal choice. He never had the problem of having a shortage of material to present to his World History or American Problems classes. Rather the opposite was true; he had an overwhelming abundance of material. The challenge was to select the best material while remaining current and conducting continuous research. The fact of the matter was that Madison made history interesting because he enjoyed it so much. Even after teaching for several years, he still couldn't get enough of it. He wasn't the only good teacher in the school, but the bad ones seemed to outnumber the good ones. Not because they weren't good people, but because they were born and raised in the local vicinity like most people in the area. This limited their perspective which limited their teaching ability. Still, Madison was able to entertain his classes with student competition in current events. Today was such a day. Students loved the game as it stressed participation and the opportunity to demonstrate knowledge. Answering questions quickly was as essential to answering accurately.

Madison was mild mannered, yet strict at the same time. He was the type of person that you wouldn't want to mess with because you wouldn't have the desire to, nor would you want to. Some people described him as a south-paw even though he wasn't left-handed. He was the type of person that anyone could whip but could knock your block off. If someone beat him in a fight they wouldn't have anything to brag about but then again, that person may also get beaten to a pulp. That was the mystery about Madison; no one could ever recall him losing a fight even though he looked beatable. He orchestrated his class competitions as if they were highly organized missions. While students were excited, they were under control.

Elwood Taquard had never been on the winning team in the previous Current Events competitions while he was in World History. Bonus questions within questions allowed team members to discuss possible choices before answering. Team One was faced with a bonus question and the possibility of taking the lead, possibly winning the game.

"For 50 points, who was the actor who portrayed Mr. Mooney in the hit TV series *I Love Lucy*, and Mr. Wilson in TV series, *Dennis the Menace?*"

"Wait! I think I know this one," Taquard would interject to the group.

"Those shows aren't current," another student would say.

"Maybe he died or something," another would say.

"Look, I think it's Ross Gordon," Taquard would say to the team captain.

"Okay, if no one else has any ideas. Our answer is Ross Gordon!"

"Gale Gordon," Madison retorted, "no bonus points, but you don't lose any points either."

Team One still had a chance of winning this event with the help of Steve Mumm and his knowledge of sports. In the sports category, he was the class expert. Baseball, basketball, football, he knew them all. With the beginning of a new football season and ten Super Bowls behind, the latest category addressed historical as well as current football trivia. "For ten points, name the only player to win the Super Bowl MVP (Most Valuable Player) award while playing for a losing team. Okay, Steve."

"Chuck Howley of the Dallas Cowboys, in Super Bowl V where Baltimore won 16-13 on the last play of the game. And it looked as if Bob Lilly was about to eat his helmet after O'Brien kicked that field goal."

"Correct. Ten points goes to Team One. If there was ever a Current

Events MVP award, I'm sure that you'd get it even if you were on the losing team. Okay, Team One, for 20 points, who was the leading passer in the NFL last year, this is determined by touchdowns not yards gained?"

"Fran Tarkenton," declared Mumm.

"Once again, Steve, you are correct. Twenty points for Team One."

With a tied score and only a few minutes before the second period bell rang, it would be Taquard who would compromise the victory with an incorrect response. Correct responses resulted in being awarded points, no response resulted in no points, but incorrect responses resulted in losing ten points.

"For 20 points in the category of entertainment, who wrote the novel *Gone with the Wind* which the popular movie was based on?"

"Martha Mitchell," announced Taquard.

"Margaret Mitchell," Madison corrected. "You are having a lot of near-hits with names today. Close only counts in horseshoes and hand grenades, maybe atomic bombs too."

Team One lost by ten points. The rivalry continued between Team One and Team Two. The largest margin of victory never exceeded 20 points.

If the purpose of life is to influence the course of history, then it would be a memorable event to play Current Events. It was another thing to be the subject matter of such a fray. What he couldn't plan for or even imagine would be a matter of remote chance that defied logic beyond the greatest realms. The overwhelming odds against such circumstances were no consolation of what would occur, nor would it make it any less real. One day in the unforeseeable future, Taquard himself would be the subject matter of a Current Events game.

# Chapter Three
## *Summer 1980*

"Bitcheye! Bitcheye! Advance to engage. Enemy vehicle sighted in the valley beyond the wood line. Engage!"

Taquard was leading a patrol during the ROTC Advanced Camp Leadership Lane Evaluations (LLE).

He began saving money for college since he was twelve years old; however this only provided him enough to make it through his sophomore year. Official employment also meant official deductions. Even at barely above minimum wage at the local "Stop and Rob," deductions were plentiful. Actually, the less you made, the more deductions you were faced with. For calculating savings, Taquard had to go with true income. That is what you netted after deductions. There were also hidden deductions that had to be considered as well. The buzzards always took money out of your paycheck before you even saw it. There were deductions for service charges, union dues for a union that claimed to increase your pay as long as you paid them money, the IRS, charity donations that you had to agree to as a condition for getting hired, and Big Ed.

As a clerk, Taquard's job was to collect money from patrons who purchased gas and items from the store. This applied to everyone except robbers, cops, and Big Ed. On the second day on the job the store was held up. Taquard, who had factored in true income and had calculated his value as an employee, did what any dedicated employee would do. Upon recognizing that the store was about to be held up, he ran into the cooler and hid while the manager had to contend with the perpetrators by herself. When a car pulls up sideways and a driver remains with the vehicle while smoke is coming out of the tailpipe, and a passenger exits wearing a long jacket in July, then it is time to assume the worst. If it was a little more apparent then it would be considered a clue by FBI standards. Taquard figured that he wasn't getting enough for his time to thwart off any would-be robbers. He wasn't getting enough to even consider taking a remote chance of facing off with perpetrators of any kind.

The masked thief used a gun to put the manager into submission and used a sledgehammer to open the safe. Although he missed hitting the combination knob on his initial swing with the sledgehammer, the knob fell off anyway. The thief aligned the tumblers and opened the door in less than 30 seconds. He even took the charity bottles for "Kerry's Kidz" and the money that the manager had on her. Afterwards, she ran to use an outside public pay phone with money that she borrowed from Taquard. The store didn't even have a phone of its own.

The police did arrive, but there wasn't a whole lot that they could do. However, they did take their complementary coffee, snacks, magazines, comic books, and any other goodies that they desired. The police had the same effect on the business as did a shoplifter. In either case, the store was going to lose money. As far as the balance sheets were concerned, it didn't matter how the money was lost. Whether the money was lost by voluntary forfeiture or was stolen without the owner's knowledge the end result was exactly the same.

Between the robbers and the policemen's regular visits, the store was challenged to turn a profit. At the end of the month Big Ed would stop by. He helped himself to whatever he wanted. Not only did he not have to pay for anything, the cashier was ordered to give him a big fat envelope that was kept under the counter. He and his sidekick both wore suits and dark sunglasses. Suits were rare in Monument. Ties were unheard of. Heck, suitable clothing was rare in Monument, as were stores with phones. But when Big Ed came to collect, the police were never around.

He decided that working the convenience store wasn't for him.

Although he knew how to spot armed robbers in advance, he knew that it would only be a matter of time before he was caught off-guard and would be looking into a barrel of a gun that was held by some desperate asshole. Even if he was careful and watchful, he was under the supervision of a manager who apparently didn't seem to learn from the incident. His manager could put him in a compromising position. There was no way of predicting what a desperate person would do. Instead of trying to figure it out, he decided to quit. He found an immediate temporary job at a ranch.

As it turned out Taquard made more money shoveling horse manure than he did at the convenience store. Not only that, but he was paid in cash which meant that the money was his to keep. Not only that, but he worked without supervision. He earned more money from the ranch than his student counterparts did.

Unbeknownst to Taquard or anyone else, his grandfather began a college savings program since before his birth. He steadily bought US Savings Bonds every month without fail. Usually he would buy a $100 bond, but sometimes for no particular reason he would buy bigger ones. Occasionally he would splurge and buy a $1,000 bond. He bought them and kept them in a shoe box. At the time that he was purchasing bonds, the bonds didn't have a maturity ceiling. That meant that they kept on growing in value after reaching maturity which took four years.

He also enjoyed the portraits on the bonds. The $50 bond had Washington, the $75 had Adams who was not depicted on any currency, and Jefferson was the most common portrait because he was on the $100 bond. Granddad enjoyed collecting currency, coins, and other valued monetary instruments. He had a $200 bond to accommodate a $5,000 bill because James Madison was depicted on both of them. Like the sawbuck, the $500 bond and the old series $1,000 bill featured Alexander Hamilton. Grover Cleveland was on the new $1,000 bills. Grandpa had to have such monetary instruments on hand to settle bets. Some people were unaware that $100 dollar bills even existed. The new $500 bill had the portrait of William McKinley as did the $500,000,000 bond, which was the largest bond ever produced. Though Grandpa had the note, the bond was a little out of reach. The $100,000 bill with Woodrow Wilson's portrait was also out of reach. Only four were made and two of them were secured in Colorado Springs. They were specifically made for bank transactions and were never released in general circulation. Grandpa continued to buy bonds and collect notes for Elwood's education. While he never forgot to purchase bonds and save money he lost track of Elwood's academic progress. It wasn't until Taquard was a Captain in the Army that he realized that he forgot to give him the money for college.

He bought bonds as a young boy beginning with the first year that they came out. He saved for decades yet he never cashed any. He just hung onto them while they continued to increase in value.

He had a philosophy about money and spending it. He also didn't trust banks. In 1933 he experienced what could happen with banks and correctly figured that if it happened once it could happen again. Because he never trusted anyone else with his money, he always had it. *Never buy anything on impulse*. That was another money management philosophy of the old man. If he saw something that he wanted he would assess whether or not he could afford it. If he could afford it, then he would wait for at least seventy-two hours before rendering an affirmative decision. Most of the time he would decide against buying the item of consideration in spite of the fact that he once wanted it. Another gem of financial wisdom from grandpa was to never settle for second best. If you wanted a Rolex watch, don't buy a Breitling because you can't afford a Rolex. Keep saving your money and do without until you can afford the Rolex that you wanted in the first place.

**OLD JEW MONEY MANAGEMENT TIP NUMBER 1: If you can't afford it, you don't need it.**

**OLD JEW MONEY MANAGEMENT TIP NUMBER 2: Pay your debts as soon as possible. Paying them is much easier and cheaper than avoiding them.**

**OLD JEW MONEY MANAGEMENT TIP NUMBER 3: The first judgment is usually the best.**

**OLD JEW MONEY MANAGEMENT TIP NUMBER 4: Don't settle for second best when you can't afford first rate. Keep saving until you can afford the best.**

**OLD JEW MONEY MANAGEMENT TIP NUMBER 5:** It is better and cheaper to build it right the first time than to go back and fix it later.

**OLD JEW MONEY MANAGEMENT TIP NUMBER 6:** Don't commit to anything that you can't see your way through.

**OLD JEW MONEY MANAGEMENT TIP NUMBER 7:** The best way not to break a promise is not to make one.

**OLD JEW MONEY MANAGEMENT TIP NUMBER 8:** One of the best ways to lose money is to give it to someone who promises to turn your investment into a fortune overnight. The best manager of your money is you, not a stranger.

**OLD JEW MONEY MANAGEMENT TIP NUMBER 9:** Remember that insurance is a form of gambling. Purchase accordingly.

**OLD JEW MONEY MANAGEMENT TIP NUMBER 10:** Don't borrow money. Don't lend money.

**OLD JEW MONEY MANAGEMENT TIP NUMBER 11:** When you see something that you want, sleep on it for a night before actually buying it. Never buy on impulse.

**OLD JEW MONEY MANAGEMENT TIP NUMBER 12:** Remember that there is no such thing as a once-in-a-lifetime deal. Don't give into sales pressure.

By the time Elwood was a junior his savings were running low, but he remembered the financial advice that his grandfather gave to him years earlier. He continued to enroll with maximum credit loads as he pursued graduation. During registration he found himself in search of an elective. He ran into the ROTC table and was greeted by a cadre member. Within minutes he was accepted into the program. ROTC would pay for his college in exchange for four years of service. All that was required was a firm handshake. In those days, they had standards.

The new commitment meant taking an ROTC class which included the study of basic military skills, leadership, map reading, and military history. The down side of the contract included forfeiting some weekends and free time. On the other hand, it also paid his tuition, provided him with $100 a month, and a summer job. This solved Taquard's financial needs.

It seemed like everything about ROTC Advanced Camp was more like Gomer Pyle than anything a motivated future officer would want to aspire to. Most of the cadets were overweight, sloppy, and simply didn't give a crap. As one looked at the situation even further, it was obvious that the cadre was a bunch of losers as well. ROTC was a bummer assignment and a dumping ground for zeros. The majority of the cadre consisted of average, run-of-the-mill ne'er-do-wells who happened to be boring. It was bad enough to be repulsive, but to be repulsive and boring at the same time was more than anyone could take. No one ever wrote about them.

Many writers who wrote about the military wrote books about war, operations, and concepts that were admired by Taquard. Many were either veterans or obviously subject matter experts who wrote about the fine men who served their country in their non-fiction books. Even the novels about war caught the imagination although they weren't as flattering as the non-fiction books. Literary works of art that were never about ROTC did something that the cadre could never, they provided inspiration. They could convince a college student to sign up for ROTC. Taquard did just that. Unfortunately, it was Army ROTC instead of Air Force or Navy.

Units at ROTC Advanced Camp participated in competitive field exercises in the battle of attrition. The object was to graduate. Although only one in 500 didn't make it, the cadets were under the impression that only a few would see graduation. Though unprepared in most aspects of summer camp, Taquard managed to get top-notch scores in all categories except peer ratings. He qualified as an expert with the M16 rifle, scored above 490 on the PT (Physical Training) test, and got three perfect scores on the leadership lanes.

The peer rating system seemed to be helter-skelter. Most cadets behaved like Adolph Hitler when they were in a leadership position and more like Donald Duck when they weren't. Oddly enough, this was what the cadre encouraged. There was no way to predict the outcome of a peer rating. Those who applied themselves to ensure that everyone did well did not get good peer rating scores. It was an area that defied Taquard's logic. Not only the peer ratings, but ROTC itself.

The conflicting information that the Army spewed out on a continuous basis was more than enough to confuse anyone at an impressionable age. A lot of people were in denial about the Army and simply refused to believe anything against their desires. Taquard was impressionable but was somehow convinced that it was better to seek the truth than to believe a lie. While it was true that he had been assigned to a Sad Sack platoon, it was also true, with the cooperation of the other members, that they could outperform the other elements within the battalion. Among ROTC cadets, the difference between the bums and the crème de la crème was paper thin.

Third Platoon seemed to lack innovation, imagination, and creativity. Their unit motto was "Third Leads the Way," although "Third Platoon is good," was a serious contender that came in at a close second. While student counterparts back at the university subscribed to the concepts of "Work smarter, not harder," and "If it isn't broke, don't fix it," the Army was thinking more in terms of "Work harder, not smarter," and "If it ain't broke, break it." Thinking outside the box was their way of telling someone that they were on their own. The Army, like ROTC, didn't believe in supporting their own. Another response to the needs of the cadets and soldiers was to do more with less. Taquard, who was in the minority, couldn't help but feel that it was better to think inside of the box and that it was better to do less with more.

As events progressed, some cadets in Third Platoon made attempts to revise their Sad Sack image. A lot of ideas and concepts were put forward but without majority support it went nowhere. A new name for the platoon was also in order. During an exercise, the cadets were challenged to rescue nonexistent oppressed people in a mock village named Millersville. The challenge to liberate the village from its captors was graded a success. From that, the unit was self-named as the "Millersville Liberators." As the Millersville Liberators progressed, green and white T-shirts were printed up and worn during off-duty sessions. The Millersville Liberators stood ready to free the oppressed in all ways and forms. They brought forth freedom, liberty, and the American way of life to all. This self-glorified mission added to the esprit de corps of the platoon and motivated cadets to keep on trying. Somehow this also became affiliated with the Women Liberators (also know as Women Libbers) of the ever so popular Women's Lib movement of that era. Yes, the Millersville Liberators (like the Army itself) who once stood up for truth and justice suddenly decided to support Women's Lib and abandon their founding principles. They embraced the Women's Liberation movement with a fever that was a reflection of Army. Not only did the Army endorse Women's Lib, they enforced it. Jeffy Meyers from Arizona State University decided that other oppressed groups needed liberating as well. He proposed that the Gay Liberation movement needed a boost from the Millersville Liberators as well. At six feet, two inches and weighing in at 342 pounds, Jeffy introduced Gay Lib into the Millersville Liberator arena by wearing green panties with a matching bra, garter belt, and green stockings. Even his high heels were green. He made his announcement and proposed to endorse Gay Lib as part of the Millersville Liberator mission. The proposal was approved by an overwhelming majority. Third platoon, not only had a new name, but also had a mission.

Cadets embraced vulgarity with a passion. Vulgarity was equated with courage and valor. The more uncouth a cadet could be the better. Cadences, songs, and language reflected the gauche desires of the ROTC corps. Cadets exceeded everyone else when it came to vulgarity. In addition to being vulgar, cadets were also offensive. They would downplay the significance of others in either their words or tone. One of the marching cadences was modified to reflect the attitude of the Millersville Liberators.

*Whoa Rangers,*
*Airborne Rangers,*
*Don't you even talk to me,*
*I am R O T C*

A memorable song dedicated to ROTC was sung to the tune "My Bonnie Lies over the Ocean."

*R O T C,*
*Sounds like a big bunch of shit to me,*
*R O T C*
*That's what it turned out to be.*

Even female cadets demonstrated their vulgar ways in conspicuous ways. They created a song containing lyrics such as "You got a hole and I got a pole." Nothing was too vulgar or uncouth for ROTC. Even though the Millersville Liberators were on a course at full speed ahead, the mission lacked substance.

There is an unwavering universal truth that has remained constant on firing ranges throughout the world among the military and law enforcement agencies. There are two things that a firing range must have, and will not function without:

1. A lot of unwarranted hype about how females are better shooters than males.

2. A female who doesn't qualify on the range.

ROTC was certainly no exception to this rule as they embraced the Women's Liberation movement at a fever pitch momentum. Even after most of the females failed to qualify on the range, there was still a lot of talk about what great shooters females were.

The highest score for a female that day was sharpshooter. There was only one female sharpshooter that day. In spite of the facts, the hype about females being superior to men in shooting continued to the point of being repeatedly endorsed through the camp cycle.

The scoring was simple. Each participant has 40 shots for targets at various ranges from 25 to 300 meters in distance. A score of 36 hits or better earned the rank of expert, 32 or higher was a sharpshooter, 28 or more was a marksman, and 16 or above was considered qualified.

*Sex has nothing to do with marksmanship.*

Taquard scored expert with the M16 rifle. Throughout his career, he would constantly score expert on the ranges. Although, Taquard was consistently an expert shooter, he was no match for many others. The conditions for the national competitions were a lot stiffer; they had smaller targets at greater ranges and less time to shoot. They had two categories above expert: Master and High Master. There were fewer High Masters than there were recipients of the Congressional Medal of Honor.

Females were in high regard in ROTC, as well as the Army itself, for no particular reason. Determining the value of the females was beyond anyone's grasp of understanding. They were continuously elevated at the expense of meritorious males. Their mannerisms were crude even by male standards. They chewed tobacco, spit openly, belched gratuitously, farted loudly, and indiscriminately picked their asses. Discretion was not even in their vocabulary. But for some unknown reason, ROTC endorsed their uncouth behavior by putting them on a pedestal.

Recondo Day would be enhanced later on in Taquard's career. It consisted of a river crossing during the day while the water was still frigid, going down a sixty-foot Slide for Life cable, and walking a three-foot wide platform that was twenty feet above the water before going on to a rope to drop. Most of the cadets would accomplish these challenges although attempting any of them was strictly optional. This was arguably the best day that Advanced Camp had to offer. Cadets accomplished more than they could even imagine unless they were in Boy Scouts.

The day began with a river crossing. First the cadets would pair up and get their ponchos and boot laces. The two ponchos were snapped together and then the cadets stripped down to their swimming suits. Everything went on the ponchos. Then the ponchos were folded over and wrapped tightly around the personal effects. The boot laces were used to secure various parts of the ponchos to ensure that water wouldn't seep in. Taquard and his partner Boyles took the poncho configuration into the river and traveled the required distance.

"I don't know about you, Boyles, but I want to get the heck out of here as soon as possible."

"Me too. This water's freezing."

"I don't have anything to prove by staying in here any longer than I have to."

"I'm glad that I didn't get some gung-ho partner like Charlie."

"I can't believe how cold this water is."

"I know what you mean, I'm freezing."

"It doesn't look cold. The sun's out, it's July for crying out loud."

"Maybe it's because it's Washington."

Although they had to traverse a rocky bottom in their bare feet and negotiate water obstacles which included pesky tree branches coming out of the water, the river crossing went well for both Taquard and Boyles. They didn't waste any time getting both in and out of the river. There was nothing for either one of them to prove and there wasn't anybody around who was worth showing off to. Their belongings were perfectly dry after the ordeal. This was a big deal to those who managed to get their belongings wet, especially after emerging out a cold stream and being without a dry towel.

The next obstacle was the Slide for Life. This consisted of climbing up a telephone pole with a ladder attachment. Cadets were instructed to yell and scream while they climbed up the pole because it was believed that screaming reduces fear. Cadets climbed up sixty feet to a platform. They were instructed to stand on a milk crate and hold on to a handle assembly that was attached to a cable. Then the cadet was instructed to do a pull up. With that he began sliding down the cable. At the bottom a flag man signaled when it was time for the cadet to let go of the handle assembly. Then the cadet would fall into the lake.

The third and final obstacle consisted of walking a platform that was about three feet wide and forty feet long. This platform was also located on the lake about twenty feet above the water. After walking the platform, the cadets would climb on a rope and hang from the middle until they were instructed to drop in the water. Many cadets stumbled to the point of falling into the water from the platform. They never made it to the rope. The cadets would continue to stumble their way through Advanced Camp while yelling and screaming. The logic is that if you yell and scream, then you will be hardcore.

The Twilight Zone hit Fort Lewis during the eruption of Mount Saint Helens. The smoke looked like it was made of marble. It was cloudy and dirty, but it didn't move. It looked like a picture. The eruption created a heat wave that hit the garrison. Taquard felt like he was suspended in time when he woke up in the afternoon and noticed that everyone else around him was asleep. He was the only person awake at about one in the afternoon. Everywhere he looked, people were asleep. Even outside people were on the ground asleep. Taquard did what any other reasonable cadet would do. He went back to bed and went to sleep.

Classes in garrison took place in the field. There were no classrooms. Cadets went back and forth to the field for their classes during garrison time. There were no tests during the classes. Instead the material would be covered in a comprehensive final exam that followed the last field exercise.

One of the things that became very apparent at Advanced Camp was the fact that this generation had no use for integrity. Honesty and loyalty meant nothing. The previous Age of Aquarius generation wasn't much of a role model for anyone to follow. As Taquard's do-nothing generation steered away from the faults of the previous generation they failed to incorporate any values to fill the void. Instead of coming up with something better they simply went in another direction. This generation was not to be trusted. They became a gaggle of back stabbing blue falcons. Blue falcon is the phonetic substitute for buddy fucker.

Other nuances in the unit included Koonders who would fart throughout the C-Ration lunches. This was usually followed by laudatory responses by the female cadets. "Oh, Koonders, you're so brave." As crazy as it may have seemed, female cadets liked farts. And when Koonders farted they all wrestled each other as they scrambled to get a close whiff.

"I just don't get it," Taquard would remark.

"Well, he cuts cool farts," one of the female cadets would respond.

During PT, Koonders would be at the front of the formation passing gas. By the end of the half-mile run most of the cadets would fall out. They would blame Koonders' farts as the reason they fell out of the run. Factually speaking, while his farts didn't help any, the cadets were basically out of shape. Fortunately, passing a PT test wasn't a requirement for graduating from ROTC Advanced Camp.

Koonders had another long-lasting effect on the unit with his introduction of a game called Stacker. Stacker, which was an immediate success that became an institution synonymous with ROTC, consisted of several people taking BMs in the same toilet without flushing, ergo the name stacker. Stacker competitions took place among the platoons and companies. Stacks were usually adorned with a business card of a person who was disliked.

Explosive ordinance was also taught. Cadets learned how to fire light anti-tank weapons, set land mines, engage Claymores, use mortars, call for field artillery fire, throw hand grenades. They got exposure to a myriad of other weapon systems. Cadets didn't always get the opportunity to engage the weapons that they wanted. While cadets set up model Claymore mines during a simulation, only one actual Claymore was allocated to the entire camp. Cadets competed for the opportunity of being the one and only cadet to actually fire a live Claymore. Cadets were graded and evaluated. Surprisingly, it was the worst cadet who would get to fire the Claymore as opposed to the best. One cadet from another company emplaced the Claymore backwards. The Claymore mine has the words "FRONT TOWARD ENEMY" configured on it. The wording is part of the mold itself. It is the epitome of and idiot-proof concept. However, it wasn't idiot-proof enough for ROTC.

"As everyone has hoped for the opportunity of being selected to be the privileged one to actually fire a Claymore, Cadet Derek Farmer has been selected. Not because he performed well during the simulation, but because he didn't. He managed to point the 'FRONT TOWARD ENEMY' side at himself and the rest of us," Major Bristol would exclaim. "The point here is that we are here to learn, and while mistakes are made we can correct them here and now. Okay, Derek, are you ready? I bet you don't ever make that mistake again."

"No, sir."

Farmer went out to the site and emplaced the Claymore. "Don't you want to double-check to see if I did it right, sir?"

"I have faith in you."

The damage of the Claymore was experienced firsthand as Farmer depressed the trigger. Steel ball bearings flew mercilessly with speed and force with the impact of their C4 explosive thrust to give them both power and range. Farmer was ripped to pieces as countless numbers of steel balls tore through his body. Even the steel pot that he was wearing was obliterated in nothing flat. Upon hitting a body, Claymore bearings lose their range, but there is no doubt that they have enough momentum to go through a body. Major Bristol's legs separated from his body as bearings flew towards the cadets and cadre. There was no time to react. Those who were in direct line of sight with the Claymore died before they ever knew what hit them. Taquard and several others sat behind a small hill near the spectator area. He reasoned that if he couldn't see the Claymore, why try to wrestle for a glimpse? Oddly enough, only 14 cadets and cadre were killed in the incident and the injuries were moderate. Injuries resulted mostly from grazing, being behind an object like a filled A.L.I.C.E. (All-purpose Lightweight Individual Carrying Equipment) pack, or a ricochet. Cadets were forced to walk back to garrison since the vehicles were in the line of fire as well.

"I wonder what school he went to," Taquard would ask.

"I don't know, but he ain't going back," another would respond.

"My captain told me that it's okay to pull your head out of your ass in ROTC," Taquard would continue.

"Who's your captain?"

"He's no longer with us anymore. He actually volunteered for an ROTC assignment, but then he left because he couldn't stand all the bullshit."

"One more field exercise and the mil skills test and we are done."

"With all the people we are losing, I doubt if anyone will fail now," another cadet would interject.

"Well, the Army still has standards."

"And the Army still has a quota to fill."

"Well, I'm doing my best."

Taquard would add, "There's nothing wrong with doing your best. Besides, I've only been in the ROTC program for four months now. I'm surprised they sent me to Advanced Camp so early."

"Don't get a swelled head over this. Look at all the screwballs they got here. Some of them have yet to enroll in ROTC."

"How could that be?"

"Hell, these Nasty Guard units send their kids to camp and get them commissioned without them even stepping into a college."

"I thought you had to have a college degree to get commissioned."

"Not in the National Guard you don't. Each state has different requirements."

"I always knew the Guard was fucked up. What I didn't know was how fucked up ROTC was."

For someone who had no previous background in the military, ROTC Advanced Camp provided a fairly adequate introduction. Branch Orientation Day (BOD) provided the opportunity for cadets to view several branches in the Army before making their formal requests. While enlisted members are assigned an MOS (Military Occupational Specialty), officers are assigned a branch, not an MOS. While an enlisted person concentrates on one single aspect of a branch, the officers are trained in several functions of the branch. For example, in the artillery there are several functions: forward observer, fire direction, and the manning of a howitzer. An enlisted person will be assigned to just one function and remain there for the rest of his career. An officer will be trained in all areas as his career will begin in performing in that branch, managing the branch, and incorporating the branch with other branches. While it is common for enlisted men to ask each other what their MOS is, it is an irrelevant question to pose to an officer although they will usually answer with their branch designator.

BOD was supported with a formal introduction to the branch orientation configuration. The Army has three functions supported by branches. The functions are Combat Arms, Combat Support, and Combat Service Support. Each branch has an assigned color and insignia.

**Combat Arms**
Infantry Light Blue Crossed Rifles
Field Artillery Red Crossed Tubes
Air Defense Artillery Red Crossed Tubes with a Missile
Cavalry Yellow Crossed Sabers
Armor Yellow Crossed Sabers with a Tank
Corps of Engineers Red/White Castle-like Building
(The Engineers are the only branch to have special buttons for their Class A uniform.)
Aviation Ultramarine Blue/Golden Orange A Set of Wings with a Propeller

Special Forces Jungle Green Crossed Arrows

## Combat Support
Corps of Engineers Red/White Castle-like Building
(The Engineers are the only branch to have special buttons for their Class A uniform.) Engineers are both Combat Arms and Combat Support.
Signal Corps Orange/White Crossed Flags
Military Police Green Crossed Pistols
Chemical Corps Blue/Yellow Crossed Flasks with a Hexagon
Military Intelligence Oriental Blue/Silver Gray Flower with a Knife

## Combat Service Support
Adjutant General Dark Blue/Red Shield
Finance Silver Gray/Yellow Diamond
Ordnance Crimson/Yellow Ignited Bomb
Quartermaster Buff (Peach)/ Wheel with Sword and Key and an Eagle on Top
Judge Advocate General (JAG) Dark Blue/White Wreath with Sword and Quill
Transportation Brick Red/Golden Yellow Wheel with Shield
Medical Maroon/White Staff with Snakes and Wings
Dental Maroon/White Medical Insignia with a D
Veterinary Maroon/White Medical Insignia with a V
Nurse Maroon/White Medical Insignia with an N
Medical Specialist Maroon/White Medical Insignia with an S
Medical Service Maroon/White Medical Insignia with an MS
Chaplain Black Cross
Jewish Faith has the Ten Commandments with the Star of David

## Branch Details
Officers from most branches can be assigned to details.
Generals Aide Shield with Eagle (the amount of stars on the shield signifies the rank of general the aide works for)
General Staff Army Eagle on Star
Inspector General Wreath with Battle Ax and Sword

USMA Professor Scarlet/Silver Gray West Point Shield with Eagle

Branches were set up differently and had a variety of displays and presentations. Most branches were represented. The Infantry Branch was conspicuously absent since many cadets were gung ho to the point of selecting Infantry no matter what. The medical and legal branches were also absent. Doctors and lawyers are recruited from medical and law schools as opposed to undergraduate programs. There were no detail representations either. The BOD was designed to help the undecided cadet select the best branch for him. Not only where not all branches represented, the cadet didn't have time to see all of the orientations.

Taquard's first orientation was finance. The choice was determined by a tent (GP Medium) that didn't seem to be too crowded. The display consisted of a board with a pen and pencil mounted on to them.

"There's not much to say about finance. It's all paperwork. The model of this black pen is an M60. We have and M60 machine gun and an M60 tank. Well we also have the M60 pen. I guess all branches have an M60 something. Look around and enjoy yourselves. Are there any questions? Well that's about it," the First Lieutenant said to the group. "You have fifteen minutes before you can go to another branch."

The second tent was a Chaplain's tent. The Chaplain was a captain and had a foot pump powered field organ on display. He went into much more detail than the finance officer. He spoke about the services that a chaplain provided to the troops and what he had to do to provide them. He also stated that the Chaplaincy was no place to go if you wanted a free ride. He said that it was more work than glory. He said that avoiding work takes more work than work itself.

The Adjutant tent consisted of a captain sleeping on a cot.

"Oh, somebody actually showed up," he surprisingly stated. "Uh, well, I didn't exactly prepare anything. I didn't think anyone was going to show up. Uh, I got some popsicles in the cooler. Anyone want one?"

The cadre saved the best for last. The Field Artillery presentation was mandatory for all to attend and took place in a set of bleachers. It was more of a show than a presentation. It was apparent that the Field Artillery put in more effort into their presentation than did anyone else.

It consisted of a group of captains and a couple of their wives. They really took the Artillery slogan, "The King of Battle," seriously. Instead of telling the cadets about how the branch functions, the captains put on more of a comical sketch. They showed how Artillery officers lived it up in the Army. They even had a sissy boy who was a captain who wore flower pattern cut-offs and the color pink. No one really understood what the purpose of the sissy boy was, but it was a prelude of the direction that the Army was about to take. They horsed around in front of the cadets for about thirty minutes. Although it didn't do anything to orient a cadet to artillery, it did show them that not everyone in the Army was without a sense of humor. This alone, convinced many to request the artillery branch. Each cadet had to make a preference list consisting of five branches in order of preference the day before graduation. Taquard selected Field Artillery as his first choice and forgot what his subsequent choices were. One of the most beneficial concepts to come out of Advanced Camp was the Communications Electronic Operating Instructions (CEOI) Authentication Table Block of Instruction (BOI) and Practical Exercise (PE). The instructor addressed the cadets with the aid of handouts and posted illustrations. Although Taquard didn't know how to apply it outside of the Army, he knew that it was important.

"The important thing to remember is that this is an established code that allows you to communicate with each other without others knowing what is being said. This will be of no used to you if you do not know how to encode or decode messages. The first thing that I want to talk to all of you about is root vibration. Does anybody here know what root vibration is? Of course not. Don't bother trying to look it up in the dictionary. Just pay attention. Root vibration is the adding of numbers until you arrive at a single digit number. For example, root vibration involves adding every digit within a number or series of numbers. With root vibration, you will end up with a number between one and nine."

**ROOT VIBRATION**
$$23 + 317 + 4{,}741 = 2 + 3 + 3 + 1 + 7 + 4 + 7 + 4 + 1 = 5 + 11 + 11 + 5 =$$
$$16 + 16 = 32 = 3 + 2 = 5$$

## The Root Vibration of this series of numbers is 5.

"You will need to remember this. But root vibration also applies to words as well as numbers. For example if I begin or end a message with 'Yellow Cab,' that would mean that I am telling you what number you will need to used to off set an obvious code where root vibration applies. Now look at the second illustration."

## MN Yellow Cab
## Fbp mzb aji yov v

"Yellow Cab is the root vibration. Each letter needs to be converted to the number that it corresponds to in the alphabet. Y is 25, e is 5, the l's are 12 a piece, o is 15, and w is 23. Cab adds up to 6 by itself. Yellow comes to 30 plus 24 and 38. It doesn't matter how you add the numbers. It will always come out the same. You can omit the 9's at any time unless it happens to be the last number left. Nine and two is always two. Nine plus 2 is 11. Eleven is 1 plus 1. Anyway, getting back to yellow, 68 + 24 or 14 + 6 or 20. The root vibration of yellow is 2. You can add it up another way but you'll still arrive at same answer. Two plus 6, or Cab, gives you 8. Remember this number. Now look at the next illustration. Note the columns and rows. The number at the bottom is the code series identification number. You will need to refer to it from time to time because there is a plethora of coded sheets out there and you need to ensure that you and the person with whom you are communicating with are using the same coded reference. Refer to MN in your message. Remember first right, then up in map reading? Well, in CEOI encoding and decoding it is left then down."

"Hey! There's no K's on your chart, Sergeant," Waldo shouted at the top of his lungs.

"I know that," the instructor responded. "I was going to get to that. Class, use the letter C in lieu of the letter K if you need to. The first letter, in this case, doesn't change. In the case of Yellow Cab MN it would. Root vibration is applied to the second letter."

"That means that N becomes V because 14 plus 8 equals 22," another cadet shouted.

"That is correct. Now take notice where M and V intersect."

"And I will fuck the girls," Waldo exclaimed.

"Will you kindly shut the hell up," another cadet responded.

Waldo was always spewing out garbage without provocation.

"For those of you who are still with me, who knows what is at the intersection of M and V," the instructor continued. "Remember that M is the left sided header."

"S," answered a cadet.

"Yes. The S line is your encoding/decoding line. Use the S line on the left, not the top. If you refer to the original message and go to the S line, and follow it until you get to the letter F, you will refer to the letter above the F on the top header line to decode what it means. In this case, F stands for S."

"Wait a minute," a cadet shouted. "Why are they all three letters apiece?"

"The words themselves vary in length just like they always do. The format selected in this case just happens to be three letters apiece. Messages aren't always read across. Sometimes they can be read in columns like a newspaper article. First, decode each of the letters. Where the breaks between the words themselves actually are is something that you'll have to figure out yourself. You will also have to figure out when a letter is either a C or a K. If you absolutely positively have to use a K, like in a serial number for instance, then just use K for K. Other than that, use C for K."

"What if the root vibration takes you past Z?"

"Keep going back to A and continue. Remember the title can be anything you want, so are the letter designators."

"And I will feed the rabbits," Waldo stated emphatically.

"Shut the fuck up, you stupid Mormon," another cadet responded.

"I have some exercises for you to complete during this block of instruction. You will find this useful in many ways. Think about how many ways you can apply this skill to everyday events and real life. For example, somebody may want to coordinate as to how they are going to beat the hell out of motormouth here. Has anyone decoded the message?"

"I have," a cadet enthusiastically shouted. "It says, 'Send help quick.'"

"Good job. If you can decode, you can encode. It's exactly performed the opposite way decoding is. You will need a little practice but it won't take too long for you to get it."

"Man, I still don't get it, Sarge!"

"Let's take another look at the CEOI," the sergeant stated while referring to the training aid again.

The CEOI consisted of rows and columns of letters and numbers. It looked impossible to follow or even read. Once a person learned how to use it, it was as simple as it was complicated.

"As you can see, the columns are labeled repeatedly as you progress down the rows. That way there is less of a chance of misaligning the intended encoding or decoding lines. Also note that the numbers may repeat themselves in some cases as in rows A and B. Zero is designated with a 7, but the similarities end there. Don't get too excited if you discover a repetition here and there. Ensure that you follow the entire decoding sequence through."

The cadets practiced using the CEOI with each other as they came up with their own encoded messages. It didn't take long for them to master their newly acquired skill. It was also a lot of fun in addition to being education. The CEOI was a great skill that one hoped that he would never have to rely on. Nevertheless, it was worth learning.

Before the cadets departed the specialized block of instruction, the sergeant gave out the cadets CEOIs of their own complete with designated series numbers.

**ABCDE FGHIJ LMNOP QRSTU VWXYZ 12345 67890**
**A** POIUY TREWQ LJHGF DSAZX CVBNM 65498 30217
**B** UYTRW EQLPO IDSAZ JHGFM XNCBV 45210 36987
**C** MJULI PONHY BGTVF RCDEX SWZAQ 74103 69852
**D** ZAQXS WCDEV FRBGT NHYMJ UILOP 20145 89637
**E** VFRCD EXSWZ AQMJU NHPLY OITGB 98763 02541
**ABCDE FGHIJ LMNOP QRSTU VWXYZ 12345 67890**

F TGBYH NRFVU JMWSX ILZPA OQEDC 08263 19574
G QAZXS WEDCV FRTGB NHYUJ MLIOP 35768 90214
H LPOIU JMNHY TGBVF REWQA SDZXC 46973 01582
I XZSER DCFTA VGWYQ BHUNJ IMLPO 59026 83741
J LOPIJ NUHBM YTGFV CREDS XZQAW 87923 06145
**ABCDE FGHIJ LMNOP QRSTU VWXYZ 12345 67890**
L CTFVY GBUHN XJMOI PDLRZ WASQE 57630 98412
M RAZQX DEWSP TOYIU MCVNB FLGJH 80527 41963
N LAJSH DGFMZ NXBCV PQOWI EURYT 94610 32578
O HGFSD ANBVC XZUYT REWQI OPJLM 73542 90618
P PLOMI JNUHB YGVTF CRDXE SZWAQ 09516 28473
**ABCDE FGHIJ LMNOP QRSTU VWXYZ 12345 67890**
Q DSFAG HNJML BZPXO CVUQW YETRI 47586 90132
R RTGIV FCDEY HNXSW QZMAJ UOPLB 95162 03478
S UHBYG VTFCI JNRDX OMESZ LWQPA 07964 13285
T IJNVU HBTFC YGARD OPXEL MSZQW 85274 10963
U WAOME SZNIJ PLRDX UQHBT YFGCV 34612 50978
**ABCDE FGHIJ LMNOP QRSTU VWXYZ 12345 67890**
V BHUYG VCFTR DXNMO IPLJA ESZQW 08231 79654
W WAQPL ESOZM XNIDJ RUTYH FBCVG 45193 06287
X JNBHU IFCVG YTMRL DXPOE SWQZA 35760 24981
Y TFCVB HUYGR DXZAQ WESIJ NOPLM 73469 85021
Z UMYNT BRVEC WXQZP OILJA HSGDF 95162 03874
F10476020B K75781497 C 9 15 22 35 37 . 18
3, 9, 8, 56, 43, 68

During another field exercise, the term Bitcheye surfaced. Once it surfaced it was repeated repeatedly. How it came about or who came up with it is still unknown. In Taquard's mind, the term Bitcheye had more of a ring to it than Millersville Liberator. Besides, the Millersville Liberators, who were in the same category as the Women Libbers, were fast becoming known as the "Faggots" by the other platoons. And no matter how hard they tried to convince others about the merits of homosexuality, 1980 was still a couple of years too early for coming out of the closet.

Bitcheye seemed to catch on easily. It was used for "challenge and password," member identification, and dispensing information on the radio. Although the evaluators would monitor radio traffic to keep track of all movements, they were not familiar with the word Bitcheye. This was an inspiration to developing codes that would put victory within their grasp. Aggressors would use their tracking information to set up ambushes. As units would communicate with each other of where and when they would move, evaluators who were monitoring the transmissions would arrive at the given location by vehicle, set up for an ambush, get out the lawn chairs, make coffee, and wait for the cadets to come. Cadets would call in grids to each other in accordance with (IAW) a map. Grid coordinated would be used to coordinate movements and actions. Evaluator aggressors had the same maps and radio frequencies were established in advance.

Call signs and frequencies would change every twelve hours. As a result of not comprehending the procedures of call signs and grid coordinates the Sad Sack unit, Third Platoon, would develop the most secure means of communication of any other summer camp unit. While other units were using call signs such as Bravo 12 or Whiskey 7, the Bitcheyes stuck with Charlie, Joe, or Atwood.

"Hey, Joe! You know where the objective is supposed to be?"

"No, let me check."

"Wait, guys, I found it."

"Where is it?"

"Let's see, it's on the card that they gave us. Grid 3457 8732."

"Where is that on a map?"

"How am I supposed to know?"

Together, the cadets were able to surmise the grid on the map which provided them with their assigned objective.

"That's gonna be near a lake or river or something like that."

"You know that the aggressors will be around. I mean if they told us where to go then it is likely that they know where we are going."

"Wait a minute. Where the heck are we on the map?"

"You got me there."

"Does anybody know how to read a map?"

Together, the cadets tried to determine their location on the map.

Fortunately, they were able to find a recognizable landmark which was in their vicinity and depicted on the map. They had been in the area previously and it began to look familiar.

"Look over here, there's the monument that we just passed."

"Wait, look at these terrain features. They're just like the ones on the ground."

"Steve, where you at?"

"Beats me, Charlie," replied Steve over the radio.

"We need to all get together."

"Yeah, but we don't know we are. This map ain't much good. And don't give me none of that grid shit either. It just don't make no sense."

"All right, Bitcheyes, I've got an idea. Does everyone know where the slide for life tower is?"

"Yeah, I think I can see it from here."

"I remember."

"I'm sure we can find it."

"But it's in the wrong direction, at least I think it is."

"We got compasses, we could use the compasses to find our way out of this."

"We can all meet together, then go to the objective."

"Where we gonna meet?"

"I got an idea. You remember a couple of weeks ago when we were on a field patrol?"

"Yeah, so what?"

"Remember that big tree where we saw those two lesbian spec fours making out?"

"Yeah. They were ugly as hell. Yeech. Big fat bitches."

"We'll meet there. Whoever gets there first will wait for the others."

The aggressors didn't know how to respond to the Bitcheye coordination.

"Sarge, did you catch all that?"

"Yeah, but I wasn't on that patrol. I don't know what they're talking about."

"I got an idea, maybe we could call them and ask for a grid."

"You mean they know how to read a grid?"

"Well, how do we set up an ambush if we don't know where they'll be coming from?"

"Shit, I don't know."

"We got to find out where they're coming from."

It has often been said that the most dangerous weapon in the Army was a Second Lieutenant and a map. This situation was even worse: a bunch of cadets with maps and compasses. The Bitcheyes were able to all remember that location. As it turned out, it was the ideal place to regroup. Difficulty with map reading was overcome with the use of recognizable landmarks and reference points. Radio frequencies were solved in the same manner. At midnight, they began with the lowest frequency possible. Every six hours, they would move the right dial one notch. This was not done to throw off the aggressors, it was done out of necessity. The cadets couldn't remember how to read the frequency schedule. Aggressors were able to monitor most of the radio traffic, but not always.

The aggressor's job of compromising the cadets was complicated in two of the most critical areas. Not only did they not know where the cadets were or where they were going, but they were about to lose their eavesdropping ability. Upon regrouping, the Bitcheyes decided to find the objective while the cadre was trying to figure how to thwart their efforts. The objective was near a sparsely occupied building. The mission was to capture the enemy flag and return to camp.

"Well, Captain Buttholes, do you have any idea where your cadets might be?" asked Lieutenant Colonel (LTC) Steinweber.

"Sir, I have no idea. And, sir, it's pronounced Bucholtz. Sarge! You got any ideas how we can find them?"

"I say let them come to us. We can ambush them as soon as they arrive near the parking lot."

"Which part of the parking lot? We don't know what direction they're coming from."

"I say we wait right here. We're bound to hear them coming."

"Yes. Captain, what if they are lost or even injured?"

"That happens all the time."

"It's no big deal, sir, we have deaths every year and nobody ever got excited about it before," First Sergeant (1SG) Glasscock would interject.

"But we are supposed to win this engagement. No cadets have ever won this engagement before since summer camps began and I don't intend to lose the first. If I were to lose this, I'd be the laughing stock of the entire cadre. My friends would laugh at me. They'd make up jokes about me. You'd better send out some patrols to go look for them."

"But, sir, I don't have enough people to send out patrols. Besides, these dumb fuck cadets will probably come in the front entrance as they always do."

"But what if they don't? What if they are smart?"

1SG Glasscock stated, "These are the dumbest fucking morons I have ever seen. They couldn't find their asses with both hands."

"Look, Colonel, it's getting late, they won't be near the objective until tomorrow afternoon. Besides, there's already another group in the area."

"Send out a patrol first thing tomorrow morning. Check with the other units and see if anyone knows the whereabouts of those cadets. I will not be made a fool of. Remind me to coordinate some air support tomorrow morning. Maybe those choppers will find them."

The Bitcheyes, who went unnoticed, did see some aggressor activity while the two groups were passing through the same vicinity.

"Wait! I see some people in the far wood line," one of the cadets would announce.

"Yeah and there's a car driving by."

Taquard had an idea. Attack the group and run in the opposite direction. The Bitcheyes took their positions.

"Bitcheye! Bitcheye! Advance to engage. Target in the vicinity. Engage on my command. Engage!"

The opposing force returned fire and began to advance on Taquard's squad even though they were caught completely off guard. The other group was a heavy platoon opposed to Taquard's eight. As his team ran away the opposition had to negotiate a hillside. The group, which turned out to be another group of opposition cadets, advanced in the manner in which they were taught. However this proved to be futile. The three-second sprint (running as fast as you can for three seconds and hitting the ground) worked well on practice fields. However, in real life the terrain wasn't always favorable for diving onto. There where other factors to consider besides the three seconds being up. Ant mounds in Washington

State were no joke and could be as much as six feet high. It was also advised that they shouldn't be used for diving into. One of the opposing cadets did exactly this during his three second sprint. He was told during training to hit the ground after three seconds regardless. Other cadets threw artillery and grenade simulators uphill. This too proved to be a disaster. As they charged up the hill, simulators would roll downhill and go off. Cadets rolled down the slope and fell into other cadets. The snowball effect was well demonstrated in this fiasco.

One of the artillery simulators fell in a dry grassy area and started a fire. The other cadets who were sustaining injuries were now caught in a fire that they couldn't put out. Blazes continued to erupt with each passing breeze. Gusts of wind made it even worse. Trees caught on fire and the fire spread in all directions. The wind continued to blow. The fire approached a car that was in the vicinity.

"Shit! We got to get out of here."

"Holy mackerel, it's coming right at us."

"Drive, you idiot! Drive!"

"This trail ought to get us out of here."

"Damn turns. That thing is gaining on us. What's the hold up?"

"Mud. But not enough to stop us from leaving."

"Well, do it quick."

"Here we go."

The vehicle maneuvered around the forest at high speed. As it sped up a slight embankment it flipped over. Elsewhere a deuce-and-half (two and a half ton) truck responded to the spreading fire (at high speed) by accidentally launching itself off of a point affectionately known as "Ski Jump Pass." The one thing that the Army emphasized was speed. Regardless of the terrain, soldiers were taught to move fast. Like the three-second sprint, soldiers were told to follow procedures without question. This Army Mental Conditioning (AMC) did not help the injured soldiers in the disabled deuce and half that wound up going over a cliff. Many rescuers were disabled before they even got close to the area where they were supposed to render assistance.

Taquard's team was advancing according to their own plan. This also turned out to be the safest course of action. The cadets scattered as they ran from the roaring fire. The University of Nevada Reno cadet dove in the ant mound and had ants crawling all over him as he did all he could to escape the fire. Several weapons and articles of field gear were abandoned. For some strange reason cadets had the tendency to dive into ant mounds.

Eventually the fire reached the overturned abandoned vehicle. With the explosion that resulted, the post was aware of the fire and responded. Helicopters transported water. Emergency vehicles and fire trucks arrived. The incident resulted in the burning of 162 acres of forest land, eighteen cadets were hospitalized from injuries ranging from broken arms to excessive ant bites, and twenty-two lost M16 rifles. Another twenty-two were stolen when a group of soldiers found the cadets and transported them to safety. A lot of other losses were entailed as well.

"Are you hurt?" exclaimed a soldier to the cadet.

"Very much so," answered the cadet.

"Look, we're here to help you out. Where are the others?"

"They're nearby I think."

A few NCOs gathered the cadets with a truck then unloaded them off in a safe but heavily wooded area.

"Fall in!"

"How many cadets do you have?"

"Forty-four."

"Okay, let's form up and get accountability."

"Yes we have forty-four. They're all here."

"Some of them are injured pretty badly," a sergeant exclaimed.

"Look, we need to get an assessment."

"Stack all the weapons here and get a count," one of the sergeants ordered.

"There are only twenty-two weapons, what happened to the others?"

"I don't know," replied the cadet.

"Hey, Sarge! They want us to requisition the cadets to help fight the fire."

"Okay. We need to get you guys reassembled. Sorry, guys, but orders are orders."

After moving the group, the sergeant informed them that he would be right back.

"Listen, I need you to assess injuries and separate the injured cadets from the uninjured ones. This is not a drill. We'll be back soon."

After a while cadets were asking each other about the sergeant's whereabouts.

"Where could he be?"

"He said that he'd be right back."

"Somebody go and check."

After climbing up the small ravine the cadet returned. "He's gone!"

"What do you mean he's gone?"

"That's what I'm telling you. He's gone."

"He can't just be gone."

"Well, he is. And so is the truck. And so are all the weapons."

"Wait a minute. Do you mean to tell me that they took our weapons and just left us here?"

"That's what it looks like."

"What a mean thing to do. That was a mean thing to do. That's a mean thing to do to somebody," another cadet added.

"They stole our weapons."

"That was a mean thing to do," he repeated.

The command post was having their share of trouble as well.

"Hey, Buttholes! Any word of where your guys are at?"

"No, sir. Haven't heard a thing. Glasscock, what have you heard?"

"Nothing. The only cadets involved in the fire were all from the second phase group. Nobody from our group."

As it began to get dark, Taquard's team realized that there wasn't a flashlight among the group. They decided that they would bed down for the night while walking under a forest canopy which made the darkness even blacker. The only thing that they could do was sleep and wait for sunrise. Another rule to remember while camping is to go to the bathroom before going to bed. This was a rule that Taquard would learn, and never forget. During the middle of the night he was having a hellacious bowel movement that wasn't about to wait. The darkness was so great that you couldn't even see your hand in front of your face.

Without a flashlight or matches he made do with what he had under the circumstances. He assembled his gear tightly. Stood straight up, did an about face, marched thirty paces, did an about-face, and relieved himself. Upon completion, he marched thirty paces and knelt down. His gear was there. The maneuver was carried out without a hitch. Except for one thing, Waldo. Taquard relieved himself in the immediate vicinity where Waldo was sleeping. During his sleep he managed to roll over into Taquard's pyramid and got it all over himself, including his face. He lent a new visual meaning to the term "shit face." "Hey man, get out of other people's shit." It seemed that the euphemisms and corollaries to shit were endless.

As usual, Waldo expressed his disapproval of his predicament at the top of his lungs. Everything that Waldo did was at the top of his lungs. At Advanced Camp cadets were instructed to do everything loudly. Cadets were always shouting even though they didn't do anything else very well. Cadets screamed all of the time about anything and everything. Waldo was one of the worst screamers of all. After each and every class Waldo would go to the instructor, get about half an inch from his face and scream at the top of his lungs, "THANK YOU, SERGEANT!"

Waldo was always doing something stupid from constant yelling at the top of his lungs to something else that had no apparent rhyme or reason. Waldo would scream for no apparent reason. He would see something and just scream. Sometimes he would just look at a person and scream. The other thing of notable record was the fact that Waldo willfully dove into one of the ant mounds. As far as anyone knew, while many cadets dove into the ant mounds, he was the only cadet to deliberately dive into one. He was told by another cadet that if he dove into an ant mound that he would receive a medal of valor. It didn't take a lot of convincing before he was up to the challenge. Some of the other cadets even tried to persuade him out of doing it. Another cadet told him that he would get a medal for doing it. So he took off his gear and shirt and screamed as he dove into the ant mound head first. He was taken to the clinic for treatment and although he didn't get a medal or citation for jumping into the mound he did get a medal at the end of camp for being the loudest cadet. They actually gave out a medal to the loudest cadet in the camp.

Jumping into the ant mound wasn't a factor.

The question of guarding the objective was on LTC Steinweber's mind. Never before had he lost an ROTC engagement. His impatience got the better of him. He decided to conduct search parties for the cadets.

"Glasscock! You got any idea where them cadets went off to?" Steinweber would shout.

"Not really, most of them are lost. I doubt that they are even seeking the objective."

"Buttholes, I want you to call the evaluators and tell them to declare us the victors."

The objective was a red flag waving on a tall pole. Taquard's group could see it from a distance and contemplated on how to take it. Upon positive identification of the flag, one of the cadets came up with a plan. The plan was to get close enough to the objective to observe the guard detail. Then they would determine on how to approach the objective. They would substitute a decoy flag in place of the actual one to avoid alerting any of the guards.

"Hey, Charlie," exclaimed Taquard. "I got an idea."

"What is it?"

"On the other side of their outpost is their parking lot."

"So?"

"Nobody's watching the cars."

"Yeah. Okay, so what?"

"Maybe if one is unlocked you could honk the horn or come up with an idea to draw everyone's attention to the cars."

"All right. Sounds like an idea. I'll meet you back at garrison."

Charlie circled around the command post area until he came to the parking lot. He was wondering about what type of distraction he would have to come up with. He didn't buy the possibility that someone would be stupid enough to leave their car unlocked. But there was one thing about Charlie: He was reliable. No matter how ridiculous a given task may be, he always figured out how to accomplish it with flying colors. Not only did Charlie manage to find an unlocked vehicle, he found one with their keys in the ignition. He opened the door, placed a book that was also in the van on the steering wheel in such a way that it steadily honked the horn.

Naturally, the cadre rushed to the parking lot in response to the noise. It didn't take too long for Taquard and his team to retrieve the flag. Replacing it with a decoy wasn't an ordeal either. In about one minute, the swap was made and the cadets were fleeing back to garrison.

"Sir," CPT Bucholtz said. "Just got off the horn with Old Man Tipton, the war games have been called off due to all of the commotion caused by the fire."

"Good. We are undefeated in war games. Nobody's ever been able to defeat us. Once again, we are victorious. My superior leadership skills and quality of management has once again prevailed. It is time for me to once again bask in the glory of victory and success."

"Glasscock, get the flag and turn it in."

Later, Glasscock walked in the post exclaiming, "It's gone!"

"Gone? What do you mean it's gone," exclaimed Bucholtz.

"Gone?" shouted Steinweber. "What do you mean gone?"

Glasscock held up a blue flag with the Department of the Navy seal. "This is what was there. The real flag is gone."

"Dammit! Where's the real flag?" Steinweber was furious. "How in the hell are we going to live this one down?"

Bucholtz interjected, "Sir, this is the only loss out of who knows how many. Nobody's perfect."

"Nobody's ever lost out to a bunch of cadets in a war game, not ever. We're the first. How on earth did they ever manage to pull this off? I'm going to be the laughing stock of this whole damn fort. They'll make up jokes about me. No telling what they'll come up with. Now what am I going to do?"

For the first time in ROTC Advanced Camp history, the cadets actually beat the cadre.

Back at garrison cadets did cleaning, attended classes, and took time off. One of the rules in the Army is that you don't clean your weapon too quickly. Weapons cleaning followed returning from the field for those who didn't lose theirs. Some cadets wrapped their weapons in plastic and refrained from firing them in order to enhance field recovery. After a thorough cleaning in a timely manner, they were still rejected as being too dirty. No matter how clean a weapon was it was considered to be too dirty if it was turned in too early. However, there was another side to the same coin. The arms room inspectors couldn't leave their post until every weapon was accounted for or listed as lost. Lost weapons reports could not originate from the arms inspectors themselves. After being turned down the group of cadets who believed that their weapons were inspection-ready took put their weapons to their wall lockers, locked their lockers, and went out and got drunk. They went to town in their uniforms because they weren't allowed to put on civilian clothes until their weapons were turned in. They returned at three the next morning. The arms room was still open while waiting for the weapons. Though the cadets didn't do any additional cleaning whatsoever, their weapons passed the subsequent inspection without any shortcomings.

As screwed up as Advanced Camp ended up being, there were positive aspects as well if one was willing to learn from other people's mistakes and if one was willing to look hard enough. The values to be gained from Advanced Camp had to be deliberately sought out by the individual because they weren't available to the casual onlooker. It was easy to understand why ROTC wasn't a preferred assignment. The truth of the matter was that ROTC, like recruiting, was the assignment that everyone avoided. It wasn't glamorous and there was very little recognition even when programs were successful. Most people who were assigned to an ROTC post inherited a disaster that was beyond repair. ROTC was a trash hauler detail that was only one rung above being a recruiter. Recruiters were considered to be the worst of the worst. ROTC was only slightly better.

One of the challenges that the cadets were faced with was to determine if there was anything of value that was taught at Advanced Camp that could be used in the civilian sector. Actually, there was, The Duty Roster. The Duty Roster was a fantastic tool that could benefit both the military and civilians alike. In the military it was used to keeping track of who performed specific details and more importantly, it was valuable in determining who should perform it next. It can also be used in the civilian sector in numerous ways as well.

The Duty Roster consists of several rows and columns. The first column is where the names of the unit members would go. The heading of the subsequent columns would consist of applicable dates in which duty was to be performed. Each person's row would be assigned a number. At the beginning several people would have the same number. On the day or rotation that duty is actually performed, the person performing duty would have the number 0 by his name on the day that he performed duty. Everyone else's numbers would increase by 1. If it was a new Duty Roster then everyone would have a 1 by his name except the person who did duty. He would have a 0. On the second duty day, for example, everyone who did not perform duty would have a 1 added to his previous number. The person who performed duty would get a 0. In this case where a different person performed duty there would be a 0 in the column, a 1, and everyone else would have a 2. As time goes by, the person determining who would get the next duty assignment would look to the person with the highest number. Other considerations, such as availability, would have to be factored in but the numbers would continue to increase for those who didn't perform duty. People would also be able to volunteer for additional duty in order to reduce their number down to 0. The Duty Roster proved to be an effective tool in both the military and civilian worlds. The sad thing about it was that most people never knew what a duty roster was or how to use it once they were in a position to make decisions or assignments. They based their decisions on politics rather than on solid information that both improved and enhanced management techniques.

## DUTY ROSTER

| Name/Day | Monday | Tuesday | Wednesday | Thursday | Friday | Saturday |
|---|---|---|---|---|---|---|
| Joe | 0 | 1 | 2 | 3 | 4 | 0 |
| Ed | 1 | 2 | 0 | 1 | 2 | 3 |
| Frank | 1 | 0 | 1 | 2 | 3 | 4 |
| Roy | 1 | 2 | 3 | 4 | 0 | 1 |
| Al | 1 | 2 | 3 | 0 | 1 | 2 |

During the final field exercise something began to happen, something difficult to describe. A bonding began to seep in. It crept in slowly and sporadically, but nevertheless, it began to make an appearance. All of a sudden Reggie Snyder wasn't such a bad guy after all, even if he did annoy everyone with his camera. He was always attempting to take pictures of four people taking a dump in the barracks latrine. The latrine had four toilets with no privacy walls between them. At first cadets would hold it until the middle of the night in attempts to gain privacy. By the end of the first week cadets would be doing their business while carrying on conversations. Afterwards, cadets brought in something to read then later something to eat. Some of the cadets would crap and eat at the same time. Later still, female cadets would come into the male latrine informally while someone was sitting on the pot. Neither broke stride in conducting their business.

Bonding didn't always take hold. After a tiring and lengthy ordeal in the field Taquard came across Waldo. Looking at Waldo, he began to acknowledge that maybe there was some hope in learning how to get along with others. Without saying a word Waldo let out a goofy scream. While the situation for bonding was set, it would take cooperation on the part of the cadets to make it work. While it did come, it came late. In the case of Nelson Johnson, Taquard knew that he was a first rate soldier, but he realized it on the final day of camp. He would be the one that Taquard would want to see again, but never did. He reminded him of the refined class of people that he was surrounded by during his years at Rowland-Hall St. Mark's. Nelson would have been regarded highly regardless of what path he took.

Some of the cadets came up with a Bitcheye Commando Handbook just prior to graduation. The concept was simple. Everyone who wanted to would contribute something to the handbook. The cadets were allowed to solicit information elsewhere. Many went to Rangers, cadre members, and instructors. With forty cadets in the platoon, the handbook was developed in record time. Initially there was an argument of using the term Bitcheye instead of Millersville Liberator. Somehow the word Millersville Liberator didn't seem to have a lot of oomph behind it when it came to a handbook title. Many cadets initially protested the development of the book but later changed their minds for fear of being left out. The book consisted of basic military skills and information. It was edited to ensure that information wasn't duplicated. It included information pertaining to class categories and symbols to shining your shoes to a high gloss shine to rank insignia of all branches of the service to Boy Scout and Ranger skills to configuring a water tight poncho raft for transporting clothes and equipment down a river to a wide variety of other interesting bits of information. Taquard added illustrations to the book since he wasn't able to come up with any ideas that had not already been previously submitted by somebody else. He was able to create the Bitcheye logo that consisted of a skull without a jawbone, Airborne wings, and a file and claw below it. He copied ideas from other sources but the end product was original. Another thing that was added to the handbook was a motto, creed, slogan, secret challenge and password, and a signal for Bitcheyes to recognize other by.

The end result was impressive even though it was a last minute impulse. It probably wouldn't have been a whole lot better if they had a lot more time to argue over the details. Instead of discussing and voting on the motto, creed and such, one cadet simply made an unchallenged contribution. There was no time to debate the logo or anything else. Everything that was submitted was taken on its own merit.

Bitcheye Motto: Success through perseverance

Bitcheye Slogan (a direct Jefferson Davis quote): Never be haughty to the humble, never be humble to the haughty.

A couple of the cadets managed to get enough copies of the handbook printed off just in time to pass them out prior to graduation. Everyone autographed each other's book. This resulted in the creating a keepsake that was more valuable than the yearbook. There were some extra copies that were given to the cadre.

"We forgot to dedicate a patron saint for the Bitcheyes," one of the Catholic cadets added.

"Choose one then," another cadet answered.

He chose Saint Rita who was also the patron saint of impossible dreams. There were no objections.

The entire Bitcheye Platoon graduated on time. This was an unexpected surprise for the cadets and cadre alike. Every Bitcheye was either commissioned on the last day of summer camp or advanced in their school's ROTC program. And in their own way, each one gained an identity to overcome the impossible in spite of overwhelming odds. Other groups like the Rangers were better recognized and had far more members. However, the Bitcheyes came into a right of their own with only forty members.

# Chapter Four
## *Airborne*

What Advanced ROTC Camp was, Airborne School was anything but. Advanced Camp was difficult in the sense that standards and requirements were ambiguous and political. All females graduated in the upper third regardless of numerous absences and egregiously piss poor performance. One female cadet was absent for six weeks of the six week course and still graduated in the top third of the platoon. Defying all facets of reason and logic was the main staple of ROTC. ROTC instructors were typically not Airborne-qualified and didn't like seeing cadets accomplish something that they themselves couldn't. While they couldn't challenge Taquard on his strength or physical capabilities, ROTC instructors criticized him for having a poor work ethic. Wimps tend to attack another's work ethic. Airborne was the exact opposite of ROTC. It was professional. Unlike Advance Camp that consisted of a cadre of slovenly misfits, Airborne was the epitome of professionalism. Tasks, conditions, and standards remained constant among classes from year to year. The status quo was perfection. The fact was that when you graduated from Advanced Camp all you had was a certificate that by itself amounted to nothing. When you graduated from Airborne School you were awarded a set of wings.

Airborne was Taquard's introduction to Saint Michael. Saint Michael was the patron saint of the paratrooper. He was an archangel who was a warrior. It seemed that every branch of the Army or badge had a patron saint. At that time neither Rangers nor Air Assault had patron saints. Later on, the Rangers would assign Saint Andrew as their patron saint. Saint Andrew, who was a martyr, was a disciple of John the Baptist. The ROTC patron saint may as well have been Judas.

Elwood's father even advised him not to go to Airborne. He himself was subject to a parachute malfunction while bailing out of an airplane in North Viet Nam during the war. He was shot down in combat. The automatic systems were destroyed by enemy antiaircraft fire during combat. The systems that were guaranteed not to fail did. During a spinning nosedive the pilot screamed for a bail out. Pulling the handles on the side of the seat launched the seat upwards into a canopy that didn't deploy. The impact of being launched into the canopy at high speed nearly broke his neck and back. Though it did not open the canopy, it twisted the helmet about ninety degrees. While wearing a helmet sideways, he wrestled to deploy the canopy. Taquard's father was able to eject out the disabled B-57 on the second attempt. One malfunction led to another. Though he was able to eject out of the airplane he was still attached to the seat as he was falling fast. He had to wrestle out of the seat and manually open his parachute without sight. There was no time to wrestle with the helmet. The pilot did not eject out of the airplane. The plane crashed in the ground and exploded. Taquard drifted towards the wreckage after getting his chute open. This was his first jump. It was a malfunction that had risers running behind his back and between his legs while he was falling head first. The landing (feet, knees, and face) was followed by enemy rifle fire directed at him. He quickly removed his helmet while cutting his face and ran away from the advancing enemy. The secret to surviving the ordeal was to plan out the response before the situation happened. He always wondered how he would respond to a spinning nose dive with a disabled parachute system. He mentally rehearsed his responses before getting into the airplane. This thinking may have been the difference between him and the pilot. Another nickel's worth of free advice is to watch where you are going when you are running. He hesitated when he came to an incline. Instead of jumping over it, he slowed down to go over it.

Even with the enemy chasing him and shooting he paused because he couldn't see what was beyond the incline. Fortunately, he did pause when he did. A blind leap would have landed him some logs that were in a small ravine. Falling on them would have crippled him for sure. His pursuit to escape the enemy was observed by a helicopter that was passing by.

Airborne was everything that ROTC was not. While it was becoming increasing more difficult to distinguish the officers from the enlisted based on behavior, there was a notable difference between those who were Airborne and those who were not. Even though the drop-out rate was considerably higher at Airborne than at Advanced Camp, Taquard enjoyed it a lot more. Airborne was always accompanied with a myriad of horror stories and was highly discouraged by most ROTC departments; however, Taquard found it to be a cinch. It was downright easy. Factually, Taquard was also prepared for it. It just seemed like the place for him. At first he wanted it to be over and done with while he envied those in Jump Week. Later he would look back and wish he were back in Ground Week.

Females were not an issue at Airborne as a result of their limited population. Like Advanced Camp, the females at Airborne were unattractive, sported tattoos, and displayed the most undesirable behavior among the human race. Elwood Taquard was able to secure an ROTC Airborne slot from his school. He correctly reasoned that if the school had any slots for Airborne, he should be selected. The university had seven Airborne slots, five of which were cancelled by the senior cadre member. He reasoned that he didn't have seven cadets who could make it through Airborne. He had already selected two cadets when Taquard expressed his interest in attending. Taquard was the top cadet at his university both physically and mentally, and he knew it. Although he was extremely popular among the student body, he wasn't well-liked in ROTC. Acquiring the slot involved a conversation between Taquard and the senior cadre member, LTC Posey.

"Sorry, but the slots are already taken."

"Then take one of the slots away from someone else and give it to me."

"I can't. Besides, only the best cadets get to go."

"There isn't a single cadet in this program as good as me. Not one. Give me the slot."

"Well, if we compare PT test scores then we will see that there are other aspects for determining who the best cadet is."

"Grades. Compare the grades. See who is making the President's List. See who is on the Dean's List. If my grades were lower, I'd be on the Honor Roll. Compare the courses and see who is taking the hardest courses."

"Well. There are more important things in life besides good grades. We were considering the spirit of the cadets."

"Give me a break. You have more Aleister Crowley wannabes in this program than any other category. Your cadets are shit. They are a reflection of the cadre. I will graduate from Airborne, guaranteed. If I don't I'll take back everything that I've said."

"It just so happens that no one from this school has ever graduated from Airborne before fuck stick. It ain't never been done before."

"I'll be the first."

"If you're not, you owe me $1,000."

"Why?"

"That's what it costs you for me to give you a slot. Take it or leave it."

"I said I'll make it."

"Have it your way, you motherfucker."

There is one thing that a jump student needs to understand as soon as possible. Acknowledge understanding with "clear" instead of yes. Follow the acknowledgment with the rank of the person to whom you are addressing. This is all followed with an enthusiastic "Airborne!" A common statement that was heard was, "Clear, Sergeant! Airborne!"

A year of free weights at the Iron Den seemed like the ticket to making it through Airborne. Day 1 of Airborne began with a physical fitness test that consisted of doing forty-five perfect push-ups in two minutes, forty-five sit ups in two minutes, and running two miles in boots in under sixteen minutes. When Taquard reported for his test, SGT Brown, a Black Hat, looked at him and said, "I know you'll make it." After doing forty-five push-ups SGT Brown ordered, "Recover!" The sit-ups had the same results. While doing the two-mile run, Taquard experienced a problem. At the halfway point he couldn't find his evaluator. He ran back and forth looking for his evaluator among several Black Hats until he was ordered to keep going. The two-mile run was followed by the requirement of eight pull ups from the dead hang position. Taquard was able to accomplish all of these requirements with ease. Those who failed the test were sent to Zero Week while the others went to their first class in a set of bleachers.

The Airborne student body included Navy SEALs (Sea, Air, and Land). They could be considered the special operations forces of the US Navy. Jesse Ventura, thirty-eighth governor of Minnesota, was a SEAL. The competitive SEAL physical fitness standards consisted of swimming 500 yards in eight and a half minutes or less, 100 push-ups in two minutes, 100 sit-ups in two minutes, fifteen to twenty pull-ups from a dead hang, and a one-and-a-half-mile run in under ten minutes. The Black Hat explained that jewelry was not to be worn during Jump School or on any jumps. He explained that dog tags were to be worn in the left rear pocket of your pants. He clearly stated that watches, bracelets, necklaces, or any other type of jewelry was not to be worn, period. His lengthy explanation was followed by a question and answer session. He asked if there were any questions.

One of the students raised his hand and asked, "What about wedding bands?"

The Black Hat responded, "Get down here! Get your ass down here right now!" The student was put in the front lean and rest (push-up) position in front of the entire class. He remained in that position until the class was over. He continued to explain, "No watches, no bracelets, no necklaces, no jewelry of any kind whatsoever. No exceptions! That includes fucking wedding bands! No fucking jewelry! When I say no fucking jewelry, I mean no fucking jewelry! You can either remove the wedding bands or you can get out of Airborne. Does anyone else have any questions?"

"What about religious medallions?" another student asked.

The Black Hat responded, "Get down here! Get your ass down here right now!" The student was put in the front lean and rest position. "No watches, no bracelets, no necklaces, no jewelry of any kind. No exceptions! That includes fucking wedding bands, and fucking religious medallions! No fucking jewelry! When I say no fucking jewelry I mean no fucking jewelry! You can either remove the wedding bands and religious medallions or you can get the hell out. Are there any more dumb-ass questions? Remember, the only stupid question is the one that is asked."

"What about medic alert bracelets?"

Again, the Black Hat responded, "Get down here! Get your ass down here right now!"

The student was put in the front lean and rest position. "No watches, no bracelets, no necklaces, no jewelry of any kind. No exceptions! That includes fucking wedding bands, fucking religious medallions, and fucking medic alert bracelets! No fucking jewelry! When I say no fucking jewelry I mean no fucking jewelry! You can either remove the wedding bands, religious medallions, and medic alert bracelets or you can get the hell out."

This was followed by no further questions from the students.

There is a saying in the Army: The only stupid question is the one that isn't asked. Actually, that's a misnomer. What they meant to say was: the only stupid question is the one that **is** asked. You can't ask a stupid question if you don't ask a question.

There was a nagging feeling that stayed with Taquard for both Ground and Tower Week. That was knowing that he was going to quit. He knew that he wasn't going to stay in Airborne. He knew that he was going to quit when the Black Hats asked the students if anyone wanted to quit. Throughout the course, they gave students ample opportunities to quit. Although Taquard decided to quit, he also decided to postpone his quitting until the next time they asked. He kept postponing it until the end of Tower Week. When he got to Jump Week, they stopped asking.

Not only did Taquard agree with the Black Hats, he got along with them. There was a myriad of horror stories about Black Hats and SEALs. The stories barely amounted to be anything more than sheer bullshit. Factually, the Black Hats were the epitome of professionalism and were serious about carrying out their duties to elite standards.

Taquard was placed next to a SEAL in his assigned stick. The SEAL drew attention away from him, but he didn't seem to mind. Students were assigned roster numbers and a dedicated place in the formation. Taquard was C226. The logical sequence of separating individual SEALs placed 171 next to C226. The SEAL kept the tempo light while making Airborne seem more like a Sunday picnic than a challenge, only funnier. SEALs stood out in the formations because they were the only ones who did not cut all of their hair off like the rest of the students. Having 171 in the class was like a teenager on a carousel constantly asking, "When does the ride start?"

Black Hats struck fear into the students with constant inspections and yelling that rivaled Sam Kinison. Everyone, except for the SEALs, tried to stay out of the "gig pit." Taquard kept a black magic marker in his pocket to touch up his belt buckle during oncoming uniform inspections. He never saw the gig pit.

On the second day of Airborne, the cadre taught the students a song that was to be sung every morning until the end of the course.

*Airborne, Airborne all the way,*
*Airborne, Airborne all the way,*
*We like it here, we like it here, we finally found a home,*
*We like it here, we like it here, we finally found a home,*
*A home, a home, a home away from home,*
*A home, a home, a home away from home.*

While the Black Hats constantly harassed the students, Taquard hardly got yelled at nor did he feel any wrath that the Black Hats dealt out. Their focus was diverted to 171. Airborne consists of four weeks of training. Zero Week is dedicated to the enlisted and those who fail the PT test, and consists of doing PT and cutting the grass. Ground Week is where officers and cadets who pass the PT test begin their training. Tower Week is then followed by Jump Week.

During Ground Week, the Black Hats reprimanded the entire student company from the beginning. The class leaders who dropped like flies were required to come up with a class motto. The class motto ended up being, "Class 37, Death from Heaven, Airborne." The PT requirements were strenuous. The students averaged more than 200 push-ups daily. The length of the runs gradually increased to a five-mile run that Friday. Calisthenics were numerous along with large amounts of repetitions that had to be performed accurately. In addition to PT, students were punished for making mistakes or answering questions inaccurately. They were required to either do more push-ups or beat their boots. After doing the additional push-ups the students stood up in a parachute stance simulating the looking up the skirt or parachute. They would remain in that position until they were told to recover. Looking up at an open parachute was the best skirt that anyone could look up. This was definitely a course that built up a person both physically and spiritually. It was designed to make you a better person and to challenge you to do something that you never imagined yourself ever doing. In spite of the continuous harassment that was designed to convince students to quit, it was a very professional course.

SFC Pratcher was the senior Black Hat for Ground Week. He put the company through rigorous work outs and was constantly on everyone's case. He had a sense of warmth and compassion that could be felt throughout the jugular vein. He addressed the student company, "You guys never listen. That is your problem. You never pay attention. You have your heads so far up your asses that you can't hear shit! You had better start paying attention and stop fucking up. Now pull your heads out of your asses and start listening!"

The entire company was silent. It was so quiet that you could hear a pin drop. Or in this case, it was so quiet that everyone could hear 171 asking, "What did he say?"

One of the cadets made the untimely mistake of farting during one of SFC Pratcher's fireside chats. As a result of the students being tight-jawed, noises seemed to carry throughout company formations.

"Who did that?"

True to the supportive character of the Army, about seven students simultaneously pointed at the culprit and shouted in unison, "He did!"

The cadet was called out of the formation.

"Are you trying to fuck with me? Are you? If you're going to shit your pants, you're not going to do it in my formation!"

Pratcher escalated his tirade against the cadet before placing him in the gig pit. This was a prelude to the formal inspection. Violations ranged from not being clean shaven (the emphasis of being clean shaven could not be overstated), to boot shines (shine could also not be overstated), to having the correct color of socks. Socks had to be olive drab (OD). Roster number 171 had the audacity of showing up in formation in white socks. In addition to being sent to the gig pit, he was nicknamed Disco Socks for the rest of the day because the Black Hats thought that he was dressed up for going to a disco instead of jump training.

As it turned out, the SEALs did go out for a night on the town after their training day. Following the 1700 formation, the SEALs took off to town in their uniforms. They departed and by 0400 hours the next morning they were nowhere in sight. By the 0430 first formation the SEALs came running in just in time to make it for roll call.

"Damn, you smell like you've been drinking," C226 would say to 171.

"So?"

"The Black Hats will catch you."

"Who cares?"

"You forgot to shave too."

"I didn't forget, I just didn't do it."

During the formation, 171 belched in the Black Hat's face. He was told to drop. This meant that your hands had to hit the ground before your feet to assume the front lean and rest position. When performing this maneuver, look to where your feet will land. 171 managed to put his feet on a Black Hat's boots. While the Black Hats surrounded 171, the SEALs surrounded the Black Hats. As potentially unpleasant as the situation could have been, nothing ever came of it. Once again, 171 went to the gig pit.

Having 171 around made Airborne go quickly. Not only did he keep people's spirits up while making them laugh, he took attention away from others while drawing it on himself. Not everyone was close enough to a SEAL to laugh their way through Airborne. The thirty-four-foot tower and parachute landing falls (PLF) came relatively easy for Taquard. Although he was right handed, the right PLF was the most difficult for him. Left PLFs were a cinch. The thirty-four-foot tower is thirty-four feet high, but it initially seems a lot higher. Eventually, it feels like fifteen feet. Anything beyond twenty feet is difficult to judge, especially if there are no reference points. For that reason, you should not release your parachute before your feet get wet when you are jumping into water. It is not out of the ordinary to be sixty feet above the water while feeling that you are about to hit the water. Students dawned on airborne gear that simulated the wearing of a parachute. They would walk up several flights of steps to the top of the tower where they would assume the exit position and demonstrate their exit capabilities.

The first time at the top of the tower was frightening. The Black Hat below who served as the grader looked like he could fit on a bottle top.

"Sound off with your name and roster number," the Black Hat said as he put the student in the tower exit location. Taquard forgot both his name and roster number. This hesitation resulted in him being thrown out of the tower by the Black Hat.

"Get the hell out of my tower!"

After receiving his "No Go" rating, he went to remedial training along with hundreds of other students. Remedial training consisted of standing in a mock frame and jumping off of a step that was about three and a half inches high. Instructors coached students on their form. Form was vital in assuming the exit position and during the exit itself. When the Black Hat slapped the back of your leg you performed the exit. The challenge was to advance six inches with perfect form. Six inches was all that you had to move forward once you were in position. The Black Hat would slap the back of the student's leg and he would jump while concentrating on his form. The Black Hat continuously reprimanded the student on his form. Reprimands came directly and were also addressed to groups.

"What is wrong with you guys? We tell you how to do something. We show you how to do it. We tell you what you're doing wrong. And you still fuck it up!"

Taquard never gave up. Remedial training continued for two weeks. The thirty-four-foot tower began to feel like just a few feet and Taquard could sound off with "Taquard C226," while positioning for exit. Tower form and exiting without being forcibly prompted by a Black Hat became easy.

August was hot in Georgia, especially with parachute gear. While advancing up the steps to the top of the tower, he decided that the normal position of attention was not for him. As soon as he got above eye level of the people on the ground he started slouching. He would lean against the tower foundation, cross his feet, and relax. It took about thirty minutes to get to the top of the tower. Taquard slouched for almost twenty minutes before he was discovered.

"C226! Beat your boots," the Black Hat yelled.

Beating your boots was a punishment for an infraction. It consisted of putting your arms out to the side, bending your knees, and touching your boots. Although, he got caught, it was worth it. Beating your boots ten times was a small price to pay for sheer relaxation. It was worth it. Since he was also one of the first students to qualify on the tower, he didn't have to go up that many times.

The exercises became more rigorous during Tower Week as opportunities to quit increased. The task that scared Taquard the most was going up the 250-foot tower to be dropped for a simulated parachute jump. Daily runs increased from three miles to five while exercises were added to the PT program. Elwood was prepared for Tower Week long before he even had an Airborne slot.

The 250-foot towers were no joke. They scared everyone except the SEALs. The towers themselves were rumored to have been exhibits at a world's fair prior to World War II. They were old and rickety. Students were strapped in a parachute that was temporarily fastened to a metal ring. The ring was attached to a cable that would lift the student from the ground to 250 feet at one of the tower arms. There were three towers, only two were operational, each with four arms. The requirement was to perform successful PLFs from the tower at least 50% of the time. Each student was required to go up the tower at least twice and for a maximum of four times.

As Taquard was taken up with the sound of a stretching cable by an old engine, he was afraid of falling prematurely. There were jolts in the raising of the cable. It felt like the machine was about to break. Then it came to an abrupt stop. Understanding the commands from the Black Hats on the ground was acknowledged by spreading your legs apart and closing them again. The student was too far for verbal responses to be effective. Once a student was in position, the Black Hats had to determine the release time. If the wind could blow the student into the tower, the student had to hang there and wait. When the release time was acceptable, the student was hoisted up to a release mechanism where he would begin his descent. It was Taquard's luck to bust his first descent. He had to go up a second, except he had to pass the next try. Many were successful on their first attempt. They had to go up for a second time but not for a grade. Elwood's second attempt was successful but subject to a compromise. He was so excited that he entangled himself after landing. The Black Hat told him that if he moved again before being untangled, that the "Go" would be changed to a "No Go" rating. He froze.

Another SEAL prank occurred in the middle of the night. The arms of one of the towers had bed sheets hanging from them. Each sheet had a large letter written on it. Together they spelled, "GO NAVY." While no one knew exactly who put the sheets up on the arms, everyone knew that it was the SEALs. No one in the Army had the guts to pull a stunt like that.

Airborne was progressing for Taquard while he continued to postpone quitting. End of the day formations at the barracks included mail call. More mail began to arrive. Room inspection results and announcements didn't apply to him. Officers were never subject to room inspections. Neither were cadets it seemed.

MSG Graham conducted the end of the day formation.

"One of the rooms was swept. It was a clean room, except for one thing. Some dumb-ass Private swept the dirt into a nice neat pile but forgot to put it in the trash."

He would comment on the discrepancies of the inspections in a direct manner.

"We found a room with a made up bed. The deficiency was that there was a fuck book on the bed. And next to the fuck book was a Bible."

There were penalties for room deficiencies, but Taquard never received a single gig throughout his tenure at Airborne so he never knew what the gig pit was like.

The class itself would change as time progressed. Students would fail, quit, or be transferred. Other students would be transferred into the class. Three-digit roster numbers on the helmets would be preceded by letters. Officers had the letter A as a designator, while cadets had a C. Enlisted had no designators. Those who failed the PT test would have a P placed in front of their roster number. Those who were recycled through

Ground Week would be given a G. An officer who failed the PT test, recycled through Ground Week, repeated Tower Week, and missed a jump during Jump Week would have a new roster number reflecting his secondary attempts and may look something like PGTJA336.

Jump Week was completely different from the two proceeding weeks. PT consisted of a two-mile run at a moderate pace. No one asked if you wanted to quit. And of course there was jumping instead of training.

The first jump was the most memorable. The feeling that you were about to actually jump from an airplane didn't set in until the door of the airplane was opened. It was hard to imagine that you were going to actually jump from an airplane. Even after putting on the parachute and reserve, it still didn't seem possible.

**JUMP RULE NUMBER 1: Before putting on the parachute, always mentally rehearse what you will do during a malfunction.**

Elwood mentally rehearsed what he would do in case of a malfunction. This was advice that was passed on to him from his father. He thought about every possible malfunction and what he would do to correct each and every one before dawning on the parachute.

Before walking to the tarmac he noticed a placard that was posted inside the parachute dawning shed. It read:

***The sky, moreso than the sea, is unforgiving of the slightest mistake.***

Getting on the plane was easy. Sitting with several others had a less regimented format than did the previous two weeks. There were Airborne students, Black Hats, Rangers, Golden Knights, and others who were making jumps as well. Everyone, to include experienced jumpers, seemed nervous. Even Black Hats were nervous. Unlike an airline, the loading of jumpers was immediately followed by the airplane taking off and becoming airborne. When the door was opened Elwood could feel his heart beating and feel the rush of cold air sweep around him while it made an evil hissing noise. He was sure enough nervous and ready to quit. No one was asking. Nervousness turned into fear. Everyone was scared. The routine began.

Even with the roaring of the C-130 engines, he could hear the Jump Master announce, "Six minutes."

"Six minutes. Six minutes. Six minutes," the jumpers responded while they nudged everyone beside them with their elbows as previously rehearsed.

Taquard's heart started beating even faster. It was beating too fast as it was, but the rate increased. He felt as if he could hear his heart beating.

"First pass, stand up!"

Taquard couldn't believe that he was actually doing this. However, everything went in accordance to the procedure. He stood up with the rest of the pass. Even though he wasn't wearing a watch, he was certain that he wasn't getting his six minutes worth. Time sped by.

"Hook static lines!"

Factually, the Jump Master paused between commands. However, Taquard perceived the Jump Master to be a jabber mouth. Each command caused his heart to leap into an increasingly rapid rate of beating. He could feel his heart beating in his head, and it was loud.

"Check equipment!"

He proceeded through the motions while trying to respond to his fear. His heart rate was so rapid he could taste it. There was no where to go except forward.

"Sound off with equipment check!"

Each man in the pass inspected the man in front of him. The last man in the pass slapped the right rear thigh of the man in front of him with the command of "Okay," when it was determined that everything was okay. This proceeded to the front of the pass. For Taquard, the inspection was more of an automatic response than an inspection. As soon as the man behind Taquard slapped him, he automatically slapped the person in front of him while announcing, "Okay."

The front man in the pass, Second Lieutenant Hadfield, motioned to the Jump Master with his right hand commanding, "All okay!" Taquard could hear Hadfield from the middle of the pass and in spite of the engine roar. His heart felt like it was six inches out in front of his chest beating loudly. The first jump would be an individual tap-out jump as opposed to a mass jump. There were several types of jumps, but this was preferred for first time jumpers.

"One minute!"

The command was passed from the Jump Master down the line to the end of the pass. Each person in the pass would turn his head and look at the person behind him and repeated the command while signaling with one finger.

"Thirty seconds!"

It didn't seem like thirty seconds to relay the command. This command was addressed with the same procedures as the previous one with the exception of the signaling of one finger. Instead, the signal was the small sign made with the index finger and thumb.

There was a red light next to a green light next to the door. He could see that the red light was on. Taquard could actually hear the red light go off. There was a pause. The green light went on making the same sound that was made when the red light went off.

"Stand in the door!"

Hadfield postured himself in the jump position.

"Go!"

Hadfield was gone. The line got significantly shorter and proceeded to move forward. Taquard didn't want to move. It felt as though he was being pushed forward. Why couldn't lines at the theatre or amusement park ever move this fast? Each jumper postured himself in the door until the Jump Master slapped him on the back of the leg and commanded "Go."

When he got to the front of the pass he handed his static line to the Jump Master who grabbed it in a manner as to impatiently say "Give me that!"

"Stand in the door!"

Taquard assumed the jump position that he rehearsed several times before. His form was perfect. It couldn't be anything but. They rehearsed to the point where everyone was perfect. The challenge was to advance six inches. While he looked down on the ground he noticed that the buildings were significantly smaller than the houses that you would find on a Monopoly board. Semi trucks were small enough to do doughnuts on a postage stamp. One thing was for certain. There was no way that he was going to jump out of this airplane.

The Jump Master slapped his leg. The response was to automatically jump out. There wasn't the slightest tinge of resistance whatsoever. Scared out of his mind one instant; out the door the next. It couldn't have been easier.

The air was cool and quiet that he had never experienced before. The experience was peaceful. As Taquard basked in the tranquility of his peacefulness he heard a screaming from a bullhorn in the distance.

"Check canopy!"

He savored his moment of solitude.

The frantic yell was repeated.

"Check canopy!"

The cool air and quiet was a perfect feeling unlike any other.

"Check canopy!"

Sometimes you get the feeling that someone is addressing you. That feeling happened to Taquard. At first, Taquard was only interested in enjoying his own private world. Moving six inches was a momentous challenge in and of itself. After that accomplishment, his fear was consumed with peaceful bliss. And although he practiced it many times before, he did not check his canopy upon exiting the airplane. In response to the screaming Black Hat on the ground, he decided to take a moment to check his canopy.

The parachute did not open. It came out but it didn't open. It was twisted in what is commonly known as a Roman candle or cigarette roll. He never felt himself falling. He struggled frantically in what seemed to be the last few moments of his life. His moment of bliss was replaced by doing all that he could to open the parachute to stay alive. Deploying the reserve would introduce the possibility of an entanglement. The best option in this case was suspended agony. Luckily, he had mentally considered the options before putting on the chute. There was no time for that now. Suspended agony consisted of extending the arms out to the side (this is known as the Iron Cross among Olympic gymnasts) while gripping the risers and putting the legs in a bicycle motion. This was practiced during Tower Week. It was difficult and agony to perform the drill. This time however, Taquard was able to yank the risers below his waist rapidly with his arms fully extended. The simultaneous bicycle leg motion was performed rapidly at chest level. His rate would be the envy of any Tour de France competitor. He moved his arms up and down rapidly like a bird taking flight. This procedure performed at a high rate of speed resulted in air being trapped at the lower end of the parachute. Repeated efforts resulted in more and more air filling and opening the canopy. No agony was felt throughout the ordeal. The parachute began filling with air as it was untwisting. He kept looking at the progress of the canopy while performing vigorously. Eventually, the canopy was completely open. At that precise moment he looked at the ground and landed. The land was hard as a result of falling faster than normal. Although the land arrived abruptly, Taquard performed a flawless left sided PLF. Before getting up to celebrate a successful jump, he felt for possible fractures. No broken bones or any problems of any kind whatsoever. He looked at the Rigger's Card that was enclosed in a pocket on the parachute pack. It had a female's name on it.

**JUMP RULE NUMBER 2: Check the Rigger's Card before drawing a parachute. If it has a female's name on it, exchange it for another one.**

It may be sexist to refuse to jump with a parachute that was packed by a female but who gives a damn what a bunch of overweight lesbian Women Libbers think when it comes to a life-and-death situation? Come to think of it, it didn't matter what the Diesel Dykes thought in any other situation either. This was Airborne, not ROTC where everything was run by a bunch of clowns. Taquard's opinions were beginning to solidify in a way that neither he nor anyone else would have predicted earlier. He could not worry about the feelings of a bunch of obese slags who somehow managed to get the support and endorsement of the Army. Factually speaking, it wasn't sexist at all to insist that females earn the respect that they were seeking. The opportunities are abundant, as were their miserable failures to deliver. No matter how much the Army lied about it, there was no way to mandate either respect or morality. No matter what anyone said or how loudly they said it, reality always came through. There was no way of changing it. Reality was the same for everyone in spite of delusions and resistance. The reality of the situation, no matter how much a person didn't want to admit it, was that the Army was filled with liars and often put out bad advice.

Surviving a parachute malfunction is all that it took to become a member of the Caterpillar Club. This club has no meetings, no dues, no newsletter, and everyone is a lifetime member. Taquard joined the Caterpillar Club on his first jump. He would be the only person in the class to join the club. Joining the club was not much of an honor, surviving a jump was. It felt good being alive.

Jumping makes a jumper thirsty. After a safe landing, all the jumper can think about is getting something to drink. It was unbelievable how thirsty jumping made a person. At the edge of the DZ was a collection point (CP). Nearby was a water pipe sticking out of the ground with a valve on it that was made for securing a garden hose. Though it was far from being conspicuous, the students found it and turned it on. They took turns either cupping their hands to gather water or by putting their mouth on the valve opening itself. Either way, no one was too particular about sanitation.

In addition to the one and only water source at the CP, there were the vultures. They were private venders who sold cans of ice cold soda pop at several times its retail value preying on thirsty jumpers. Taquard never bought.

The first jump was an individual tap-out jump. The rest of the jumps were mass-exit jumps. Mass jump exiting took a lot less time. The Basic Airborne Course provided five jumps with four different types of jumps; the day individual tap-out jump, a night jump, a day combat loaded mass tactical jump, and two day mass exit jumps. As it turned out, an additional day mass exit jump was substituted for the night jump. The night jump was scrapped due to unfavorable weather conditions. Nevertheless, all of the students in Class 37 who made the five jumps graduated and were awarded their wings.

Day two of Jump Week consisted inspections and PT. Instead of a two-mile run, they did a one-mile run at a moderate pace. The inspections weren't nearly as strict as they were the previous two weeks. The morning began by the students putting on parachutes and waiting for a plane to go up. Due to a cloud covering and haze, the airplanes would not fly for a jump mission. The students sat down in the parachute dawning shed and waited. After waiting for hours, they waited some more. No jumps were made before lunch. Even though the students didn't do anything besides sit and wait they were exhausted. A lunch break was a welcome change from the routine of just sitting and waiting. The students ate lunch and helped themselves to ice cream. Ice cream sandwiches were always a favorite. After lunch the students returned to the shed and donned on their parachutes once again. Taquard inspected the Rigger's Card once again to ensure that it didn't have a female's name on it. He wasn't about to take any chances with some dyke on spikes. Once again the students sat and waited and waited some more with their parachute gear on. Wearing the gear and doing nothing was tiring. They continued to wait throughout the afternoon but the weather conditions remained impermissible. When it was time to eat dinner the students took off their gear and were informed that they would try again the following day. Day two of Jump Week had no jumps.

While Taquard would experience a myriad of jobs throughout his career, he would see KP duty once. During day two of Jump Week, the long lunch line in front of the mess hall was something that Taquard didn't want to tolerate. He and another cadet cut to the front of the line. Cutting in the mess hall line has been an Army tradition for centuries. It was part of our proud military heritage. He reasoned that if someone else could cut in line, so could he. He found out that he was not a privileged person to such an entitlement. The mess hall had suspended opening for lunch because they needed some kitchen help. They were looking for two volunteers. A captain who observed the infraction, voluntold the two culprits for the detail. Operating behind schedule precluded any orientation to details or instruction. Taquard began his detail as a chili server by forgetting to wash his hands. He served three people when this was addressed.

"Wash your hands," the mess sergeant yelled.

Startled, Taquard dropped the ladle into the chili tray. He managed to splash chili onto the floor.

"Watch what the hell you are doing!"

He quickly washed his hands and returned to his position. He retrieved the ladle.

"Don't put your grubby hands in the chili!"

"It's okay, I just washed my hands."

"Damn it! Go wash your hands again."

"Okay."

He washed his hands again and returned to his station. He quickly started to serve chili again. He served the chili by reaching over the glass partition and aiming the ladle over the bowl and dropping the chili into the bowl. This created a chili trail.

"No! Damn it! You're supposed to take the bowl and then serve it from there. Give me that!"

Taquard reacted.

"Don't touch me with that. Damn it!"

Taquard accidentally let go of the ladle and got chili all over the mess sergeant while dropping a ladle full of chili on the floor. The place was a mess.

"Shit! You...uh. You got chili all over my pants. Damn it!"

"Oops."

"Damn it! Get this, uh. Go get, uh. Put a hat on, damn it!"

He put on a white paper mess hat and grabbed a new ladle.

"Can I get another bowl of chili?"

"Sure," responded Taquard.

"And I'd also like a bowl of chili," another student added.

"Okay."

"No! No, damn it! One bowl of chili, just one," the mess sergeant yelled.

"Okay," continued the student. "Well, how about some chili for my hot dog?"

"Sure thing," Taquard replied.

"No! No, no, no," yelled the mess sergeant. "You get just one bowl of chili! If you want chili on your hot dog then you don't get a bowl of chili. You can have a bowl of chili or you can have a chili dog, but not both."

"Give me back that chili dog," Taquard said while grabbing the student's plate.

"Forget it," the mess sergeant yelled. "We have people to feed. Now hurry up."

Taquard accidentally dropped a bowl into the chili tray as his hat fell off in to the chili tray. Chili splashed onto the mess sergeant and got on the floor. He grabbed the bowl out of the tray and dropped it on the floor. More chili was on the floor and the mess got bigger.

"Damn it! Damn it! Get the hell out of my mess hall!"

Taquard cleaned up and spontaneously put on another mess hat. Miraculously, he never got any chili on himself.

"Get out! And stay out! I want you the hell out of my kitchen right now!"

"What about my watch?"

"What watch?"

"It fell in the chili."

"Get the hell out of here!"

He left the kitchen realizing that his watch was back in his room as watches were prohibited during Airborne training. This marked Taquard's first and last mess hall detail. He grabbed a meal and helped himself to several ice cream sandwiches.

"Hey! One! You're only allowed one ice cream," screamed the mess sergeant. "Other people have to eat too. Can't you read?"

The sign on the ice cream freezer said "Don't be a Blue Falcon! Only one ice cream per person." Blue Falcon was a euphemism for Buddy Fucker. There were signs all over the mess hall. The one by the paper towel dispenser above a sink said "Don't take two if one will do." Another sign at the beginning of the serving line said "Take what you can eat and take no more; If you don't like it, there's the door."

The mess hall episode was immaterial compared to the two successful jumps that followed that afternoon. Taquard earned his wings the following day. It was another two jump day which enabled the class to meet its graduating requirements. The airframes were also filled with Rangers who were taking a refresher course during their second day of Ranger school. Black Hats were all over the Drop Zone (DZ) awarding silver wings to the graduates as they completed their fifth jump. The personal one on one recognition had a gratifying touch to it. SFC (Sergeant First Class) Byrne presented Taquard with his Airborne wings.

The morning following Taquard's graduation the cadets were called in to be addressed by the commandant of students. He was upset by the fact that the cadets arrived at airborne school without their Class A uniforms. He informed the cadets that they had arranged to have a special ceremony dedicated just to the cadets who were in the class.

"Your ROTC departments have done you a great disservice. They were instructed to ensure you that you brought your Class As with you to Airborne. We all know that ROTC is not a preferred duty for anyone to have. The important thing to remember is to be an individual. The Army moves you around in a heard and from one heard to another. As an individual you will stand above and beyond the group and you will be able to define and keep your principles. Groups don't have values. The Army will do everything that it can do to keep you from being an individual. It is one thing to work together as a group, but not at the expense of your own identity. Groups become more interested in conformity rather than purpose. People don't give a damn about you as clearly demonstrated by your ROTC cadre. You have got to learn to think for yourselves and stop blindly following people just because they are in a position of authority. Your ROTC cadre leaders are not worthy of your respect. They haven't earned it. I venture to say that they are not even Airborne. If you don't take anything else with you from Airborne at least remember that most people are not Airborne and that you should never forget to be an individual."

The Captain was right. Not only was Taquard Airborne, he was also an individual. He was an individual who knew how to jump out of airplanes and how to stand on his own two feet.

# Chapter Five
## *Ranger*

North American Rangers began in the seventeenth century wars between colonists and Native American Indian tribes. Rangers were full-time colonial soldiers who were dispatched to range among frontier landmarks and fortifications. Their role was to provide reconnaissance to providing early warnings of raids or threats. They consisted of scouts and guides. They would locate targets for colonial forces or militia troops. Captain Benjamin Church took the Rangers to a new level when he created a unique unit composed of both white frontiersman and friendly natives.

During the French and Indian Wars (1754-1763), Major Robert Rogers took the Ranger concept a step further when he organized a group of woodsmen to work under the British domain. The Ranger companies operated against the Canadian French. They were very knowledgeable in wilderness warfare and were rendered by many as the epitome of what military units should be like. Major Rogers recorded concepts for Rangers and other military units to follow. His knowledge was reflected in his Standing Orders and concepts of maintaining discipline. Despite their success in the French and Indian Wars, General George Washington considered frontier security a local responsibility, limited the Rangers involvement in the Revolutionary war. He favored more traditional military units over special ones. The Rangers were unconventional in their nature. Several conventional warfare units that had nothing to do with Rangers or their concept of operations called themselves Rangers during the Revolutionary War. Several other groups and organizations also called themselves Rangers. The Rangers themselves basically practiced guerrilla warfare.

Rogers Rangers went forward covertly and terrorized the French and their Indian allies during the French and Indian Wars while the British and American units adhered to fortifications. One of the most frequent operations that they performed was the ambush. This was extremely effective and inspired the British to form light infantry regiments. While the Rangers concentrated on the unit's main forces, supply columns, and components, they avoided French and Indian scouts at all costs. In December of 1862, John Singleton Mosby, a scout on General Stuart's staff, left the unit and formed his own partisan unit that operated like Rogers' Rangers. They would operate behind enemy lines. Several years after they ceased to exist, they would be famously known as Mosby's Rangers.

On 6 June 1944, on Omaha beach during the Normandy Invasion, General (GN) Norman Cota asked, "What outfit is this?"

Someone yelled, "Fifth Rangers."

Cota replied, "Well, Goddamn it then, Rangers, lead the way."

From this the Ranger motto, Rangers Lead the Way, was born. This was followed by a Ranger Creed and accompanied the existing Standing Orders.

**The Ranger Creed**

**R**ecognizing that I volunteered as a Ranger, fully knowing the hazards of my chosen profession, I will always endeavor to uphold the prestige, honor, and high esprit de corps of my Ranger Regiment.

**A**cknowledging the fact that a Ranger is a more elite soldier who arrives at the cutting edge of battle by land, sea, or air, I accept the fact that as a Ranger my country expects me to move farther, faster and fight harder than any other soldier.

**N**ever shall I fail my comrades. I will always keep myself mentally alert, physically strong and morally straight and I will shoulder more than my share of the task whatever it may be. One-hundred-percent and then some.

Gallantly will I show the world that I am a specially selected and well-trained soldier. My courtesy to superior officers, neatness of dress and care of equipment shall set the example for others to follow.

Energetically will I meet the enemies of my country. I shall defeat them on the field of battle for I am better trained and will fight with all my might. Surrender is not a Ranger word. I will never leave a fallen comrade to fall into the hands of the enemy and under no circumstances will I ever embarrass my country.

Readily will I display the intestinal fortitude required to fight on to the Ranger objective and complete the mission though I be the lone survivor.

**RANGERS LEAD THE WAY!**

## STANDING ORDERS ROGERS' RANGERS

1. Don't forget nothing.

2. Have your musket clean as a whistle, hatchet scoured, sixty rounds powder and ball, and be ready to march at a minute's warning.

3. When you're on the march, act the way you would if you was sneaking up on a deer. See the enemy first.

4. Tell the truth about what you see and what you do. There is an army depending on us for correct information. You can lie all you please when you tell other folks about the Rangers, but don't never lie to a Ranger or officer.

5. Don't never take a chance you don't have to.

6. When we're on the march we march single file, far enough apart so one shot can't go through two men.

7. If we strike swamps, or soft ground, we spread out abreast, so it's hard to track us.

8. When we march, we keep moving till dark, so as to give the enemy the least possible chance at us.

9. When we camp, half the party stays awake while the other half sleeps.

10. If we take prisoners, we keep 'em separate till we have had time to examine them, so they can't cook up a story between'em.

11. Don't ever march home the same way. Take a different route so you won't be ambushed.

12. No matter whether we travel in big parties or little ones, each party has to keep a scout twenty yards ahead, twenty yards on each flank, and twenty yards in the rear so the main body can't be surprised and wiped out.

13. Every night you'll be told where to meet if surrounded by a superior force.

14. Don't sit down to eat without posting sentries.

15. Don't sleep beyond dawn. Dawn's when the French and Indians attack.

16. Don't cross a river by a regular ford.

17. If somebody's trailing you, make a circle, come back onto your own tracks, and ambush the folks that aim to ambush you.

18. Don't stand up when the enemy's coming against you. Kneel down, lie down, hide behind a tree.

19. Let the enemy come till he's almost close enough to touch, then let him have it and jump out and finish him up with your hatchet.

## MAJOR ROBERT ROGERS 1759

Ranger had three phases: the Benning Phase, the Mountain Phase, and the Florida Phase.

Each phase had two sub-phases, the Benning Phase had the City Phase and the Darby Phase; the Mountain Phase had the Lower Mountaineering Phase and the Upper Mountaineering Phase; and the Florida Phase had SERE (Survival, Evasion, Resistance and Escape) Training and the twelve-day patrol.

The City Phase consisted of physical training, hand to hand combat, bayonet training, confidence building, explosive ordinance, the Airborne refresher course, land navigation, a church service, range patrolling, and classroom instruction. The Ranger students were at the mercy of the Ranger Instructors (RI) except during the classroom classes where the speaker was usually not a Ranger. Students could do anything and everything to try to stay awake.

Rangers were assigned Ranger Buddies. The concept was that a Ranger would look out for his buddy. The Ranger students tended to look out for each other even if they weren't assigned as buddies. This concept of looking out for one another didn't necessarily take hold in other military organizations.

The Airborne Refresher Course couldn't've been any easier. It was taught by the same Black hats that Taquard knew from Airborne school. Instead of yelling at the students, the treated them politely and with respect. They seemed to respect the Rangers. Even though the Rangers wore sanitized uniforms (no patches, no rank, no awards; nothing other than the name tag and US ARMY tape) they were recognized as paratroopers by the Black Hats. Taquard was recognized by an off-duty Black Hat who implored where his Airborne wings were. He was amazed that the Black Hat knew about his Airborne wings and was able to remember him from thousands of previous students. At the Airborne Refresher Course the Rangers were required to do two PLFs off of a platform. Taquard messed up his right PLF. For some reason, although he was right handed, he had an extremely difficult time doing right PLFs. His left PLF was a textbook role model. After his two PLFs (he did not have to redo the right PLF) he went out of the thirty-four-foot tower in a mass exit formation. The following day he jumped out of an airplane with Airborne students.

There were two main ways that Ranger students tried to stay awake in the classroom. The first and foremost method was to tell jokes. When a student had a joke to tell he would get up out of his seat, walk on the stage, and interrupt the instructor to tell his joke. This could only happen if the instructor wasn't a Ranger. Students had no qualms about interrupting instructors. Some instructors protested, but to no avail. When a Ranger was determined to tell a joke, then he told a joke: no instructor was about to stop him. A student would politely intervene in the presentation with a request such as, "Get the hell out of my way you stupid fuck head, I got a joke to tell."

The other way of staying awake during class was to play a game called Fag Tag. The game began when anyone at anytime called out "Fag Tag!" Then each person would hit as many people around him upside the head that he could.

On the second day of Ranger, the cadre taught the students a song that was to be sung prior to PT during the City Phase.

*Rangers, Rangers, lead the way,*
*Rangers, Rangers, lead the way,*
*We like it here, we like it here, we finally found a home,*
*We like it here, we like it here, we finally found a home,*
*A home, a home, a home away from home,*
*A home, a home, a home away from home.*

Unlike ROTC, PT was rough, and the land navigation courses were difficult. Instead of having the punches located beside a road where the evaluators drove up to a place to set up the punch station like they did in ROTC, the Rangers went deep in to the woods to set up their stations. A compass wasn't required on the ROTC land navigation courses, but at Ranger a compass as well as an accurate pace count was a must. Victory Pond was the site for both the slide for life and the forty-foot drop. When compared to similar tasks at ROTC Summer Camp, it wasn't a comparison at all. The slide for life was much higher and the rail for the forty foot drop (instead of the ROTC fifteen-foot drop) was only nine inches wide. Ranger was much harder in every shape and form. The Rangers were constantly doing something physical from extremely early in the morning until late at night. For many, Ranger would be the hardest experience that they would ever have to endure. If this were only true, Taquard would have had it made.

There were four church services throughout Ranger school, including the survival meal service. The service at Harmony Church was led by a First Lieutenant Chaplain and consisted mostly of singing.

Camp Darby was named after Colonel William O. Darby who commanded the 1st Ranger Battalion when it was first activated on 19 June 1942. He trained about 500 Rangers. Darby was killed in Italy two days before Germany's surrender. He was promoted to Brigadier General posthumously.

There were classes that were held in covered bleachers during the Darby Phase. The Rangers welcomed the instructors by mooning them and slapping their butts. The students in the class referred to them selves as Third Bat as in the Third Ranger Battalion which actually came into being at a later date. The Third Bat greeting was to turn around drop your pants and slap your butt many times really fast. Camp Darby was taking its toll on the Rangers and they were noticeably losing weight. The Rangers were lucky if they could get three hours of sleep a night.

After the completion of the Benning Phase, the Rangers were given an eight hour break. Since Taquard brought his own vehicle to Ranger school he used it to go into town. There was a cleaners that would do your laundry for you in a matter of hours for a fee. The arrangement was set up to address the need of Ranger students. Most students took advantage of that offer. The next item on the agenda was to go to the mall to get something to eat. While the group that Taquard was in was deciding on where to eat a young child walked out of Baskin Robbins 31 Flavors with a double scoop of butterscotch vanilla swirl ice cream on a cone. He obviously didn't like the way it tasted and proved this by tossing it into the trash basket after taking a lick in front of the Rangers.

"Are you crazy?" one of the Rangers said to the kid. "You don't throw food away. Do you realize how much value food has and how many people not too far from here are deprived of food?"

He scared the kid right out of his mind. The scolding didn't last long as the Rangers decided to get some ice cream while deciding where they wanted to eat. No one ordered butterscotch vanilla swirl. Taquard ordered pistachio almond fudge. After they got their double scoop ice cream cones they saw another Ranger from their class. The other Ranger dutifully turned around, dropped his pants, bent over, slapped his butt really fast many times, and yelled out, "Third Bat!"

"Man, don't you wear underwear?"

"Heck no. I got used to not wearing any."

While the Rangers tended to draw attention to themselves, the locals seemed to tolerate it. They had become accustomed to Rangers on their breaks.

"Hey isn't this where Calley works?" one of the Rangers asked another while they were passing a jewelry store in the Peach Tree Mall.

"I don't know. Seems like I did hear something about that."

"Who cares? There's a restaurant. Let's eat."

The location for the Mountain Phase was at Camp Merrill in Dahlonega, Georgia. It was named after Major General (MG) Frank D. Merrill who commanded the 5307th Composite Unit, known as Merrill's Marauders, in 1944. Riverside Military Academy (RMA) was located nearby in Gainesville, Georgia. They had a Ranger program as well. Though the black and gold Ranger tabs were identical, the Riverside Military Academy Rangers had a subsequent tab to clearly identify themselves as being separate from the Army Rangers. Although RMA was actually a private school as opposed to a military academy, they possessed military traits that were the envy of all of the services. While other units copied the Rangers and called themselves Rangers, RMA stood on its own merits and didn't need the Ranger image. Later on in life, Taquard would come to admire and respect the RMA Ranger tab far more than the Army one. A lot of things would happen that were beyond his imagination. While RMA was an exceptional aspect to its surrounding communities, it was all that was positive about the area. Dahlonega approached the vicinity of the area where the movie *Deliverance* was filmed. The similarities didn't end there. Camp Merrill didn't have any black RIs at the time for fear of the locals shooting at them. All Ranger students wore face camo. That way all students would look alike to would-be hillbilly snipers. Some of the Ranger students who saw *Deliverance* were concerned about the redneck mountain boys who lived in these parts of the hills. After all, if they were attracted to Ned Beatty, who knows what else they might go for? As it turned out there was never an incident with the locals and the Mountain Phase was Taquard's favorite. The only encounter that the Rangers had with the locals was when they moved their patrol through a party that some kids were having in the woods.

The mess hall at the Mountain Phase of Ranger School was better than the one at Fort Benning. The food was good. During one of the meals (Rangers take eating food very seriously) an announcement was made. The mess steward came into the dining area to address the Rangers.

"Everybody calm down. Just take it easy," he said. "Okay, everybody take it easy."

Everyone looked at him inquisitively and was wondering what this was all about. Then he made his announcement.

"Seconds."

The Rangers jumped out of their seats and ran to the kitchen knocking anything and anyone in their path down. The steward had to run back into the kitchen to avoid being trampled. This was the only time that additional food was formally offered to the Rangers.

The Florida Phase took place at Eglin Air Force Base; Camp James E. Rudder, Auxiliary Field Number 6 which was named after MG James Earl Rudder who organized, trained, and led the 2nd Ranger Battalion as a Lieutenant Colonel. This unit proved to be very effective during World War II and on D-Day. He was wounded twice. He retired in 1967 and served as President of the Texas A&M University system until his death in 1970.

Although there was a SERE (Survival, Escape, Reconnaissance, and Evasion) course set up with a mock POW (Prisoner of War) camp, some classes replaced that particular block of instruction. The Ranger students were unofficially and informally informed about an incident that occurred a few classes earlier. In a previous class, one of the Ranger students who was captured endured several bouts of forced anal sexual intercourse during his stay at the mock POW camp that was run by National Guardsmen instead of Rangers. Thoughts of Ned Beatty resurfaced when the students found out about this even though it was never confirmed to the students themselves.

One thing that was taught was how to communicate as a POW. Communicating between each other is one of the most important aspects for surviving as a POW. It is one thing that provides hope and strengthens the will to survive. Four POWs who were imprisoned together in Viet Nam in 1965 decided to make use of a simple yet effective secret code while anticipating their separation. The POWs were Captain Carlyle "Smitty" Harris, Lieutenant Phillip Butler, Lieutenant Robert Peel, and Lieutenant Commander Robert Shumaker. They vowed to maintain communicating with each other and to keep up their resistance.

Harris recalled a secret code that was made up of a five-by-five alphabet matrix. There were five rows and five columns. To set it up a person had to remember that Air Force Loves Quick Victories; there are no Ks. Each letter is communicated by two tapping sequences. The first tapping designates the row, the second the column. For example: tap, tap; break; tap, tap, tap would mean second row, third column or the letter H. For W, you would use 5-2. The letter C is used for the letter K since the matrix has no K. The letter X can also be used to end sentences. By late 1965, many POWs were utilizing the code regularly. One ex-POW said that the building sounded like a den of runaway woodpeckers.

Another aspect that the Rangers had was the utilization of this code to vet out people in two critical categories: POWs who would want to escape, and those who wouldn't. The test is simple; if you can teach the tapping code to someone within two minutes then you have identified someone that you can trust in a POW setting. It is acceptable to draw the matrix. I was a very simple design that was virtually self explanatory once a person was provided with an explanation. Furthermore, the tapping code matrix was impossible to forget once you learned it. As easy as it was, not everyone in the Army was able to grasp it. And as useful as it was simple, the matrix was nearly impossible to pass along to others, even in the event of war. The Rangers in Taquard's class got it right away.

| A | B | c/k | D | E |
|---|---|-----|---|---|
| F | G | H | I | J |
| L | M | N | O | P |
| Q | R | S | T | U |
| V | W | X | Y | Z |

Factually speaking, you don't want everyone knowing about your plans to escape even if they are Americans. Such people need to be weeded out. The two-minute drill was a great way to separate the people you could trust from those who couldn't be trusted. As ridiculously easy as it sounded it actually worked.

Initiating the tapping communication began with "Shave and a hair cut," in rhythm. The person on the other side of the wall would respond in the correct rhythm "Two bits." The reason that this ditty was selected was because of the simple fact that the Viet Cong didn't have the rhythm to mimic that beat. Orientals elsewhere are typically to perform the beat as well. POWs could also communicate the matrix with eye contact by blinking the tap code. Also the tap code could be flashed with fingers when visual contact was made in an environment where speaking was prohibited. POW stories included the banging of dishes in a tapping code to reveal information or the use of banging other things while on a detail. Coughing in code can also be used to communicate.

Another way to communicate is through the use of message drops. POWs who wish to communicate to another when relaying a message via wall tapping is impractical can use specified areas for leaving messages. Messages can be scratched in a bar of soap and left in the shower. The idea is to communicate clearly on something that can be quickly destroyed.

The Rangers taught the POW tapping code. Some units such as 3rd US Army (Patton's former unit) opposed it. Their logic was that teaching this code would reduce morale.

Other units such as the US Cavalry taught it as well and embraced the concept of preparing for battle.

While the Rangers addressed the matters pertaining to POW survival they also addressed prioritizing rescue missions.

"In today's Army, officers tend to place the importance of themselves and their friends over the importance and needs of everyone else," the Ranger Instructor (RI) stated. "Sometimes this is done at the expense of others. United States Military Academy graduates tend to look out for each other before they begin to look out for other officers. They will take care of each other at the expense of others. They have been told that they are the best people on this earth. They believe it. Therefore it is paramount that you know a few things about the academy, also known as West Point, before you go into combat. Air rescue missions are often flown by West Pointers and they may have a few questions that they may want answered before they take a chance on rescuing somebody. Knowing the correct answers may have some influence on how your rescue is prioritized. Not only that, but knowing the challenges and passwords of the academy is fundamentally a good drill in exercising your brain."

He referenced Bugle Notes verbatim and provided the Rangers with the following challenges and passwords:

**How is the cow?**
*She walks, she talks, she's full of chalk, the lacteal fluid extracted from the female of the bovine species is highly prolific to the nth degree.*

**How many lights in Cullum Hall?**
*340 lights.*

**How many gallons in Lusk Reservoir?**
*78 million gallons when the water flows over the spillway.*

**How many names on Battle Monument?**
*2,230 names.*

**What is the definition of leather?**
*If the fresh skin of an animal, cleaned and divested of all hair, fat, and other extraneous matter, be immersed in a dilute solution of tannic acid, a chemical combination ensues; the gelatinous tissue of the skin is converted into a non-putresible substance, impervious to and insoluble in water; this is leather.*

**Who used artillery on his former Artillery instructor?**
*General Beauregard fired upon Major Anderson, who was stationed at Fort Sumter.*

**What is the oldest regularly garrisoned military post in the United States?**
*West Point has been garrisoned since 20 January 1778.*

**What are the names of the Army mules?**
*Crusader*
*Ranger*
*Traveller* (Yes the name is misspelled, though not intentionally)

**What is Murphy's Law?**
*(1) Nature always sides with the hidden flaw*
*(2) Things, if left to themselves, go from bad to worse*

This was actually Murphy's Law as opposed to the common belief: Whatever can go wrong will go wrong. The RI supplied the Rangers with some definitive information about Murphy. Edward Aloysius Murphy, Jr. (11 January 1918-17 July1989) was born in the Panama Canal Zone and graduated from West Point in 1940. He achieved the rank of Major. As a safety-critical systems engineer for the United States Army Air Corps he noticed that the worst possibilities always seemed to arise at the worst times. He is most famous for the eponymous Murphy's Law. Burma, India and Chinese front, flew over "the Hump," and fixed planes from Saigon to Mandalay. He was also a friend of Dr. Laurence J. Peter (16 September 1919-12 January 1990) who was an educator who was best known for the Peter Principle. He was born in Vancouver, British Colombia and graduated from Washington State University in 1963. The Peter Principle states that in every hierarchy every employee rises to his level of incompetence.

**Where are the Lucky Spurs?**
*The Lucky Spurs are on the monument of General Sedgwick. The stautue of General Sedgwick, cast from cannon cpatured by the VI Corps which he commanded during the Civil War, has rowel spurs that turn. An old legend is that if a cadet is deficient in academics, he should go to the monument at midnight the night before the term end examination, in full dress, under arms, and spin the rowels on the monument. With luck, he will not be found.*

**What did Brigadier General Henry M. Robert, USMA, Class of 1857, write that is still in use today?**
*He wrote "Robert's Rules of Order," which has guided generations of Americans through the mazes of parliamentary procedure.*

**Who headed the building of the Panama Canal?**
*Major General George Washingtom Goethals, Class of 1880.*

**What are the mistakes of the French Monument?**
*Curbed saber, straight scabbard; wind blowing flag in one direction, coat tails in the other; cannon balls larger than bore of cannon; button unbuttoned.*

**What did Sherman, Class of 1840, say of war?**
*"There is many a boy who looks on war as all glory, but boys, it is all hell."*

"There is a lot more West Point trivia and information that you might find both enjoyable and useful. If you are interested you can order a small book that is ridiculously priced from the academy called *Bugle Notes.*"

The challenge and passwords had to be memorized. This was a great way to exercise the brain as well as learn a little about military history. The RI was right, if people thought that you were a West Point graduate you received preferential treatment. Housing officers even provided better rooms to West Pointers than they did to Captains. Later, Taquard would discover just how vast the divide between West Pointers and the officers really was. It was so big in fact that Taquard would never recommend that anyone ever even consider going into the Army unless he was a West Point graduate. He felt that if you were not a west Point graduate then the Army is not an option.

The other thing that was unique about the Florida phase was the one-eyed alligator named Big John. He was in the Ranger zoo. As legend went, a private was told to cut the grass at the zoo. He cut the grass inside of the fence with a power mower. The alligator attacked the private who retaliated by raising the mower towards the charging alligator. The alligator, who was later named Big John, charged into the mower. The private escaped and the alligator lost an eye.

The Florida Phase included a twelve-day patrol at the end. By the end of the first day the Rangers were bushed. Every twelve hours, the RIs would get relieved. Oncoming RIs would do everything that they could to exhaust the students even further. This wasn't hard. By the second day of the twelve-day patrol dysentery started to set in on the class.

"Dammit, I just shit my pants," one of the students said.

Dysentery set in on the class like a ton of bricks. Unlike diarrhea, dysentery didn't give a person any warning of a bowel movement. The Ranger pulled up his underwear beyond his pants and cut each side. Then he pulled the cut underwear out the back of his pants and tossed them away. He found out that he could function better without underwear.

In the winter the Rangers found out that Florida was extremely cold especially if you were wet from being in the swamps and dirty from never changing clothes. Whatever clothes a person may have brought with him in his ruck sack was rendered useless by being soaking wet.

On one of the patrols Taquard heard music. Upon realizing that he couldn't possibly be listening to music it ceased. Later on another patrol he heard the music again. Knowing that he it couldn't be listening to music but deciding to listen to it anyway the music continued. He also was able to select the songs that he wanted to listen to. His sense of smell and hearing increased substantially. On a perimeter lookout in the middle he heard another Ranger opening a can with a P-38 can opener. All of the other Rangers heard it too. They didn't know exactly where it came from but they knew that it was another student who was trying to get something to eat. They smelled about.

"Peanut butter," one of the Rangers said.

The Rangers were constantly thinking and talking about food. While other soldiers throughout the Army were bragging about the women they were with, the Rangers never once talked about sex.

By the sixth day Taquard crapped his pants. The knife served its purpose well. There was an objective that the Rangers had to reach in a timely manner in order to make a swamp crossing during daylight. On one of the patrols the Rangers made it to the stream during daylight. They all cooperated and rushed to the objective as fast as they could. The one thing that you want to do is finish crossing the stream while there is still daylight. The Rangers did their part to ensure that this would be possible. The RIs put a stop hold on the patrol. The Rangers had to sit and wait until 2300 hours to continue the patrol. It was at this time that the stream crossing could begin. Five of the Rangers jumped in the water and swam to the other side of the stream with a rope. They secured it firmly to a tree. Although securing a rope to a tree sounds fairly easy, it involves some skill and thinking. The rope had to be secure enough to withstand heavy loads for a long period under adverse conditions. In this case that would be about twenty fully loaded Rangers at a time with weapons, heavy wet packed to the seams back packs, and gear hanging on for hours while the current of the river was pulling on them while it was raining. The knot configuration of choice was the trucker's hitch or power cinch. The trucker's hitch offers three times as much anchoring security as do the other anchoring knots. Knots had a meaning and were named accordingly. Tying the knot required a basic understanding of knots. Understanding the half hitch, clove hitch, and sheep shank were advantageous in correctly tying the trucker's hitch. Former Boy Scouts had an advantage because they learned survival skills at an impressionable age while they were exposed to something that was new to them at the time. They learned skills that they never forgot to include tying the sheep shank, clove hitch, and the end of the line Bowline. The main body would anchor their end of the rope first with a trucker's hitch. The trucker's hitch consisted of several loops (there are several variations of the trucker's hitch) including a two-loop clove hitch configuration, followed by another loop that loops through another loop created from the main body of the rope that goes through the clove hitch like a sheep shank. Once this is configured the end of the rope is taken around the tree and back through the trucker's hitch. Four Rangers pull on the rope as hard as they can while the fifth person secures a half hitch knot and slaps the hand of one of the people who is securing the tightness of the rope. He releases his hands while the first person pulls on the rope. This is repeated until the knot completed. Slip knots can be added for an anchoring configuration. D rings are also tremendously useful in producing rope anchors. The main body will use the exact same anchoring configuration before the lead body enters the water. The Rangers attached their gear to the rope with D rings and went into the water. Once the Rangers were in the water they waited for over an hour. They were in the freezing water just hanging on to the rope doing nothing except waiting for time to pass. One of the students shouted, "This is what you will remember. You'll remember this." He was right; Taquard remembered the experience very well even though he would prefer to forget it. It is a rumor that Rangers like pain, they don't. They have endured pain and don't want to endure it again.

The following day there was an air movement supported by helicopters. The crew really felt for the Rangers. They brought food. They passed out apples, Chips Ahoy cookies, Reese's Peanut Butter Cups, and more. When a package of Chips Ahoy cookies was passed to Taquard he ate the entire bag. The movement was short but the Rangers ate fast. Taquard had a Reese's Peanut Butter Cup that escaped his hand while the helicopter was flying Nap of the Earth (NOE). Although the peanut butter cup flew out of the helicopter, Taquard reached out and caught it.

On a patrol Taquard managed to corner a snake at the root of a large tree. An RI witnessed the event.

"What's on your mind, Ranger?"

"I was looking at that snake."

"Were you planning on eating it?"

"I was considering it."

"That's poggie bait, Ranger."

Poggie bait was slang for candy and junk food as opposed to the type of food that one would find at a legitimate meal. The RI picked up the snake with a stick and put it in a plastic bag. At the end of Ranger school a message was sent back to Taquard to inform him that the snake that he trapped was a rare species and had been sent to a zoo. It was the only one of its kind at the zoo. The initial appraised value of the snake at that time was $5,000 and climbing. Other value assessments were to follow. The RI added a note reminding him that he was about to eat that rare snake. Later on another private was feeding the snake and the snake tried to bite him. The private got mad at the snake and made a belt out of it. What is it about Ranger animals and privates? First it was the alligator, and then it was the snake.

Towards the end of the Florida Phase there was a survival meal that was offered to the Rangers. By that time they were so hungry they were ready to eat anything. The survival meal began with a church service presented by a chaplain who was a Captain. The chaplain was not a

Ranger himself, but was scheduled to attend two months later. He brought a guitar and it was obvious that he had presented sermons to Rangers before. A lot of preparation went into his delivery. He set up some tables with boxes on them.

"Hey, I got a question," one of the Ranger students whispered to Taquard. "I'm Jewish."

"So am I. Not by religion, but by nationality. As far as most people are concerned that's just as bad."

"What are we going to do? We aren't supposed to be here."

"We do what we always do, we keep our mouths shut and blend in."

"Do you think that they'd let us in if they knew we were Jewish?"

"Some would, some wouldn't. All it takes is for one dickhead to get offended and we're in hot water. Keep your mouth shut."

The chaplain instructed the Rangers that there was a time schedule pertaining to the survival meal. His service was not encroaching on the Ranger's eating time one iota.

"Everyone form a line single file line beginning on my right and be sure to pick up one item from each box and then return to your seats," the chaplain said to the students.

Each box had a specific item that the chaplain wanted the student's to have. The first box had Bibles. These were the genuine leatherbound Original King James Version Bibles. The Bibles even had a concordance in the back of them. They were top of the line. The chaplain was really going out on a limb for the Rangers and spared no expense or effort in supporting the Rangers. While other versions of the Bible are approved and even endorsed by the Army, the Original King James Version is not. Although it has not been officially disapproved by the Army, the chaplain was taking his chances by passing it out.

"Remember to blend in. Take a Bible," Taquard whispered to the other Jewish Ranger. "Remember the old Jewish tradition: Change your country, change your name."

The second box had copies of *Watt's Hymnal*. Isaac Watts (1674-1748) wrote hymns and spiritual songs. This was a first-rate hymnal. It, along with the Bible, was a required school textbook under the direction of President Thomas Jefferson.

The third and fourth boxes were filled with elephant bags. These were heavy duty rubber waterproof bags that worked really well. They were proven effective in previous Ranger classes. Two elephant bags were needed to secure the items that the chaplain was passing out.

The next box was filled with gospel tracts entitled *Holy Joe*. Gospel tracts were frowned upon by many, including churches. The chaplain was really sticking his neck out.

"These gospel tracts really stir up a lot of people, a lot of people hate them," Taquard said. The first time that he ever saw a gospel tract was when he met Sergei Kourdakov. People in the church were Sergei was speaking were passing them out. Coincidently, the two tracts that Taquard received were *This Was Your Life* and *Holy Joe*.

"Why are they so controversial?"

"Maybe it's because they tell the truth. Galatians 4:16 says 'Am I therefore your enemy, because I tell you the truth?' Let's face it, no two religions that doctrinally oppose each other can both be right. It's possible that all the religions in the world have it all wrong, but they can't all be right. One could be correct but no more than that. So of all the religions and beliefs that are in the world today only one or none are correct."

"So these gospel tracts oppose most churches and beliefs?"

"They simply refer to the truth of the Bible and do their best to present the word of God. All they are trying to do is save people from the damnation of hell."

"No wonder everyone's so upset."

"Apparently, they have also challenged the legitimacy of some religions. And they feel that the Jews are the chosen ones."

"I bet that pissed off a lot of people."

The next box was filled with pencils for note taking. The box next to that one had small notebooks. The last box had Pop Tarts for the Rangers to eat while they were waiting for the time that they would be allowed to eat. Eating was a precious event at Ranger school; the chaplain understood this very well. The chaplain understood a lot about Rangers, the Bible, and history. This knowledge was reflected in his sermon. The Rangers were a fantastic audience and could handle controversy much more than a typical congregation. One thing that could be said for Ranger school was that the Rangers were subject to an extremely fine sermon.

"Rangers," the chaplain addressed, "you have undergone training and ordeals that most people will never even consider. I will be frank with you and provide you with information that the general public cannot handle. Sermons are usually sanitized and tailored to a specific audience. Today's sermon is directed at a receptive audience that doesn't mandate what the service should and should not contain. Ranger services are not screened for content although other services are. My intent is to generate your interest in the items that I gave to you. If you don't want anything that is being offered don't take it. Take what you want but keep all you take. If you are going to do something, do it with pride and do it well. I would like to reference David Barton's book entitled, *Original Intent.* Our country was founded on the principles of Christianity. Our forefathers understood this well and forged a country that was the epitome of perfection. They did it with hard nerve, courage and by seeking the Lord's guidance. That's right, our forefathers were Christians. Not every single one of them, but enough subscribed to Christian values that it would be unfair to dismiss the Christian foundations of this country. This is reflected in their establishment of formal education and laws predating the Constitution. Free public education began in the 1600s in the new territory. The bedrock of education was that of learning how to read the Bible. Learning to read the Bible and education was important to our founding fathers but not for the reasons that you might think. Throughout history many people have been murdered, tortured, deprived of property in the name of God. Heinous crimes have been committed under the banner of Christianity. The Spanish Inquisition is a prime example. Many pilgrims experienced firsthand the atrocities committed by the crown all in the name of professed Christianity. It was important, in the minds of the early settlers, for people to learn how to read the Bible so that they would know the difference between actions that were truly based on Christian principles and those that were perpetrated by apostates. This was so important that a law was established to address this concern. The Massachusetts Bay Colony legislated a law into action 1647 and called it the Old Deluder Satan Law. I will read an abridged rendition of the law which stresses how important this law concerning compulsory education actually was. 'It being one chief project of the old deluder Satan to keep men from the knowledge of the scriptures as informative nears by keeping him in an unknown tongue so in these latter times by persuading from the use of tongues so at least your true sense and meaning from the original may be clouded by false glosses of saint seeming deceivers learning may not be burdened in the grave of fathers in the Church and commonwealth, the lord assisting our endeavors it is therefore ordered in every township of this jurisdiction after ye lord have increased your numbers to fifty households, shall then forthwith appoint one within their town to teach all such children as shall resort to him to write and read, whose wages shall be paid by either parents or masters of such children, or by the inhabitants in general, by way of supply, as ye major part of those that ordered by prudentials ye town shall appoint, provided, those who send their children be not oppressed by paying much more money than they have for teachers in other towns, and it is further ordered where any town shall increase to one hundred families or households, they shall set up a grammar school therefore being able to in such youth as far as they shall be fitted for the university, provided that if any town neglect this performance more than one year then every such town shall pay five pounds to the next school until they shall perform this order."

"Other New England colonies followed suit enacting similar laws of their own. They viewed ignorance as being Satanic. Harvard College was established by Reverend John Harvard whose intent was to prepare men for the ministry. The Puritans of that era wanted to ensure that people were educated so that the old deluder Satan could not keep people from personal knowledge of the scriptures by means of illiteracy. They also stipulated that the teachings of the Word of God should be taught by proper authority to avoid the inducement of deception under the guise of Christianity. Education was revered with the utmost importance to ensure that the new world would not fall victim to the atrocities of the old world. It was as moral as it was a means to survival. Many are deceived by deluders. The Bible is the Word of God. Reading it will endorse your education. There are many Bibles on the market on the market today;

some are contradictory to the Authorized King James Version, some are deceptive and not to be confused with the real Word of God. The Mormons have books that supercede the Bible. Is there some deception taking place under the guise of legitimate Christianity? Sure there is. Who would want to deprive honest true believing Christians from the genuine Word of God? Satan would, that's who. The most successful type of deception is that of a wolf in sheep's clothing. Our founding fathers consisted of men who had values. The aim of the teachings in the townships was to teach children how to read the Bible. A wise man will know the difference between a legitimate Christian and an apostate. In pursuing knowledge of the Bible we developed great institutions of learning. Though you wouldn't guess it today, Harvard, Yale, and Princeton were all founded on Christian principles. The clergy was once a very influential facet in higher learning. I will provide you with a basic litmus test to determine which Bibles are legitimate and which ones are not. Most corrupt versions of the Bible will tamper with 1 John 5:7. It reads, 'For there are three that bear record in heaven, the Father, the Word, and the Holy Ghost: and these three are one.' If that verse is tampered with, then watch out. The Bible also says in Matthew 24:35, 'Heaven and earth shall pass away, but my words shall not pass away.' You will notice in the Bibles that I have given to you that the verses haven't been tampered with. You see, our forefathers were Godly men who wanted us to know the Word of God and how to differentiate it from imposter versions. They pursued this need by establishing an education system that was based on Christian principle. In the process, Noah Webster produced the first dictionary in the English language. Up until that time there was no formal way to spell or pronounce English words. Spelling was based on the sounding of the word instead rules of grammar. For this reason people spelled the same word differently. Many didn't use 26 letters. The dictionary has proven to be a universally accepted authority of the English language. Noah Webster was a devout Christian who gave us the dictionary. It has been said of him that he was a great man who taught thousands to read, but not one to sin. This is how he was once remembered though it is very doubtful that you would be taught this in our schools today."

The chaplain continued his sermon but made sure that it was within the allotted time frame that he was told not to exceed. The cadre used the sermon time to prepare for the survival meal. His sermon was both educational and inspiring. It was too bad that sermons like this were only heard by a select few. The Rangers were proud to have been privileged enough to hear it. Every Ranger kept everything that the chaplain had to offer. The Rangers listened attentively even though they were hungry. While they chunked down their Pop Tarts in record time, they secured their other handouts in the elephant bags. One thing that was for sure, Ranger offered a lot of things that a person couldn't get anywhere else including a no-holds-barred sermon.

The Rangers were required to kill for their meal. A rabbit and chicken were allocated to each Ranger. This was a survival meal that was offered to the Rangers. They would have to kill and cook their meal. The cadre demonstrated how to kill a goat by blasting its brains out with a 45. The goat was divided among the Rangers. The rabbits had to be held by their hind feet by one person while another person delivered a hard karate chop with curled fingers to the back of the neck. The chickens were placed on the ground with their head facing forward and a line was drawn in the dirt. The chicken would freeze in place and stay there even after he was released. The Rangers, although they had the option of releasing their animals, killed their animals and began cooking them on the fire as fast as they could. They knew that their time was limited and they were also extremely hungry to begin with. They also knew that they were about to undergo additional rigorous patrols soon. Although the food was burnt, they enjoyed their meals. Vegetables and sauces were also provided to each Ranger group. The groups consumed everything that was given to them. If it was edible, they ate it in record time. This was the part of Ranger school that everyone was looking forward to. They had a few days left before the end of the course and they knew it.

The Army always had a screwed up perception of women and the women that it attracted tended, with few exceptions, to be extremely uncouth. On the very last night of Ranger school, the cadre threw a party for the students. They had music, food, and a stripper from the University of Florida. The cadre was concerned about potential problems that may arise from 138 men who hadn't seen a woman in fifty-eight days. The Rangers were told to keep their hands off. She got on stage and took off her top. She showed her breasts. The Rangers kept on eating. There was fire barbecued chicken, white bread, milk, and beer. They were talking to each other about the chicken, bread, and milk. Taquard got and entire loaf of bread and shared it with his Ranger buddy, Cole.

No one cared about the beer or the stripper. She began complaining about the inattention that she was receiving. She yelled at the Rangers and tried to gain attention. She even got off of the stage and sat in Rangers' laps. The Rangers were still focused on the chicken, bread, and milk. She wondered if Taquard and Cole were brothers. They did look alike with their skin heads and black Army issue glasses. Rangers were hardly in a position to criticize anyone for the way they looked.

Taquard lost thirty-nine pounds at Ranger school. He was unable to hold down any food for several days. The Army was a way of life that could consume a person. Priorities and missions changed frequently and often without rhyme or reason or intelligent consideration. The Army was no better than the people who were in it. Not only was the Army a dose of the unimaginable to Taquard, so were the places where he would go. The Army successfully put Taquard in a mood that people aren't accustomed to. He drove from Fort Benning, Georgia, back to Colorado. He had to make a lot of pit stops along the way to address his bouts with diarrhea. When a restroom wasn't nearby he simply pulled his car off to the side of the road and did his business there. It was no big deal. He drove in a manner to travel as far as he could in a short period of time. Even though he had just completed Ranger school, he wasn't about to find lodging at some dumpy hotel. He still had some class. His first stop was at a Hilton Inn in Shreveport, Louisiana. The room next to his was occupied by four band members of a rock and roll band. They were playing their instruments and were keeping Taquard awake. Other customers tried addressing the situation without success. The arguments could be heard from within other rooms. The band had their way with the other patrons. Taquard decided to take the matter into his own hands. Realizing that he was no match for anyone in his current condition, let alone four people, he dawned on two handguns with concealed weapons holsters. He also packed a knife. He was ready. He never did any extensive traveling without weapons and he made up his mind that he was going to kill every person in the next room. He banged loudly on the door until it was answered. Before any of the band members could ask him what he wanted, Taquard presented them with his ultimatum.

"You guys will quiet the fuck up right now. If you want I will take on all of you motherfuckers on right here and now. Wake me up again and I will be back."

However they read Taquard, the band decided not to keep him awake.

After Ranger, Taquard was in the process of traveling to his basic course when he got so sick that he was admitted to the Air Force Academy Hospital. His dysentery was severe and he wasn't able to hold down any food. In the Air Force physician's assistants (PA) were captains instead of warrant officers as in the Army. The Air Force didn't have warrant officers. The physician's assistant (PA) surmised that Taquard had a tape worm. His only remedy was fasting for the next forty-eight hours.

"Are you out of your mind, Captain? You expect me to stop eating for forty-eight hours right after Ranger school?"

"Well, yeah. If you don't the tape worm will keep on growing."

"No way. Not after Ranger. There's just no way."

"You keep mentioning Ranger. Is that like Smokey the Bear or something?"

"No way. Airborne Ranger. Not Smokey the Bear, Ranger, Airborne Ranger. Army. Get it?"

"No, I don't get it. What does Ranger have to do with the Army?"

"It's an Army school that starves you and keeps you up all of the time. No food, no sleep. It's a leadership course that teaches you to lead people under adverse conditions."

"I still don't see what that has to do with Smokey the Bear."

The argument continued between Taquard and the PA.

"Shit, can't I at least eat soup?"

"No, the tape worm will get it. No matter how much you eat you will still be hungry. Eating won't help you out one bit. You have to starve the tape worm and digest it out. You may have swallowed a tape worm while you were in the swamps. From what you've told me about this Ranger school it's likely that you came in contact with tape worms. I still don't understand what you were doing in the swamps though. I though that Smokey the Bear was from the forest."

"Ranger, as in Airborne Ranger, as in what I've been trying to explain to you doesn't have a damn thing to do with Smokey the Bear. Everybody seems to think that it does, but it doesn't."

"The La Grange Parker High School has a basketball team called the Rangers."

"This has nothing to do with those dickheads either."

"Do they ever win a game? Bunch of rednecks. They even have a rodeo team. Talk about a bunch of sod busters. And speaking of which, I need a stool sample."

"That won't be long, I could give you one fairly soon. And no, I once again must emphasize that the Rangers have nothing to do with Redneck High. They even have a bull barrel at one of the bus stops."

"Bull barrel?"

"Yeah, it simulates riding a bull. It's used to train bull riders. It's the predecessor to the mechanical bull. Actually, the school recently purchased a mechanical bull. The cheerleaders got it. Something about those cheerleaders and that mechanical bull. All they do is spend time on that mechanical bull."

"Oh, sounds like a lot of laughs. Here's a container for your stool sample. When you're finished with it, return it back to the lab."

"Can't I have anything at all? How about water?"

"Water is okay. You can drink as much of that as you want."

It wasn't long before Taquard provided the lab with the sample that they were wanting. The countdown continued. Taquard began the time from when the PA first breathed the beginning part of the sentence that assigned him to the fast. He hated Air Force PAs. All that he could do was wait and count down the hours before he would be allowed to eat again. All he could do was think about food. When he watched television it seemed as though all of the advertisements were about food. The shows had food in them. Magazines had food on the cover, in the pictures, ads, and inserts. An insert that fell out of one of the magazines that Taquard was looking at was an invitation to an offer for purchasing an outdoor grill. Naturally, the picture had to include shish kabobs cooking on the grill. The shish kabobs included a choice select of plump juicy steak cubes and fresh vegetables. Even the thought of eating hospital food was appealing.

When he went outside for a walk he saw candy wrappers, billboards advertising food, posters for functions where food was mentioned, and smelled food cooking from the smoke that came out of the mess hall or other nearby places that were cooking something. There were reminders about food everywhere he went. All that he could think about was food. No matter how hard he tried, he couldn't get food off of his mind.

Another stipulation that the doctor placed on Taquard was to set up another appointment with him before the forty-eight-hour fasting period expired. The mark would occur during the appointment. Taquard had food ready to bring to the appointment. Taquard held out for forty-eight hours without eating when he found himself back in the captain's office.

"I'm afraid that we lost the stool sample. Can you give us another one?"

"Actually I can't."

"We need it to determine whether or not you have a tape worm."

"I can't shit because I haven't been eating."

"There's only one thing left to do."

"What's that?"

"You have to fast for forty-eight hours."

"I already did that."

"No, I mean for another forty-eight hours."

"Are you out of your mind? Fasting after Ranger school?"

"I'm afraid we don't have any other options. You keep mentioning Ranger. Was it like a big deal or something?"

"It's one of the biggest fucking deals that the Army has. I need to eat something right now."

"If you do the tape worm will get."

"I'm about to starve to death right here and now."

"There are no other options. Oh, by the way, you can check into a hotel if you want. You don't have to stay here."

"I have family that lives close by."

"I'll see you in forty-eight hours."

Taquard went to his parents' house which was close by. He decided to fast there for an additional forty-eight hours. This was a rough task. He had a severe headache from the fasting. As much as he tried to sleep he couldn't. Hunger kept him awake. He used a black grease pencil to mark off the passing time on the kitchen oven clock. He did everything that he could to pass the time. Everything reminded him about food. Even the Wacky Packages reminded him of the food that the parody was dedicated to. He wrote on the clock and whipped it off with his fingers as time passed. He was at all hours of the night trying to occupy his mind with something else besides food. It was midnight and he had twelve hours to go. He looked at a loaf of bread that was on the counter and thought about Dan Aykroyd eating toasted white bread with nothing on it in the movie *The Blues Brothers*. At this point of the fasting Taquard didn't see what one piece of dry white toast without anything on it would do. He updated the clock with black grease pencil. He looked at the loaf of bread. He thought about Dan Aykroyd eating dry white toast with nothing on it. It sure sounded good. The loaf of bread that was next to the toaster oven hadn't been opened. Taquard opened the loaf of bread. Bread never smelled so good. This was store bought, not freshly baked, bread. The bread smelled so good. Normally, people could care less about store bread and no one takes the time to smell it. But Taquard could smell it. His sense of smell was very acute. He could smell anything even at long distances.

He took one slice of bread and put it into the toaster oven and smelled the aroma of hot bread that was becoming toast. It smelled so good. Taquard was eighty-four hours into his fasting that was prescribed to him by the PA. He had twelve hours, which was depicted on the kitchen oven clock in black grease pencil, to go. He felt that one slice of bread wouldn't make any difference. When it was toasted he savored the flavor of his toast. While he was violating the PA's orders he didn't care. As far as he was concerned it was worth it. He had the delicious taste on his mind, not the opinion of some Air Force captain. He ate his toast and enjoyed it so much. In fact, he enjoyed it so much that he decided to have another piece of toast. After all, if he had already had one piece of toast, what difference would two pieces make? He enjoyed the second piece of toast as well. He could never remember toast tasting so good. The second slice of toast tasted so good in fact that he decided to try two additional slices of toast. Even though he enjoyed eating four pieces of toast without butter he was still hungry and craved more food. He decided to overcome his hunger with an additional four pieces of toast, this time with butter. Taquard continued eating to the point that he decided to pursue his deliverance from hunger in lieu of following the PA's orders. After finishing off one and a half loaves of bread, including the heels, he made himself a thick rich chocolate malt to go with his meal. Additional chocolate malts were made to accompany Taquard's feeding frenzy. He also ate an entire package of Keebler Fudge Stripe Cookies. He ate and ate until he didn't feel like eating any more. It was delicious. Taquard couldn't remember a better meal. He managed to turn a slice of bread into a feast and didn't care what the captain would have to say about it later on. As scheduled, Taquard did report to the PA and informed him about what he did.

"Listen," he responded, "I've been doing some research about this Ranger school that you mentioned. One of my colleagues has informed me that it is a physically challenging course where students are deprived of both food and sleep for long periods of time. After Ranger school, I'm surprised that you held out for as long as you did."

"That's what I've been trying to tell you, Doc."

"Well, I didn't get it. I thought that it had something to do with Smokey the Bear."

"I keep trying to tell people that it doesn't but they don't listen."

"Well, I never dealt with a Ranger before. I usually deal with Air Force, not Army. Oh, we did find your stool sample. You're suffering from a virus, not a tape worm. The best thing that you can do is to eat and sleep. The virus will have to take its course, but you need to keep on eating or else you won't recover. You will continue to experience diarrhea, but that is normal. As you recover, your stool samples will harden."

Taquard left the office and decided to take his records with him.

"Well, before we can release your records to you permanently we need to make sure that a few requirements are met," the clerk informed Taquard.

"What are those? And be quick about it, I'm hungry."

"First you must be eighteen years old or older."

"Here's my ID card. My birthday's on it."

"Okay, good. Next we will need a form of ID to prove that you are eighteen. Oh, this military ID card will do the trick. Third and lastly, we need some type of proof of employment to show us that you are no longer living with your parents. Oh, yes, this ID card. Okay, here are your records. Sign right here."

# Chapter Six
## *OBC*

Upon college graduation, Taquard was commissioned as a Second Lieutenant in the United States Army. His first duty assignment was to attend the Officer's Basic Course (OBC). In his case it would specifically be the Field Artillery Officer's Basis Course (FAOBC). Fort Sill in Lawton, Oklahoma, served as home of the Field Artillery. For all practical purposes, Fort Sill is Lawton. Lawton is a local camp follower community that feeds off of the Army. Fort Sill was staked out on 8 January 1869 by Major General (MG) Philip H. Sheridan. Sheridan earlier led a campaign into Indian Territory accompanied by frontier scouts. Among the scouts were "Buffalo Bill" Cody and Wild Bill Hicock. The garrison was initially called Camp Wichita, but Sheridan renamed it in honor of his West Point classmate and friend Brigadier General (BG) Joshua W. Sill who was killed during the Civil War. Colonel (COL) Albert Gallatin Boone, grandson of Daniel Boone, was also assigned to Fort Sill as an Indian agent.

The Field Artillery had a mission, traditions, and a controversial patron saint. The mission of the artillery is to destroy, neutralize, or suppress the enemy by cannon, rocket, and missile fire and to help integrate all fire support assets into combined arms operations. The Artillery officially began on 17 November 1775 because that is the day that the Continental Congress unanimously elected Henry Knox as

"Colonel of the Artillery Regiment." The regiment formally entered service on 1 January 1776. The Artillery produced two official branches: Field Artillery and Air Defense Artillery. Other notable birthdays included:

U.S. Army: 14 June 1775

U.S. Navy: Friday 13 October 1775

U.S. Marine Corps: 10 November 1775

U.S.M.A.: 16 March 1802

U.S. Air Force: Thursday 18 September 1947

The Field Artillery is also referred to as the "King of Battle." This is a nickname that resulted from the fact that during World I and World II, the field artillery weapon systems produced more casualties on European battlefields than any other. Field Artillery members are called red legs because the Artillery wore red stripes on their pant legs during the Civil War. The Artillery uniform that included red trimmings and a red plume on the hat was developed around 1777. Red was later designated as the official branch color.

An Artillery tradition that was not introduced at the Basic Course was Artillery Punch. Artillery Punch is a concoction of alcoholic drinks, motor oil, dirty socks, and anything else mixed in a punch bowl. The challenge is to drink the punch that is created for the purposes of being undrinkable. Vomiting is not an uncommon response to drinking it.

This tradition would be introduced to lieutenants when they were indoctrinated into their units. Other tidbits of military tradition and knowledge were introduced to the new lieutenants. The military terminologies were unique and took getting used to. Urinals were referred to as pissers, toilets were called shitters, and sleeping bags were fart sacks.

Acronyms were also in abundance as well. Some of the lesser known ones were TED; typical enlisted dude and DWI: Dependent wife. Everyone knew what a GI was without knowing that it stood for Government Issue.

Saint Barbara is the Patron Saint of the Field Artillery. This is a controversial issue because St. Barbara is considered on good authority to be a false saint. Some claim that she does not appear on the original St. Jerome's list of martyrs or any known authenticated Christian antiquities that predate the ninth century. Veneration of saints was very common from the seventh century. According to legend, Barbara was the daughter of Dioscorus, a wealthy heathen who lived near Nicomedia in Asia Minor. Barbara lived and died around 300 AD. She was secluded in a tower by her tyrannical father. He locked her up to eliminate her exposure to the outside world. It was in the forced solitude that she had to endure that she sought Christian beliefs through prayer and study. She had heard the teachings of Christ while her father was away and spent her time in deep contemplation. She observed the surrounding countryside from her window. She decided that manmade idols made of stone or wood that were worshipped by her parents must be condemned as false. Eventually, she started accepting Christian beliefs. Before departing on a journey, he contracted to have a bath house to be built for her. She told the builders to add an additional window so that the bath house would have three windows instead of two. When her father returned from his trip he was infuriated by the alteration to the plans and her repeated refusals to get married. When she informed that she became a Christian, her father denounced her before a civil tribunal in the province of Martinianus. It was decreed that she would be tortured and put to death. She was whipped, beaten, burned, and called names. The torturing was followed by a beheading that was mercilessly executed by her father. On his way home from the execution he was struck by lightning and consumed. Some say that the reason that she was beheaded is because she was ugly. The legend that her persecuting father was struck down by lightning has also resulted in St. Barbara being regarded as the patron saint in time of danger from thunderstorms, fires, and sudden death. When gunpowder was introduced to the Western world, St. Barbara was invoked for protection from accidents resulting from explosions.

Artillery utilized gunpowder in their operations and had volumes of accidents. Somehow, through the accidents and trials of artillerymen, St. Barbara became their patroness. December 4th is the traditional day that recognizes St. Barbara and is celebrated by the military with a formal Dining In, Dining Out, or dinner, and the consumption of Artillery Punch.

The Field Artillery has three distinct components: The forward observer (FO), the fire direction center (FDC), and the firing line. FM 6-30 is the artillery reference. Because artillery fire is deployed indirectly, observers have to be staged in positions to observe the impact of the rounds that are fired. FOs will make adjustments when required. FOs are also known as bastard children. For all intensive purposes, they are bastard children.

The FOs communicate directly with the FDC (the brains of the Artillery). The FDC receives the FO information, computes the firing data (deflection and quadrant) and sends it to the guns. In this process, accuracy is sacrificed for speed.

The last component of the Artillery is the firing line or guns. The FO sends commands to the FDC. The FDC determines what data need to be sent to the guns to hit the target. The guns take the data produced by the FDC and fire.

The Artillery uses mils instead of degrees to measure deflections and quadrants. There are 6,400 mils in a circle which enhances accuracy greatly when compared to the typical use of degrees. One degree is approximately 17.77777778 mils. One grad is 16 mils, one point is 200 mils, one mil is 3.375 minutes, and one mil is equal to 202.5 seconds.

Beyond the scope of the Artillery world was Lawton, Oklahoma. Oklahoma was populated with rednecks that never left the state while professing that Oklahoma City was the biggest city in the world. Lawton was a reflection of this inbreeding that went wrong. During the early 1980s Lawton sported a plethora of strip joints, bars, a pool hall, porno theatres, and UCLA (University of Cameron in Lawton America). The only things to do in Lawton besides going to a strip joint was to drink freshly squeezed lemonade at the mall, eat at the Plantation Restaurant, eat a burger at Meers (Meers was the name of a restaurant, a person, and a town with a population of one), give blood, drive to Wichita Falls, Texas, or go to the Oklahoma City Zoo to watch a gorilla throw up.

One of the most memorable moments of being in Oklahoma took place at the Oklahoma City Zoo. They had a gorilla that always threw up. This gorilla sat at one side of the cage and faced the other side of the cage and threw up. Airborne vomit went across the cage and hit the wall on the other side. Splashing vomit in gorilla quantity was enough to make any observer want to toss their cookies as well. The amazing about the gorilla is the fact that he managed to throw up every time a lieutenant went to see him. As stories about the vomiting gorilla circulated, lieutenants laughed and drove to the zoo to see for themselves. Without fail, the gorilla would throw up. The quantities of vomit didn't disappoint although it occasionally resulted in causing an observer to vomit as well. There was something about lieutenants and the gorilla throwing up that was beyond mere coincidence. Other than that, there was very little that Lawton had to offer. Another off-post memory that Lawton had to offer was the Baker Bean Bar that was just outside of the front gate. For fifty dollars a lash, you could whip one of the girls of your choice. The whipping was done with a belt rather than an actual whip. It seemed like a real turn on for some of the locals and GIs alike. Everyone watched while the girl, who was not tied up, held on to a horizontal wooden rail while she got whipped. She would scream loudly every time. Previous whip marks on her body were highly visible. Some felt that this was a sick endeavor and looked forward to the day that they would be leaving Fort Sill, Oklahoma, for good.

When someone was considered to be screwed up they were referred to as being "out to lunch." Another expression used to address such people was "steak and eggs." "Biscuits and gravy," was considered going over the line. Although the newest Second Lieutenant (O-1) in the Army outranked the Sergeant Major of the Army (E-9), sergeants were used as instructors. They carried around sticks that were called "Lieutenant Adjustment Rods," and threatened to use them accordingly. Although it may seem unfair for a twenty-two-year-old Second Lieutenant to outrank a Sergeant Major who has been in the Army for twenty-four years, any attempts to rectify this injustice proved to be far more disastrous than the original intended organizational model. Sergeant Majors were enlisted men even though sergeants and even corporals tried to distance themselves from the enlisted men by referring to themselves as NCOs (noncommissioned officers). If the Army was in the bullshit business, the Field Artillery was determined to lead the way.

Artillery traditions were also observed by the United States Marine Corps (USMC). Sometimes the traditions were carried out to absurdities.

One example of this was demonstrated by a band of marines called The Blade and Wing that performed at a club also called The Blade and Wing. The lead singer wore red stockings, a red garter belt, and red pumps to honor the red leg tradition of the artillery. The red panties may have been in honor of the USMC tradition. Red is used a lot by the USMC. The hit song that spread throughout the local area was entitled, "Paul McCartney, Where Are You Going to Go?"

The lyrics included:

*Paul McCartney, I'm not impressed with your performance,*
*Paul McCartney, I've never seen you perform PMCS on a howitzer,*
*Paul McCartney, I bet you don't know how to lay a battery with an aiming circle,*
*Paul McCartney, you had better move like you have a purpose in life,*
*Paul McCartney, where are you going to go?*

The song consisted of similar verses that sounded like a lot of nagging that one would expect from an old woman. Also, it didn't even rhyme. However the song did gain enough local notoriety and support to be aired on the radio. When the band, The Blade and Wing, performed at The Blade and Wing, the local audience would go wild. For some reason, the band had a serious hard-on for Paul McCartney. It was doubtful that Paul McCartney was concerned about a bunch of Oklahoma rednecks who spelled it Beetles instead of Beatles. On days that they didn't perform, hefty middle-aged strippers would keep the GIs entertained. Taquard knew that if he had it to do all over again, he would've selected any other branch besides Field Artillery.

Towards the end of Taquard's tenure at Fort Sill they built a brand new theater, pool hall, and pizza joint in Lawton. This was the biggest thing to hit Lawton America since the first McDonald's restaurant opened in Oklahoma. Not only did the theater show six movies simultaneously, they had video games such as Donkey Kong and Pac Man. They even had Centipede. Before the end of the week, lieutenants were seeing movies that they had already seen as a means of entertainment. Video games were catching on. The lieutenants were playing the newest games available while the locals were warming up to Space Invaders. And since nobody, with very few exceptions, played pool, tables were always available. At a dollar an hour for a table, there was never a time when all of the tables were all filled.

Oklahoma had its own nuances that infected the Army. Oklahoma OBC was just plain weird. Oklahoma can be best described as a boring version of the Twilight Zone without the punch. It's not so much that people who get assigned there are weird, but when someone starts liking it, it's just plain bizarre. It is true that many people are a product of their environment. Oklahoma is a proving ground for this. Oklahoma is also proof positive that the majority can be wrong.

# Chapter Seven
## *Korea*

Taquard arrived in Korea in December of 1982. Arriving in Korea seemed like being in the Twilight Zone all over again. It just didn't seem real. He would never forget the smell of kimchee in the air that nearly gagged him when they opened the airplane door at Kimpo International Airport (KIA). The stench was unbearable. It was late at night and pouring down rain, but the smell of kimchee was in the air. Going a short distance from the terminal to the buses resulted in the new arrivals being soaking wet. They piled on to buses, exceeding the intended capacity, and went to Camp Coiner at Yongsan Garrison. When they offloaded the buses, they went to a reception station that was no more than an empty orderly room. A sergeant pointed to a building and told them to find a bed. He said, "We don't work past five around here."

Three lieutenants found a room and decided to bed down for the night. The building had plenty of beds but no blankets or sheets. Though the buildings were unmanned they were filthy, disorderly, and smelled like kimchee. Some people threw up from the kimchee smell. The next morning they looked for someone who might know something. The three lieutenants reported top the orderly room in their Class A uniforms. "Nobody wears Class As around here," the desk sergeant responded. He answered their questions and told them to stand fast until further notice although he had no idea when further notice would be.

The mess hall had terrible food. The eggs were the worst that he had ever tasted. The problem was that he was assigned to Korea for a year he was going to have to eat. The only way that he could eat the eggs was to smother them in pepper and gulp them down with a glass of water.

Although he vowed never to leave camp until his tour of duty was complete, he went off post his first day there. When exploring Korea beyond the base perimeters, it was highly advised to be with someone who had been there before. While most of the GIs went to the businesses of ill repute in Iitaewon, Taquard and the two other lieutenants went to the Lotte luxury hotel/shopping center in Seoul, the capital of South Korea which is about thirty miles from North Korea that was officially established. Seoul was officially established the capital in 1948. It was their first of several excursions. This was the place where the rich and famous Koreans spent their time. Lotte was the classiest place in Korea. Even though there were about 200 soldiers sent to Camp Coiner, nobody showed the least amount of interest in them for nearly two weeks. The stay at Camp Coiner was excellent because you were free to do absolutely anything that you wanted whenever you wanted albeit, the quarters themselves were atrocious. The order was given to fall in, and get in formation. The unit was separated into two groups. Names were called out to determine who would go in what group. Everyone was hoping to be in the group that would stay at Yongsan. The other group would go to 2nd Infantry Division at Camp Casey in Tong Du Cheon (TDC). Taquard and the two other lieutenants got picked to go to 2nd ID.

Camp Casey was both the in processing and out processing site of the division. This place was affectionately known as the Turtle Farm because the in processing and out processing buildings were right next to each other. It took a full year to go from one building to the next. That was a long time, hence the term turtle. New soldiers were affectionately known as turtles. Anything that a new person had to endure was labeled turtle in some way, shape, or form. Concrete ditches that unsuspecting new arrivals fell into were known as turtle traps. During the course of the following week soldiers drew their equipment and gear. After processing, they remained in a barracks and waited. Unlike Seoul, the only thing to do in TDC was to go to the bars. The Korean girls were all over the GIs like flies on a carcass. They did anything and everything that they could think of to get a GI to part with his money. While in the barracks soldiers would informally be informed of what unit they would be going to. At this point, everyone was hoping that they would remain at Camp Casey. It was about eight at night when a first lieutenant came into the barracks.

"Taquard! Taquard! Where the hell is Taquard," he yelled.

"Here I am."

"Get your stuff in the vehicle. Let's go. We haven't got all night."

"Where are we going?"

"Camp Stanley. It's in Uijeongbu. We're already late as it is. Captain wants to see you first thing in the morning."

"What's going on?"

"You're going to be the new target acquisition officer."

After about an hour on the road the lieutenant said, "I got to pick up another lieutenant tomorrow. I have no idea where he could be. Drinkwater? What kind of a damn name is that?"

"Wait," interrupted Taquard. "I know a Drinkwater. Did you say that he was a lieutenant?"

"Yeah, an engineer."

"I met a Lieutenant Drinkwater at Camp Coiner. He's an engineer. Maybe we are talking about the same guy."

"Where is he?"

"At the Turtle Farm."

"Driver, turn this jeep around. Pronto."

When they got back to the barracks at the Turtle Farm the two lieutenants looked for Drinkwater.

"Where could he be?" asked Lieutenant Benson.

"Probably at one of the clubs in the ville," answered Taquard.

"I'm going to have to come back tomorrow and look for him then."

"Here's his bunk. Do you want to leave him a note or something?"

The lieutenants and their driver were once again on the road to Camp Stanley to what Taquard believed to be his first unit. The next morning, 1LT Benson introduced Taquard to the captain.

"Nice to meet you," said CPT Hastings. "Look there is a lot of things going on right now. Why don't you come back later?"

"Sir," Benson interjected, "why don't I take him with me to the Turtle Farm to help me find the other lieutenant that we just got assigned?"

"No problem."

Taquard and Benson returned back to the Turtle Farm in a search for 2LT Drinkwater. Remaining in a holding pattern on your first assignment was nerve wrecking. On subsequent assignments, it was a cinch. Finding Drinkwater was a lot easier during the day than during the night. Night life in TDC was filthy yet enticing. Ten dollars got a GI enough time with a Korean girl to get relief, twenty got him an overnight. Female GIs, according to rumor, paid a lot less.

Benson returned to Camp Stanley with the two lieutenants. As far as anyone was concerned, this was their final destination. It wasn't much, but it would be their home for the next year.

The day and night was uneventful and consisted of being introduced to other officers and listening to their war stories and philosophies on how to be a great soldier. Listening to others turned out to be a nuisance and had to be tempered with selectivity. About 95% of what you heard was pure bullshit. This seemed to be true throughout not only the Army but other places as well.

The following morning, Taquard reported to the headquarters. Although he had traveled extensively he was not assigned a room and still needed to settle in. While waiting the commons area a meeting adjourned in the next room. Another First Lieutenant, 1LT Blues, came out and told Taquard to get his gear. He informed him that he would be taking him to Camp Pelham. Once again, Taquard found himself in the moving mode. Every move was to a worse place than he was before. Camp Pelham was closer to the enemy than any other installation that the US had, it was within five kilometers of North Korea. Blues took Taquard to dumpy building where the lieutenants stayed.

"Here's your room. Hurry up and unpack. Get what you need, we'll be leaving soon."

"Leaving? Where are we going?"

"You're going to the field."

"Okay, I'll get ready. When do we leave?"

"Wait. You'll be leaving in a few days on very short notice so make sure that you have your bags ready. I have a detail for you."

Duties in the Army include details, dangerous missions, difficult tasks, achieving important objectives, and escorting the Dallas Cowboy cheerleaders around Camp Pelham. He was assigned a specific cheerleader; his task was to keep the soldiers from becoming too familiar with her. In some cases the question was who would keep the cheerleaders off of the soldiers. Although the detail got a lot of publicity and attention, it wasn't much of a task at all. In fact it was downright debasing to give such a detail to any lieutenant. Even though they were the Dallas Cowboy cheerleaders, they looked rather plain in person. They didn't measure up to their promotional pictures or what one would expect. They weren't ugly, but they weren't beautiful either. They also couldn't compare with the Korean ladies. The Koreans were much better looking. According to the Koreans, the best food in the Orient was Chinese, and the best-looking women were Japanese.

In another attempt to acclimate to his environment Taquard purchased a large economy size bottle of 100 proof (50% alcohol) Southern Comfort. This bottle was close to half of a gallon. He noticed how much drinking went on at Camp Stanley and decided to get with the program. Part of being in the Army at that time was drinking. Drinking was a good thing once you acquired a taste for it. Taquard was still in the process of acquiring a taste for alcohol. He had yet to get used to beer. He knew that it would only be a matter of time before he would be able to drink alcohol like the rest of the officers. The one hurdle that Taquard didn't count on was ajossie. If there is one thing that the Koreans do blatantly and continuously it is to steal. It costs more to live in Korea than it does in Japan when you factor in the rampant theft that the Koreans engage in. Ajossie also has acquired a taste for alcohol. What ajossie did not know was that there is a difference between a typical alcoholic drink and a liqueur. While regular whiskey can be guzzled down indiscriminately, liqueurs have to be sipped. Southern Comfort qualified as a liqueur and was not intended to be guzzled. Because of the alcoholic level of Southern Comfort, it was not advisable to drink too much at one time. The ajossie house boy, who was probably in his early sixties, stole the Southern Comfort by drinking it all. Taquard broke the seal on the bottle but barely tasted it. Ajossie guzzled down nearly two quarts of Southern Comfort in one sitting. Maybe ajossie intended to fill the empty bottle with colored water to disguise his theft. The problem was that ajossie had a sudden heart attack and died before he could do something about the empty bottle. Needless to say, Taquard was assigned a new house boy. Nobody gave a damn about a dead ajossie. Another lieutenant set a rat trap covered with won (Korean currency) bills inside of his desk drawer. When the ajossie house boy entered his room the lieutenant left. The lieutenant didn't get three steps out the door when he heard the clasping of a rat trap accompanies by a bellowing scream by the ajossie. Taquard decided to forgo any thoughts of purchasing any more alcohol, not because he was concerned about the possibility of another dear house boy but because he knew that it would be a waste of money with ajossie around. He gave up his attempts to acquire a taste for alcohol and remained a non-drinker although he was known to have a social drink on occasion. Taquard also had a briar root pipe and a special blend of Noble Bachelor and Twilights Dawning tobaccos that was also stolen along with his Southern Comfort. No telling what ajossie manager to do with it. Taquard resorted to smoking cigarettes.

Being assigned to an infantry unit was desired only by a few, and was certainly not desired by those who were not infantry. The worst assignment by far in the Field Artillery is that of being assigned to a FIST (Fire Support Team) team. Fisties were branched Field Artillery, but were attached to an Infantry unit. Their job was to provide artillery support to the Infantry by calling for fire and making adjustments based on observation. The question was who did FIST actually belong to? It wasn't so much that the question had to be resolved; the truth was that nobody wanted them. They obviously didn't belong to a Field Artillery firing battery. They really weren't part of the Infantry Company either. The Field Artillery Headquarters and Headquarters Battery (HHB) did everything in their power to disown the fisties. Being a fistie was like walking down the middle of the highway where the people on the right side wouldn't let you go there and neither would the people on the left. The fact is that nobody wants a FIST. Nobody. A very common and appropriate term referencing a fistie is bastard child. The other problem with being a fistie was that you were at the beck and call of both the Artillery and Infantry. When the

Infantry went to the field they brought FIST. When the Artillery went to the field they brought FIST. Fisties spent more time in the field than anyone else, yet received the least amount of recognition for their efforts.

While the FIST was attached to the Infantry to provide artillery support there was hardly an opportunity to call for fire because the Infantry, unlike the Artillery, was constantly on the move. Even when they decided to settle down, they were usually away from an impact area that could take artillery rounds. Fisties would deploy repeatedly, yet never fire a round. Logistically speaking, FIST was simply ignored. The Infantry never felt compelled to support a bunch of "red legs." And like never firing a single shot, the Infantry never provided logistical support for their FIST. That meant that if you were a fistie you better bring your own chow, otherwise you would not eat. When deployed with the Artillery, the FIST was stationed at an isolated and remote site away from the battery. And like the Infantry, the Artillery never provided logistical support for their FIST. That meant that if you were a fistie you better bring your own chow, otherwise you would not eat. HHB carried FIST on their unit roster but they received their directives, not from

HHB, from the firing batteries and the Infantry. HHB didn't want FIST either and was under no obligation to support them.

FIST is the organizational role model of what something should not be. It is a pool of outcasts and a bummer assignment. It was the lowest assignment that an Artillery officer could have. For the enlisted, it was even worse. That meant slow promotions, few awards, and always having to suck on it. Even if a fistie was lucky enough to get an award from the Infantry, the Artillery would override the recommendation and ensure that it was disapproved. It was common knowledge that the lowest element of society was assigned to FIST. If you were a shithead, you were going to be assigned to FIST. New Lieutenants to the unit were considered shitheads.

Infantry commanders constantly blamed the FIST for slowing down or compromising their movements even when it wasn't true. FIST was an excellent scapegoat for everything. Artillery batteries blamed FIST for poor firing missions.

Celebration and health and morale tours were scarce and usually occurred when the FIST was in the field. When the Artillery had an opportunity to go on an outing, FIST was in the field with the Infantry. When the Infantry had their opportunity, FIST wasn't invited. FIST was faced with a problem that they weren't capable of resolving.

The Army was loaded with misconceptions that were about to become revealed to Taquard during his tour of duty. Infantry movements were constant and often occurred with little or no notice. This was something that artillerymen were not used to. The FIST Chief was responsible for supporting the Infantry. That meant getting his people out of the sack in the middle of the night. This was a common occurrence in the field.

While a Second Lieutenant, affectionately know as "butter bars," had no support or authority whatsoever. Taquard would eventually discover how to turn butter into gold. In the true Bitcheye spirit, he would accomplish something that would run counter grain to the norms of the Army. The Army was more wrong than it was right. It is said that there are three ways to do something: the right way, the wrong way, and the Army way. The preferences seem to run in the same order. The new lieutenant was constantly challenged by the enlisted men below him and crapped on by the officers above him. In ROTC, cadets were taught and continuously reminded of the value of NCOs (enlisted men E-4 to E-9). Their value was overrated to an extreme. Although the NCO had experience and had been in the Army longer, the lieutenant assigned to him was his boss. While it is a problem having twenty-two-year-old Second Lieutenants outranking forty-four-year-old Sergeant Majors who have been in the Army longer than the lieutenant has been on the earth, the remedy is even worse. The Army has been trying to remedy this for decades, all with options that worsened the situation. Factually, there are as many types of NCOs and officers as there are types of people. The military is a reflection of the general population, it is no better. Some NCOs are great while others are shit. It wasn't until the Officer's Advanced Course (OAC) that instructors would address NCOs in a negative manner. During the Basic Course, several instructors were NCOs and continuously flattered themselves in a glorified fashion. They carried sticks known as Lieutenant Adjustment Rods.

Korea was extremely cold and windy during the winter season. The field produced several amounts of cold weather casualties. Infantrymen slept in tents even in the extreme cold. The infantry went many nights without sleeping altogether. The challenge was to set up the tents at night in the blistering cold where canteen water turns to ice. A soldier fought against cold temperatures, nature, and his command. Infantry field exercises lasted for over a month at a time. The soldiers wouldn't have the opportunity to ever change their clothes during this time. No matter how insulated the packed gear was, it would be compromised (usually by extreme cold). The clothes would freeze, get wet, get dirty, or all of the above. The clothes that a soldier could change into during a field exercise would become a worse alternative to the filthy clothes that he was already wearing. For the lower ranking soldiers, tents were as closest thing to a shelter available. In the freezing night during early February, Taquard found himself in the field with the infantry. The soldiers managed to erect a GP (general purpose) medium tent. By itself, it wasn't enough. Soldiers have learned to adapt and improvise according to the situation and their environment. Unfortunately, they don't always produce favorable outcomes. After the tent was set up, some of the soldiers found several Korean handmade straw mats. The mats seemed like a good idea. They were dry and provided a good buffer between the occupants and the muddy ground. They were infested with bugs and rat shit which resulted in soldiers getting sick and dying. The disease was referred to as "Rat Shit Fever." Although the straw provided heat, it wasn't enough. A pot-bellied stove made for GP medium tents was emplaced. The search for wood resulted in finding a lot of wood that was either iced over or too wet to burn. Experienced NCOs had improvised to overcome that problem as well. Mogas, gasoline, benzene, or whatever the Army used to refer to plain leaded low octane fuel as. While the forest provided wet wood, the gas would rectify the challenge of lighting it. The stove was filled with wood and then gas was poured over the wood. The NCOs were not taking any chances. They not only filled the stove with five gallons of gas, the had two additional five gallon cans filled with gas on hand in case they needed more. The additional gas as well as additional wood and straw mats was stored inside of the tent near the stove. For some odd reason the NCOs felt that the stove needed five gallons of gas. That was the way it had always been done. After all, these were five gallon cans. Although this concerned Taquard, the NCOs remained confident and told the new lieutenant to mind his own business.

"This is NCO business LT (El Tee)."

After the stove was prepared came the moment of truth or time of reckoning. A lit match was dropped into the stove. The stove lit up instantly. The stove pipe turned a bright cherry red. It was at this time that the importance of leveling the part of the ground that the stove was resting on was discovered. It was too late to correct that situation. The stove was burning hot. Heat was felt throughout the tent. The rubber molding at the top of the tent, made for insulating the pipe from the canvas, was melting as the burning shaft began leaning. The weight of the tilting pipe caused the stove to tilt as well. The medic, another person who was not branched Infantry but assigned to them, was sleeping at the base of the hot burning stove. It was just past midnight and the occupants were basking in their blissful warmth. Foreseeing the obvious, Taquard packed his gear while others began warning the medic of the circumstances.

"Hey, Doc. I'd move if I was you."

"Yo, Doc. The stove's falling over."

"You're gonna get burned up."

Warnings went unheeded as the stove began to topple over slowly but surely. The burning hole at the top of the tent grew bigger and bigger while the pipe remained burning hot.

Another lieutenant gave the order to evacuate the tent. Taquard calmly gathered his gear and left. The key to sleeping in the field was to never homestead anywhere and to keep your possessions packed as much as possible at all times. Only use what you need when you need it. Taquard learned this principle from his father who was once in a hotel fire. Pack light and never use the drawers. He not only survived the fire unscathed, but he did it with all of his belongings.

Homesteaders were frantically attempting to retrieve their gear in the dark. They were scrambling in the tent trying to locate their junk while simultaneously trying to pack it. Everyone knew that time was running out as the stove leaned further and further. Discombobulated soldiers were bumping into each other, scattering gear, and compounding the situation. So much for letting NCOs handle things.

"Has anybody seen my boots?"

"Who stepped on my face?"

"My gloves, where are my gloves?"

"Watch it! You damn near bumped me in the damn stove!"

Several minutes after the order to evacuate was given, only two of the forty or so occupants were out, the two lieutenants. Before any of the others could get out the pipe fell to the ground while burning a huge hole in the tent that went from the top and down the side. This caused the stove that was filled wit gasoline to tip over. The straw and tent were engulfed in flames instantaneously. Prior planning prevents piss poor performance was repeatedly stated throughout the Army. Perhaps the original intent of this philosophy was lost in translation. The extra fire wood and gasoline that was stored inside of the tent turned out to be more of a hindrance than an asset. During the confusion of trying to escape the fire, the five gallon gas cans were kicked over. As expected, gasoline spilled and ran downhill in a top speed trickle. It's amazing how fast things can travel when you don't want them to. The tent was the only thing on the massive slope. Below were other tents, but the odds of the gasoline trickle hitting one of them was almost zero. Stopping the trickle of gasoline wouldn't be necessary because it was likely to be absorbed by the ground. Luckily the fire from the tent didn't make contact with the gasoline even though the origin of the spill was inside of the burning tent. Taquard stood quietly on the hill in the cold wind watching the burning tent catastrophe. Some people ran out the front, some out the back, and others ran out the sides. Some ran through places where there were no openings. Some were on fire and others were dragging out burning gear. In spite of such an affair, there were few injuries though most of the gear was lost. The snow and frost prevented the fire from spreading to other tents.

Moments later, the fire reached the fire spill. Fire lit up along the trail of gas that trickled down the slope. There was a tent below that was so quiet that Taquard wondered if it was even occupied. The end of the inquiry came as the burning gas trail led into that very tent. When the tent caught fire, there was a ruckus that echoed throughout the mountain ridges. Apparently the subsequent had an empty gas can in it as assumed by the explosion.

This was hardly any way to begin a field exercise. It was the first night with thirty more remaining. This type of mishap would be seen repeatedly in decades to come. Safety was an arena that took lots of work, supervision, and attention. Taquard would not only discover the value of safety, but how to operate safely. Safety is an arena that demands respect. The minute you lose respect for safety, the minute you wish that you never took it for granted. Taquard was in fires before. Seemed like they never went out of style. When he was 11, his friend was playing with matches while they were walking to the bowling alley. He accidentally burned down a cemetery. As a cadet on an exercise, he found himself in the middle of a fire that was started by an artillery simulator. It consumed over 160 acres of Fort Carson forestry. Although Taquard had acquired an appreciation for safety, he also found himself to be in the overwhelming minority. At this point he had no idea how to ensure operational readiness. He was about to learn. It was evident that most people were simply unreliable and intended to remain that way. Some accidents were accidents (Type I Accident), most were deliberate (Type II Accident). The second type was far more difficult to handle.

In this case in the freezing night there was only one thing to do, pull rank. The two lieutenants walked to another tent that was completely filled.

"Alright, we need two of you to leave, we need this tent."

Although the problem for the two lieutenants was solved, the other soldiers were without a place to sleep while being exposed to frostbite conditions. The second tent also had a heater though it was much smaller than the first. However, the top flap was left open and by the time the two new lieutenants were bedded down no one in the tent had the intestinal fortitude to get out of bed to go outside to close the flap so the occupants froze.

Field movements were constant and usually occurred at night.

Movements and meetings. The Army was never an organization to function without meetings. Rest periods were never scheduled so it was up to the individual to take up the initiative to rest when he could. Although, Taquard was not only attached to the Infantry and not assigned to them, he was obligated to attend meetings. He and the company commander would drive through unforgiving terrain and hostile weather conditions to the lieutenant Colonel's Command Post. Driving there in the jeep took hours while countless natural obstacles had to be negotiated. Unlike the soldiers in the company, the commander's quarters were extravagant. The lieutenant Colonel had seven GP medium tents to himself. The tents were lined with wooden floors that were built up off of the ground to ensure that mud would never get in. Heaters were emplaced throughout the post. The quarters included a meeting room with chairs, charts, podiums, tables, and a desk where the stenographer sat. Unlike the typical soldiers who relied on flashlights for a light source, the commander's post was supported by generators and the tent was well lit. He even had a bathroom set up along with a heated shower and a sink. Taquard peeked into another tent in the command post and noticed the colonel's sleeping quarters equipped with a bed and a rack of uniforms that were still wrapped in plastic from the cleaners. The private dining area had a nice dining table with a table cloth, china, silverware, and what appeared to be the remnants of a steak dinner.

Meetings occurred every night and while the companies moved continuously, the command post didn't. During the meetings exercise enemy information was fabricated to support the missions. Everything else was created as well, even the weather reports. The weather reports always stated favorable weather conditions to support the company movements even though it was always snowing and movements were scheduled in the middle of a blizzard. Lieutenant Cornelson closed each meeting with his harping about shaving. He wanted everyone to have a clean shave. He spent several minutes complaining about the possibility of soldiers not shaving in the field. He harped about shaving so much that he became known as the "Get a Shave Colonel." It wasn't that anyone was apprehensive about shaving, the question was how. Water was scarce even when it wasn't frozen in the canteens, cold batteries didn't generate any power to operate the electric razors. Taquard used snow to facilitate his dry shaving. Most soldiers would shave periodically instead of daily in order to preserve their faces. Taquard was relieved when the Get a Shave Colonel didn't want artillerymen attending his meetings anymore.

The truth of the matter was that most infantrymen didn't recognize the value of artillery support. The situation was exacerbated by the fact that the fisties themselves didn't know how to call a fire mission. Taquard himself hadn't called a fire mission since OBC. Since dry fire missions were never exercised Taquard found himself to be the most experienced person on his team. Even his NCO had forgotten how to call for fire. Taquard was the newest member in his team yet the most capable of delivering a fire mission. The other problem that Taquard has was integrating the Artillery into the Infantry. As an Airborne Ranger, he understood the Infantry mindset.

During the day, the exercise went slow. The infantry slept. This made sense to Taquard because moving during the night was a means of staying warm. Sleeping during the day was considered a good idea since night movements were usually unannounced. This was something that the artillery did not comprehend.

Somewhere in the artillery it was taught that one should always keep busy during the day or at least look busy. This was a concept that became a religion to the artillery. During the day the FIST NCOs would make sure that everyone was awake and had plenty to do. When there was nothing to do they began digging. In the artillery when there is nothing to do, dig. When in doubt, dig. Heavy machine gun positions were dug; burying wire involved digging, and then there was digging for no other reason other than to dig. The infantry never dug. They performed vehicle maintenance and slept during the day.

"Rise and shine, El Tee. Get your ass outta bed," Sergeant (SGT) Dingus said to Taquard at the beginning of a new day in the field. NCOs liked to use the term El Tee instead of Sir or Lieutenant, yet got upset when someone referred to them as Sarge. While Dingus was insubordinate, mouthy, and incompetent, he was considered the crème de la crème among artillery NCOs. He was idolized by many.

"What's the matter, El Tee, too good for the rest of us? Haven't you ever heard of setting the example?"

"What the fuck are you doing Dingus?"

"We are all out here digging fighting positions. It's your turn to dig."

"You need to start up the vehicle and fill it with gas. We haven't had a night movement in a couple of days, so expect one tonight."

"Shit, El Tee, we got that all taken care of."

"Did you run the engines? They're hard as hell to start up if you haven't run them."

"Look, El Tee, don't tell me how to do my fucking job. That's NCO business."

"Don't delay the movement."

The fisties dug for hours creating fighting positions, barriers, and heavy machine gun positions. By afternoon, they were exhausted. The captain came over to Taquard.

"Lieutenant, I don't understand why you guys always have to dig everywhere you go."

"They were digging fighting positions, sir."

"We're not allowed to dig in this area. The Koreans consider this sacred ground. Tell your men to fill it back in the way it was."

"Yes, sir."

"Have you run your track today?"

"No, sir. My NCO assured me that it was ready to go though."

"One of my NCOs took the liberty of checking your batteries. They're completely dead. Expect a night movement. Keep someone awake at all times, we don't want any delays when it's time to move."

"Yes, sir. I understand."

"I found a weapon lying on the ground unattended. It belongs to one of your guys."

"Thanks, sir."

"Look. NCO business is our business. When an NCO says it, it is a euphemism for telling someone to fuck off. Your sergeant will let you down and frankly speaking he is not even good enough to be considered mediocre."

There was a long pause.

"Next time you trust an NCO with anything, remember Calley."

Fixing the mess created by the digging of the fighting positions took constant supervision on Taquard's part. As soon as he turned his back the fisties stopped working. He had to ride the NCOs constantly to repair the position. The repair wasn't completed until after midnight.

"SGT Dingus, do you have all of our weapons?"

"Yeah, El Tee, we got 'em all."

"Then whose weapon is this?" Taquard asked as he held up an M16 rifle.

"Fuck you."

"Get everyone out here now, with their weapons."

"You do your job and I'll do mine."

"Your job is to do what you're told."

"Bullshit. You fucking El Tees think you know everything. Fucking college boys, that's all you are."

Taquard called the formation himself. Sure enough, one of his people didn't have his weapon.

"SGT Dingus, start the track."

"It don't need starting."

"Do it anyway and do it now."

"I told you that the track is fine and it don't need no starting."

"The battery is dead. Prove me wrong. Start the damn track. Now!"

"Yes, sir, if it's going to be a big deal."

Repeated attempts to start the track failed. Even with a jump start, it took over an hour to get the engine to run. Taquard had one of the infantry NCOs fill the track with gas during the ordeal.

The Infantry NCO asked Taquard, "What the hell is wrong with all these Artillery NCOs? They never want to run their vehicles or top them off with gas. All they ever want to do is dig."

Taquard decided to take first watch, but it wasn't long before movement. Waking up artillerymen wasn't easy. It was damn near impossible.

"What the hell we moving for," Dingus would complain.

"Everybody, let's go. We're moving," Taquard would shout repeatedly.

"Fuck the movement," Dingus would respond. "We just went to sleep and it's dark outside."

SGT White had the same attitude as Dingus. Gear was scattered everywhere and Taquard found another unattended rifle. While the Infantry was moving, the fisties were still packing. Taquard was scrambling to get the team moving. Luckily the track started, but the Infantry was out of sight. They attempted to catch up, but noises were misleading throughout the night. The infantry movement took about six hours, but it took the artillery over 12 hours to look for the unit and catch up. They were able to find additional fuel along the way.

"Look, sir, it is my job to train lieutenants," Dingus would say.

"It's my job to keep this team deployable because you are not doing your job. Don't you ever miss a movement again."

The seven man FIST team returned from the field with two permanent cold weather injuries including SGT White.

It was Taquard's first field exercise outside of training. It was a miracle that no weapons were lost. He fought with his NCOs throughout the entire exercise and came to the same conclusion as the infantry captain. The term "NCO business" was no more than a euphemism for shoddy performance.

While Taquard's team was assigned to the Infantry for an exercise, they were reassigned to the Artillery two days before the Infantry was due to return back to garrison. That meant that the FIST teams spent more time out in the field than both the Infantry and Artillery. The Infantry was constantly on the move while the Artillery avoided it as much as possible. It was no wonder when Taquard observed how the Artillery conducted their movements.

First Lieutenant (1LT) Hand orchestrated a consolidated APC convoy that consisted of the entire fire support element, nineteen APCs in all. The convoy included a river crossing. The convoy looked awesome. Taquard's track was near the end of the convoy. He was taking in an impressive sight of the convoy successfully negotiating the challenging terrain of Korea in unison. Even the steepest of muddy inclines didn't break up the convoy. The APCs made four wheel drive vehicles look sick. The convoy traveled through woods, icy roads, up and down steep icy slopes, and thick mud without a hitch. The sight was memorable. The inspiration came to an end when the convoy had to descend down an extremely steep icy narrow incline to approach a rushing river that was about 200 meters wide.

Taquard approached Dingus with his inquiry. "We're going to cross this river?"

"Yes."

"It's too deep to cross. We'll never make it."

"Yes we will, you stupid mutherfucker."

"These things don't swim."

"Yes they do, you dumb son of a bitch."

"They swim? These things actually swim?"

"That's what I've been trying to tell you, but you just don't listen."

"I had no idea that they swam."

"Well, try listening to your NCOs for a change."

The APCs were stopped just prior to approaching the steep embankment that led to the river. Prior to swimming, the wooden extension on the front of the APC had to be set in the required position for swimming. It didn't take long to put it in position, but the track couldn't swim without it.

"So that's what those things are for," Taquard exclaimed.

"That's what I've been trying to tell you all along, El Tee," Dingus responded without solicitation.

Tracks started to bunch up prior to going into the river. This shortened vehicle intervals from about 500 feet to about forty. This didn't affect Taquard's vehicle that was near the rear of the convoy. Just before entering the great slope, that was covered in ice and was about 700 feet long, that approached the river, they were stopped by two sergeants who were on foot.

"What the fuck, over," Dingus shouted.

"We're setting the swim extensions for you," one answered back.

"So you don't have to get out of your track," the other added.

"The vehicles are too close together. It's dangerous," the first continued.

"Only my crew is authorized to set the extension on this track," Dingus interrupted.

"Okay. Be careful and don't get too close to the other tracks."

"Hey, I know what the fuck I'm doing," Dingus exclaimed.

"Thanks for your help," Taquard added.

"Oh, and one more thing. Is your drain plug in?" one of the NCOs asked. "A lot of people have been forgetting their drain plugs."

"We know what we're doing, you fuckhead," Dingus shouted.

Taquard grabbed SGT White and asked, "How many drain plugs does this thing have?"

"One."

"Where does it go? Show me! Show me now!"

As he had guessed, the drain plug wasn't in place. After scrambling around the inside of the track Taquard managed to find the drain plug on the other side of the track; is wasn't even close to the drain.

"White! How do I put this in?"

"You just put it in."

"Does it need a seal? Does it require a certain amount of torque?"

"What do we need a seal for?" asked SGT White.

"Does this need a seal?"

"No, why would it?"

"Okay, show me how to put this thing in."

"Whut fer?"

"Put the damn thing in now. We're running out of time. Do it now!"

"Okay, if that's whut you want."

After putting the drain plug in place, Taquard continued asking questions concerning his first river crossing in an APC.

"Sergeant White, is there anything else that needs to be done to prepare for a river crossing?"

"Why do you keep asking all these questions?"

"Stop arguing. Are we forgetting anything?"

"Like what?"

"Like anything that is needed to prepare for a river crossing. Are we forgetting anything?"

"No, not that I know of."

"How many drain plugs does this thing have?" Taquard asked again.

"One. I already told you that already."

"Yes, I know. I'm just double-checking."

"You need to have confidence in your NCOs."

"If it weren't for me that drain plug would still bouncing around the APC instead of where it should be. You should've thought of that before I even asked you about it. As far as confidence in NCOs goes, you haven't earned it."

Just then SGT Dingus stomped on the accelerator causing a jolt through the APC. In response, Taquard stood up through the open hatch. The track was sliding down the ice. The rate of sliding was relatively slow but there was no way of stopping it. It turned sideways before impacting the APC in front of it. A frontal his would have destroyed the extension assembly. Though it was a hit that derived from slow speed, the impact sounded like thunder. While the impact caused Taquard's vehicle to come to a complete stop, the other vehicle slid into the vehicle in front of it causing a chain reaction that continued all the way to the lead APC. APCs were knocked into the river prematurely as a result of Dingus' maneuver. Taquard watched what was going on through his binoculars. A couple of the APCs went into the water sideways facing each other and one went in backwards after being spun around. Another APC managed to slide in the river without its extension. Fortunately, it wasn't all the way in and there was enough time to extend it. Unfortunately, this was just the beginning of a chain of fiascos to follow. The two tracks that were in the river facing each other both started their engines simultaneously. They also accelerated simultaneously without any type of prior coordination whatsoever. This resulted in a head on collision that destroyed the swimming extensions of both tracks. The two tracks that collided both appeared to be front heavy. One of the tracked vehicles seemed to slowly descent deeper into the water front first. Once the front was completely immersed in the water the track went perpendicular to the water as soldiers jumped out in a mad frenzy. The driver jumped out into the cold water then the rest of the crew followed as water filled the hatch. The APC just seemed to stay still for a few seconds with the rear half sticking out of the water before plummeting completely into the water. The second APC went through the same gyration as did the first. The men from both downed APCs swam for the other track that was in the water.

The extra weight on the APC didn't cause it to sink. This was a surprise to everyone. However, the track had to negotiate the current to face itself forward. The additional weight complicated the maneuver significantly. It miraculously made it to the other side although it missed the re-entry point by several hundred meters. It was not able to secure itself on the steep embankment. It continued to float with the current until it was completely out of sight.

Taquard couldn't believe what he just saw. Of the nineteen tracks in the convoy, three of the first four to enter the water were lost. Dingus repeated his previous acceleration stunt and hit the track that was in front of him with greater force than before. The chain reaction fiasco was repeated once again. The crew cussed at Dingus.

"You fucking dingus, Dingus," Taquard yelled at Dingus. "Knock that shit off! White, put the extension in place now. I mean now."

White and another soldier put the extension in place in about four minutes. Vehicles piled up in the river and began drifting. Although the current was slow, it was strong enough to pull the APC down stream if it missed the re-entry point that was flat and shallow and perfect for accessing the shore. The APC pile in the river was drifting as the NCOs made a mad scramble to correct their situation without coordination. Some of the soldiers stood on top of the tracks to relieve themselves in the river. While most of the soldiers urinated, one was actually taking a dump. While his pants were pulled down they got caught on protruding objects from the APC. Not only did his turd fall directly into his pants, he fell into the river.

Taquard ordered Dingus to stay put. He decides to wait until the cluster fiasco was uncorked before letting Dingus drive the APC into the river. At times like this it paid to be patient. He watched and waited. When Dingus protested the wait, Taquard took off his helmet and smacked it up against Dingus' head. Fortunately, Dingus was wearing his helmet.

"Not yet! I'll tell you when we move," Taquard said to Dingus.

Taquard watched Canerra's vehicle as they entered the water and noticed that the one in front of it that was sinking slowly. Although the swimmer extension was emplaced properly, it was sinking. It was obvious that they forgot to put in their drain plug when the crew abandoned the track. They swam for Canerra's track. Canerra didn't want them boarding his vehicle. Wet men meant wet equipment and extra weight and more crowded conditions. In short, nobody wanted additional men on their vehicle. Just like the Infantry didn't want the fisters, the FIST teams didn't want additional fisters. Canerra did the honorable thing that anyone else would do in a similar situation. He diligently did all that he could do to prevent anyone else from boarding his APC. One of the swimmers grabbed the APC moments before Canerra smacked his hand with a helmet. Another soldier tried to get on as Canerra butt stroked him in the face with an M16 rifle. Then he grabbed the tool bag and threw tools at anyone who might gain access to boarding his vehicle. Gates threw a rope to one of the swimmers; Canerra cut the rope. Canerra then aggressively kicked another soldier in the face as he was trying to get on the track. Swimmers attempted to bypass Canerra's track and get on Taquard's.

"If any of those assholes tries to get on our track, clobber them," Dingus stated.

"We'll let them on," Taquard overruled.

It was obvious why some men were officers and others weren't. This distinction would become cloudier as time went on. The Army had the knack of mismatching compatible officers and NCOs. Taquard preferred Gates over Dingus while Canerra preferred Dingus over Gates with the NCOs having mutual feelings about the officers.

Fortunately, most of the soldiers from the previous track were able to make it to Taquard's track. The ones that didn't make it froze in the frigid water and ended up drowning.

Only four tracks were lost during the river crossing. This was considered successful by Artillery standards and exceptional by stateside units. The FIST teams completed the river crossing and set up a consolidated camp. Medical Evacuation (MEDIVAC) mission were conducted with helicopter air support. It was beginning to make sense to Taquard how many units managed to lose more men through training they did in combat. Two large tents were set up in the area although no one knew who set them up. Korean vendors were also on hand to provide the soldiers what they wanted. This usually consisted of a bowl of ramen, a bottle of Coke, a moon pie, and kimchee. The downside to having the vendors around was the fact that they were also infested with slicky boys. That meant that you really had to watch your stuff.

One thing that became apparent early in the tour was that nothing seemed to cure the cold like kimchee. While the soldiers despised kimchee, a lot of them ate it when they were in the field. It was a stinky remedy, but a remedy nevertheless.

During Team Spirit, which was also affectionately known as Team Stupid, the 25th Infantry Division (ID) from Hawaii was conducting maneuvers. As expected, they deployed without preparing for the cold weather conditions of Korea. Their encampments surrounded the 2nd ID FISTs. The FISTs set up camp and waited for further orders. Orders wouldn't arrive for another three days. The soldiers passed their time by smoking, joking, reading fuck books, playing cassette tapes, wandering around, homosexual experimentation, and playing with themselves.

Taquard would wander off by himself as a way to kill time. He didn't desire hanging out with his troops. He understood more and more as to why officers despised their soldiers. Taquard sat by a brook while consuming a moon pie and a Coke. He observed a black captain from the 25th ID pull up to the brook in his jeep. He got out and assessed the situation. It was obvious that he had no appreciation for the topography or temperature variances of Korea.

"It's not that deep. We can make it," he said.

The jeep slowly negotiated the shallow river with its wheels just barely covered beyond the halfway point. When it reached the middle of the river, it stopped. The driver did everything that he could to move the jeep, but the jeep just wouldn't move. The mild current didn't appear to pose ant problem for the jeep crossing. The water was only about a foot deep. As the wheels spun, the back of the jeep shifted in the downstream direction. The captain continued hollering and cussing at his driver while the wheels kept on spinning. Then the entire jeep moved sideways. The driver stopped the jeep. The jeep stood still for a moment, then it moved downstream again in a small spurt. Then it moved a little more. Then the water level on the jeep began to rise. The captain cursed even louder. The water rose even more and the jeep moved further downstream. Finally the water level rose to the point where it got inside of the jeep and it was slowly but steadily moving downstream. The captain and driver got out of the jeep and stood on the hood. The jeep was sinking while picking up speed. The captain grabbed the drover by the coat and pants and threw him off of the jeep. However, the captain found himself in the water soon afterwards while the jeep continued to sink. Taquard was hoping that this observation was of something that wasn't typical of a unit that appeared to operate like a Mexican whore house. He wasn't sure which unit the captain and his driver came from since they had additional jackets covering their division patches. All that he knew for sure was that these boys were definitely from out of town from a stateside unit. The 25th ID had an unofficial motto: "If it ain't broke, break it." These idiots appeared to be capable of breaking a steel ball. While 2nd ID was "Second to None," the Second of the Eleventh Field Artillery Battalion from 25th ID was "Second to Last." Their concept of discipline was to tear up work areas with a stick, denying them sleep, and urinating on them. Commanders would urinate on their soldiers while they stood at attention and took it. The soldiers had professional pornographic photos of each other's wives. Commanders were notorious for placing their soldiers on restriction so that they could get over to their house to have sex with their wives. Some of the ignorant wives were stupid enough to believe that they were doing it to help their husbands. Commanders would threaten the soldier's wife as well as the soldier himself. Some of the soldiers, with the overwhelming approval of their commanders, were even pimping their wives. Homosexuality was rampant throughout the unit and was practiced openly. It was even practiced out in the field. This was even beyond Canerra. Even he was embarrassed when he came upon two homosexual soldiers going at it when he walked into what he believed to be an empty tent while searching for unattended valuables. The homosexuals, without missing a beat, told Canerra to get out.

To make matters worse, Fort Carson (at that time) had a worse reputation than Schofield Barracks. Camp Casey had the best reputation, although the soldiers who were on their first tour couldn't believe it. The more that Taquard saw of 2/11th the more he was grateful to be assigned to Pelham. Unfortunately for him, he never observed any division patches. At least the soldiers who were assigned to Korea knew how to go into the woods to relieve themselves, at least for number twos. Not Hawaii, when they had to go they went. One of their soldiers even took a big hairy dump inside of a tent. As unbelievable as this was, it turned to be a fairly common practice throughout the Army even among officers. Most of it was deliberate as opposed to dumb ass. Turds were strategically placed at someone else's location. For new lieutenants, this was both appalling and unacceptable.

Surprisingly enough, the Hawaiian division was well equipped with vehicles. Although they didn't have a lot of cold weather gear for their soldiers, they were well stocked in other areas. The Army rarely gave anything new to Taquard. The 2/11th boasted a brand new deluxe field mess hall that was located at the bottom of a hill. It was the latest innovation in the arena of battalion field kitchens. It was awesome. When Taquard saw it, he just stood there and looked at it in amazement. He decided that he would see what the meals there would be like. It was lunch time and the arrangement looked as if it could spare an extra meal for a passerby. This would also give him the opportunity to observe the kitchen close up. He had nothing else to and he was hungry. Taquard approached the field dining facility with great anticipation. As he got closer he was met by an armed guard who presented him with the challenge.

"Cable," the guard challenged.

"Oh I forgot to look it up today, I missed breakfast," Taquard replied.

"Then I can't let you go in," the guard replied.

Taquard turned around and walked away. When he came upon some approaching soldiers he challenged them with, "Cable."

"Grape," one of them responded.

Taquard turned around again followed the other soldiers. This time when he was challenged he knew the password and accessed the field mess with ease.

The inside was more impressive than the outside. The food was awesome and the menu included steak and crab legs and lots of it. Taquard loaded up his plate with food and stuffed even more food in his pockets. Another officer from the 25th ID noticed Taquard's 2nd ID patch.

"Hey, what the hell are you doing here in our mess hall? You don't belong here. Get the fuck out of our mess tent."

"Wait. I'm in this unit now. I PCSed from Korea a couple of months ago. I decided to wear this jacket here since I couldn't wear it anywhere else."

"I never seen your face before."

"I'm with the target acquisition battery. Anyway, the challenge and password is set up to keep imposters out. It never fails. Have you ever been to Korea before?"

"No."

"Well, I have and this is my second Team Spirit (TS) exercise. Last year I was on the opposing side. If you have any questions, just ask me and I'd be more than happy to help you out."

The separation ploy worked and Taquard commenced to finding himself a place to sit down and enjoy his meal. He spotted Canerra who managed to have more food than he did, which was saying a lot.

"How'd you manage to get in here?" Taquard asked.

"I walked in," Canerra responded.

"I had to go through an interrogator."

"Not me. There was no one posted when I came in."

"Beer? You're drinking beer in the field?"

"Sure. They have plenty in that cooler over there."

"They have beer in the field?"

"Yeah. This unit does things a little differently than we do."

"I noticed that," Taquard said while observing beer at several of the other tables. "What if Hand finds out?"

"He downed a few just before you came in. He just left. You just missed him. He said it was okay."

"So, are we allowed to eat here as well?"

"No, we're not. So don't tell any of your guys. If they see too many of us in here they'll throw us out."

"How many of us know about this?"

"Maybe four or five, possibly six."

As they left they spoke about returning back later that night for the evening meal. They agreed that they would come back separately to be less conspicuous. And like the rumors that they had heard previously, the observed a black captain urinating on a soldier who was standing at attention.

"I fucked your wife," the captain said to the soldier. "I fucked her socks off. Do you understand me? I fucked her while I put you on restriction."

He shouted reprimands to the soldier while he was urinating on him. The soldier took it.

Both Taquard and Canerra felt that the unit, although it had a great field mess, had officers who were way out of bounds. Taquard and Canerra approached the top of the hill when the notices a two and a half ton truck with a running engine and no occupant.

"I don't see a driver," Taquard said.

"Me either," Canerra responded.

They continued back to camp.

The wheels of the truck rolled slightly forward toward the field mess facility and stopped. Then it moved a little more and stopped again. The driver was off to the side in the tree line taking a number two while he left the engine running while the truck was parked on an incline. Even though the brake was on the truck still nudged forward. The truck slid forward in the mud. Eventually, the incline applied too much stress for the brake. The truck rolled down to the bottom of the hill and crashed into the field mess facility. When it hit the butane storage tanks that were behind the kitchen an explosion erupted. The gas ranges explodes and the truck was tossed about 150 feet in the air. Exploding vehicles were thrown into the air like they were no challenge at all for the explosions. They went up like rag dolls that were tossed in the air by Neanderthals. The entire facility was in flames and the frantic mob was running for their lives. People who accidentally ran into each other ended up punching each other in the face. The behavior of the discombobulated crowd created additional injuries. The slightest resemblance of order, which was beyond anyone's grasp, would have resulted in far less than it should have. The injuries would have easily been reduced by half. Abandoned ammunition began exploding. Compressed cans of food exploded. The field mess facility was converted into a massive inferno accompanied by a long drawn out series of explosions. The fire lasted for hours, but although the fire posed a great threat to everyone it was contained. The snow covered ground and wet foliage that surrounded the fire accounted for its containment. The Army itself had nothing to do with that. Fortunately, the other tents were far enough away not to be effected. The aftermath was a series of MEDIVAC rescues. This was a difficult maneuver for the helicopter pilots. Smoke filled the air and landing spots were extremely tight.

"Well, I guess we don't have to worry about the others finding out about this place," Canerra said to Taquard.

"They don't call this Team Stupid for nothing," Taquard responded.

All that everyone could do was to look forward to ENDEX (End of Exercise). In those days there was no AARs (After Actions Report) that's were an additional exercise in and of themselves.

The following afternoon Taquard was in his established routine of eating and drinking a bottle of Coke at the brook. He noticed a familiar captain with a new jeep. On further observance he noticed that it was the same driver too. The jeep stopped short of the creek but was posed in a ready position. The captain got out and paced around while surveying the situation.

"Excuse me, but there's a bridge about two miles upstream," Taquard said to the captain.

"Two miles," shouted the captain. "I'll be late for the meeting. No thank you."

"Better late than losing another jeep."

"Why don't you mind your own business, honky?"

"I was just trying to help."

"What's wrong, cracker? Don't think I can make it?"

"All I know is that you didn't make it last time."

"We didn't have a running start last time, whitie."

"How in the world did you get honky and cracker to mean white? I can understand whitie, but honky and cracker."

"Cracker is the crack of the whip that the white man used on my ancestors."

"Judging from your attitude, I'd say that he didn't use it enough."

"And judging from your attitude, I'd say that you are full of shit. You think that you can bring the black man down but you can't."

"That creek might bring the black man's jeep down."

"Aw fuck you!"

"Well, good luck crossing that stream anyway."

"Luck is for suckers."

With a running start, the jeep entered the creek at high speed. This time it made it beyond the halfway point. It kept on moving as the speed decreased. The effort was impressive. The front of the vehicle nearly made it to the other side. The driver kept on trying. The rear of the vehicle slid in a downstream direction. Even with four wheel drive the jeep wasn't moving. The captain began cussing out his driver as usual. His hollering was louder than the engine that was being taxed to no end while attempting to negotiate the creek. The captain got out and stood on the hood of the jeep.

"Get the fuck out here, you fuckin' bastard."

The driver got out onto the hood of the jeep as well.

"Get the winch cable and take it to the other side. Well don't just stand there, reach down there and get the cable."

"This water's freezing sir."

"Get the fucking cable, you white mutherfucker!"

"I'm trying, sir."

"After you get it, I want you to swim to the other side and tie it to a tree."

"Swim, sir?"

"Yes, you stupid white honky mutherfucker," the captain said to his driver as he kicked him. The captain kept on kicking his driver until eventually he fell into the stream. The driver drifted downstream. The captain continued to yell at the driver as the jeep began nudging downstream. "Get your white ass back here you lazy bum. I need for you to get the cable. We're sinking, you stupid mutherfucker! I'm going to fuck your wife!" The jeep sank while it drifted downstream and the captain was once again in the water himself.

The exercise continued with a race among artillery batteries to selected firing points. The FISTs would not be participants. The 2/17th had 198 155mm howitzers while 2/11th and 7/8th only had 102 105mm ones. The 198s were heavy and had to be towed. The Hawaiian units had a tremendous advantage. Not only were the 102s lighter and easier to move, they could also be airlifted with a CH-47 Chinook helicopter. Even with these advantages, units should not be in a hurried rush like the ignorant Hawaiians. While 2nd ID tended to travel at a leisurely stroll, 25th ID ran in a mad panic. The two and a half ton trucks that were towing the 102 howitzers did so at high speed over very rugged and uneven terrain. Hugh bumps that were negotiated at high speed resulted in bouncing howitzers. One could only hope that the howitzer would bounce back right side up.

**HOWITZER TRANSPORT RULE NUMBER 1: The more you bounce a howitzer during a transport, the greater the chances of it falling on its side.**

Other batteries were in the process of sling loading howitzers while the lead unit made a mad rush to the firing point via land movement. Driving like hell through Korean terrain was never advisable. Hawaii was never much on taking advice. The land movement battery had two immediate mishaps. One of the wheels came off of one of the howitzers. Naturally, it fell off while it was at the top of a hill and managed to stay upright as it rolled down the hill as it approached Ski Jump Pass. It wasn't long before the wheel was out of sight and out of reach as it soared off of the road rise and over a cliff. As expected, no spare tire was available. It didn't matter as the sudden loss of a wheel from a howitzer in motion. Another howitzer, to no one's surprise, landed on its side during the transport. The truck kept on moving as the driver attempted to keep up with the convoy. The damage to the howitzer was tremendous and beyond functioning by the time the truck eventually stopped. The air lift was even more disastrous. While it is technically possible to sling load three 102 howitzers simultaneously it is not advisable. The conditions have to be perfect. Wind stresses the tension on a sling load as does air density resistance and temperature. Every condition matters. Loading two howitzers isn't even advisable in most cases. The aviators were trumped by the ranking major from the artillery unit. They insisted on sling loading three howitzers simultaneously. The lift went smoothly. Getting airborne wasn't nearly as difficult as the aviators imagined. The howitzers reached their maximum mission altitude when they were about halfway to the destination. They encountered a gust of cold wind. The slings stretched and the howitzers began to bounce. The sling configuration was dependent as opposed to individual configurations. This was done to reduce the possibility of the howitzers bumping into each other. The tension of the slings gave way to stretching. Bouncing created greater tension. The sling configuration separated and the howitzers began clanging against each other. They spun around and banged against each other even harder. One of the slings broke. The helicopter pilot was monitoring the situation and tries to steady the load. One of the howitzers dropped. It fell about 2,000 feet and crashed into the Korean landside. It broke up into countless numbers of pieces upon impact. It didn't take long for the second howitzer to drop. There was no stopping the third howitzer from dropping at this point which it did shortly after the second. Everyone, including Taquard, saw the howitzers drop. It was definitely something to talk about. The 2nd ID made it to the firing points first and occupied the positions that 25th wanted. They scored many more points than 25th could ever hope for. While the 2nd ID had more than its fair share of problems, they were nothing compared to the 25th. Gomer Pyle had nothing on the 25th ID.

Taquard's group made another movement to a new location later that day. The weather got even colder than it was before. As usual they made the best of the new site. Canteen water froze, and Taquard was amazed at the fact that people were surviving in below freezing temperatures all day long for days on end. The inside of the track was covered with ice. Two days later he was strolling at another stream that was frozen over. He saw a familiar captain and his driver with yet another new jeep. The captain got out and carefully walked out onto the ice. He walked out a little further. Soon he was confident about the situation. He jumped up and down on the ice a few times. After returning back to the jeep his driver got out and grabbed the winch cable. Then he ran with the cable across the frozen stream. He ran until he ran out of cable which caused him to fall down backwards on the ice before he could reach the other side. The driver returned and both of them got back inside of the jeep. They slowly drove across the ice. When they were almost halfway across the stream, the jeep slid. Even though they were going slowly and cautiously, the tires spun on the ice. The driver tried speeding up but the tires kept on spinning and the jeep kept on sliding. Then the spinning wheels cut into the ice a little. The driver got out and attempted to tie the winch cable to a tree. The cable was so cold that securing a tight knot wasn't possible. The knot was large and loose. The cable didn't want to bend. Even with the anchor hook on the end of it the knot was anything but reliable. In an attempt to secure the knot the driver returned to the winch and reeled in the cable. As the knot wouldn't hold, the cable loosely wound back around the winch cylinder. When the end of the cable wound up on the ice the captain started cussing at the driver. He got so mad that he posted the driver at the position of attention. Then he unzipped his pants and urinated on the driver. The driver complied with the order to shout "Red Dragons" while he was being urinated on. The captain appeared to enjoy pissing on his driver and abusing other. He was a role model for the artillery units in his division. The captain and driver returned back inside of the jeep without securing or reeling in the cable. The wet driver attempted to move the jeep but the wheels just spun slowly. Then the tires cut into the ice even deeper. The driver got out and operated the winch and made yet another attempt to secure the cable around a tree while the captain stayed in the jeep next to the heater. This time the cable appeared to be more secure. The driver made another attempt to drive the vehicle after tightening the cable. The tires spun again and the jeep fell in a little deeper into the ice. Then the jeep fell in further. It became obvious that they were going to lose another jeep. The occupants got out of the jeep and the captain picked up a stick and beat his driver with it. The driver operated the winch while being beaten with a stick. The tight cable got tighter and tighter. The jeep fell completely through the ice into the river even though the cable held taunt. The cable cut into the ice as the jeep was being dragged downstream. The ice began breaking up around the cutting cable. Then the cable snapped and the jeep was lost. The captain and his driver ran back while the ice was cracking and breaking up.

"Hey, Captain. How many jeeps have you lost so far?"

"You shut the fuck up, you white honky muther," the captain responded.

"It seems that the way you keep losing jeeps you would have figured out how to use a bridge or something."

"You white mutherfucker. I know what I'm doing."

"You know with all the breaks and free rides that you people have been getting you haven't been worth a shit."

"You white fuckers have been holding us down."

"From what I've been observing, it's a mistake for a white man to listen to a colored guy."

Taquard left while the captain screamed racial slurs at him.

The Artillery group didn't spend a lot of time in the field compared to the Infantry. After spending another night at a consolidated camp site they headed back to garrison. Infantry deployment was rough, but no matter how bad the infantry was, it was never as bad as artillery garrison.

# Chapter Eight
## *Artillery Garrison*

"SGT Dingus is one of the best men that I have ever met in my entire career. He is trying to give you the best training possible, if that's possible. You are interfering with him every step of the way. As far as I am concerned, you are the worst lieutenant that I have ever seen," LTC Absalom shouted at Taquard. The one-sided reprimand continued. "Your statements have no substance here. When SGT Dingus tells you to do something, you do it!

SGT Dingus stuck his tongue out at Taquard when Absalom wasn't looking.

"SGT Dingus had five ARCOMs (Army Commendation Medal), two of which I gave to him personally. How many do you have?"

"None, I just came in the Army."

"That's right, asshole! You don't have any ARCOMs and you're brand new to the Army which means you don't know shit. Not only do you not have any ARCOMs, you ain't going to get any either. SGT Dingus is ten times the soldier that you will ever be."

SGT Dingus just stood by with a big smile on his face.

"I graduated from West Point and I am telling you to follow SGT Dingus' orders to the letter. Don't question, just do. And one more thing Lieutenant. Get the fuck out of my office!"

Taquard had a problem that was compounded by another problem.

He tried to address the Dingus problem but to no avail. Dingus was out of control and had the old man in his pocket. When Taquard was at OBC he was told that there was a 99% chance that a Second Lieutenant would make First Lieutenant. This battalion, under the command of LTC Absalom, had three lieutenants that Taquard knew personally that did not make it. They were known as the one per centers. Taquard felt like he was about to join the club. SGT Dingus was assigned to monitor Taquard and his Officer Evaluation Report (OER) would be based on Dingus' counseling reports. The other three lieutenants who got passed over for first were also under the supervision of an NCO. The best that a Second Lieutenant could hope for in this assignment was to get promoted to First Lieutenant and get an ARCOM. It didn't look like Taquard was going to get either.

Returning from the field was worse for Taquard, and was about to get even worse. Being under the supervision of an NCO was a new Army concept that was practiced repeatedly regardless of how stupid it proved to be. As if Taquard didn't have enough to deal with, he was appointed to two additional positions: the Battalion Safety Officer and the Battalion Fire Marshal. He was selected by the S-1 who was not in his immediate chain of command. 2LT Taquard's captain decided not to intervene on his behalf. Of the seven FIST Chiefs, Taquard was the only one to have additional duties. The positions had been vacant for the previous six months so there was no transition. As usual, Taquard found himself building an office from scratch from the ground up. First he would have to learn the positions, and then he would have to perform the missions involved. Unfortunately for Taquard, the realm of Fire Marshal had an area of interest that got MAJ Coldhammer's attention. This meant that Taquard would be working for two bosses simultaneously. Coldhammer was new to the unit, but although father was a full General he came into his own. His presence was felt and it was obvious that Coldhammer was someone never to be crossed. Taquard felt like he was between a hammer and an anvil while at the wrong place. Camp Pelham (AKA Camp Peyton Place) was short on sympathy, but had an overabundance of grief even though it housed just an artillery battalion with a few attachments. Camp Pelham may have been appropriately named after the right person.

Camp Pelham was about twenty-four acres in size (about five acres larger than Alcatraz) and named after Major John C. Pelham, a Confederate artilleryman who died while leaving three pregnant surviving fiancees. He was born on 7 September 1838 and died on 17 March 1863 (St. Patrick's Day) at the age of twenty-four. He resigned from West Point in 1861 just a few weeks prior to his graduation. He fought in over sixty battles and came up with ideas of enhancing artillery mobilizing methods to increase effectiveness. He was struck in the head with an artillery fragment at Kelly's Ford and died soon afterwards. He was posthumously promoted to the grade of Lieutenant Colonel.

While Taquard tried to find some morsel of guidance concerning his new duties there was an accident. On his first day on the job as the Battalion Safety Officer there was a twenty-nine-vehicle pile-up at the bottom of an icy hill. The accident included both US military and Korean civilian vehicles. Investigations by themselves were a real pain in the ass, but adding Koreans to the equation made it even more unbearable. The ajossies (Korean men) would do anything and everything to steal every last penny they could from everyone that came near their sector. This was very much like, just off of the highway in a remote area of Hick Town, Americans but more egregious. The ajemas (Korean women) and aggessies (unmarried Korean women) behaved likewise. By Korean standards, the US owed them millions of dollars just for being there. At the time, the US was giving the Koreans about $2 billion annually. They still wanted a lot more. Even in cases where the ajossie was drunk and obviously at fault for causing an accident, the US paid a hefty sum of money to compensate. Korea turned out being more expensive than Japan when thievery and absence of quality was factored in. Taquard did the accident investigation and report. Even though he determined that the US drivers were not at fault, the US still paid off the Koreans.

Korean prostitutes would cry rape if they were shortchanged. The bartender at Camp Pelham drove a Cadillac. Little Camp Pelham was the only installation in the military where the unit commander and the base commander where the same person. As small as Camp Pelham was, the outer ville, Sun Yu Ri had about forty different night clubs with convenience rooms. That's a lot of clubs for a unit with only about 500 people. That's about a club for every twelve people. The ville was off-limits to officers except for official business. Camp Pelham was manned with indigenous Korean guards who were constantly asleep while on duty. Theft was as common in Korea as was the stink on kimchee. Koreans in the western corridor would scream and go into crying fits and tirades over financial disputes for as little as a dollar. As far as the residents of Camp Pelham were concerned, Korea was the armpit of the world. The ville, Sun Yu Ri, certainly endorsed that sentiment. Sun Yu Ri looked like it was about 400 years behind the rest of the world. It consisted of one main road and lots of alleys. Instead of commodes, the ville had two ditches that went down the main road. These ditches were the public toilet. While the ditches served as waste consolidation sites, other areas both imaginable and unimaginable were used for fecal deposits. The ditches would overflow during heavy rain storms. Human waste byproducts produced by the consumption of kimchee made for a nasty stench that never went away. A person could never get used to this smell no matter how long he was exposed to it. Kimchee comes in many varieties, but they all smell bad. Kimchee ferments in the ground between four to six months. The ferment site that Taquard recalled was next to the porta potties.

The kimchee-eating prostitutes in Korea were worse than the stench of kimchee farts. The problem was exacerbated by the US. While the Army responded to problems logically they created more problems while fueling the present ones. Courtesy Patrols (CP) were conducted by junior officers every night to address the fights and a myriad of other problems that GIs were having while in the ville. Soldiers were beaten, robbed, poisoned, cheated, and occasionally killed. The ville and the soldiers were made for each other.

Blues would socialize with Taquard on an occasional basis. When Taquard first arrived to Korea he was encouraged to drink. Everyone was offering him a drink during social occasions. He had never taken up drinking before since he hadn't acquired a taste for alcohol. Taquard went to the class six store and bought a large economy size bottle (½ gallon) of Southern Comfort. Blues would share a drink with him from time to time. Blues' consumption amounted to less than a cap full on a rare evening.

The way Blues consumed alcohol; you would never guess that any was ever consumed. Blues sipped Southern Comfort slowly and in great moderation, they way it was meant to be consumed. Koreans were not familiar with liqueur or the fact that they should be sipped, not guzzled. Taquard's house boy, a sixty-three-year-old ajossie, stole his Southern Comfort by guzzling the entire bottle in one sitting. He also stole his Noble Bachelor/Twilights Dawning pipe tobacco and briar root pipe. After finishing off the entire bottle, minus what Blues and Taquard consumed, of Southern Comfort the ajossie had a heart attack and died. Upon finding a dead body in his room Taquard informed Blues. Blues acknowledged and informed Taquard that this was not the first time that something like this had happened. His secretary, Miss P, was a resourceful person who always knew who to contact in the Korean community when the need arose. Another house boy was found within the hour.

"Say, that reminds me," Blues said to Taquard, "you're on CP duty tonight. Be here at 1700. Oh, and by the way, I'm making you the new Battalion Safety Officer. And you're also going to be the Battalion Fire Marshal too."

Taquard's first CP was directed by the S-1 and was considered a training session. His second CP was solo and much more eventful. While the CP had duties to attend to the Staff Duty Officer (SDO) was overall responsible for what went on in the evening. The SDO was also responsible for responding to alerts. While pulling CP and alert went off. Taquard didn't know about it. The SDO who happened to be Taquard's immediate supervisor didn't know about the alert either. He didn't even report to duty. As a result the battalion failed to respond to an alert. When higher command initiated the alert they demanded answers when it was missed. The SDO was in his room sleeping at the time. MAJ Poindexter, MAJ Coldhammer's predecessor, consulted the SDO Roster which also included the CP Roster. 1LT Hand was called in.

Poindexter chewed Hand out up one side and down the other while reprimanding him. Hand's response was to do the only thing that anyone in that situation could do, blame it on someone else. He informed MAJ Poindexter that he switched SDO dates with Taquard. "Of all the damn people you could've picked why did you pick Taquard? You are a worthless liar that can't be trusted. First, you fail to report to duty, then you lie about it. The fact that you were so dumb about lying about it is even more insulting."

Unbeknownst to Hand, Taquard was on the CP list at the same time that he was assigned to the SDO assignment. The duties were not to be pulled by anyone simultaneously. At this point Taquard was undergoing training before he would be authorized to pull SDO duties. While patrolling the ville, Hand ran into Taquard and then it occurred to him how Poindexter knew so much. Hand came up with another bright idea. He tried to convince Taquard to go to the XO (Executive Officer) and plead his case while mentioning a misunderstanding. In other words he wanted Taquard to get in trouble for something that he wasn't accused of doing. Sacrificing men needlessly was not an option. It was also inexcusable. Taquard didn't like the idea of being sacrificed for something that wasn't his fault. The bad thing about it was that Taquard would look back on his career and wonder where all the good men like Hand went. Comparatively speaking, Hand would be among the Army's best. All that Hand could do was count the days until Poindexter's DEROS (Date Effective Return from Overseas). Little did he know that his replacement, MAJ Coldhammer, would be much harsher to deal with.

As soldiers continued to die in the whore houses in Korea, the responsibility of their deaths fell upon second lieutenants. During this time dictionaries lost their purpose in the Army. Eventually this idiocy would infect the entire United States at a fever pitch. The US would embrace this stupidity with unbridled enthusiasm. Whore houses were not to be called whore houses; instead they were called convenience rooms. If there was anything convenient about a case of VD, the soldiers were hard pressed to identify what it would be. Whores were called "Business Girls." Any GI caught using the word whore to describe a whore was summarily disciplined and seriously reprimanded by his commander. Dictionary definitions no longer applied. That is unless you happened to be a Bitcheye. A whore was still a whore no matter what anyone called her. Calling her a virgin wouldn't have made it so. Shakespeare once said that a rose by any other name would smell the same. Taquard applied this same logic to the Army by saying that a turn by any other name will still smell just the same. The problem was that most people in the Army never read anything that Shakespeare ever wrote. This was unfortunate since Shakespeare was the greatest psychologist that has ever lived and the Army was overflowing with practical exercises worthy of psychological review. Such subjects were also known as "Freudian Delights."

The Korean word "ondol" had a unique meaning as it could generate heat during the winter and/or even death. An ondol was a clay brick cylinder that was about five inches in diameter that was soaked in oil and was burned in a stove as a means of providing heat. It had several holes down the middle and was black in color prior to use. After use it was a dull muddy orange in color and very fragile unlike its original form. Although ondol bricks were extremely common throughout Korea, caution had to be exercised to ensure that there were no leaks in the stoves or pipes. A burning ondol would give off carbon monoxide which was colorless, tasteless, and had no odor. Leaks, that were very difficult to detect, often resulted in death. Sometimes leaks would develop during the middle of the night while occupants were in the room.

The whore house influence on the Army was significant. Many categories on the status reports were the result of the whore houses. Unit status reports included categories of how many GIs were infected with VD or any other type of disease caught from the business girls, and how many GIs died in convenience rooms. The main gate posted a wooden sign listing the top five clubs that produced the most cases of VD or other diseases from the previous week. While commanders could care less about their soldiers, they did care about the unit status reports. While unit administrators and statisticians were told to be creative in computing the data while exercising artistic license with the perennial "magic pencil," there was nothing that they could do with the medical data. The medical data which included VD cases and death came directly from the medical staff and was provided directly to the battalion commander before the units knew how they fared. One of the duties included with being the Battalion Safety Officer was ensuring that GIs didn't die in convenience rooms. That meant that Taquard had to inspect every heater in every bar and every convenience room. Leaks were detected by soaking a small rag in used motor oil, lighting it on fire, dropping it in the stove, and closing the stove. This gave off a very black and dirty smoke that was easy to detect.

Going down in the trenches was the best way to understand your men. This was something that was instilled in Taquard repeatedly by people who never practiced such a concept. While it was good to a point especially when it came to developing standard operating procedures it had to be used sparingly. Inspecting whore houses was about as close as one could get to the rank and file of the battalion. It seemed that the more that Taquard got to his soldiers the less he liked. He felt morally obligated to despise them. To avoid being blamed for the death of some stupid GI, Taquard commenced to inspecting ondol heaters. He did this during the day which not only identified those who were on liberty, but also those who were AWOL (Absent Without Leave). He learned a lot about the bars, whores, and their customers. He learned a lot more than he cared to. In this job you literally caught people with their pants down. On his first bout of ondol inspecting, Taquard discovered that many were not cooperative to have their rooms inspected. As Koreans were not in the business of making secure locking systems, a locked proved to be more of a minor inconvenience rather than an obstacle. Upon forcing a door open, Taquard was confronted with a screaming customer that was recognized by the enlisted men who were with him. Taquard knew that he was out of his element, not only was he new to his unit, he was new to the Army.

Sergeant Storm yelled at Taquard with a ferociousness that added credit to his name and was in keeping with his reputation. His tattoos and overall bearing rivaled the toughest Marines. Storm demanded that Taquard identify himself and explain what he was doing there. This was standard throughout the Army. Sergeants were always yelling at lieutenants. On the last day of Ranger school Taquard was faced with a similar situation. The Rangers were given a short break. Taquard and a couple of other Rangers went to the main PX at Fort Benning to grab something to eat. A drill sergeant was offended by Taquard's appearance. Although Taquard lacked any resemblance of personal hygiene and the abundance of dysentery stains in his pants coupled by the fact that he looked like a zombie may have attracted some attention. Taquard was wearing a sanitized uniform as required by the Rangers. The sergeant threatened to write up Taquard to which he told the sergeant to go fuck himself. If there was one thing that Taquard knew, it was that lieutenants did technically outrank sergeant majors. Someone tried to explain to the drill sergeant about the condition that Rangers are subject to. Although he was stationed at Fort Benning, he had never heard of the Rangers.

The situation with Storm was similar to that of the drill sergeant. Coincidentally, Storm himself was also a drill sergeant. Storm demanded answers. "What are you doing with her?" Taquard asked. Storm continued yelling. Taquard continued, "I know what you are doing, but why her of all people?" Storm's anger was elevated. While Storm was mad, he was also embarrassed. He had been caught sleeping with Clyde. Taquard saw her earlier and wondered how she managed to stay employed. Now he knew. Taquard remembered seeing her on his first CP, while he was not yet certified to pull the SDO assignment. While making his rounds, Taquard had difficulty remembering everyone's names so he occasionally came up with nicknames. It seemed that the majority of the Korean whores dyed their hair red that resulted in a brownish reddish color. This girl whose name he couldn't remember had a striking resemblance to the orangutan from the movie, *Every Which Way but Loose*. Her teeth had a remarkable resemblance. So he nicknamed her Clyde. The name caught on and stuck. This was the first of many encounters that Taquard would have with Storm. Instead of being afraid of Storm like everyone else he simply remembered him as the sergeant who slept with Clyde.

Field duty could be best described as injury and garrison is best described as insult to injury. While officers were told to get to know their men they also had to refrain from fraternizing. It seemed like the more that he knew his men the more he despised them. Factually speaking, most officers insulated themselves from their men and for good reason. Taquard knew his men in the field; he was too busy with his additional duties in garrison to interact with them. His team was sorry. His NCOs were both lazy and incompetent, and the junior enlisted weren't showing any promise. They seemed to idolize the sergeants. One of the enlisted even had the audacity to ask for time off in the field so that he could rape one of the Korean girls from a nearby village. She was about ten years old. This was followed by demonstrated disappointment when Taquard denied his request. When this was relayed to the sergeants, the sergeants were baffled by Taquard's denial. They knew that there was enough time for a raping or two. Taquard was surprised, although he shouldn't've been, at the request to commit rape and the consenting NCOs. He heard about similar incidents at Fort Carson while he was a cadet, but he was still shocked by the request and response. He didn't want to hear of such incidents and certainly didn't want to believe them. Some units and assignments seemed to bring out the worst in people. The artillery apparently lead the way when it came to abusing soldiers and their families. The artillery seemed to engage in abnormal psychological activities on a regular basis. Such activities included but were not limited to homosexuality, soldiers pimping their wives, NCOs putting their soldiers on restriction so that they could have sexual intercourse with the soldier's wife, captains and commanders putting their soldiers on restriction so that they could have sexual intercourse with the soldier's wife, pedophilia with another soldier's child, and bestiality. The MPs, not the artillery, seemed to be the top dogs in the bestiality arena with dog handlers having sex with their dogs.

SGT Dingus responded by writing Taquard up in the form of an official counseling statement. The formal written counseling included a highlighted statement: "Second Lieutenant Taquard is a detriment to the morale of the troops, prevents opportunities of leisure and he makes things bad."

LTC Absalom was the one who put SGT Dingus in charge. Naturally, the team missed their first night movement with the infantry. Taquard was able to find the company later on with a map, the help of the infantry lieutenants who provided him with information in advance, and a lot of luck. Missing a movement didn't have the consequences that Taquard was expecting. There was no significance in an artillery unit missing an infantry movement. The infantry didn't need them in the first place since they never called for live fire anyway. Nobody wanted the fisties in the first place. The more the red legs stayed away from the infantry the better.

The routine of remaining secluded and tagging along became SOP. During the day the FIST team would sit idle, but away from the infantry. PMCS, Preventive Maintenance Checks and Services, on the military vehicles and equipment was conducted before, during, and after movements because digging was not allowed.

Returning from the field seemed like another ordeal that would begin with SGT Dingus' formal counseling statements going to LTC Absalom. However, news of charges against SGT Dingus seemed to offer some hope to the situation. SGT Dingus was being charged with illegal drug possession for the second time within six months. He was found guilty of possession of illegal drugs about six months earlier, but he got off with a warning.

LTC Absalom addressed the drug charges directly after field recovery operations were completed. The charges were heard in a meeting in lieu of a trial and addressed. SGT Dingus plead guilty to the charge of possession of illegal drugs. He said that he had a cold and that other forms of medication wee not available. It was egregiously obvious to even the most casual observer that SGT Dingus had to go. Taquard was a member of the board and made the recommendation to do just that.

After hearing the case and receiving the recommendations from the panel, LTC Absalom decided that the best thing that he could do under the circumstances was to once again drop the charges. Everyone was excused except Taquard. It was apparent that enforcing the rules was a bigger crime than breaking them. The Age of Aquarius generation left their mark at West Point while forgoing conservative values. This reminded him of a story that he had heard earlier about a soldier who was the only one in his company who didn't take drugs. The wild stories that Taquard had heard earlier, although backed up with factuality, remained on the realm of unbelievable.

"Once again, Lieutenant, I am trying to keep you from being a fuck up. What the hell do you mean recommending the maximum punishment? I don't see why the charges were made in the first place. What the fuck is your problem?"

Lieutenant Taquard was stunned at the level of corruption and unprofessional behavior that was egregiously displayed by a senior officer who graduated from the United States Military Academy. Unfortunately, Absalom would not be the last of his kind to be in a position of authority in the Army.

"Sir, I don't know exactly what I did wrong or what corrective action you are seeking."

"You are a son-of-a-bitching fuck-up! That is what you are and that is the problem. I am fed up with your bullshit and shoddy performance. You are to do what Sergeant Dingus tells you to do. You are to do exactly what he tells you to do. Motherfucker, if he says "shit," you had better have a load in your pants before he takes his next breath."

Absalom took Taquard out from under 1LT Hand's supervision and put him under CPT Finch. Finch was known as The Fat Fucker until *Return of the Jedi* came out when he was affectionately known as Jabba the Hutt. He was fatter than Absalom and shared his opinion of both Taquard and Dingus.

"Another thing Taquard, Sergeant Dingus has provided me with counseling statements that he wrote on you. I'm not impressed with your performance."

"One of the soldiers wanted to rape one of the Korean girls during a field exercise."

"Aw bullshit! It doesn't say that here. I don't see it in any of these counseling statements."

"Dingus got mad when I denied the request."

"Well, he should've gotten mad. I'm sure he had a good reason to."

"Raping a ten-year-old girl is deplorable. That's what he wanted to do."

"I don't believe you. Nobody would do that. Besides, even if he did do it, what's the problem? We're talking about a Korean here. So who gives a flying fuck if they get raped or not?"

"Sir, rape is wrong."

"Says you. Who the fuck cares if one of these Koreans gets raped? If it does happen, I don't want to know about it. And you don't need to be interfering in things that are none of your business."

A few weeks later every lieutenant in the battalion was charged with insubordination. No one had any idea whatsoever what provoked

Absalom, but all of the lieutenants were reprimanded. Apparently one of the lieutenants was insubordinate to Absalom. Either that or he was just plain out of his mind.

A few days later CPT approached Taquard and asked why he wasn't at PT that morning.

"I was there, ask Colonel Absalom, he was there also."

"It was Colonel Absalom who was asking why you weren't there."

Taquard was wondering about the sanity of Absalom. He was wondering if Absalom had him confused with someone else, or if the old man was just getting too old. Other lieutenants were making the same observations. One thing was for certain: colonels weren't above and beyond being just flat out crazy.

"There is a way that I can prove that I was there," Taquard interjected. "I can tell you everything that Absalom did during PT this morning. I can even tell you where he was when he fell out of the run."

"Forget it."

# Chapter Nine
## *The Fisting of the Fisties*

Fire and safety duties and responsibilities consumed nearly all of Taquard's time, but there were FIST duties to attend to as well. 1LT Hand's departure created a vacancy in the Fire Support Office. The Fire Support Officer position followed that of a FIST Chief. There was a lot of FIST down time in the spring of 1983. The FIST members, or fisties, were treated like bastard children as usual. Their presence in garrison was unwanted and unwelcome. Finch made sure hat Taquard was even more of a bastard child by assigning him to support a cavalry instead of an infantry unit and giving him the worst NCO that he could find. The init that he would support was 4/7th CAV, which turned out to be Custer's old unit, at Camp Gary Owen. There were seven FIST teams in all: three for the 1/31st IN, three for the 1/9th IN (Manchu), and one for 4/7th CAV. The cavalry hadn't had a FIST team since anyone's recollection and weren't even aware that there was such a support element. For all practical purposes, Taquard's team was without a purpose or a function. This was the ideal dumping ground for the worst of the worst. Taquard could devote his time to fire and safety if it weren't for the fact that he had date of rank on all of the other FIST lieutenants.

Finch moved all seven of his FIST Chiefs to an abandoned Quonset hut with the acquisition of two new NCOs. Two thirds of the hut was barracks space, the other third was and office and an empty area. The office was given to a Sergeant First Class (SFC) while the rest served as the work area of seven lieutenants. The furniture was divided up accordingly. Of the four desks, one went to SFC Cool while the seven lieutenants would share three desks. SFC Cool was SFC Swackhammer's assistant.

Taquard took one desk for himself since he was the only FIST Chief in the battalion to have additional duties. The other six lieutenants had to share two desks. When the other lieutenants complained about the arrangement, Taquard offered to give up the desk if someone would share the load of additional duties. There were no takers. That still didn't stop them from complaining. Taquard ordered seven telephones, one for each lieutenant. Another lieutenant decided that one phone would suffice while realizing that not having a dedicated phone of his own would result in having less work to do. Taquard took the phone for himself while the others did without.

Being a FIST meant backstabbing other FISTs in an attempt to fit in. FISTs would cut each others throats in a heartbeat. Recreation and relaxation (R&R) tours were scheduled for the entire battalion minus the FIST teams. The FSO component only had about sixty soldiers so it didn't really matter to the rest of the battalion. Batteries scheduled tours for their batteries. Although FIST teams were assigned to Headquarters and Headquarters Battery (HHB), their affiliation to the Infantry generated a lot of logistical confusion. It served the battery a lot better to assume that the Infantry would take care of them. In an effort to establish equity, some of the FIST NCOs decided to arrange an R&R tour of their own. Scheduling a tour meant committing busses and dedicating at least 40 members for the tour. Each bus carried forty-four people, so the tour configuration needed other people besides FIST. Arrangements were made to allow for other batteries to provide people for an R&R tour to occupy two dedicated busses. The 4/7th FIST was not invited. Volunteers and standby members were on hand to address any unforeseeable vacancies. One shortage and the entire tour would be cancelled. Partial loads were not acceptable. The arrangement was set and the busses would arrive at HHB to pick up the FISTs, then they would go to the parking lot near the installation entry/exit point to pick up enough people to fill the tour quota. The ajossie bus drivers got confused as usual and made their initial stop at the entrance/exit parking lot. Once the busses were loaded up they departed without even bothering to go to the HHB area. The loaded busses were bound to the R&R venue without a single fistie on board. A subsequent attempt for a FIST R&R tour had a similar outcome. This time the fisties waited at the front parking lot like everyone else. As approximately 150 people attempted to board two busses a fight broke out. A captain was called to the scene. He did the only honorable thing that a captain could do under the circumstances; he unloaded the busses and filled them with his own people.

"But, Captain," one of the FIST NCOs said. "This is a FIST tour."

"Nobody gives a shit about FIST, you should know that by now," he responded. "Besides, you bums don't deserve Jack shit. You fisties get to party hardy with the Infantry, now you leeches want to take a free ride with the Artillery? I don't think so!"

Once again the busses departed without a single fistie on board.

One of the biggest problems that Taquard had in garrison was Coldhammer. The troubles began with a simple question one afternoon as Taquard was walking back to the office.

"Are you the Fire Marshal?" Coldhammer asked Taquard.

"Yes, sir."

"Well, I noticed an empty fire extinguisher in one of the barracks."

The short conversation resulted is a sense of urgency imposed on Taquard. Prior to this conversation, he had never thought about Fire Marshal duties. He was given some old beaten up black binders when 1LT Blues selected him to be both the Safety Officer and the Fire Marshal. Blues made the additional duty assignments based on a coin toss. The additional duties would consume more time than being a FIST Chief. He had made a dent in the Safety Officer requirements with the ondol inspections, but he didn't know where to begin in the fire arena.

Lieutenant Taquard also found out that he had a fire and safety NCO. Staff Sergeant (SSG) Miller was very opposite from the type of person that Dingus was. He was an example of what an NCO should be and glorified the grade. It became apparent to Taquard that not all NCOs were bad just as not all officers were good. The merits of an NCO relied on the man, not the rank. NCOs were not the backbone of the Army, people were. People of all ranks and backgrounds.

The work week at Camp Pelham consisted of a five and a half day work week, sometimes more. This made for a very long assignment for Taquard who was under the Hammer of Coldhammer. Prior to the afternoon of being asked about the Fire Marshal, Taquard was just another forgotten person in the battalion. Following that, Taquard was the subject of wrath from Coldhammer. Nobody, but nobody, wanted to be subject to the wrath of Coldhammer. No matter how much legwork Taquard performed there was just no way of legitimizing the fire extinguishers. The soldiers loved playing with them too much. Fire extinguishers were instrumental in all types of horseplay.

Taquard's additional duties surpassed his primary duty as a FIST Chief in a matter of days. Taquard solicited the help of the batteries to help him ensure that fire extinguishers were up to standards. Two of the five batteries didn't even have safety officers or NCOs. The other three batteries let it be known that Taquard could take his fire extinguisher concerns and stuff them up his ass.

Another day meant another ass chewing from MAJ Coldhammer. Ass chewings, like pain and misery, were beyond inoculation. No matter how many you had, you never wanted any more. No matter how much Taquard tried to avoid Coldhammer, he never could. No matter how much he tried to rectify the safety concerns, he never could. Facing Coldhammer became a daily routine for Taquard.

CPT Finch's sergeant, SFC Swackhammer, occupied a private office and was put in charge of the seven FIST lieutenants. Swackhammer wasted no time in letting the lieutenants know where they stood and how the lines were drawn. He let them know how the cow ate the cabbage. He assembled the lieutenants, addressed them firmly, and gave out the orders. It was apparent that Swackhammer ran the lieutenants with an iron fist and no one dared to cross him.

Taquard didn't worry about Swackhammer. His concerns were with Coldhammer. In trying to deal with a situation he searched anywhere and everywhere for help, advice, and any type of productive guidance he could muster. He even approached Swackhammer for anything that he could help him out with in the arena of fire and safety.

"First of all, Lieutenant, I don't want you barging in my office unannounced. Second, that's not my job. When I told you that I would be more than happy to help you out, that didn't mean that I would do your job for you. Now drive on, Lieutenant," Swackhammer stated authoritatively.

Leg work wasn't paying off as the batteries repeatedly told Taquard to fuck off. And no matter how many times Taquard tried to rectify the fire extinguisher problem, Coldhammer kept finding violations. In sheer desperation, Taquard called the Division Inspector General (IG). He asked about the IG inspections and inquired about his arena. The IG had dedicated inspections for both Safety and Fire Marshal areas. Upon being informed as to how large and involved these areas were it was obvious to Taquard that there was o way possible that they would ever pass an inspection. Taquard asked for a courtesy inspection. The IG was so impressed with the request that they decided to grant him one right away.

The Division Safety Officer was ecstatic to find someone who was actually interested in safety. This was a break for Taquard because there were areas, policies, codes, regulations, directives, rules, and standards that the battalion didn't even begin to address. Meanwhile, Taquard continued to get his ass chewed by Coldhammer while lacking the will to inform him of how the batteries were responding to his efforts. He was so upset by the situation that could be worsened by the presence of the Division that he called his dad in yet another moment of desperation. His dad's response was contrary to Taquard's expectations. He stated that Coldhammer was the man and that he should do everything possible to support him. He further stated that he was fortunate to have Coldhammer. He praised Coldhammer in several ways.

"But, Dad, you don't understand, this guy is tearing me apart."

"Everything that I have said is true. If you don't believe me, give him the integrity test."

"Integrity test?"

"It's easy. Ask him if you can have his support. If he says 'yes,' then he is for real. If he says anything else at all then call me back. If he says, 'that's what I'm here for,' or 'that's my job,' then he fails the test and is no good. Give him the test and call me if he fails."

The next morning Taquard reported to Coldhammer as usual. During the conversation, Taquard posed the question.

"Sir, can I have your support?"

"Yes."

That was the answer that he was hoping for and from that moment on he knew that he wouldn't have to absorb the blame for derelict battery Safety Officers and Fire Marshals. Taquard informed Coldhammer about all of the attempts of cooperation that were treated with abuse and hostility.

True to the level of integrity stated by his father, Coldhammer responded to the information by calling in the battery commanders and dismissing them without their backsides. Taquard's butter bars turned into gold. When Taquard arrived at the units he was no longer dismissed as that pesky lieutenant. Instead, he got what he wanted.

A few days later, the IG conducted the courtesy inspection. The battalion failed miserably. However, corrective actions were outlines and checklists were supplied as well as the latest required publications. Another courtesy inspection was requested and approved for the following month. Battery points of contact were established and information began to get disseminated. Taquard even attended Division Safety meetings to facilitate his efforts.

There was a third R&R attempt for the fisties. Unfortunately, there was an alert on the morning of the tour. An alert meant that everyone had to arrive at designated assembly areas with their vehicles and full field gear. The units assembled during the unannounced muster and people and equipment were accounted for. The alert occurred early in the morning and was completed before the tour buses arrived. The FIST teams, minus 4/7th CAV, approached the buses when they were stopped by an artillery captain.

"The Artillery is cleared for this alert, but we haven't checked with the Infantry. Did you?"

"No," answered one of the FIST NCOs.

"Until you get clearance from the Infantry you're still on alert status."

"But if we get clearance from the Infantry, then we're free to go on the tour, right?"

"That's the fact, Jack."

The NCO made a mad dash to notify the Infantry counterparts and ask for clearance. Clearance came as quickly as the requests. The Infantry units weren't alerted nor were they even aware that an alert even took place. By the time the fisties returned to the parking lot, they were greeted by the back view of departing busses. And as before, not a single fisties made it on the R&R bus.

Taquard had his own idea of R&R. Instead of relying on the artillery to come up with a tour bus that would include fisties, he decided that it would be far better to go out on his own. Seoul was a good place to start, especially the area around the Lotte Hotel. This was where the upper 7% of Korean society hung out. They were rich and knew how to live it up. Near the Lotte was the World Cup Restaurant Theatre. This was the type of experience that America would do well to learn from. Entrance into the World Cup Restaurant Theatre required an exclusive membership or a member escort. Elwood was lucky enough to meet a young lady whose families were members. The dress code was strictly coat and tie. In addition to the entrance control measures, prices were outrageous. A six-ounce class of Coke was about $15.00. He didn't mind splurging in this case although he wasn't about to spring for a full seven-course meal. The couple sat in one of the balconies with a fantastic view of the huge stage. In front and below the stage was a full fledged live orchestra. Entertainment consisted of live performers from around the world who made their presentations in their native language. Songs that were sung were sung in the language that the song was famous for. *From Russia with Love* was performed in English by a Korean who was nothing shy of remarkable. He sounded exactly like the soundtrack. Other than his appearance, one would never surmise that he was Oriental. The selection of songs was first rate even though it wasn't in vogue contemporary. No concert could ever beat it. This was his first time of ever seeing an orchestra and between a well performed classic song with an orchestra and a concert that was typically loud, Taquard would take the former any day. This was a case where he discovered something that he appreciated greatly. This was not the type of excursion that anyone would find on an R&R tour with a bunch of GIs. In addition to singing the entertainment included a circus. The circus on stage consisted of one act at a time but the quality of the act made up for the lack of the big tent atmosphere. Acts included bears driving small cars, riding on motorcycles, and riding unicycles. The trapeze artists and acrobats performed their act above the audience. The magic acts added to the enjoyment of the evening. One of the magicians admitted to being new to the arena of magic and even divulged his secrets. His son climbed into a box and emerged from a different box. The thought of using identical twins was nullified by the dismantling of the original box. The panache was taken out of the act when he revealed his secret. By turning the boxes around the audience could see that there was a way to open the back of the boxes. All the son did was to simply climb out of one box into the other while the magician stood blocked the space between the boxes with his body. Upon dismantling the original box and turning the second box around, he admitted that he still had a few bugs that he needed to iron out of his trick as his wife emerged instead of the anticipated son. It was very apparent that while the Koreans in the ville acted like a bunch of animals, the upper level of Korean society really knew how to live and appreciated the finer things in life.

The Lotte shopping center, within walking distance from the World Cup, had a special place that catered to the very rich. The products were from around the world and were the ultimate in high-grade quality. Instead of the imitation junque that the Koreans are well known for fabricating, this was the place to get the genuine article although prices were prohibitive. Dunhill belts began at over $100.00. Alligator hide products were also available at much higher prices.

The upper level of Korean society did not mingle among Koreans nor did they buy Korean products. It wasn't that they were snooty; it was just that they preferred to keep to themselves or possibly the engagement of a few others who shared similar interests. They didn't act like typical Koreans. A night at the World Cup Restaurant Theatre was an evening to remember.

Infantry units didn't need FISTs, neither did the Cavalry. However, the Artillery units did. Firing Artillery batteries in the battalion needed forward observers, ad did other artillery units that were rotating to firing points in the Western Corridor. Firing points along the DMZ had an abundance of ammunition that was about to expire.

One phone call was all that it took to get the artillery units back in business. The call would give the FIST teams missions to perform. Fire support requests would normally go to CPT Finch, but he was nowhere to be found. The fact was that he didn't want to be found, neither did SFC Swackhammer. Taquard had no choice but to support the request of the person who called. Taquard assumed the duties of CPT Finch. Finch had it made in the shade, he not only didn't have to show up to work when he didn't feel like it, and he also had a scapegoat to blame his incompetence on.

There is a saying in the Army that goes: You can delegate authority, but not responsibility. Delegation of blame and responsibility is practiced continuously Army-wide. Another saying: The maximum range of an excuse is zero meters, is also false. The Artillery says that the maximum range of an excuse is zero mils. Both are false. Depending on whether or not someone is a Good Ole' Boy will determine how much range an excuse will have. In many cases, "I forgot" or "Somebody forgot to remind me" will go to the moon and back for some while hospital emergencies didn't hold water for others.

The only saying that did matter was "Think DEROS." Another one that seemed to make sense was: "Why take life seriously, you're not going to get out of it alive anyway?"

Simplicity was the concept of managing seven FIST teams to support the oncoming high volume of fire support missions. There were thousands of rounds to be fired in a very short period of time. Every forward observer in the battalion could be an expert in any type of fire mission imaginable. The concept that Taquard devised consisted in a three month cycle. One month would be dedicated to supporting the Infantry and/or Cavalry. The other two months would follow a rotational cycle that included all seven FIST teams.

Blank space, also referred to as white space, could be up to the FIST Chief's discretion. Taquard's team would set the example by beginning the cycle the following Monday. The Artillery cycle went as follows:

Field Duty
Field Recovery
Garrison Training
Additional Duties
Maintenance and Field Preparation
Recover, Recuperate, and Recreation
To Be Determined

The schedule was simple, flexible, equitable, realistic, and received with a bunch of bickering and bitching from the other lieutenants. Their idea of a preferred schedule was to be in the recreational mode until the end of their tour.

"Why should we be doing any of that shit?"

"You're not our boss."

"Fuck you, I ain't doing any of that shit."

"We work for Captain Finch, not you," Canerra added.

Taquard couldn't get any of the lieutenants to support him, but he couldn't ignore the request for fire support that came from Division Artillery Headquarters. There was no way possible to get the lieutenants to get off of their asses. Naturally, Finch couldn't be found. Taquard reluctantly turned to Swackhammer.

Swackhammer cut him off with, "Do you know where the impact area is?"

"There are lots of them."

"How about the firing points?"

"Not all of them, but the FISTs don't go to the firing points."

"Do you have the vaguest notion where the observation points are?"

"There are bunches of them."

"Well, shit. You'd better get with the program, El Tee."

"You said that you were available to help us out at any time, I'm asking you for help."

"You mean you want me to do your job for you while you sit around scratching your balls. El tee, pull your head out of your ass. I believe that the colonel has told you that as well. He told you, now I'm telling you."

"Could you at least tell me which observation points are dedicated for DMZ fire missions?"

"I could, but I won't. I wouldn't be helping you if I did. It is my job to train lieutenants not baby sit them. If I do everything for them, they won't learn."

"Forget it. I'll see if I can find anyone who knows."

"Your attitude sucks, El Tee. Have you ever wondered why you are such an outcast? It's because you don't know what the fuck you are doing."

Swackhammer called one of the other lieutenants on Taquard's phone. Soon, 2LT Rose arrived. He stood at attention, saluted, and shouted, "Lieutenant Rose reporting as ordered Sergeant!"

Swackhammer returned the salute.

"Rose, do you know where the firing points are?"

"Yes Sergeant, I do," he responded with enthusiasm.

"See, everyone knows except you," Swackhammer said to Taquard.

"Where is 4P1?" Taquard asked Rose.

"Who?" Rose replied.

"I don't suppose you have a map of the impact areas, do you?" Taquard said to Swackhammer.

"Did you see the way Rose reported to me? Who in the blazes of blue fuck do you think you are barging in on me in my office? What gives you the right to demand information from me? You are one insubordinate motherfucker. Yeah, I have the map but I ain't going to give you one," Swackhammer stated in his tirade.

Taquard left without wasting any more time. He went down the hall to see CPT Case. Taquard explained the situation, but Case interrupted him.

"We've got at least three maps of everything for every element in the battalion and then some. Follow me."

Case led Taquard to the back of the long office to a steel bureau that was covered in dust and spider webs.

"I haven't opened this thing in months. We haven't fired a single mission since last year's ARTEP (Army Training Evaluation Program). I was wondering when someone was going to get these missions rolling again. Well, here you go. This is what you'll need to support the firing batteries. I'll send these out to the firing batteries and built up firing points so that everyone is using the same map series," Case said to Taquard. "These maps are about five years old but they're the latest ones that we have. They are also made in Korea and have shit loads of mistakes. The impact boundaries have been reduced to account for the errors. These are the most accurate maps available at this time. They're not at the standards that they should be, but it's all we have."

"Sir, the fire support shop wasn't able to show me a map. Do they know about this?"

"I doubt it. Where else would they be getting their maps from than besides me? They haven't checked out any in almost a year. Okay, here are the 1:50,000 series and the 1:25,000 series. How many people do you have in your team?"

"Five."

"Including you?"

"Yes."

"Here you are. That comes to three of each series for each person. You don't even have to sign for them."

"Can I get some with more accuracy?"

"No. Believe it or not, these are the most accurate that we have."

"Does the fire support office have anything better?"

"No. They would get their maps from me."

"Can you show me where the impact areas are?"

"We have two for our area. These will be the ones that you will be using. Here are the overlays."

"Where are the firing points?"

"You won't be going to those, but they are surveyed sites designated by the numbered crosshairs on the map. The one that you need to be concerned with the most is 4P1. It's right here."

"What about the observation points?"

"They are pretty much anywhere you want them to be as long as you can see the impact area. I can give you a couple of overlays with some OPs on them. They seem to work pretty well."

"Thanks, sir. I really appreciate help. The FSO shop wouldn't lift a finger to help me."

"You're welcome. Look, there's nothing sorrier than a red leg."

Taquard stopped by Swackhammer's office.

"Your maps are out of date. The fact of the matter is you don't know what the fuck you're doing. We've been out of commission for almost a year, but we're about to go back into business and you're full of shit. And by the way, you're welcome"

The FIST chief office was a reception station for protesting Taquard's training schedule. The only way to accomplish the artillery support missions was to do it without the other FIST teams. Taquard's team and only Taquard's team would provide all forward observation artillery fire support for the entire division. Training would take place in the field while recovery would be limited to two days. Down time was not scheduled. The revised schedule was set and implemented without delay. Taquard had a new team and a new NCO who he never got a chance to get acquainted with. He contacted his NCO, SGT Zimmerman.

Instead of creating busy work, Taquard's team had a mission and a lot to do. They were the only game in town when it came to fire support.

"Get the APC ready. We're leaving tomorrow. I wanted to wait until Monday, but we need to get out in the field as soon as possible. There are about 700 rounds that need to be fired before the end of next week. These are 155mm rounds. That means a wide variety of missions."

"What time do we leave tomorrow?"

"0600."

"How long are we going to be out there?"

"We should be back by Wednesday evening. Can you handle that?"

"Yes, sir. I'll get everything ready. I'll pick up some C rations to bring along. We had a lot of food shortages in the field in my last unit."

"Good idea. We've had our share in this unit as well."

Taquard went to the S-3 shop to pick up the latest editions of FM 6-30, FM 6-20, and even A-10 for the APC. Then he went to the library and checked out a book by Stephen King. The book was Cujo. He swung by

Swackhammer's office before departing for the day.

Instead of creating busy work, Taquard's team had a mission and a lot to do. They were the only game in town when it came to fire support.

"Just in case anybody asks, we're going to the field tomorrow. We'll be gone for about a week," Taquard informed Swackhammer.

"Why am I going to the field?"

"By we, I meant 4/7th FIST team."

"Why are you going?"

"Division Artillery has called for immediate fire support. Somebody has to do it. If we don't do it, it won't get done. If you don't want us to go, tell me now. Do you want to cancel the mission?"

"No, no. That's okay. Go ahead. Tell me how it goes. And if there's anything that you need, just let me know."

"I need the other teams out in the field in about two weeks. That's what I need."

"That'll be up to Captain Finch."

"That would be a 'no.'"

Later that evening another turtle bus arrived at Camp Pelham. The new arrivals were allocated to the units within the battalion. SGT Zimmerman, who happened to be in the parking lot when the bus arrived, was given a turtle. He just happened to be the only FIST out there when they were giving out the turtles and no one saw a problem in letting him have one. He asked for a turtle and got one. It was that easy.

The first order of business was to introduce him to the lieutenant. He managed to catch Taquard just as he was about to leave the office for the day.

"Sir, I'd like for you to meet PFC Reynolds, he's been assigned to us."

"Great. Do you want to go to the field tomorrow morning or spend some time in garrison?"

"Well, sir, garrison," Reynolds replied.

"Great. See you first thing tomorrow. We'll all be leaving for the field no later than (NLT) 0600. Yes you're going to the field too. Oh, and by the way, welcome to Camp Pelham."

Zimmerman was a fine NCO who took care of the team, the equipment, the vehicle, the training, and even Taquard. Taquard had his fill of rotten NCOs and felt fortunate to have Zimmerman on his side.

The following morning was successful as the team departed on time without a hitch. It was the first exercise for the new team and everything went as planned. It was the dumping ground for the undesirables with the worst equipment in the battalion, yet it was the best FIST team that Camp Pelham had at the time.

The team went to 4P1 to make acquaintances and validate radio frequencies and establish coordination procedures. Following that they went to Heartbreak Ridge to set up an OP. Heartbreak Ridge had a few firing points, OPs, some small compounds, and some people. The Koreans avoided the area because it was on the border of North Korea and was extremely dangerous. The people in the area were extremely poor. When President Carter disbanded two battalions in Korea two US installations were closed. Korea, more so than Oklahoma, thrived off of the US military. Many towns in America are military towns. They live off of and survive solely on the military base. Gate brides are a common sighting. When the installation closes the town dries up and deteriorates when everyone leaves. In Korea, the situation is much worse. A battalion may have its own installation and also be the only lifeline that a village may have. When two of the battalions were disbanded the vacant installations served no purpose. The people abandoned the villages that thrived off of the installation. They also abandoned their children in the process. With the overflowing orphanages, the children had no choice but to remain in the villages and fend for themselves. Being a lone FIST team without a convoy or guide to follow can result in getting lost which is easy to do in Korea. During one of the movements Mad Dog FIST got lost. In some cases the unit doesn't want their people to get lost for obvious reasons. In other cases they don't want people to see certain things. This resulted in seeing firsthand what the aftermath of an action can really be like. They were so poor that they left their children behind. Mad Dog FIST accidentally drove through an orphan village. As Taquard's team drove through the villages, thousands of orphans ran to the track begging for food. This was the case regardless of what time of year it was. The streets were filled with children, many who had no clothes whatsoever. The oldest person in town was about fourteen years old. This was an amazing sight that was beyond anyone's comprehension: an entire town with no adults. There was no industry, no employment, nothing that was clean, just a bunch of starving unsupervised children who were as young as three years old. In addition to being an abandoned village with no name, it was dumping ground for unwanted children. It served the same purpose that a foreign neighborhood would serve for dumping off unwanted puppies and kittens. Taquard remembers the idea being addressed in a Richie Rich comic book. Richie Rich built a town with no adults where the children could roam freely and enjoy themselves without being bound to any rules. The result was a fiasco. Richie Rich put the dilapidated unpopulated town up for sale. He realized what a mistake that he made and abandoned any notions of a town without rules. He wished that he never considered a town without supervision in the first place. The true life result was far worse than the comic version. In the comic book, the children came to the town voluntarily and had fun. Later Richie Rich threw them out of town and the returned back to their homes. Here, the children had no choice in the matter and there was no other place for them to go to. They begged for food as the FIST team drove through town. Some were completely naked, all were filthy. They did anything that they could think of to attract the attention of the FIST team members. Taquard knew that they had to keep on driving without handing out any goodies of any kind. It seemed heartless but the sight of food and the possibility of getting some could result in the children rushing the track. This could also result in some of the orphans getting killed. Stopping the track would certainly result in the orphans climbing on and in. They would take everything that they could get their hands on. Killing the team members would also be a possibility. Ownership of an APC was also a potential form of commerce. Although arriving at an abandoned orphan village was the last thing on anybody's mind, Taquard was able to respond to the situation quickly and accurately. He ordered the sergeant to maintain the speed of the track. As long as the track was in motion and as long as nothing was thrown to the children, the team would be okay. As much as he would have liked to help, he knew that he couldn't help the children but he and his team could get compromised. The mission at hand was to push forward with the team in tact.

An amazing fact about the village was that the children spoke English very well. They didn't have books, teachers, classrooms, or any type of viable resources to utilize, but they still spoke English in an impressive manner. There was no formal education whatsoever.

Seeing the children in the streets surviving made the team realize how cruel the world was. Taquard saw the pettiness of the bullshit that the Army was self-inducing for no purpose whatsoever. The Army's way of operating was a reflection of their immorality. The Korean orphan villages, a sad sight that had an impact, were in the vicinity of Heartbreak Ridge which was appropriately named. While Taquard saw vast differences between the US and Korea, he noticed a lot of similarities but to a greater extent. What happened to Korea could happen to the US. He knew that the US needed to clean up its act or face similar damnation.

There was no time to think about unfortunate orphans or wonder how such events could be prevented, Taquard's team had a mission to go to and a timeline that had to be followed. They no more than got away from the village when they came upon a cemetery. The cemetery had thousands upon thousands of happy mounds, markers, and tomb stones. This was a cemetery that was dedicated to the Koreans who were killed by the Chinese during the Korean War which lasted from 25 June 1950 to 27 July 1953. Taquard stopped the APC and had the team disembark to take a look around the cemetery. This was history. It was a history that should be remembered. Although it was recorded it wasn't remembered by those who didn't experience it firsthand. The team noticed a lot of US graves with tombstones that were both in English and Hangul. Taquard was amazed by the demonstrated involvement that the Chinese had in the war. When people think about the Korean War they never consider China. This was even more proof to Taquard's team that China was a viable threat to the US.

On 7 October 1950 the US troops crossed the 38th parallel which may have motivated the Chinese to enter into the war though there were earlier signs and warnings that their involvement was imminent. Mao was under the impression that America's attack on Korea was a prelude to a war against China. The Soviet Union provided aid, albeit very limited aid, to China in their attacks against US forces. The Soviet assistance to the

Chinese assault was known to the UN and US but was not publicized. This was to avert a possible escalation that could lead to an all out nuclear war.

On 25 October 1950 the US and Chinese troops (about 270,000) made contact with each other. China saw its role against the US a means of protecting national security.

The US troops proved to be more skillful in the art of warfare and drove the Chinese forces back. The US and UN forces advanced their forces to the Yalu River against the Chinese forces that posed no threat. The Chinese were viewed as weak and lacked fighting credibility. This was supported by previous CIA investigations that clearly stated that the Chinese would not get involved in the war. MacArthur himself did not see China as a threat either. He stated that they may have been able to support North Korea but knew that such assistance would lead to their own slaughter.

The Chinese marched three divisions on foot from Manchuria to the north side of the Yalu River. This distance of approximately 286 miles was covered in about nineteen days. They traveled undetected by allied forces because they traveled during the hours of darkness. During daylight travel the Chinese troops were ordered to remain perfectly still if aircraft was observed in the area. Violators were shot.

In late November the Chinese forces committed a surprise attack along the Chongchon River that caught UN forces off guard. The Chinese overran several South Korean divisions and defeated the US Eighth Army. The oncoming defeat of the US Eighth Army resulted in the longest retreat in US military history. At the Battle of the Chosin Reservoir the 7th Infantry Division (30,000 man strong) was unexpectedly surrounded by Chinese forces. The division fought hard and eventually managed to escape encirclement, but at a loss of over 15,000 casualties. The Marines were also defeated at the Chosin Reservoir. This particular group of Marines was known as the "Chosin Frozen" and the "Frozen Chosen." Most people are under the impression that they were victorious.

What became evident to Taquard and his team was the fact that they were not invincible. While Americans thought of themselves as being the best at everything as well as being invincible, they were wrong in spite of their beliefs. Americans dodged reality while ignoring the truth. This was arrogantly displayed by those that never considered that our prosperity came at a great price. Taquard could see what could happen by ignoring the truth. Seeing the aftermath was a sobering dose of reality and of what could happen again. Korea was a plethora of examples of what could happen if you let down your guard. Unfortunately, history always repeated itself and mankind resembled itself everywhere in spite of racial and traditional differences. Knowing the future did nothing to prevent calamities. Like Cassandra, people didn't believe anyone who was the bearer of bad news. Although she accurately foretold the future she wasn't believed. These are the same people who are the cause of history repeating itself. Ironically, they are also the ones to believe a fast sales pitch that is designed to take their money. The recognizable sign can be seen in their enthusiasm to win money in Las Vegas or on horse races or a myriad of other cons.

Even though the team was sidetracked in their movement they managed to arrive in time to commence artillery firing on schedule. By 1000 Taquard's team had established a functional OP and were firing live artillery missions and began to deplete the 700 round cache that was about to expire. Missions were rough and slow. Transmissions were lengthy. It was obvious that they needed the training.

"Uh, yeah, uh L14, this is, uh, D49, over."

"All right D49er, this is L14, we read you loud and clear, over."

"Yeah, fire mission, over."

"What kind of fire mission would you like, over?"

"We'll do the adjust fire mission just like we talked about, over."

"Right, one adjust fire mission, over."

"Grid 3700 6500, just like the one we talked about earlier, remember?"

"Yeah, I remember. Grid 3565."

"No wait! I thought it was supposed to be 3765."

"Yeah, you're right it was supposed to be grid 3765."

"Armored company with dismounted troops in the open, HE (high explosive) over."

"Hey this is also going to be a registration, okay?"

"Okay."

"By the way, what's your direction?"

"2790 mils."

"All right, we're going to give you splash (a five-second warning before the round impacts)."

"Okay."

The first mission took what seemed forever, but it was a start. It was this preparation time that Taquard called for just for ironing out the wrinkles that units in the field experience.

One of the biggest problems in the Field Artillery (FA) is computing firing data known as gunnery. Most artillery officers can't do it. One of the most basic and fundamental errors that a forward observer can make is to tell the FDC where he is.

**FORWARD OBSERVER RULE NUMBER 1: Never tell anyone where you are.**

**FORWARD OBSERVER RULE NUMBER 2: Never tell anyone where you are.**

The Officer Basic Course teaches the observers to notify the FDC of their location. The school also teaches the FDC to plot the FO location on their chart. The Fire Direction Officer (FDO) used a blank grid chart for computing manual gunnery data. A pin was used to mark the battery location. An instrument that pivoted on the battery location pin would be used to determine the range and deflection from the firing battery and the target. This instrument resembled a ruler with a protractor built on to it. Targets were also plotted with pins as was the FO location.

Taquard's team was located between the firing battery and the target. While the FDC was moving the instrument from the firing battery pivoting pin, it was stopped by the FO pin instead of the target pin. Once the instrument is stopped by a pin, computations begin. Safety is sacrificed for speed in the Army. Corners are cut and shortcuts are taken. During a mission there is lots of yelling and screaming while everyone is frantic about speed.

Taquard and his team were sitting beside the APC during their fire missions. Although the team, like the other teams, needed improvement, progress was being made relatively fast. The FDC error of directing fire on the OP instead of the target was a common mistake that usually resulted in injuries. Fortunately, this was an adjust fire (AF) mission instead of a fire for effect (FFE). The first round would be classified as a kill although no one was actually killed. The round impacted about 10 meters from the APC, but on the other side that the team was on. The team was surrounded by a shower of flying 155mm HE shrapnel that passed in front, behind, and above them at high speed. Although the APC was hit several times, it was not disabled. Taquard's first inclination was to tell Lewdvick how screwed up he and his unit were.

"Sir, we got to get out of here and fast. I heard about Lewdvick in my last unit. He's shit," Zimmerman said to Taquard. "He's a real goofy son of a bitch and fucks things up constantly. You'll never get any resolution out of him."

"Let's go," Taquard responded.

The team put the APC in motion. By the time the FDC asked for an adjustment, the team was out of the OP. While they were moving to a new location Taquard ordered that they would not respond to radio traffic until further notice.

After relocating, Taquard responded to the radio traffic by informing Lewdvick about what had happened. Lewdvick denied that such an incident ever occurred. The FDC questioned as to the whereabouts the new OP was located. Taquard gave an erroneous location that wasn't anywhere near where they were actually at. With Lewdvick in charge, the team had to extremely cautious about giving out information. Information to Lewdvick could easily result in a fatality. Forward Observer Rule Number one went into effect and stayed in effect.

Moving to a new location didn't take long. However, when the FIST team was ready to fire, the firing battery called for a Class 1 delay. In other words, they decided to take a lunch break. FISTs never had Class 1 assets or scheduled meals. They developed the ability to work and eat at the same time. It wasn't much of a challenge, but it was more than a firing battery was able to do. Unlike other firing points, 4P1 was accompanied by a barracks and a mess hall. The FDC operated from inside of a building instead of a vehicle. They had offices, and education center, library, and were in the process of building a swimming pool.

Fire missions continued throughout the day into the night. Coordinated illumination fire missions were tricky at first, but ended up being a lot of fun. A full day of fire missions in the field made all the difference in the world. The team picked up the pace with greater accuracy.

"L14, D49, 6 rounds fire for effect, over"

"Roger."

"Grid 36596408, over."

"Grid 36596408, out."

Taquard and Zimmerman predominately called the fire missions during the first day in the field. They managed to fire nearly 200 rounds that day. The second day was dedicated to Zimmerman and the other team members. Day two exceeded 250 rounds in fire missions. By day three, Zimmerman was a casual observer. The forth day incorporated training the KATUSAs (Korean Augmentation to the United States Army). Taquard's team was the only team to have two KATUSAs. The truth was, nobody wanted them. What others didn't want, Taquard got. The 700 rounds were completely expended on the forth day. The assessment was positive. Even the KATUSAs were mastering the art of forward observation.

"Hey, D49er, we just got word. Another 750 rounds that is ready to expire just arrived. Can you support?"

"Sure. Can we begin firing now?"

"Yeah."

Coordinated illumination missions continued throughout the night. Although Taquard's team ended up staying in the field longer than they had anticipated they didn't mind. At least they didn't have to put up with the bullshit that garrison had to offer. By the end of the fifth day every member of Taquard's team was an expert. The field exercise included driver training. Even Taquard learned how to drive the APC. As the exercise was extended, rations were consumed. A nearby ROK post supplied the team with food to sustain operations. Measures to conduct field recovery exercises were implemented to make recovery more manageable. Six days in the field was great for innovation. Although the Army once stressed initiative, they didn't really mean it. At the beginning of the exercise the uniform was the standard load bearing equipment (LBE), M16 rifles, steel pots, and all of the other accessories that the Army felt that a soldier couldn't do without. By the sixth day it was T-shirts and sunglasses. The reasoning was that there was no reason to encourage heat exhaustion. It wasn't as if the North Koreans didn't know where they were. The FIST team and the North Koreans could clearly see each other without binoculars. During the night, the North Koreans would play Beatles music loudly. Another OP was in the vicinity of an entire North Korean city that had no occupants. It had lights, music, and a national flag that was about 100 feet long. It was known as Propaganda Village and the music was referred to as Singing Sam.

Garrison recovery was a cinch. Taquard was occupied with another IG courtesy inspection and his additional duties while Zimmerman and the crew performed maintenance and trained in areas not exercised in the field. The second courtesy inspection was an improvement over the first, but Taquard was striving for a perfect score. The battalion went from an unsatisfactory rating to a satisfactory. Taquard requested yet another courtesy inspection to take place the following month, and it was granted.

"As a matter of fact, there's a division safety conference next week. I'm going to list 2/17th FA BN as the most improved unit in safety. Actually, I think I am going to list it as the unit with the best safety program," the inspector added. "Oh, by the way, your submission to the Division Safety poster contest took first place. We're going to print them up and distribute them division wide. Actually, we thought that it was so good that we decided to send it up to Army level for review. However, there is one thing that we wanted to check with you on. The wording is rather lengthy. We wanted to change it, but we wanted to talk to you about it first."

The inspector was referring to the statement on the poster that said, "Of All the Fire and Safety Problems in the Army Today, CANERRA is the Worst." The acronym CANERRA was explained at the bottom. It stood for Careless and Needless Endangering Ridiculous Reoccurring Activities.

"We thought that the acronym was a little rough. How about if we simplified it a little?"

"Sure, but it has a nice ring to it once you get used to it. I wanted to generate something that would be remembered. If it's too simple, people may forget it."

"The G-1 was wondering why you decided on a bunch of fat guys to illustrate your theme."

"Artistic exaggerations catch the eye and enhance the memory."

"Okay, we'll go with it as is."

Fire extinguishers were a problem, but points of contact were assigned to the fire extinguishers to ensure serviceability. Taquard made so much noise about fire extinguishers that the fire station decided to facilitate his needs. With a new shipment of fire extinguishers that had recently arrived, every fire extinguisher in the battalion was replaced. Not only were the fire extinguishers replaced with the latest models, but the areas where the fire extinguishers were mounted or emplaced were refurbished. Even the tags and lead seals were replaced. The fact was that Taquard was the only person to bother the fire department about anything. That is why they supported him so much.

For some odd reason Taquard was required to do PT with MAJ Coldhammer. This wasn't all that bad unless you happened to miss PT. Though the areas of fire and safety were manageable, Taquard made the mistake of oversleeping one morning. Coincidentally, it was the same morning of the day that Coldhammer ceased the semi-daily safety reports from Taquard. Taquard avoided Coldhammer and the new S-1, 1LT John Blunt (JB). However, escaping Blunt was never easy. He was a lawyer by profession who had an uncompromising integrity and a good nature. He was also an ace when it came to finding things or people. He came upon Taquard in an obscure shed on remote part of the installation.

"Elwood, the XO wants to see you."

"Yeah, I guessed as much."

"Why did you miss PT?"

"I overslept. I tried out this new clock and I set it wrong. There is really no excuse for oversleeping. I know that's not what you want to hear, but it's the truth."

"Let's go see the major."

"JB you could probably find a Swiss battleship."

Other people, like Canerra, could get out of doing PT. Other people could get out of doing a lot of things, but not Taquard. Taquard couldn't get away with anything.

The inevitable happened as expected, Taquard got his ass chewed.

"Sir, Lieutenant Taquard reporting," Taquard stated as he saluted MAJ Coldhammer.

"Why did you miss PT this morning?"

"Sir, it's just like I told you," Blunt offered.

"I happen to be speaking to the gentleman standing next to you."

Taquard informed Coldhammer of his misdeed and was reprimanded. Taquard was now assigned to lead PT instead of simply being a participant.

"Sorry, Elwood, I tried to help you out," Blunt said to Taquard while they were in Blunt's office. "Maybe you had better tell him about the IG visits before he really gets upset."

"IG? What are you talking about?" Evidently, Coldhammer had acute hearing abilities.

"Sir, Elwood called the IG."

"What?"

"He requested some inspections."

"You did what?"

"They have been here twice already."

"I happen to be speaking to Lieutenant Taquard."

"Yes, sir. I did. They have conducted two inspections already."

"Why the hell didn't you tell me about this?"

"Sir, he wanted it to be a surprise."

"Blunt! What the fuck happened?"

"Sir, when we had our conversations I felt that the only thing that I could do at the time was to make things happen as soon as possible. I also knew that I was responsible for the fire and safety areas that were no where near the standards that they should be at so I asked the IG for a courtesy inspection."

"You should never go over my head to division without telling me."

"Sir, we are now at a satisfactory rating," Blunt interjected. "We would've never been able to get there this soon without their support. Taquard has made some significant contributions."

"I still need to know about the division coming down here before they get here."

"I guess this is as good of a time to tell you. They're on their way back," Blunt continued.

"What?"

"Yes, sir. Next month. I'm going for a perfect score, sir," Taquard explained.

"What?"

"Yes, sir. Lieutenant Taquard has made arrangements for the inspectors to come down here every month until the end of the year."

"What?"

"Don't worry, sir, the division has been down here twice and nobody even knew it."

"That doesn't look good on us. We should've known."

"Just be glad that one of the enlisted swine didn't badmouth one of the inspectors," Blunt added. "Could you imagine what would happen if Sergeant Dingus ran his mouth off to one of those inspectors? Or if Captain Finch had another one of his dumb attacks."

"That does it. We're calling a safety meeting tonight. I need to see the inspection sheets. Blunt, get every commander here at 1700 hours. The colonel has a Division Artillery safety meeting tomorrow. The only way to get the IG off of our backs is to impress them to the point that we bore them. We have to be so squared away that they won't want to keep coming down here."

The arena of fire and safety, though once forgotten, was now the pinnacle of the division. With the support of the IG and other agencies affiliated with fire and safety and the support and participation of the unit commanders, the battalion was in ready shape. They were being noted for their successes by the division. When Absalom returned from the safety meeting he addressed Coldhammer.

"Well, we have the best safety program in the division. Can you believe it?"

"Well, that's good news, sir," Coldhammer responded.

"Is it?"

"Sure it is. Why wouldn't it be?"

"Well, first of all, I'll be leaving soon. That means that I won't be reaping the awards and recognition that comes with having the best fire and safety battalion in the division. And second of all, some asshole at division put Taquard in for a safety award."

"Even so, that will reflect favorably on you. And in addition to that, Taquard has made a lot of progress."

"Fortunately, I was able to block his award."

"Sir, he did earn it. Even though you may hate his guts, he does deserve it."

"Fuck him. He doesn't get along well with Dingus."

"They don't even work with each other anymore."

Absalom handed Coldhammer a copy of the division safety poster. "Take a look at this."

"So, he used Canerra as an example of what not to be. Good for him."

"The G-1 put the battalion in for a safety award."

"A battalion award would be great, especially when the inspectors come around."

"I blocked it. Let the new commander get his own award I tell you. I'll be leaving in three weeks anyway."

"Obviously, this poster is part of Taquard's handiwork. These posters will generate more recognition than the awards will."

"We won't be displaying them."

"Okay."

"Do I have to spell it out for you? These posters are a mockery of the unit. Look at that obese bastard there. That's Lieutenant Canerra. Hell the acronym CANERRA came from Canerra's name. And this guy here. He's a dead ringer for Captain Finch."

"This artwork is remarkable. No wonder it got so much attention. Maybe we need to notify division to rescind these posters."

"The hell you will. They have printed 500 copies so far and there going to run another 3,000. The colonel has received a lot of laudatory recognition for these posters. He was very excited. We can't stop the posters, but I am not about to let this snot nosed lieutenant get away with trying to make a jack ass out of me."

"Colonel, look at this figure here. Is that you?"

"Hey, I got more hair than that. And I'm not that fat either. And why the hell is my ass on fire?"

"I can certainly see why this poster got so much recognition."

"The colonel congratulated me on setting a new division record."

"What record?"

"Apparently, we fired over 1,450 rounds from 4P1 last week."

"In one week?"

"And the colonel is under the impression that it was done by one team."

"Just one?"

"Yeah."

"Which one?"

"I don't know yet."

"We need to find out. The colonel's going to want some answers on this one really soon. I'll get Finch."

"We need to get confirmation or denial on this one ASAP (as soon as possible). Apparently, someone is going out again real soon."

The following morning PT was conducted by Taquard. Coldhammer was absent because he overslept. Blunt even had the nerve to ask Coldhammer to report to Taquard for an ass-chewing.

The problem with bastard children was that they were conditioned to staying out of sight. They conducted their business in a detached fashion. Either they stayed away or found some way to stay away from everyone. Although Taquard operated in a clandestine manner, he made the division highlights. Absalom approached Finch about the recent news of the 4P1 missions.

"Are you aware that our battalion has adjusted over 1,400 rounds in just one week? That's a new record," Absalom said to Finch.

"My FIST Teams are reliable. All except Taquard's that is."

"The Division Artillery commander was under the impression that it was done by one team."

"That would mean that six teams were doing absolutely nothing at the time. That would be gross dereliction of duty not to mention a total disgrace to the entire FSO (Fire Support Office). That can't be true. It must be the other way around."

After Taquard's team was in garrison for a few days they departed to the field again. Upon his departure, a new battalion commander arrived. The firing point had acquired an additional 750 rounds of ammunition that was about to expire and were expected to expend it in three days. Coldhammer called Finch in to address his concerns about the mission.

"Listen, I just got word from Division Artillery that there is another mission going on at 4P1. I understand that we're supporting it. Can you account for your teams?"

"Yes, sir, they're all here."

"Shit. I wonder how these rumors get started. I'd better call the colonel and tell him that we are not supporting that mission. Wait. Did you know that Taquard wasn't at PT this morning?"

"He overslept again, as usual."

"Blunt! Get in here! I thought you told me that Taquard was taking his team out to the field this morning?"

"Yes, sir. That's why I led PT this morning. Don't you remember seeing his track this morning? Everyone was wondering about the Mad Dog logo he had on his track. And you might be asking yourself with great impatience, 'What is the significance of this drawing on the side of his track.' Well, I'll tell you. First thing you got to do is read Stephen King's novel *Cujo*. Taquard read it and it inspired him to name his team Cujo FIST."

"That's right. We did see the track passing by. Where are the other teams?"

"They're in the office reading *Hustler* magazine. They got this catalog that specializes in ceramic dildos. And let's not forget about the Penis Festival. They've been really talking that one up. They're excited."

"Shut up, Blunt! I was talking to Finch."

"Sir, I'll get to the bottom of this right now. As far as I know, Taquard isn't in the field, he's hiding."

"Sir, there are six chiefs in the office and I know for a fact that Taquard's team is supporting 4P1," Blunt continued.

"Check out the FIST chief office and somebody call 4P1. We need to get to the bottom of this right now."

"Sir, I already checked," Blunt said to Coldhammer. "There are six FIST chiefs grab-assing in the office and the phone's ringing like crazy."

"Who's answering the phone?" Finch asked.

"Nobody. That's Taquard's phone. For all we know, it could be the division IG calling us again."

"Get those idiots to answer that phone now," Coldhammer ordered Finch.

"He doesn't like anyone messing with his phone, that's why he keeps it locked up in his desk," Blunt responded.

"Well, hell. Get the combination and answer the phone."

"He uses padlocks that require keys."

"Captain, find Taquard, get that key, and find out what the hell is going on out there with these fire support missions. And no more unanswered phone calls."

"Yes, sir."

"And find out what in the hell the other teams are doing. I wonder how many rounds 4P1 has for this exercise."

"750," Blunt answered.

"750? That's 107 rounds per team. Every swinging Richard in the FSO should be out there," Coldhammer responded.

"Sir, there's a possibility that they will receive an additional 750 this Thursday," Blunt added.

"Damn. That would make every forward observer an expert." Finch responded.

"With the upcoming ARTEP we would be in great shape," Coldhammer said.

"Taquard's team is fully qualified," Blunt exclaimed. They fired over 1450 rounds last week alone. HE, smoke, coordinated illumination, white phosphorous, high angle, time on target…."

"How come you know all of this and I don't?" Finch asked.

"I don't know, I thought it was common knowledge. How does anyone manage to fire 1,400 rounds of artillery in a week without anyone knowing about it?"

"Or maybe you're just making this up to cover Taquard's ass."

"Or maybe we could go to the vault and listen in on the fire missions to see if these fire missions actually exist. Or maybe we could walk across the street and observe six lieutenants jacking off in the FIST office. Or maybe we could call Division Artillery and ask them what's going on at 4P1. Naturally, they might be a little concerned when they find out that one of our units is supporting the biggest artillery firing exercise that anyone has ever heard of and we don't know anything about it."

"Shut up already," Coldhammer interjected. "Is there anything else going on that may affect us?"

"Alpha Battery is going out tomorrow. Taquard will be supporting them as well," Blunt said.

"Any more surprises, Lieutenant?" Coldhammer asked.

"Yes, Bravo will be going out on Wednesday. Taquard will be adjusting their rounds too."

"Sir, I didn't know anything about this," Finch protested.

"You make the assignments, not him," Coldhammer retorted.

"Sir, if I may speak," Blunt interrupted.

"What's keeping you? You always blurted out everything before whenever you felt the urge."

"Sir, a few weeks ago Division Artillery called with an urgent mission assignment concerning 4P1. Finch wasn't in the office so they called the FIST Chief's office. Taquard took the call and gave out assignments to the other chiefs. They told him to get bent. Besides they had more important things to do like play with ceramic dildos."

"Finch, get those keys to his disk and find out exactly what's going on here."

CPT Finch and his driver went to 4P1 in a jeep. The drive took about forty minutes. He received a grid location to the OP. Since the grid was erroneous, Finch spent the next two hours scouting for the OP. In spite of the unknown location, he was able to find the OP. His first order of business was to reprimand the team.

"This isn't a Sunday picnic, get your LBE on!" Finch reprimanded Taquard in front of his troops at length for about half an hour. "Taquard, where's the key to your desk?"

"I gave it to Lieutenant Russell."

"Why did you do that?"

"He was bellyaching about not having a phone and I knew that I was going to be away so I gave him the key."

"But Lieutenant Russell hates your guts. It seems that a lot of guys hate your guts. Ever wonder why?"

"He asked if he could use the phone so I let him. All he had to do in return was take my calls. He agreed."

After Finch's departure, a ROK Lieutenant Colonel who witnessed the ordeal approached Corporal Kim. After conversing for a while Kim addressed the issue with Zimmerman.

"The colonel said that he witnessed the reprimand."

"Everybody did," Zimmerman responded.

"He feels that it was most unprofessional. He wants to help out."

"There's nothing that he can do."

"He feels offended by the reprimand."

"Yeah, I know."

"He says that the captain never supplies us with food, yet he reprimands us in public."

"There's nothing that he can do about it."

"That building over there only has four people. It was designed for twenty. He says that we can use it."

"We can?"

"He says that there's a barracks room on the third floor that we can use. He says that we can see the impact area from there very clearly. We can call our fire missions from there; they have a 292 antenna on the roof. We can park the APC inside of the garage so no one will see us."

"I'll tell the lieutenant," Zimmerman replied.

Zimmerman and Kim informed Taquard about the offer.

"Tell the colonel that I appreciate the offer, but we are moving to a new OP tonight. We'll be using the other impact area tomorrow. Kim, ask him if we can take him up on his offer later on, we'll be coming back."

After the night missions, Mad Dog FIST departed. They occupied a new site that overlooked another impact area. Behind them was Propaganda Village with the sounds of Singing Sam. While the team members slept in tents, Taquard and Zimmerman slept in the track. As time went by, Taquard and Zimmerman got along better and better. They passed the night away with cigarettes and jokes. The problem was that they couldn't stop telling jokes. This encroached on their sleep time. They ragged on about how dicked up Charlie Battery was. Charlie Battery was another dumping ground for misfits. Zimmerman's previous unit also designated Charlie Battery as their dumping ground as well.

Then it was rag on the Korean wives time. Many soldiers purchased wives from clubs. Even officers purchased wives though on a much smaller scale. One lieutenant caught gonorrhea from a girl twenty-nine times in a seven-month period and ended up buying her for $2,000.00 then marrying her. Since spouses weren't allowed to reside on Camp Pelham, he had to rent an apartment for her. Her nickname was "Rim Job" and she continued to work at the club. How could anyone support Women's Lib after seeing the Korean club girls in action? These women behaved like animals.

Taquard and Zimmerman laughed at the military television network's sexual harassment commercials. How was it even possible to sexually harass women in Korea? Outrunning them might have been considered harassment.

West Pointers were subject to ridicule as well. Cream wasn't the only thing that floated in the Army. Taquard told Zimmerman about the West Pointers that he dealt with. They seemed to be just like anyone else. Some were fine people, while others were just flat out assholes. Taquard relayed a story that he had heard from a West Point fiend of his.

After nearly four years at West Point a disappointed cadet exclaimed to a cadre member, "Sir, we're supposed to be living by a code of honor. We're supposed to be the product of standards that transcend human nature. We are not to lie, cheat, or steal, nor tolerate those who do, yet you can't trust anyone in this place. Everybody here lies, cheats, and steals constantly. This entire honor code is just one big lie. There's nothing real about it. The whole honor system is nothing but one big lie."

The cadre officer responded with, "Are you just now figuring this out?"

"I got a piece of trivia for you, Sergeant Zimmerman," Taquard exclaimed. "What is the order of precedence of an armed forces parade?"

"I have no idea."

"It starts out with the United States Military Academy Cadets. Second comes the United States Naval Academy Midshipmen. Third, the Air Force Academy Cadets followed by the United States Coast Guard Academy Cadets, then the Cadets from the Merchant Marine Academy. In other words the cadets come first. Army, Navy, Air Force, Coast Guard, and the Merchant Marines. After the cadets come the Army, Marines, Navy, Air Force, and Coast Guard. They are followed by the Nasty Guard, Army Reservists, the Marine Corps Reserves, Naval Reserves, Air National Guard, Air Force Reserves, and the Coast Guard Reserves. Then you have Nasty Guard organizations, whatever the hell they might be. They are followed by the Marine Corps Reserve organizations, don't ask me to explain. Let's see. Next comes the Naval Reserves organizations, and after that comes the Air Reserves organizations. These organizations may include the Veterans of Foreign War and Disabled Veterans Association, who knows? After that I guess the grand marshal of the parade will prescribe what order the veteran and patriotic organizations will follow in. Sometimes you have foreign soldiers who may participate in a parade. They will be positioned in front of the US soldiers. The police, whose job it is to clear the parade path, are in front of everybody. The grand marshal and his staff are in front and lead the parade itself. Naturally all of this is subject to change."

Jokes continued throughout the night well into the next morning. Ethnic jokes, sexist jokes, dirty jokes, jokes about Captain Finch, and lots of other jokes filled the time.

While most women used garters, Finch's mom used inner tubes. They joked about everything imaginable until they eventually fell asleep at about four in the morning. Waking up by eight was an impossibility. Although the alarm clock woke them up, they weren't in any shape to call for fire. Taquard called the firing battery on the radio.

"Right now we have fog in the impact area. We are unable to observe. We'll get back with you when the area is clear."

"Roger, out."

"That ought to buy us a couple of hours," Taquard said to Zimmerman.

"Okay, I'll leave the radios on in case they call us again."

Two hours were nice but they passed too quickly. Taquard called the battery again.

"The fog is still in the impact area. We're still watching it. We will get back with you when it's clear."

"Okay, out."

Zimmerman picked up the alarm clock. "Two hours, sir?"

"Better make it one."

At about 1130 they decided to call the battery again. They were still too weary to engage in fire missions.

"You're not going to believe this, but the fog still hasn't moved. We should be getting some wind soon. We'll let you know when we are able to observe."

"Okay, out."

Obviously, the unit didn't believe Taquard. At about noon the Bravo Battery Commander opened the door to the APC. He caught Taquard and Zimmerman napping.

"Fog at noon my ass. What are you guys still doing in the sack?"

Taquard got dressed and walked with the captain to the edge of the OP site. He explained that he was periodically checking the area and was about to check again. Together they checked the impact area. It was a bright clear sunny day all except for the impact area that was completely covered with a thick fog.

"I didn't believe you when you said that it was all fogged in," said the captain. "Let's give it another two hours and check again. I'll notify the other units. Everyone thought that you were making this up."

"Actually, sir, the other impact area is probably clear."

"No, we need to get experience on this one."

"I didn't know what else to do, so I decided to get some sleep."

"There's nothing else that you can do, except maybe eat."

Taquard finally caught a break. Later that afternoon, Taquard's team began firing missions for three separate units simultaneously. Missions were stacked and there were no limits to implementing creativity.

Everything was going well until Alpha Battery lobed an unobservable round. This meant that the round could've landed anywhere or may have been a dud. Either way, it ended the fire mission. Alpha double-checked their firing data and fired again. The second round was also unobserved. The commander himself intervened.

"Just say that you saw the round."

"Negative," replied Taquard, "we have six people on the hill and no one saw either round."

Alpha made a third attempt producing yet another unobservable round. This created tension and additional people to the OP. CPT Finch was summonsed to the OP along with others to investigate the incident of unobservable rounds. Finch questioned Zimmerman about his location. There was a survey marker on the ground that was depicted in the wrong location on the Korean made map.

"Show us where we are, Sergeant."

Zimmerman stood next to the survey marker and pointed to the survey marker that was on the map.

"Don't you know how to read a map? That's not where we're at, at all."

"The map is incorrect. The terrain feature depicted on the map is also incorrect. These maps are Korean. They're the best we have. As inaccurate as they are these are the top of the line," Taquard intervened.

"I was talking to the sergeant, not you."

"That still doesn't change the fact that the rounds were not observed. Here's the grid of the fire mission."

The grid and data were verified again and Finch himself called the fire mission to Alpha Battery. Splash was used. The round was still unobserved. Finch didn't see it either and an investigation was underway. Within an hour the S-3 arrived with a verdict: FIST was at fault. As usual FIST was blamed for someone else's mistake. Finch stated that Taquard's team was substandard and needed more field experience. With the benefit of hindsight, time in the field was actually a blessing in disguise. Problems that remained unsolved were forgotten until they resurfaced. Taquard's desk was such a problem. Finch informed Coldhammer that Russell may have had Taquard's desk key. Taquard locked his phone up in his desk drawer. He also received calls from division headquarters from time to time.

"Lieutenant Blunt, you'd better see if Lieutenant Russell has Lieutenant Taquard's desk key. We'd better make sure," said Coldhammer.

"Yes, sir."

Blunt accounted for six FIST Chiefs who where goofing off as usual.

"I thought I told you to get rid of those magazines," Blunt said to the chiefs.

"Well, shit JB, we don't work for you. So why don't you just get the hell out of our office and go back to where you belong?"

"I like *National Geographic* for the same reason you like your magazines. I get to see things that I'm never near," Blunt said to Canerra.

"I happen to be married, you asshole," Canerra responded.

"And all this time I was thinking that Mama Cass was dead."

Blunt was no one to argue with. No matter how things went he always managed to get the upper hand. Blunt addressed Russell.

"Hey, buttface! Do you have Lieutenant Taquard's desk key? Well, do you? Either you do or you don't. Well which is it?"

"Yeah, asshole, I do, but you sure as shit ain't gonna to get it."

"You make sure you answer his phone when it rings. That means that you put down your fuck book and answer the phone. You take the call and do what you're supposed to do. And don't jack off while you're on it either."

"Fuck you, JB!"

"Do you need the key? If not I'll take it."

"As a matter of fact I do need it, you horse's ass."

"Why, so you can steal something that doesn't belong to you?"

"In case I need to use the phone you jackass."

"Then why haven't you been answering the phone when it rings?"

"I ain't no damn secretary. I may be black but that don't make me nobody's boy."

"You need to answer Tauqard's calls when they come in. I know that that may cause you some great inconvenience while you are beating your meat but the call may be important."

"Fuck him. He can answer his own calls."

"When he's in the field like he is now you need to answer them."

"Fuck him, I ain't his secretary. And fuck you too. We can handle things just fine without you telling us what to do."

"Just remember what we talked about," Blunt said as he departed.

"And another thing, get your sorry ass outta here and don't come back," Russell shouted at Blunt as he was leaving. "I took care of you, you chickenshit mutherfucker."

Blunt returned to his office which was situated next to Coldhammer's. It became apparent that Blunt had spoken to Coldhammer when CPT Richards arrived at the FIST Chief Office.

"Russell, the XO wants to see you."

"Why?"

"Perhaps you misunderstood my order. Come with me now."

Richards escorted Russell to Coldhammer.

"Do you have the key to Lieutenant Taquard's desk?"

"Yes, sir," replied Russell.

"Then why haven't you been answering his phone?"

"He didn't get any calls, sir."

"Are you telling me that Blunt is a liar? He informed me that the phone was ringing while he was at your office and that you ignored it."

"Then I would have to say that Lieutenant Blunt is a liar."

"Funny, I never said when Blunt was in your office. This happened yesterday, where were you?"

"I was in the motor pool."

"Lieutenant Harris didn't see you there. I'd say that your chances of making First Lieutenant are pretty slim."

Russell returned to the FIST Chief Office. Blunt arrived soon afterwards.

"Give me the key, Mr. Loudmouth."

Blunt unlocked the desk, took the phone out of the drawer and put it on the desk, and secured the drawer.

"When that phone rings, you answer it," Blunt said to Canerra. "That means that you get off of your fat ass and answer it. And you get off of your black ass and come over and get me," Blunt said to Russell.

"That's a racist remark, I'm going to report you," Russell said to Blunt.

"Actions speak louder than words, boy," Blunt retorted.

"That's it, I'm reporting you to CPT Finch."

"Since he's not here you'll have to go to the XO."

"I'll wait until he gets back."

"You'll report it to the XO now," Blunt insisted.

"Okay, I will. You're not getting out of this one, you peckerwood."

"He's expecting you."

"Sir, I have a complaint to make about Lieutenant Blunt," Russell said to Coldhammer.

"I am processing the paperwork denying your promotion to First Lieutenant."

"But, sir, I have a complaint."

"I don't want to hear it. I don't want you to even open your mouth. You'll be getting a copy of this soon. Get out and stay out."

As Russell departed Blunt gave him something to ponder. "Come here. Come here. If any of the other chiefs want to forgo their promotion, you know where to send them."

Meanwhile, the fire missions continued without an incident. Fire missions went well in to the late evening approaching midnight. When Alpha and Bravo Batteries were finished expending their ammo, they returned back to garrison. However, 4P1 had a lot of ammo remaining. Taquard decided to make a night move to the ROK compound. By midnight, the Cujo FIST team was embracing a well deserved slumber in the ROK installation. Missions wouldn't commence until noon the next day.

Major Coldhammer's reputation was spreading throughout the Western Corridor. He was known as being hard and exactly the person who you wanted to avoid. The undeniable fact was that Coldhammer was the best major the Army had seen in a long time. He lived up to his reputation as he instilled fear in the minds of many.

"Captain Finch, I want to see Lieutenant Taquard's call for fire sheets on the unobserved rounds at Crab Island. I want that grid surveyed. We're going back and we're going to fire it again."

"Sir, that was yesterday. I wouldn't expect him to have it anymore."

"I wouldn't expect him to have it either. I expect you to have it."

"No, sir, he didn't give it to me."

"But you were there. You initiated a mission yourself. So where's your sheet?"

"It was determined by the S-3 that Taquard was at fault."

"You were there, did you see the round impact or not?"

"Sir, Lieutenant Taquard doesn't know his ass from a hole in the ground and his sergeant doesn't know how to read a map."

"I asked if you observed the round impact and you can't remember."

"Yes, sir, I remember."

"Did you or did you not see the round impact? The next word out of your mouth will either be yes or no. Did you, or did you not see the round impact?"

"No, sir, I didn't see it."

"Get the sheet. I want to see it."

"Well, like I said earlier, he may not have it anymore."

"He still has it," Blunt added as he stuck his head in the office. "I just confirmed it from the TOC (Tactical Operating Center) radio. I guess they don't call me Mr. Helpful for nothing."

"I can think of a lot of words to describe you and helpful isn't one of them. Finch, get the sheet."

Finch departed in search of finding Taquard. As he rode in his jeep he could see lots of smoke and hear several rounds impacting in the area. Cujo FIST was firing multiple missions simultaneously and wasn't shy about expending artillery shells. Finch arrived at the Crab Island OP only to find it unoccupied. Then he went to 4P1 to acquire a new location on the FIST team. The bogus location that was relayed to Finch resulted in him engaging in another wild goose chase. He could see the exploding impact area with lots of smoke, but he could not locate the OP. He went to every potential OP site imaginable while enduring the tremendous and constant noise created by the explosions. Finch returned to 4P1 to try to get a fix on Taquard's location. He was wondering if Taquard was even in the field in the first place. He heard Taquard's voice over the radio as he called for a battery twenty-four-round smoke mission. That meant that a gross of smoke rounds would be deployed in less than 20 minutes. Finch validated his grid location again. He was at that grid location previously, but he didn't see anyone. Finch called Taquard on the radio and demanded his position. Taquard's team did not respond. Blunt radioed Taquard from the TOC vault.

"Jabba the Hutt is headed your way," he informed Taquard.

"Yeah, I know, he's been looking for me. Look I need some help."

"What is it?"

"Fat Dave is asking for my location from 4P1. Last week they fired on the OP instead of the target. Lewdvick buried the incident. They got us confused with the target and damn near killed us."

"Wow."

"From then on we never gave away our position. Now we are inside of a Korean compound. If they shoot this place up and kill Koreans…"

"I got it. I'll tell Major Coldhammer at once. Can you give me the fire mission data verbally?"

"Yes. Can you get Major Coldhammer to intervene on my behalf so that I don't have to give our position away to Fat Dave? Do you have any idea what a bunch of 155mm rounds of high explosives can do to a Korean installation?"

"Yes."

Blunt took the fire mission data to the XO while Finch was trying to reach Taquard on the radio. Coldhammer verified the mission data and confirmed the grid location. He then sent the ammo officer to get the ordinance records of the mission. Finch called Coldhammer telephonically.

"What do you mean AWOL? Blunt just spoke to him," Coldhammer said in response to Finch's accusation.

"Sir, I've looked everywhere for him and…"

"Dave, come on back here. Never mind about the mission data right now. I need you back here."

Although Finch acknowledged, he wasn't about to give up that easily. He remained at 4P1 as fire missions reconvened. When the mission was completed, Finch broke in demanding an accurate grid to his location. Taquard requested Blunt via the TOC radio frequency.

No matter what he did there was no way for Taquard to redeem himself in the eyes of Finch. There was no way that he would ever get a garrison assignment over the field. For the next three and a half months,

Cujo or Mad Dog FIST was in the field providing fire support while the other six teams remained in garrison. Other units rotated in and out of 4P1 while ammunition that was about to expire was identified. From May to August, Mad Dog FIST would fire over 9,000 rounds. The Korean barracks that was used for an OP for "No Name" impact area would never be discovered.

Coldhammer solved the mystery of the unobserved rounds. He lived by a philosophy that if a question remained, then information was missing. And while questions remained he searched for answers until he found out exactly everything that had happened and why. He reviewed all of the data and took in to account every factor that could have affected the unobserved rounds. He factored in powder temperature, muzzle velocity, air density, and much more. He noticed that it was a time on target mission with the impact at 100 feet above the ground. Major Coldhammer validated the use of Joyner's Law of Interpolation as it applied to the range from the battery to the target in accordance with the Tabular Firing Tables. As it had turned out, the lot of the time fuses from the contractor had an anomaly that the contractor failed to mention. While the fuses usually function normally, their functional ability is subject to compromise if the projectile flies over water. There was a large body of water, the Imjin River, between the firing point and Crab Island.

Crab Island actually isn't an island at all, but rather a piece of land that is surrounded on three sides by the Imjin River which flows from North into South Korea passing through the DMZ and finally meets the Han River near Seoul. It was the site of two major battles and two infiltration attempts. The battles took place in 1592 and during the Korean War; the infiltrations both took place in 1983.

A third IG courtesy inspection was a resounding success. The results were nearly perfect. The inspectors gave Taquard a new set of binders, fresh documents, typed dividers, and a $50 bond for winning the Safety Poster Contest. Extra blank forms for suggestions and identifying areas for correction were enclosed in one of the binders as were requisition forms, and additional checklists. The latest regulations and directives were posted accordingly. As far as the paperwork of the fire and safety program was concerned, Taquard had a perfect role model of what the paperwork should look like. "This is the epitome of what every one's books should look like. Everything is perfect. I guess if you want to make it better you could take your $50 bond and have the books bound in leather," the inspector informed Taquard. "You've made a big improvement over the last inspection, only four gigs for the entire battalion. You've got the number one fire and safety program in the entire division."

The inspector also presented Taquard with the Outstanding Safety Excellence Award which came in the form of a plaque.

"Normally, I would give this to your colonel myself, but I want you to give it to him."

"When can we have another inspection?" Taquard asked.

"Never, it won't be necessary."

"But I am shooting for 100%."

"I know and I think that you'll get it."

"Oh before I forget. Here's something for you," Taquard told the inspector. "It's a game. A board game. It's a fun game to be sure, but the theme character is also in the safety poster. I was hoping that this would enhance safety awareness or in some cases generate interest."

"A game. Hmmm. Well, the poster has turned out to be a great success. People can't get enough of them. A game would be something to consider especially if everyone likes it as much as they like the posters. A game might work, then again it might not. I am open to suggestions though."

"You mentioned earlier that you were seeking ways to enhance safety awareness."

"Yes I did. There's even a $100 bond award to the winner who comes up with the best idea."

"Well, I thought that a game..."

"Wait a minute. The Slim Jim Game? How does that promote safety? It looks like a regular game to me."

"Well, sir. I didn't want to be too forward with this because it might be dismissed as something too boring to consider. You see GIs don't always respond well to terms like safety, discipline, and responsibility. So, I created a game that was both fun and included a recognizable figure from the safety poster. It is a regular game in many ways, actually in all ways, but I was hoping that the recognition of Slim Jim would generate some recognition to the safety program. We're starting with nothing with these GIs."

"You've got a point. So far your ideas have worked remarkably well. I suppose that we could print up some games for distribution. The posters are in such high demand that I can't even get them out to distribution once they get printed."

"I forgot to consider the costs of producing a game. I'm sure that your budget is already stretched to the limit as it is with the posters."

"Are you kidding me? We have a blank check on anything we want. There is no budget, we're part of the federal government, remember?"

"Well, in that case we haven't lost anything in trying. That's a comic book that goes with the game. Maybe one of the soldiers might read it while the others are playing the game. Rumor has it that some soldiers actually know how to read. You see, drawing comics is a hobby of mine. And I also happen to be extremely enthusiastic about safety. Putting the two together makes the job both fun and productive."

"Well, I am beginning to see your point of view but there is hardly any resemblance between your comic book and fire and safety awareness. It doesn't seem to have any connection with the intent of a promotional item. Although money has never been an issue, time and energy is. I understand your enthusiasm, in fact I like it, but I want to avoid going off on tangents that will take me out of the realm of the intent of our original."

"Actually, you're right. It doesn't have any resemblance at all. I was hoping however that it could become a recognizable figure affiliated with safety or the epitome of what not to do. Sometimes the direct route will not get you to your destination. Of course, if these items are in demand they might get circulated around. What if soldiers liked these ridiculous comics and asked for more? Where would a soldier go do ask for his own comic book or game? They would go to the Division Fire and Safety Office. They would come to your office. Who knows, they might be calling you for a change. It sure beats running around like a chicken with its head cut off trying to convince people to be safe. We have both seen where that gets us."

"Actually, I'm open to anything that will interest anyone in safety matters. Considering all of the accidents and injuries that we have going on around here; it would be worth it to get people interested in safety for a change. Let me see if we can get these published and distributed. I'm willing to try anything at this point."

"And I also produced a perpetual calendar to accompany the safety poster. Not only will they have a poster, but they will also have a calendar to go with it. Oh, and I also designed some stickers to be given to the GIs all in the name of safety awareness. They resemble the old Odd Rod stickers that were once popular about fifteen years ago. We always got a kick out of them. Maybe we could spark up some interest with them. "

"Yes, I do remember those. My son used to collect them. Okay, I have a Slim Jim Game, a Slim Jim comic book, Slim Jim stickers, and a perpetual calendar. This fat character named Slim Jim just might be the ticket to what we are looking for. The important thing is to establish some safety situational awareness. Maybe we can produce something that people will want and ask for again and again. Maybe in the process, they will solicit our help."

Remembering the advice that was given to him while he was still in college, Taquard aimed at achieving a score of 100% every time he encountered a challenge. If you shoot for a 95% you will never get it as you are accepting failure before you even begin. However, if you strive for 100% you may not get it but you will come very close. Not only that, but you will find that achieving a perfect score is an obtainable goal. The battalion post office had survived five years of IG inspections (announced and unannounced) without ever getting a single gig ever. They were perfect for five years running under the supervision of SGT Carroll who later became a Warrant Officer. Not only was his post office perfect, so was his vehicle and his uniform. Even the tool bag was clean. He served as a role model for others to follow and the epitome of what Taquard was aiming for.

In spite of battalion interests, Finch made no measures to establish a field rotation for the FIST teams.

# Chapter Ten
## *Sinking Lower*

Being a bastard child wasn't all that it was cracked up to be. Continuous field duty and operations without the support of anyone was the standard of the Artillery bastard child. No food, no fuel, no equipment, and no support of any kind were available. To make matters worse, Tauqard's M113 APC (Armored Personnel Carrier) FIST track was officially designated as the Hanger Queen courtesy of CPT Finch. That meant that anyone who needed M113 parts had permission to cannibalize parts from another M113. Cannibalizing parts from other vehicles was previously considered to be a crime. Robbing parts from FIST vehicles had no consequences to begin with because the fisties had no one that they could complain to. Being a FIST was a constant struggle and the epitome of being a born loser. They were losers by design. They did the most work and had the least to show for it. The FIST logistical motto in Korea was "Beg, Borrow, Steal, or Kimchee Rig." Kimchee was the answer to everything in Korea.

The difference between deploying with the artillery and the infantry was that with the artillery, you actually got to adjust fire for firing batteries and there was a lot less movement. Once the FIST team was emplaced Dingus put the team to work digging. When in doubt, dig. The problem was that digging became more important than the fire missions. Since Taquard couldn't make his team adjust fire, he simply left and joined the other teams that were.

Someone came up with the expression that the presence of a high ranking officer in the field boosts morale. Whoever came up with that saying didn't' know what the hell he was talking about. After several of adjusting fire from the forward observation positions, LTC Absalom arrived.

"Well, the missions haven't been going very well. There hasn't been a good mission all day. Why do you assholes keep fucking things up," Absalom demanded.

He picked up one of the radio microphones and contacted one of the firing batteries. "I'll straighten these fuck heads out if it's the last thing that I do."

When the next fire mission commenced, SGT Gates initiated.

"L85 this is B27, adjust fire, over."

"Slow," Absalom retorted

"Grid 3987 6640, over."

"Wait a minute, where the fuck did you get that grid?"

"From the map, sir," Gates answered.

"No! Where's your survey book?"

"Survey book?"

"Yes your survey book, you stupid son of a bitch."

"I'm sorry, sir, I don't know what that is."

"You stupid motherfucker! It's a book. It's a survey book. It has all the surveyed targets in it. You're supposed to get your grids from there," Absalom insisted.

"Sir," Taquard interjected, "No one from the Fire Support Office ever mentioned anything about survey books that I know of. But now that we have identified the problem, where can we obtain them?"

"You bastard, you're supposed to have them with you!"

"I understand, sir."

"You fuck heads! Where in the hell are your survey books? I don't see a single one out here! Canerra, where is your survey book?"

"Sir, I told Sergeant Gates to pick it up on the way out of the office, but he failed to carry out my direct order, sir," Second Lieutenant Canerra responded.

"But, sir, that's not true. He never mentioned anything about a survey book to me, not ever."

"And what college did you got to Gates?"

"Sir, I wasn't fortunate enough to have had the opportunity to go to college."

"I graduated from West Point which I am sure that you surmised from looking at my gold class ring. Therefore I am intelligent and you are not. Look at this ring and look at it good, because you will never get one. I'm smart enough to know when someone is telling me the truth and when someone is lying. Lieutenant Canerra told you to get the survey books and you didn't get them," Absalom continued.

"But, sir, I'm telling you that he never mentioned them ever," SGT Gates responded.

"Look, you stupid motherfucker. He told you and you just didn't understand. Does he have to give his commands to you in jive in order for you to understand? Well, I'm sorry, but the official language in this battalion is English, not any of that other crap you people are always speaking."

"Sir, where exactly were the survey books to be picked up at?" Taquard asked. "I'm sure that Sergeant Gates is doing his best to ensure that the team is ready to support fire missions."

"Did you graduate from West Point?"

"University of Colorado."

"Then what the fuck do you know?"

"Well, I did make the President's List repeatedly and I also know that there is a target marker on the map," Taquard continued. "We could use that with the absence of survey books."

"Shut the fuck up! I didn't ask for target markers. The whole exercise is fucked up. You bastards fucked it all up!"

Absalom went on a shouting binge. He looked down the side of the hill and noticed the trash that was scattered about. It looked like something from the "Alice's Restaurant" song multiplied by ten. Arlo Guthrie would've been impressed.

"Look at all of that trash. Did you do that?" Absalom asked.

"No, sir," a few of the soldiers responded in unison.

"You're a bunch of fucking-ass liars," Absalom shouted back.

Taquard informed the colonel, "Sir, the men thought that you were referring to the entire hillside of trash. They wouldn't deliberately lie to you."

"I was referring to the entire hillside you filthy bastards," Absalom retorted.

"Sir, there's no way they could have done this," Taquard said. "There's almost six tons of trash here. We've only been here for a few hours. It's out there, maybe 600 feet, maybe even more. It would be physically impossible to have done all this in a single day."

"I want it cleaned up," Absalom said.

"Okay. Men, police up your trash. Some of it is ours and—"

"Not some you motherfucker! All! This is your mess, and I want it cleaned up. All of it."

"Sir, do you mean that we have to clean up the entire hillside?" one of the NCOs asked.

Absalom answered, "That's what the fuck I mean. Do I have to spell it out to you? I'm gonna be back and when I am I'd better not see any of this trash anywhere."

"Sir, we didn't do it," Sergeant Craig answered.

"The hell you didn't! Look, look at this. Who the fuck left this cookie wrapper here? Who did that?" Absalom questioned.

"That would be Lieutenant Canerra," Gates responded.

"Sir, Sergeant Gates is a liar. He is lying to cover up for his own incompetence," Canerra interjected.

"I am not lying. I saw what you did. We all did," Gates angrily responded.

"Shut the fuck up," Absalom interrupted, "and get to work and I mean today."

"Move your ass, Gates," Canerra ordered.

"Sir, you are a liar. You are the biggest liar that I know," Gates stated in disgust.

Canerra responded with, "Hey, Sarge! What do you call a colored hitchhiker?"

It was apparent that Canerra didn't give a damn about anyone besides himself. He answered his own question sine Gates wasn't interested.

"Stranded."

"That's racist," Gates responded.

"Everything's racist to you jigaboos. Hey, Gates, what do you call a nigger in a Cadillac? Thief. And speaking of niggers, you have a job to do. I believe that the colonel made it quite clear about what needs to be done. So get off of your dead black ass and move it you scuba skin. Move it nigger boy. I said move it."

While Gates and Canerra were arguing, Absalom went to Dingus' track.

"Well, well, well. That's quite a fighting position that you have there," Absalom said.

"Yes, sir," Dingus said, "strategically located behind the track for rapid response time."

Dingus was very proud of his fighting position. The Infantry wouldn't let him dig, but the Artillery did. So when he was out with the artillery digging became part of the daily operations.

Taquard approached Dingus and asked, "Sergeant Dingus, where is the survey book?"

"Somewhere where you can't find it, El Tee," he answered back.

Absalom laughed along with Dingus.

"What color is the book?"

"What color is your asshole?"

They laughed even harder.

"In other words, there is no book," Taquard continued. "If you have it, we need it."

"Too late, El Tee. You already fucked up the fire missions," interrupted Absalom. "Now you have another mission."

The dark clouds preceded an expected rain storm. It was the rain that caused Absalom to leave. With a laudatory remark to Sergeant Dingus, Absalom departed.

The heavy rain continued for the next three days. The Artillery couldn't fire a mission even if they wanted to. It rained both day and night without a break. It never stopped, but it kept Absalom away. It also was enough to recall the firing batteries. The firing batteries returned back to garrison without informing the FIST teams. The FIST teams remained in the field for an additional three days simply because no one bothered to inform them that the exercise was cancelled. Dingus' APC tailgate was stuck in the mud. The fighting position that Dingus prepared filled up with rain and created a large mud hole. Because of the slope of the fighting position; mud began flowing into the APC when the tailgate was dropped. Taquard retrieved his gear and left.

"Hey, where the fuck do you think you're going, El Tee?" Dingus asked.

"To see how many soldiers are fucking your wife," he responded. "She's still working at the club you know."

Dingus was stunned.

"If you want to do something about it I'm right here."

Dingus remained in the track.

"That's what I thought," Taquard said as he departed.

During the several attempts to close the back end of the APC he forgot to stop the controls while the end was stuck in the mud; this resulted in stripping the gears. Now the back end was permanently opened. Eventually the mud overflowed into the track itself. The track was soon filled with mud. The irony of it all was that if Dingus hadn't've dug the fighting position n the first place this fiasco would've been avoided altogether. It was his digging that created a myriad of problems and a disabled track.

Taquard eventually made it back to Pelham, first by walking, then by catching a ride. After dropping his gear off in his quarters, he went to the Fire Support Office and addressed Lieutenant Hand.

"Mike, where are the survey books?"

"Survey books, what are those?"

"They contain the surveyed data and grids of the targets that we're supposed to be firing. Apparently we can't fire missions without them."

"Never heard of it."

"The old man was pretty upset about us not having any."

"I still never heard of it."

"Mike, we have to find them and quick. The colonel's hot about this. You'll be in trouble for this one too."

"Right, we'd better see the S-3."

"He's out in the field."

"No he isn't. I just saw him a few minutes ago."

"But he's supposed to be in the field."

"Elwood, he's here. The exercise was cancelled a couple of days ago on the count of the rain."

"The FISTs don't know that. They're still out there."

"I'll send Ball to the vault. Maybe we can reach the FISTs by radio and tell them to come back in. Hey, Ball."

"I got it, sir," replied Ball.

The two lieutenants went to the Three to inquire about the survey books.

"You stupid fucks! Get the hell out of my office."

Taquard decided to see the S-2 for further guidance. His office was at the intersection of two halls across from a water fountain. It was very hard to find and very easy to overlook. The office itself was a maze of storage shelves and storage cases. It looked more like an abandoned warehouse than it did an office. One thing for sure, it had privacy and lots of maps.

"Sir, I was wondering if you had a moment. There's something that I've been trying to track down."

"Sure come on in," Captain Case replied.

"Sir, I'm trying to find the survey books that the FIST teams use for their fire missions."

"I remember those back when I was a second Louie. They don't use them anymore. They're obsolete. The protractor and a map and a little practice and you don't need the survey books."

"But the colonel was asking about them. He was pretty sore about us not having any."

"It just so happens that I have a bunch of vintage stock on hand. I've got a bunch that you can have. There's no data in them. Like new. Never been used. How many do you need? You can have all of them if you want."

"Where do I get the data?"

"Look it up on the map."

"But the colonel was crying about a survey team compiling the data."

"We don't have a survey team. Haven't had one in the past year. We're supposed to be putting one together as soon as we get some more lieutenants. In the meantime, use map intersection for your data. Here's ten. If you need any more, just let me know," Captain Case said as he handed the old dark brown books to Taquard.

"Thanks. They sure do look old. These are dated 1951."

"That's the latest series there is. The Army doesn't use them anymore. Don't use pen in those books. Be sure to use only pencil in case you have to change any numbers. And if we ever do get a survey team assembled, they will provide you with a grid."

Taquard was never able to find a practical use for the survey books although he made a great effort to do so. They were close to being ideal but the format denied its usefulness. Absalom was approaching the end of his tour and never inquired about survey books again. Even though Taquard was prepared, it was just as well that the subject never came up again.

# Chapter Eleven
## *When Butter Turns into White Gold*

On 27 July 1953, the Korean War was the subject of a cease-fire accord between both North and South Korea. Unbeknownst to most people, neither side surrendered to the other. There was no unconditional surrender. Technically, the two countries were still at war. The accord was for thirty years, renewal was a certainty to the rest of the world. As 27 July 1983 approached, neither side was proposing a renewal conference. Camp Pelham was the most forward US military installation that existed situated five kilometers from North Korea. 4P1 and other firing points and OPs were closer to North Korea than Pelham was, but they weren't permanent duty stations. The possibility of hostile activity was extremely high as an all out war between the two countries. After all, they were at war with each other in the past. Living at Pelham made believers out the most cynical of critics. To the rest of the world, Korea was nonexistent. Maybe it was because the media was tightly controlled in the vicinity of the DMZ. Media wasn't allowed. Also, American wives were not allowed. Camp Pelham was an unaccompanied tour of duty. Access to Pelham and the rest of the area was strictly controlled and enforced.

Korean wives, although in the immediate vicinity, didn't confide in the media the way American women did. The Korean media was censored and tightly controlled. No one trusted the media.

At another base an American housewife noticed a stripper at the club.

She reported it and soon strippers ceased to exist at base clubs. However, the actions didn't end there. Additional disciplinary actions were exercised. With the leverage and push from the media, several officers had their careers compromised. This included officers who weren't involved or even remotely connected to the incident. Repercussions continued to spread for almost a year. Officers were hiding from American females who were civilian employees. Women's Lib was part of the Army.

The positive aspect of this repercussion was that Americans did everything possible to control both the media and number of American females in the area. This meant that people could for the most part do what had to be done. The units in the Western Corridor didn't have the luxury of time to establish cooperation to engage in negotiations. Without the presence of the media, a lot of extreme actions without justification occurred. Most incidents that occurred on the border were not reported. Even if an incident was reported, the media twisted the facts and altered the incident to suit their needs. The slanted story was so inaccurate that it was unrecognizable to the participants.

When 27 July 1983 came, it did so without the renewal of the original 1953 Cease Fire Accord between North and South Korea. This meant that either side could fire at the other when ready. Acts of Aggression would no longer be considered acts of aggression. This would be followed by other historical events as well. The attitude that the soldiers had was reflected by a unit T-shirt that was silk screened. It said "B 2/17, The Armistice is over, Let the Bastards Come, Bravo Bulls." The Bravo Bulls led the battalion in attitude initiative by depicting a nuclear explosion, a 198 howitzer, and a bull (all in red) on the T-shirts to accompany the statements. This was by far the best T-shirt ever produced by the Army. While wearing the Bravo Battery T-shirt, Taquard momentarily forgot about being a FIST Chief and thought of himself as a member of the battalion. This instilled him with the motivation and vigor to fight in the event of a conflict. The nice thing about actual conflict is that true feelings surface.

As the US and ROK were unprepared for any conflict, the manning of the DMZ posts was not upgraded. Some outposts were US while others were ROK. Because manpower was so limited, some posts were unmanned at times. Everyone was unprepared for war. The only people who are prepared for war are the ones starting it.

Blunt didn't have any faith in the Korean security elements that protected Camp Pelham from any perpetrators or any other threat or danger. During his SDO tours he would inspect the guards and prove that they were sleeping on duty by taking their shotguns away. He got at least one shotgun every time he pulled SDO duty. He also suspected where the loyalties of the local Koreans actually stood. South Korea seemed to have a large population of North Korean supporters. As poor as the population was it was no wonder that their loyalties might be compromised. The South Korean government and upper class treated the citizens like dirt. The elite consisted of only 7% of the South Korean population while the remaining 93% lived in abject poverty. When you are being mistreated your loyalties begin to waver. The upper 7% had endlessly exploited the rest of their countrymen at every conceivable opportunity. So much so that it was virtually impossible to make a legitimate living honestly. A casual observer might wonder which side treated their people the worst. They would also wonder what the fundamental differences in their political ideology were.

The expiration of the armistice was followed by the infiltration of three North Korean soldiers who were heavily armed. They managed to bypass many checkpoints without detection. They traveled in a raft on the Imjin River and went south of Sun Yu Ri to the town of Munsan. Unfortunately for them they were spotted by some ROK soldiers who were unintentionally manning the wrong outpost. They opened up fire without hesitation and the three North Koreans died immediately. It was suspected that the three soldiers had a lot of information to penetrate to Munsan without being detected. They had to be familiar with how both the US and the ROK conducted military security operations. Obviously they had a lot of information and they would've traveled beyond Munsan if it were not for the ROK soldiers manning the wrong outpost. Had they passed Munsan without detection they would have been able to go anywhere that they wanted without being spotted. The question was, where and how did they acquire this information. One question that had to be answered was who knew what the rotation schedule of the outposts was. There was one posted in the TOC. It was suspected that the information was being provided by the Korean wives who hung out at the TOC while their husbands were pulling SDNCO duties. NCOs routinely brought their Korean wives or girl friends or even a business girl to the TOC during their SDNCO tours. This gave the NCO a chance to engage in sexual activity while on SDNCO duty. It was a great arrangement and exercised by many. While having a Korean wife without a security clearance in a restricted operations area would be considered a security violation by even the most casual of unaffiliated observers, it would take a significant event for the Army to become interested in security.

Shortly after, the division commander completed his tour of duty. The new general wanted to see Camp Pelham. A visit by a Major General at Camp Pelham was a significant event. Even a full colonel's visit was cause for alarm at Camp Pelham. Camp Pelham only had one lieutenant colonel and that was as high as it went. The battalion/installation commander was a virtual monarch to the soldiers and Koreans in the vicinity. It was the only post in the military where the unit commander was also the installation commander. The entire camp got a dose of perfection fever in preparation for the general's anticipated visit. Anyone who outranked the battalion commander was revered with a great deal of awe. Such presence was welcomed with enthusiasm.

The question that was on everyone's mind was who was going to actually see the general. The Pope himself couldn't have established himself in higher regard. Seeing the general was considered a great honor and shaking his hand was hoping for too much.

Taquard realized that his chances of actually seeing the general were slim to none. He scheduled another fire support mission in the field during the general's anticipated arrival. The battalion commander had an idea to introduce the new general to the camp. The general's itinerary should be complete and there shouldn't be any dead time during his visit the colonel reasoned. It was better to overload an itinerary than to risk the possibility of having dead time. He put in a lot of details and functions to ensure that he general was occupied while he was on the installation.

Officer Evaluation Reports (OER) were the subject of concern for officers, even lieutenants. The belief was that an OER had to absolutely perfect or else your career would be over. All OERs needed to reflect that the rated officer didn't get his socks damp while he walked on water and was in the top 1/1000th of the top 1% of everything that he ever thought about doing. OERs should reflect the fact that the rated officer's turds belong in the Smithsonian rather than to simply be flushed down the commode. Every one of the other lieutenants who ever spoke to Taquard about OERs was without exception a water walker and was expecting their turds to be bronzed any time now. MacArthur himself was not worthy of washing the underwear of these lieutenants. Every lieutenant except Taquard was holier than the Pope. His one and only OER rated him as above average as opposed to the best that has ever been. This alone would ensure that he would never be promoted to First Lieutenant. Taquard's peer group only consisted of the best there ever was. Superman would be considered mediocre by this group's standards.

Back-stabbing lieutenants surfaced from the first day that Taquard entered the Army. The common misconception was that everything that they did as lieutenants would effect their chances of making General one day. Factually speaking, no one cared what Eisenhower did as a lieutenant.

Excitement filled the air when the battalion commander, LTC Ingel, decided to submit a frocking for one of the lieutenants that would coincide with the general's visit. A frocking leads to a brevet grade. That means wearing a rank above your pay grade and being referred to by the higher rank. Frocking is usually limited to those who have been selected for promotion. With the exception of Taquard, all of the lieutenants were sure that they would be selected for an early promotion. Ingel's next task was to produce a promotable lieutenant. He called in all of the officers who might have legitimate input. Blunt, although not considered to be significant, was also there. He considered the input from the captains. Blunt nominated Taquard.

"Are you out of your fucking mind?" Finch asked.

"Actually, no I'm not," Blunt retorted.

"I've got six lieutenants in that Quonset hut over there who are all more qualified to fill the role of First Lieutenant more than Taquard."

"Taquard's been filling your role during your absences from the office."

"He has not," Finch exclaimed.

"Taquard has fired more rounds than the other six lieutenants combined. I seem to be under the impression that Colonel Ingel wanted other teams on the hill as well."

"Wait! Finch, didn't I tell you to get the other teams on the hill," Ingel said.

"Yes, sir. I was planning a rotation schedule. Taquard's team needs more training especially after the fiasco they performed at Crab Island."

"That was the result of faulty fuses. Taquard called that one correctly," Ingel insisted.

"But the S-3 said that Taquard was at fault," Finch replied.

"Well, he wasn't."

"Don't forget that Taquard is the only second lieutenant who has additional duties at the battalion level," Blunt added.

"He already has recognition at the division level," Coldhammer added. "His safety poster is being distributed throughout the division. The IG has been very impressed with what he's been doing."

"I might add that he named his poster CANERRA after Lieutenant Canerra," Finch protested.

"Canerra is the epitome of a fat fucking slob," Blunt informed the group. "Hell, he even outweighs you. Maybe even your mother."

"All right," Ingel exclaimed. "Taquard's our man. Is there any reason why we shouldn't frock him in front of the other lieutenants?"

"Yeah, I can think of several reasons," Finch stated. "For starters he's the worst performing lieutenant that I've got."

"Are you saying that Russell is better than Taquard?" Blunt asked Finch.

"Yes I am."

"Enough of your bullshit," Coldhammer said to Finch, "Taquard's getting promoted and that's final."

When the colonel provided Taquard with unexpected news of where to be without stating why, Taquard was apprehensive.

"Sir, I'll be in the field that day."

"No you won't. You'll be here."

"Yes, sir. There is an exercise—"

"Your men can go without you. The way I understand it, they can provide any type of fire support necessary without supervision."

The colonel was right and Taquard delegated the management of the exercise to Zimmerman who proved to be extremely capable. The team was so capable that going out to the field with his men would no longer be considered. The frocking of Taquard coincided with the general's visit. The first thing on the general's schedule was to promote Taquard from Second to First Lieutenant. Finch informed Taquard to remove the sew on insignia and to wear pin on. Being promoted by a general is considered to be a big deal in the military. The most that a Second Lieutenant could ever hope for during a tour of duty in Korea was a promotion to First Lieutenant and an ARCOM (Army Commendation Medal). A promotion by a general was an honor that exceeded everyone's expectations. Taquard remembered when another Air Force General (Major General Ford) presented his dad with the Silver Star. He wound up being in the paper, the news, and a book about Viet Nam along with his dad as a result. He remembered getting dressed that morning for an event that he wasn't aware of; now, as then, he wished that he dressed better. This time he would dress better.

The promotion was set at 1300 hours on 3 August 1983. Taquard bought a new pair of jump boots and had his fatigues pressed. While the rest of the Army was wearing BDUs (Battle Dress Uniform), Second Division was still wearing fatigues and pile caps. He kept the jump boots hidden from ajossie. Ajossie always had a habit of ruining everything that he touched. He would polish boots with a furniture polish lacquer that would ruin them indefinitely.

Later on people would look at the pictures of the ceremony and ask why everyone, with the exception of Taquard, was sweating so badly. August was one hot and humid time in Korea, especially in a room without air conditioning. Between 1100 and 1300 hours, Taquard took not one but two showers. In both cases he rinsed off in cold water. This was how he managed to avoid profuse sweating. In the pictures, he was the only person who wasn't sweating. He didn't lookout of place, everyone else did. Even the general was sweating. This was a big deal because most people have never seen a sweating general.

During the promotion ceremony the general instructed Taquard that he was now ready to take on bigger and better responsibilities. He made Taquard feel as though 3 August was created just for him. It was the greatest promotion that a First Lieutenant could ever imagine. Taquard would never see another promotion ceremony that could match it. Many people were present due to the general himself presiding over the ceremony, but Taquard felt special just the same. When he was asked to give a speech, all that he could come up wit was, "I really appreciate this promotion. Thank you for coming." Everyone stood in line waiting their turn to shake his hand. It was a memorable event soon to be followed by an even more memorable one. Blunt was the last person in line to shake Taquard's hand.

"Elwood, you really deserve this. By the way you have SDO duty tonight."

Other promotion ceremonies which were much more formal and entailed a lot more pomp and circumstance could never match this one. This was the first promotion ceremony that he had ever attended. It was also the best. Although promotions are supposed to be a surprise, recipients are alerted when someone informs them not to wear sew on insignia the next day. Another leak occurs when a person is told that he doesn't have to do PT the next day. A promotion to Captain is far greater than an officer's initial promotion. The term Captain is far more eloquent than Lieutenant. While Lieutenant means one who can act in place of his superiors, Captain meant commander. Colonel's loved giving promotion speeches to captains. Captain seems to bring out the best in a man while he is still young.

"In a literary sense Captain brings to mind many things. When we think of Captain we think of Captain Blood, or Captains Courageous, or a Captain of Industry, or a Captain of a ship. These literary connotations are not shared by the grade of Lieutenant. Even when we think of Major we think of major screw up. Lieutenant Colonel has the word lieutenant in it and we all know what that means."

Promotions to Captain usually included a cake with the inscribed

"Happiness is making Captain." Somehow the grade of Captain had a lot of niceties that the others didn't have or couldn't hold. "Happiness is making Major," just doesn't have the same ring to it.

The SDO tour was upgraded. As a First Lieutenant, he now had a jeep and a driver. The usual SDO tour went from 1700 hours to 0800 hours the following morning. The required tasks made sleeping virtually impossible. This duty began at 1400 hours and required his attendance at a Hail and Farewell party. The party began at 1800, but Taquard didn't arrive until 1845. Upon his arrival he noticed that the new lieutenants to be initiated were still outside being hazed.

"What the f is going on around here? Why hasn't this thing started already?"

"Sir, there's a hold up," Second Lieutenant Watson replied to Taquard. "They're waiting on something. Actually, I think that they are waiting on you."

"Me? I'm not even sure that I have time for this. I still have a lot of other areas to inspect."

Taquard went in to the Officers Club. Blunt had made arrangements for the function to begin upon Taquard's arrival. He was greeted by a great applause. His portrait was hung above the fireplace. It was a portrait that Taquard had purchased earlier and had in his room. So much for room security and privacy. The surprise was as good as anyone could ever expect. Knowing that it came from Blunt made it all the better.

The introductions would be followed by initiations and the turkey awards. The first turkey award "Aw Shucks," went to Taquard. CPT Alston nominated him by raising the portrait and saying that a picture is worth a thousand words. It was the end of a fine day. The day was his and everything seemed to revolve around Taquard. Blunt made sure of it.

Within a few days Taquard rejoined his team in the field. Only this time, the brown insignia on his helmet was black. Zimmerman did a superb job supervising the exercise. Taquard did very little and enjoyed the field. Field duty was avoided by most but it didn't have the politics of garrison. Garrison was by design an enjoyable place of duty but people insisted on screwing it up. Dipshits seemed to live and breathe by the philosophy that things had to be miserable and that people were put on this planet to screw things up.

Garrison would be great if people minded their own business and refrained from screwing their colleagues. The FIST Chief office managed to stay occupied for over four months without a single field exercise and without firing a single shot. The six chiefs managed to successfully get under each others skin.

While Taquard was out in the field garrison life was shaken up a little by an unexpected episode. One of the soldiers decided to slice one of the KATUSA's neck, not once, but twice. By some form of nothing shy of a miracle, the PA (physician's assistant) managed to save the victim's life. It was a long shot but the doctor came through with flying colors. Never before or since would Taquard meet a PA that could measure up to CW2 Graves.

The culprit actually admitted to the throat slashing while showing no signs of remorse whatsoever. He did admit that this was simply a case of mistaken identity. It was late at night and dark outside and he mistook the Korean for CPT Blues who didn't look anything like an Oriental. He promised not to do it again; promised no to get the wrong person again that is. He informed the investigators that the next time he would get the right person, CPT Blues. The soldier remained in custody in D cell. D stood for detention. They wanted to ensure that there wasn't going to be a next time.

The soldier who attempted to kill CPT Blues expressed some slight remorse for getting the wrong man. He felt ashamed of the fact that he couldn't even kill a KATUSA. Having the attempted murderer locked up in D cell, made Blues feel a little better. Blunt tried to cheer up Blues up while he was at the bar drinking. He was sipping Southern Comfort on ice.

"Don't worry, Blues, I'm sure that most of your men would never attempt to kill you in the dark. But then again, if your men can't tell the difference between you and a KATUSA there's no telling what they're liable to do."

"Shit, they'll probably go for my XO first."

"He's probably telling them how they can get to you. With you out of the way, he'll be in command."

Blunt always had a way of bringing out the best in everything. It was no secret that 1LT Dick, like most lieutenants, would do anything to unseat his boss in the command billet. XOs correctly surmised that they would replace their bosses in the event that they screwed up or were taken out of action. Dick was especially dangerous because his level of stupidity well above average as well as his assessment of acceptable risks. He, along with Finch, was previously an FSO and he, like Finch, missed two alerts in the previous six months. He was the most hated officer in the battalion. Finch was a close second.

Blues informed Blunt that Dick would not ever get a command billet even if he needed a replacement.

"You may be correct, but Dick don't know that. There's no telling how much money he'd be willing to put up to have you bumped off," Blunt replied.

"Well, if it's all the same to you, let's talk about something else. Who do you think is favored to win the next Super Bowl?"

"You may not live long enough to see the next Super Bowl," Blunt responded.

"We have an ARTEP coming up," Blues reminded Blunt.

"The field is the ideal place to waste someone. They could cut your throat in the middle of the night and bury you somewhere. With all the movements and all you wouldn't even be missed until the ARTEP was over. And even then they wouldn't know where to begin looking for your body."

"Don't you have something else that you should be doing?"

"Don't worry. I won't give Dick any ideas. Maybe if they burnt your tent down while you were sleeping in it. It wouldn't be the first time that's happened. With all the accidents that we have in the field, who would notice?"

"Why don't you shut your big mouth? Why don't you go to your room and watch Wayne and Schuster or something?"

"Oh, do you want to leave me your TV in your will?" Blunt asked Blues.

"No. Besides nobody is going to kill anyone," Blues answered.

"Your battery is full of nobodies."

In spite of making light of the situation, every officer in the battalion was uneasy and knew that he could be the next target. Even though the culprit was apprehended and in D cell, officers were worried and took precautions. They were so paranoid that they never traveled alone.

Taquard applied for a six month extension. Korea was an assignment with mixed emotions. It was terrible, but it was also good. Normally appointments had to be made in order to see Colonel Ingel, but Taquard was called in. Colonel Ingel insisted on discussing the matter before approving an officer's request for extension.

"Lieutenant Taquard, about this request for extension."

"Yes, sir."

"Are you sure you want to do it?"

"Not 100%. I was considering it."

"I'll sign it if you want me to, but I'm not so sure that you ought to extend. However, I can't blame you for wanting to either. Your new orders leave a lot to be desired."

"Orders? Sir?"

"Yes, you're being sent to Hawaii."

"Hawaii?"

"Yes. I thought that was the reason for your request."

"No, sir. I didn't know anything about that. Actually, Hawaii sounds pretty good."

"I figured that maybe Blunt gave you a heads up on your new assignment. Anyway, I'm sorry about your assignment. It may as well have been Bumfuck, Egypt."

"But, sir, I thought that Hawaii was a choice assignment. I've never been to Hawaii before."

"Believe me, you don't want to go there. You won't like it. It's good for you to transfer to as many places as possible while you are a lieutenant. It's too early for you to start homesteading. It is my policy for me to discuss extensions with the officers before I approve them. Sometimes a little consideration will make all the difference in the world. I assume, since you now have orders taking you to Hawaii, that you don't want the extension."

"Yes, sir. Hawaii it is."

"Anyway, the orders just came in, Blunt can give you a copy."

Little did Taquard know how right Ingel was. Hawaii was considered an overseas assignment even though it operated like stateside. Overseas assignments tended to have the advantage of not operating in a stateside idiosyncrasy. There was a lot less bureaucracy in overseas assignments. Stateside units had a way of making the probable nearly impossible.

Taquard saw Blunt, picked up his orders and was now a short timer who was beyond the halfway point of his tour. For the first six months of a one year Army tour soldiers are not expected to know their jobs very well because they are newcomers. For the last six months they are not expected to do their jobs well because they were short. This was the basic consensus that didn't apply to Korea. Nevertheless, he was a proud short timer who was counting down the days until he would be going to Hawaii. News about his new assignment traveled like wildfire. While performing SDO duties in the ville, bar girls would run up to him and ask him about his new assignment to Hawaii. Usually, the bar girls knew about something before the GIs did. They even got their information before the Army Times. Usually their information was accurate. It was not uncommon for a soldier to find out about an assignment through a food vender who used a set of orders to serve greasy food in. In Korea, orders rolled up in a funnel shape were used for serving food in. It never ceased to amaze anyone how Korean food vendors managed to get stacks of orders before the GI did.

September was a challenging month because that was when the ARTEP (Army Training Evaluation Program) was scheduled. The IG inspection was scheduled in December. In August there were still high hopes that the ARTEP would be forfeited because the expired armistice was yet to be renewed. An ARTEP under the circumstances seemed like a goofy thing to do. It soon became apparent in the early part of August that the ARTEP would go on as planned. Armistice or no armistice, the ARTEP was going to be conducted as scheduled. That meant that the battalion would be deploying at the end of the month in preparation for the ARTEP. A rear detachment command was yet to be established. As the end of August approached, speculation of who was going to be the rear detachment commander ran rampant. One thing that was for sure, no one wanted that job for anything. There was a boatload of responsibility involved with too many opportunities for failure with that position. Even without the battalion, there was a tremendous of work to be done while maintaining accountability. New arrivals had to be processed, departures would have to be conducted in accordance with an established schedule, construction was in progress, and emergencies were constantly arising without notice. Many attachments were not ARTEP deployable. This included physician's assistants, dentists, weathermen, the chaplain, and others who were not line officers. Only line officers could be given command billets. The command of Camp Pelham was in question during August. Volunteers were nonexistent. Whoever had that position would be filling in for LTC Ingel. That job was difficult enough as it was for a lieutenant colonel; it would be far more difficult for a lower ranking officer. Failing at this task would be a career-ender. The only thing that the officers of 2/17th FA BN agreed upon was that nobody wanted this job.

Blunt, who was ARTEP deployable, addressed the issue with Taquard.

"I think it's going to be you," Blunt said to Taquard.

"Oh no! There are captains around. You can't tell me that he would chance this level of responsibility with a lieutenant," Taquard replied.

"Yeah, but I think you'll be the one who get it," Blunt responded.

"How do you propose to run a successful ARTEP without a high level of quality of fire support? You tell me, how?"

"Your team's going out to the field for the ARTEP, not you. From what I've heard, they can manage without you."

"We've got a bunch of lieutenants running around...."

"But you're a First Lieutenant and around here that means a lot. No one considers you a FIST Chief anymore. There's no way that you're going to get out of this one."

"They don't need Finch. My team can function better without him."

"It was already offered to Finch. He turned it down."

"How could he turn it down? Is he going out to the field?"

"He's taking leave."

"How can you take leave at a time like this?"

"The colonel approved it."

"But at a time like this, leave can be cancelled."

"Yes, but the colonel decided not to cancel it. He requested that he cancel his leave voluntarily and take leave at another time. Finch refused."

"But this is bigger than anything that he has going on back at home."

"I didn't say that he was going home. He's staying here."

"On leave?"

"Yes, that's correct."

"Major Winthorpe, yeah, Major Winthorpe."

"He's a dentist."

"But he's a major."

"Only line officers can assume command. That means no doctors, lawyers, dentists, chaplains, or veterinarians. No soft corps officers."

"There's got to be another captain around here somewhere. Wait a minute, Captain Norris, he's a line officer."

"He was already offered it and already turned it down."

"Maybe the old man can force someone to take it."

"I don't think he will. He wants somebody who he can trust. Someone who is willing to try."

As a First Lieutenant he felt a lot of difference in the level of responsibility that he was assuming. The first balloons were King of the Hill in the Lieutenant Quarters, but the potential weight of responsibility was starting to have an affect on Taquard. As the end of August was fast approaching everyone was still wondering who the Rear Detachment Commander was going to be. It was still a mystery on the day of the battalion departure to the field. That afternoon the battalion was loaded up and staged for departure. No news was good news for Taquard. He was all stressed out and was nervous for nothing. As it was, the colonel had a solution all along and it didn't even affect Taquard. Actually, he couldn't've asked for a better deal. He wasn't in charge and he wasn't going to the field. The only thing left to do was to sit back and relax. As late afternoon approached, Taquard noticed that the battalion convoy hadn't moved. He was anxious for them to get out of the area o that he could sit in the shade and drink lemonade. He could spend the next few weeks sleeping in every morning and not doing anything that he didn't feel like doing. Also, he could spend as many nights off post as he wanted. He could travel to Seoul during duty hours and nobody would be the wiser. He had no function and no responsibilities whatsoever. The battalion didn't move. While he waited with anticipation, the battalion just remained in place. It was 1440 and the battalion was just sitting there doing nothing. The battalion was over an hour behind schedule. The original departure time was 1300 hours. Taquard paced the entrance parking lot while constantly checking his watch. He knew that he couldn't begin goofing off until after the battalion was out of sight.

Blunt approached Taquard with the usual bad news look on his face.

"Hey, John," Taquard said, "When's the battalion going to leave? They're burning daylight. They need to be leaving real soon. I've been to those firing points before. First you have to find them, then you have to decide where to emplace the weapon systems, then you have to emplace them, then you have to coordinate the supply runs. They need to stop hanging around here and get going."

"The colonel wants to see you."

"Wait a minute there..."

"Right now."

As Taquard approached the colonel's office with anxiety and nervousness he was hoping that whatever the colonel wanted that it didn't have anything to do with being a rear detachment commander. What ever was going on, at least he could find out when the battalion was going to leave. Maybe he could do something to get them on their way. The thought of being a rear detachment commander of a battalion while also being the installation commander was a lot to expect from a lieutenant. He was able to convince himself that whatever the colonel wanted it had nothing to do with being in charge. Taquard reported to the colonel in a professional manner.

"Sir, Lieutenant Taquard reporting as ordered, sir."

"Would you take my place while I'm gone?"

A lot went through Taquard's mind between the time that the colonel asked him that question and the time he answered. He remembered what the general said to him about being ready to take on bigger and better responsibilities. A simultaneous battalion and installation command would definitely qualify as a bigger and better responsibility. Other thoughts with the same theme also went through his mind. Thoughts like never turn down a combat assignment, faint heart never won fair maiden, and the possibility that this could be a test. What else could his answer be?

"Yes, sir."

"Good, I don't know what I would've done if you said no. Report to the XO."

This answered his question as to why the battalion hadn't departed. He walked to Major Coldhammer's office. The door was ajar and before Taquard was in the office Coldhammer saw him.

"Well, it's about fucking time. You're in charge. Don't fuck up. Crow!"

Coldhammer grabbed his helmet and rushed out the door. His driver, Crow, followed. In a split instant Taquard found himself alone among junior officers, NCOs, and in command of both the battalion and the installation. He went from being a FIST Chief to being a commander in a flash. It was that quick. As a cadet he would ask questions about battalion level actions and responsibilities. The instructors always told him not to worry about it since he was so far away from that possibility. The truth was that the instructors themselves didn't know the answers. The noise of departing vehicles was quickly replaced by an eerie silence. The quiet was disturbing. The challenge was to figure out what he needed to do to ensure that everything remained in order. "Don't fuck up," seemed a little vague. However, it didn't rule out any excursions to Seoul. It also didn't rule out sleeping in whenever he felt like.

Coldhammer stuck his head back in the office.

"You are not to go to your room. You will sleep on the Sergeant Major's couch. Sergeant Humphries will be your Sergeant Major. You will pull staff duty every day and night. You will account for all vehicles and equipment that is left behind. You will inventory all vehicles as soon as we leave. You will hold a battalion formation to determine how many people you have left. You will maintain accountability of all of your people. Don't let anyone fuck with anything. You have to be mean in this job. There's still room in D cell if you need it. Use it if you have to. Don't even hesitate. You're no good to anyone if you let these bastards slide. If any of these enlisted fucks tries to give you any shit remember that you are a Lieutenant and a Lieutenant outranks the Sergeant Major of the Army. Be ruthless if you have to, but don't let these bastards walk on you. Your job is not to take care of your men. Their job is to serve you."

As Coldhammer departed he turned back to Taquard.

"The colonel appreciates you taking on this responsibility. You've got his full support and mine too. You're in charge not Finch."

Though he had been stationed at Camp Pelham for nearly nine months, it suddenly seemed like a different place. He was now the battalion commander of what was left after the main body departed for ARTEP preparation. Most of the soldiers who were left behind were approaching the end of their tour. Out processing consisted of delivering them to the Turtle Farm at Camp Casey once the PAC (Personnel Administrative Center) confirmed a departure window.

Taquard sat down at Blunt's desk and quietly jotted down a "to do" list. All he had to do was ask himself what Coldhammer would do in this situation. Challenges would be much greater for Taquard for the simple fact that he had neither experience nor authority. His opposition had much more experience as they far outnumbered him. At age twenty-four he was in charge of hundreds of people, many who were nearly twice his age. The mean age of Camp Pelham's rear detachment was twenty-five. He wasn't even average, yet he was in charge. He hadn't even hit his two year mark in the Army while others were in their final re-enlistment to hit twenty. Age-wise he was below average and service wise he was way below average. This was anything but a textbook scenario as the circumstances defied logic. In addition to the soldiers that he had to account for, the position also included about 500 Korean civilian employees. He also had control of the town of Sun Yu Ri because its lifeline was Camp Pelham. All of the other installations and sites in the immediate vicinity came under the management of Camp Pelham. That meant that he was also in charge of Camp Giant, RC4 (Recreational Area), a warehouse annex, a communications relay site, and an Air Defense Artillery (ADA) installation. Camp Pelham was the biggest camp in the area. Camp Giant was 23.9 acres in area, but it housed only one Field Artillery firing battery. It also had a PX (Post Exchange) and a barber shop. RC4 had a building where a person could do arts and crafts, a gym, a theatre, a class six store, a barber shop, a PX, and a library.

The task at hand was to in process new arrivals and out process those who were at the end of their tour. First he had to inventory the property, equipment, and vehicles. He also had to find out where everything was supposed to be. With all the writing that he was producing he was in dire of some notebooks. He had to establish accountability of information as well as physical items. He went to the Camp Pelham PX to stock up on writing supplies that he would certainly need.

Upon his arrival to the PX he noticed a crowd of soldiers waiting outside. He made his way to the front of the crowd to find a Korean civilian ajossie locking the entrance. It was exactly 1600 hours, but the sign posted on the door said that the PX was scheduled to close at 1700 hours.

"Hey ajossie! What the hell do you think you are doing?" Taquard asked.

"We closing store now," ajossie answered.

"Why? It's not supposed to close for another hour."

"Today we close early. Unit go to field."

"That doesn't make any difference; you're not supposed to close until 1700."

"Orders from new commander. He say we close early. We get new commander today."

"Who gave you those orders?"

"New commander. Old commander go to field today."

"Give me a name."

"No name, he just new commander. Now you get out of the way from here you fuckhead."

"You lying sack of shit! Get your lazy ass back to work, you lying son of a bitch. I am the new commander. If you don't open this place back up I will fire you."

There was a large applause from the crowd of soldiers as the PX was reopening. He encountered and won his first challenge. He hadn't been in command for ninety minutes and already the people where testing him. He knew that he was going to have to be aggressive and make some changes. When he left the PX he fired all of the Korean guards and replaced them with Americans. The American guard mount consisted of having two guards at each post instead of one. In addition to having

239

weapons and ammunition they had a radio. Instead of shotguns, the guards had M-16s. A roving supervisor was established even though it was acceptable for one of the guards to sleep at his post while the other one was still awake. A guard was even allowed to relieve himself if he needed to. It was a guard mount with a new twist. This was easy and easy to implement.

A few other officers remained on post with Taquard; they were either soft corps officers or second lieutenants. With so few officers left on post, Taquard closed the Officers Club, besides the NCO Club was closer to the office.

"Why did you close down the club?" one of the officers asked. "Why do we need to eat with enlisted men?"

"We don't need our own club. Besides, what's good enough for the enlisted men is good enough for us."

"Actually, I don't agree. We shouldn't be eating with them."

The rest of the evening was devoted to inspecting the area and ensuring that everything was secure. The new Sergeant Major was a recruited a few hours ago. Together they worked to synchronize the management of Camp Pelham. By midnight, they didn't know who the new battery commanders were. Taquard went to each battery and called for an alert. Units held formations while Taquard assessed accountability. Unit commanders were identified. This was probably the only place in the US Army where NCOs were battery commanders. The problem was that all five batteries had less than 100% accountability in their units.

Taquard called for a morning meeting at 0830 hours.

Between the unit alerts and the scheduled meeting Korean Air Lines flight KAL 007, a passenger Boeing 747, was shot down by a Soviet Flagon jet interceptor while flying through Soviet air space on 1 September 1983. KAL 902 was shot down a few years earlier while flying through Soviet air space in 1978. KAL 007 was shot down just west of Sakhalin Island. All 269 passengers and crew were killed. There were no survivors. One of the passengers aboard the flight was US Congressman Dr. Larry McDonald who was the second and current president of the John Birch Society (JBS). Taquard remembered flying the same route several months earlier on Northwest Orient. When the crew informed the passengers that there were in Russia he wondered if a violation was taking place. Now he knew.

With the amount of defecting Russians that was taking place it was hard to fathom why any one would want to go there willingly. He remembered meeting Sergei Kourdakov in October of 1972. He informed him about the plight of Russia and what the people had to endure. As a Naval officer, he was able to defect by jumping ship around 10:00 PM on 3 September 1971. He arrived on the pacific side of Queen Charlotte Island on 4 September 1971. Thirteen months later, he would meet Taquard. He was an extremely interesting person who explained his flight in great detain to Taquard. His motivation was founded on his recent conversion to Christianity. He also predicted his murder and stated that it would be made to look like an accident. On 1 January 1973 he was murdered. The media carried out this story internationally and reported his death was the result of suicide.

He hadn't even been on duty for twenty-four hours and already he was facing problems that were considered significant. The Koreans could start World War III over the downing of KAL 007. There was no telling what the ajossies would do. Nothing was beyond consideration regardless of how ignorant it was.

Everything was happening extremely fast. Changes were rapid. Fortunately, orders were being carried out. Everyone who was scheduled to arrive at Camp Pelham arrived. Everyone who was scheduled to leave Camp Pelham was involuntarily extended for an unspecified amount of time. If a war were to break out, all of the occupants of Camp Pelham would be right in the middle of it. They needed every swinging Richard that they could get. The bus that arrived at Camp Pelham full of turtles departed empty.

The morning meeting took place in the battalion conference room. Taquard sat in LTC Ingel's place. He assumed command and acted as if he had been in command for a while. His mannerisms surprised everyone including himself.

"As you probably know by we have a situation on our hands and we also have a lot to accomplish in a short period of time. This is a color coded map of the installation. Each code designates areas of responsibility. Find out how many vehicles the batteries left behind. I need to know the vehicle type, model, vehicle identification number, and where it is at. You need to know who is unaccounted for. We're going to continue these midnight alerts until we find out where everyone is. You have heard about the airliner getting shot down. Everyone stays. Nobody leaves. If a war breaks out we're going to be in it. Harden the bunkers in your area. If we fight it out it will be infantry style. That means hand to hand combat. We don't have a lot of time. Inform your men that they're restricted to post except for official business. Everything off post is off-limits. Check your arms rooms; I need to know how many weapons we have. I'll be holding a battalion formation at the entrance parking lot at 1700 hours. I'll need your information by then."

"We've got men out on pass," one of the sergeants reported.

"No passes. Recall them back at once."

"What about leave?"

"No leaves. Anyone who is about to go on leave now has his leave cancelled. Rotate your men to the dental clinic. There's hardly anybody there and everyone can get their teeth fixed."

"If we get involved in a fight between North and South Korea we won't live long enough to enjoy our fixed teeth," another sergeant stated. "By the way, what are our chances?"

"I'd say that our chances are pretty good. Prepare for the worst."

The meeting was concluded. He thought about the airliner and surmised that it was some dumb ajossie taking a shortcut. He made out a checklist to follow. He looked at the Sergeant Major's couch and realized that he hadn't slept in it. He also realized that he needed a shower, a shave, and a haircut. He needed a clean uniform as well. He was too busy to burn up time at the barber shop. The phone was constantly ringing and all the calls were for him and there was always some crises that he had to address. However, as installation commander he also had the authority to make modifications. If he couldn't go to the barber shop, then the barber shop could come to him. Three Korean female barbers came to his office and gave him a haircut and a massage. The Korean barbers knew how to cut hair and how to give a shave. They used straight razors in 1983. They would massage the face with hot towels and apply shaving cream with a boar brush then use hot wet shaving towels again. When they were finished shaving, you didn't need a shave for the next three days. They gave the closest shaves possible. After his shave, haircut, and back massage he had his lunch delivered to his office as well. It wasn't that he was being lazy or decided to push the ends of the envelope as to his realm of authority; he just didn't have time to get away. He was able to have an early lunch delivered to his office. Also, he was able to place a PX order telephonically and have it delivered to his office. He took a break at 1100 hours and went to his quarters to take a shower and change into a clean uniform. He was back in the office by 1125. Blunt's secretary was now Taquard's secretary. He gave her the week off, but she came to work anyway. Blunt was known as "Number 10 GI" by the Korean locals. Ten in this case meant the worst. Miss P was glad to have Taquard as a supervisor instead of Blunt. Taquard was also "Number 10 GI," but not to everybody. Some of the Koreans actually thought of him as number hana with was the opposite of being the worst. One thing that was certain was that no one gave a crap about what the Koreans thought.

At 1700 hours Taquard addressed the battalion formation.

"It is possible that a war could break out. If it does, most of us will probably not make it out. Our purpose is to stay alive as long as possible. Think about that while you are preparing the bunkers. Think about it always. Our lives depend on your performance and preparation. Get right with God. Call your families back at home, collect, if you get a chance. Anybody who runs after the fighting begins will be shot. Cowardice will not be tolerated. This is not Third Army."

The formation was short but it was long enough to drive the point home. The command meeting that followed consisted of answering questions that were posed earlier that day and the issuing of additional directives. "I was checking out the bunkers earlier today. Some haven't been touched since MacArthur was here. We need to fill the sandbags with gravel instead of dirt. No telling what high powered weapons we will be faced with. Sandbags must be at least six deep."

"Six deep?" one of the NCO battery commanders questioned.

"Yes, six. At least six. When the shit hits the fan you'll be wishing it was eighteen," Taquard replied.

"Look I hate to bring up a sore point but some of these GIs have families here. What are we going to do with them?"

"I'm not sure. Maybe we could start rotating them to the airport and send them back to the US. Maybe we could use unoccupied barracks."

Though it was highly unauthorized, many soldiers brought their families to Korea on unaccompanied tours. Many other GIs produced families while they were in their tour. In such cases, the dependents lived off post but near by. It was stupid to ignore families, even during a crisis. He considered using unit funds to finance flights back home on commercial airliners. However, in spite of the arm twisting and harassment that went on in the units to force soldiers to part with their money, there was no money left. The worst form acceptable theft occurred stateside and was that of the US Field Artillery Association. Officers who didn't join were threatened with derogatory OERs, shithole assignments, restriction, cancelled leave, and everything else shy of death. When you refused to join, the command took it personally and played hardball. When someone did join all they got was a promise that they would get a monthly magazine. Usually, they wouldn't deliver on that promise. The magazine, when it did arrive, was nothing more than worthless tripe. It wasn't even good enough to wipe your as with.

The problem was that the soldiers didn't have any money as a result of the Army always stealing it from them. They weren't making that much money to begin with. The problem of having money taken away from you decreased as one rose through the ranks. A new private would have to pay off his Sergeant in order to have a special request, such as leave, granted. He would also have to pay off the First Sergeant to secure his approval. Stateside units were the worst for stealing money from their soldiers. Many times a First Sergeant would threaten his men with restriction if he didn't get a pay off. One popular ploy was to walk into the barracks and claim that he left a specified amount of money on the desk in the CQ (Charge of Quarters) office (also located in the barracks building). He would also claim that the money, his money was missing. He would accuse one of the GIs of taking it, but didn't know exactly which GI actually took the money. He would deliver an ultimatum to the troops and give them time to come up with the money or else the innocent would be punished along with the guilty and be given extra duty while being on restriction. He would inform them that he would be back in 15 minutes and that the money had better be back on his desk or else. Even full bird colonels participated in ploys to extract money from their own soldiers.

Pay day was open house at Camp Pelham. The payroll officer would arrive at the orderly room with the money and two armed guards. In 1983 payroll officers would carry the entire battalion payroll in cash. This was a monthly payroll as the option to be paid every other week was not available. Direct deposit was a relatively new concept at this time. Soldiers who received their pay checks through the unit would wait in line in front of the orderly room to cash their checks. After cashing their checks they went through the gauntlet of people trying to hustle and swindle the soldier out of his money. Mamasan was always in line to collect on her hooker tab that the GIs would run up. Bars had their pick up men waiting for the GI as well. Unit officials were there asking for donations for fund raisers. Many soldiers were out of money before they could even clear the gauntlet and resumed going back on credit again.

As the battalion commander he consolidated the battalion payroll activities at one location instead of five. Some of the NCOs correctly guessed that Taquard was a Jew when he prohibited fund raising solicitation to occur on any day during the week that a pay day fell inside of. He made a lot of noticeable changes as the commander. Also, Koreans who didn't work on post, or who were fired, were not allowed on post, period. That meant that there were no mamasans, no bartenders, no hookers, and no one there to form a swindler's gauntlet at the soldier's expense. A soldier got paid and left the orderly room without being harassed or hustled.

For the first time since the 1976 hatchet murders, Camp Pelham closed the front gate of the post. Koreans were up against the chain link fence protesting. Hundreds of Koreans protested loudly as they demanded to see the new commander. Not only were Koreans not allowed on post, they couldn't hang around the orderly room on pay day. To make matters worst, the soldiers weren't allowed to go to the Korean businesses. All of the soldiers were put on restriction. That meant that all of the businesses in Sun Yu Ri were without any customers. Protesting began less than 24 hours after Taquard was in command.

"We need money so that the soldiers will have the option of sending their families back to the states," Taquard reminded the group.

"Did you know that there are a lot of Koreans at the front gate protesting?" one of the NCOs asked.

"Yes. We have to break off contact with the Koreans. We have to bring our accountability levels to 100%. That means that no one leaves post unless it's on official business. Everyone is on restriction and everything is off-limits."

"Your speech basically destroyed the morale of the soldiers."

"What little they had left," another NCO added.

"Get those bunkers ready. We're all in this together."

Ammunition status reports were consolidated. All supply classes were inventoried and recorded. He knew the location, condition, and amount of every class. Each item had people assigned to it. Responsibility was delegated as required. The perimeter guards were given an allocated amount of specified equipment and additional ammo. In addition to their M-16s, they also had two grenades and one white phosphorous (Willie Pete) grenade per guard. This accountability was reported a well.

Taquard posted a detailed poster in the meeting room addressing supply classes and to ensure that everyone knew what they were doing. It illustrated the following information:

**CLASS I: Subsistence**
A: Nonperishable
C: Combat Rations
R: Refrigerated
S: Other Non-refrigerated
W: Water
e.g.: Rations/Milk

## CLASS II: Individual Equipment, Clothing, Tools, Administration Supplies

A: Air
B: Ground Support Material
E: General Supplies
F: Clothing
G: Electronics
M: Weapons
T: Industrial Supplies
e.g.: Boots, Tents, Machine Guns

## CLASS III: POL: Petroleum, Oil, and Lubricants

A: POL for Aircraft
W: POL for Surface Vehicles
P: Packaged POL
e.g.: Gas, Oil

## CLASS IV: Construction Materials

A: Construction
B: Barrier
e.g.: Cement, Barbed Wire

## CLASS V: Ammunition

A: Air Delivery
B: Ground
e.g.: Bullets, Grenades

## CLASS VI: Personal Demand Items

e.g.: Soap, Toothpaste, Whiskey

## CLASS VII: Major End Items: Racks, Pylons, Tracked Vehicles, etc.

A: Air
B: Ground Support Material
D: Administration Vehicles

G: Electronics
J: Racks, Adaptors, Pylons
K: Tactical Vehicles
L: Missiles
M: WeaponsN: Special Weapons
X: Aircraft Engines
e.g.: Trucks, Helicopters

## CLASS VIII: Medical Supplies, Medical Materials
A: Medical Material
B: Blood/Fluids
e.g.: Litters, Syringes

## CLASS IX: Repair Parts
A: Air
B: Ground Support Material
D: Administration Vehicles
G: Electronics
J: Racks, Adaptors, Pylons
K: Tactical Vehicles
L: Missiles
M: Weapons
N: Special Weapons
T: Industrial Material
X: Aircraft Engines
e.g.: Engines, Batteries

## CLASS X: Material for Non-Military Programs
e.g.: Tractors, Seeds

## CLASS XI: Waste, Rubbish, and Water
A: Waste/Trash
B: Salvaged Items
W: Recycled Water

Taquard adjourned the meeting.

"Go get something to eat, I'll see you tomorrow. HHB will be alerted at 0200."

"Wait a minute," Swackhammer protested. "Two in the morning is pure harassment."

"Now listen to me and listen to me good, you good-for-nothing son of a bitch. You are now in a command billet by virtue of date of rank. You can still be replaced. You don't work for Finch any more. I don't work for Finch any more. You have lied like hell and have gotten away with it. You are not getting away with any thing else again. You will not get away with your insubordination. Now get the fuck out of here and unfuck your attitude, mister."

Taquard also reminded him that he still had three people missing and that he had better find them.

"Sir, couldn't you let the men go out for just a night? What would it hurt?" another NCO asked Taquard.

"No I said."

"Well, some of the other NCOs may try to let them out anyway. How would you be able to stop something like that?"

"I've got the MPs patrolling the ville."

"What if Captain Finch were to come back?" Swackhammer asked.

"That would be great except for one thing."

"What's that?"

"He's not allowed to set foot on Camp Pelham until Colonel Ingel gets back."

"But suppose he did?"

"Then I guess we'd have two people in D cell instead of one."

Taquard began opening bags of toy soldiers and spilling them out on the table. There was a bag of dark green soldiers; another had a light shade of green. There was even a bag of cowboys and Indians. The cowboys were brown and the Indians were yellow. Another bag contained white plastic figures who were not cowboys, Indians, or even soldiers. They were space men.

Taquard said, "Everybody get something to eat and get some rest, we have a long day tomorrow. Swackhammer, is Finch on post?"

"Not that I am aware of, sir."

"He is under strict orders and he knows it. I thought I saw him going to his barracks."

"I'm sure that he's not on post then."

"But if you do see him then I am sure that you will inform me at once."

"Yes, sir."

"I'm fortunate to have such cooperative people working for me. Too bad not every one exercises the level of integrity that they ought to."

He divided up the soldiers and designated what they represented. The dark green soldiers represented HHB; the light green ones stood for Bravo Battery; the cowboys were Alpha Battery; the Indians were Service Battery (AKA Circus Battery), and the white figures were Charlie Battery. A sixth pile of extras was marked with idiot ink and was used to represent the people who were still unaccounted for. Extra unopened bags would be used for the new arrivals. In Ranger school toy soldiers were used to demonstrate where people would be emplaced while securing an objective. The toy soldiers were tagged with the name of the person that was being represented. Tags also indicated who carried what systems such as radios, M60s, and other specialized equipment. Symbols were painted on the figures to signify leadership positions. The patrol leader was represented by the symbol for male while the symbol for female represented the assistant patrol leader. Triangles, squares, and a myriad of other symbols were utilized to pass on information while conserving space. The soldiers used on the sand tables at Ranger school were HO scale and the avenues of approach were lined with gunpowder. It was lit to demonstrate the avenues of approach to be utilized to seize the objective. There were a lot of lessons that were taught in Ranger school that weren't available anywhere else.

Taquard drew an outline of Camp Pelham on several sheets of butcher paper that were taped together. He drew streets, buildings, guard posts, and other significant features. He used some items to represent features as well. There were eight toy canons that came with the soldiers. Those were used to depict the eight howitzers that remained on Camp Pelham and Camp Gant after the battalion departed. Some small boxes represented the guard towers. With the exception of Charlie Battery,

Taquard wanted the guard towers to be manned by two people from different units so that they would get to know each other better. The front gate was secured by the MPs and the engineers.

Then he realized that he didn't have any toy soldiers to represent the ADA Battery. Nor did he have any to represent the medical support element, or the soft corps officers, or the target acquisition battery. He didn't even consider the US civilians that he had in the area, or the Korean employees, or specialized contractors who had a way of arriving and departing whenever they felt like it.

The more that he thought about it, the bigger his command got. It was going to take a lt more than eight bags of toy soldiers to represent what he was responsible for. Taquard ad a lot on his mind and decided to go to the NCO Club to get something to eat.

SFC Swackhammer went to the senior officer's barracks undetected. He met with CPT Finch.

"He's putting everything off-limits. There's no way that I can handle him."

"I guess the bastard's gone nuts," Finch responded.

"Why don't you step in?"

"No, not yet. Let's keep the ace in the hole hidden for now."

"He said that the colonel doesn't want you on post until he gets back."

"Boy, talk about twisting the truth. I told the colonel that I didn't expect to be on post until after he got back."

"That means that you can step in and take over."

"Yeah sure, and then I will have to put up with him after the colonel gets back. I'm still officially on leave and I still want to take care of a few things. If he screws this up I will be rid of him once and for all. I can't jump in too early."

"But he could do a lot of damage. sir, I think you should step in."

"No. That would only provide a temporary solution. You know that a mutiny isn't out of order here."

"Mutiny is illegal."

"Not if it's justified. Are you familiar with the Uniform Code of Military Justice?"

"Vaguely."

"First of all, you need to remember that you are not authorized to obey illegal orders. Second, you can detain anyone who tries to force them upon you."

"Well, he is certainly guilty of that."

"What do the other NCOs think about him?"

"They all want to hang him."

"Put your heads together. Maybe he could have an accident. After all, your very lives depend on whether or not he is eliminated. I don't know about you, but if I were you I'd do something about it. You might be able to come up with a better idea than I can if you put your heads together."

"If you stepped in you could fix things before they got out of hand."

"I thought about that. But that only provides a short term solution that could backfire. His promotion by the general has really helped him out. I can't just jump in, at least not now. This is a sensitive situation that requires timing. If I go in too early I may not be able to fix everything that needs to be fixed. I don't want to tip my hand. Taquard could fall on his ass at a critical time and get us all killed. There is only one solution. Taquard must be killed and it must look like an accident."

"Can you eliminate him?"

"Not at this time. I need to come up with a plan. I need you and the other NCOs to come up with a plan as well. Our lives depend on it. It must be believed by everyone that I am not even here. That will be a great advantage when the time comes. You guys should be able to devise a plan to eliminate him. Didn't you tell me that the other NCOs hate him?"

"Yes they hate him with a passion. Maybe we could poison him. That always works well and they'll never find out who did it."

"Where does he eat?"

"At the NCO Club like everyone else."

"That's perfect. That's a perfect location for a set up. All you have to do is turn all of the other NCOs against him."

"That won't be too hard."

"After he's dead, there'll be so many suspects that it won't even be funny. As the HHB Commander, that would make you the senior ranking person on this post. You would be the new battalion commander. You could assume command and report him AWOL if you can get a couple of NCOs to hide the body."

"We could bury him in one of the bunkers that he's having us build. We're building them six deep and seven feet high. They'll never find him, ever."

"Perfect. Now all you have to do is figure out a way to poison him."

"Yes, and we'll bury him in the rear of the post, not a bunker. He'll smell up a bunker and they'll find him. I'll have a detail dig his grave tonight."

"Tonight?"

"Sure, I'll find a couple of trouble makers and give them the extra detail. It will work out perfectly."

"But what if someone finds the grave?"

"I found some cement near the south end of post. You know the new parking lot that they're building?"

"Yes."

"We'll bury him in a hole at a secluded part of the compound where no one hardly goes. We'll bury him, then we'll cap off the burial site with concrete. Then we'll stencil some Korean writing on the dried up concrete. Nobody will ever look there in a hundred years."

"This could really work."

"It's so simple that it's not even funny."

While Finch and Swackhammer were plotting Taquard's demise, Taquard was at the NCO Club ordering his dinner. He ordered a roast beef sandwich on rye. He sat at a table by himself. While waiting for his order he went to use the latrine. When he returned from using the latrine his order was on the table waiting for him. The only problem was that there was a turd in the sandwich between the slice of bread. The drink was spilled all over the table and replaced with urine.

Taquard went to the manager and placed his order again, take out. He waited in the kitchen to ensure that there were no surprises. The next item on his "to do" list was to re-open the Officers Club.

He returned to Blunt's office and ate his meal. He outlined additional strategies and duties for the next day. Part of his mission was to prepare for an attack. He called home collect and told his family the news and how things were going. After he finished his phone call he went on patrol with the MPs. The ville was uneventful as the clubs had no customers. The alert on HHB went well, but had two shortages.

# Chapter Twelve
## *Current Events: Monday, 5 September 1983*

Retired Brigadier General Sean Taquard taught upper level math courses the previous school year. He was getting bored with retirement and decided to teach as a means of having something to do. He didn't need the money; he had plenty of additional income besides his glamorous retirement package. His house was paid off as was everything else that he had. He had no debts whatsoever. As a result, he decided to teach at the local high school which wasn't too far away. There was a job opening that he was well qualified for and he took it. While he was teaching he was concerned about his son Rodney who was still in school and who was on the basketball team. The concern was that he never got to play in any games. He spoke to the basketball coach about his concern for the situation. The basketball coach told him to stuff it. Taquard pointed out the fact that Rodney never missed a practice; in fact he wasn't even late. Yet he never played in a single game ever, not even for a few minutes. Other players, who played throughout the season smoked, drank, came to practice late, missed practice, and violated many other rules as well. Even though it was officially mandated that such violations would immediately expel a person from the team, exceptions were repeatedly made. He pointed out the fact that Rodney's performance during practice was great and often times surpassed that of the star players. The basketball coach was unmoved and beyond being convinced.

He asked that Rodney be allowed to play in a game, but the basketball coach disagreed and clearly stated that Rodney would never play in a single regardless of any circumstances. To make matters worse, Taquard was assigned the detail of operating the fund raiser sale for the basketball team. As the new teacher at the school he was tasked the detail of running the yard sale. Taquard questioned the duty assignment.

"Why do I have to run the yard sale? I'm not the basketball coach."

"Yeah, but we need someone to do it and that would be you."

"Why can't you do it? After all you're the coach."

"We have a tournament this weekend."

"Got it. What about Rodney?"

"What about him?"

"Does he get to play?"

"I thought I already made it clear to you that he ain't playing no matter what."

"I tried to convince him to quit the team, but he believes that you're going to give him a chance. He's more than proven himself. He actually looks up to you."

"What the fuck? Do those general stars make you go deaf or something? He ain't playing and that's final"

"Larson is playing isn't he?"

"Larson is one of our own. We take care of our own. You are outsiders, thinking that you're so special just because you fought in the Viet Nam war. It was just a war nothing more."

"Larson got busted for marijuana last week."

"He's our star player and therefore he plays. Marijuana or no marijuana, he plays."

"That's against your own policies."

"Policies only apply to outsiders."

"If you're not going to let Rodney play then I'm not going to run your yard sale."

"Oh yes you are, Chief. If you want to keep your job you'll do what you're told or aren't you used to taking orders. Sours is behind me all the way on this one."

"How big is it and where will it be held?"

"It's the biggest yard sale that anyone's ever heard of. One hundred and four items have been donated for sale including two brand new pick up trucks and the Estimeer Cadillac. That's right. The Estimeer donated their famous restored Fleetwood to help us out. The yard sale will take place just beyond the south side of the Industrial Arts building."

"When is it supposed to be?"

"Day after tomorrow. You decide what time."

"Where do we store the items that we don't sell?"

"You will stay there until every last item is sold."

"That could go until next Monday when school starts again."

"Now you're getting the hang of it."

"Who's going to help me out?"

"Nobody. You can do it, you don't need any help. Besides, ain't you supposed to be some kind of a hot shot general or something? Oh, let me give you a nickel's worth of free advice. You might want to look at the inventory between now and then. You'll find everything on the south end lot of the Industrial Arts building. Oh, and by the way, I have scheduled an appointment for you at the local radio station tomorrow after school so that you can tell everybody about your sale. If you don't attract any customers, you'll be out there all weekend."

"Is this yard sale a continuous thing?"

"No, this will be our first. Don't drop the ball on this one. If you mess it up we won't be able to get any more sponsors."

The following afternoon Taquard went to the local radio station. It was extremely casual and the disc jockey was as cordial as ever. The format wasn't even established. Taquard decided to pose as a salesman on the air, the jockey agreed.

"Well, ladies and gentlemen, you are listening to KSCJ, for the best in radio entertainment turn your dial to the Jack, Mad Jack that is, your host. And now let me introduce you to a man who needs no introduction, Crazy Larry, who is about to tell you about the yard sale of the century in support of our very own La Grange Parker High School Rangers. Their basketball team has set up a yard sale like no other yard sale you have ever seen. And to run the yard sale, they have hired a professional, Crazy Larry. One hundred and four lots will be on sale, one hundred and three of which will be brand new. The only used item on the lot is the notorious Estimeer Fleetwood Cadillac. Well Crazy Larry, tell us more about the yard sale."

"That's right Mad Jack we're having us a yard sale. That's right ladies and gentlemen, Crazy Larry here to tell you all about it. Perhaps you remember me from before from the movie *Crazy Mary and Crazy Larry.*"

"Wasn't that *Dirty Mary and Crazy Larry?*"

"Well, I don't know but I'm just plumb crazy enough to run this here yard sale. And remember folks, all the proceeds go directly to the La Grange Parker Cow Pokers basketball team."

"That's Rangers Larry. Wait, didn't Larry die at the end of that movie?"

"Maybe so, but I'm just crazy enough to run the yard sale anyway."

"Well, when the yard sale and what makes it so special?"

"Our sale begins tomorrow morning at the south end of the Industrial Arts building at the high school. Our doors open at 6:30 tomorrow morning."

"But what makes this sale any more special than any other yard sale."

"Our inventory and our prices. Nearly everything is brand new. We have some of the finest benefactors around. For example a couple of dealerships have been so generous as to provide us with a brand new Chevy and Ford pick up truck. This is no joke, our lot includes two brand-new pick up trucks. I have made arrangements to have a representative from the Department of Motor Vehicles on site to handle the tax and title on the spot. Oh, there is some bad news."

"I knew that there was a catch, Crazy Larry."

"Relatives of people who are employed by the Department of Education are not allowed to shop at the yard sale. Also, I have made arrangements to have an IRS member on site as well too. You will have to pay taxes on your merchandise."

"Larry, that doesn't seem like much of a yard sale to me. If I want a new pick up truck I'll just go to the dealer and get it myself."

"But I can beat their prices, guaranteed."

"Okay, Crazy Larry. How much for your brand-new Ford pick-up truck?"

"Well, since it is brand new and just so happens to be the latest model available with all of the options, I will let you have it for one dollar."

"One dollar! You mean to tell me that you are going to let someone have a brand new Ford pick up for a dollar."

"No. With sales tax it will actually come to $1.06."

"A dollar for a pick-up, that's unbelievable."

"I am pricing everything to sell. And don't forget about the new Chevy that is also available. I'm letting it go for a dollar as well."

"Holy moly, walking talking mother of Mary, Peter, and Joseph, I have never heard of a deal like that ever. What else is on the lot and how much is the Estimeer Cadillac going for?"

"Well, Mad Jack, they don't call me Crazy Larry for nothing. And the Estimeer Cadillac is going for…"

"Music please."

"One dollar."

"There must be something else on the lot besides cars."

"There is a Snap-On tool chest filled with tools that would normally sell for around $3,000. I'll let you have it for…"

"Don't tell me a dollar."

"Too high? Oh well, you drive a hard bargain. How about fifty cents?"

"Fifty cents? No complaints here. If you can find a better deal anywhere, tell me about it. Lee Iacocca says that if you can find a better car anywhere, buy it. I'm saying if you can find a better deal anywhere I'll buy it."

"There is some more bad news I'm afraid."

"I knew there would be."

"Only one item per customer, that's all."

"Well, I'm sure that at these prices, you won't have any problem finding 104 customers."

"However, five minutes after making a purchase, you are considered to be a brand new customer."

"So if only one customer shows up, you will be on the lot for almost nine hours if he wants to buy everything."

"Remember, everything goes, it's first come, first served and the doors close when everything is gone."

The day after the broadcast had all of the makings of a feeding frenzy. Even the Parson was present and eager to get access to the sale. Local law enforcement was there to keep the crowd under control. At six in the morning there was a mob of people waiting for Taquard to arrive and open the sale. They couldn't believe the inventory which also included the largest Steinway and Sons grand piano that was produced for production.

Once Taquard announced the beginning of the sale everyone went bonkers. By 7:20 AM, the sale was over. Producing the receipts of the sales took the most time. The sale generated $76.50. Everything was recorded and documented and displayed in a ledger. The following Monday, Taquard turned the paperwork and money over to Principal Sours.

"Seventy-six dollars? You mean to tell me that that's all you got from the yard sale?"

"Pretty impressive, huh? Everything's in the ledger. See for yourself."

"There were two brand-new trucks on the lot not to mention a lot of other things that were worth a heck of a lot more than seventy-six dollars. What's this? You sold a coupon for 100 gallons of premium gasoline for fifty cents. Are you out of your fuckin' mind," red-faced Sours angrily retorted.

"Do you think I charged too much?"

"Charged too much? Are you kidding me?"

"Sir, you got a call on line one, it's Mac Higgins. He sounds upset," his secretary said while interrupting the reprimand.

"All right. Yeah, Mac, what is it?"

"One dollar? Do you want to tell me what in the hell went on at that yard sale of yours? A dollar? Are you out of your fucking mind? Nobody sells a fucking brand new truck for a dollar. That's insane. Insane I tell you."

"Well, Mac, I was just talking about that with the man who was running the sale."

"You're the fucking principal! You tell me what happened."

"I'm getting to the bottom of that right now."

"How in the hell did you manage to get a tax assessor down there? More important, why?"

"Tax assessor? Nobody told me about no tax assessor."

"Let me explain something to you, fuck stick. That vehicle had a sticker price of $37,000. I was willing to let it go for $30,000, but I couldn't sell the damn thing. So I donated it to you as a tax write-off. The thing was worth more to me if I gave it away than if I kept it on the lot and tried to sell it. The fucker wouldn't sell so I donated it to your cause. But you had to invite a tax assessor to your fucking yard sale. Do you know how much tax credit I can get for that donation? Do you? Nothing, that's what. How in the hell am I supposed to cook the books now? I can't. You lost me a lot of money, you jackass. Don't you even think about ever asking me for anything again. Do you hear me? I ain't never supporting you again fer nuthin'."

The one sided conversation was followed up by countless calls from other angry benefactors. There wasn't anything that anyone could do. Taquard quit before the year was out. He didn't need the money and the bullshit was surpassing his need to confront the boredom of retirement.

Mort Madison arrived in the classroom in the fall of 1983 with the latest edition of Current Events and decided to engage the class with the competition. The Current Events envelop had a red KAL 007 stamp on it. The company always created a special stamp of a noteworthy news event and stamped it on the envelope before mailing it out to the schools. He addressed the class with the news about the tragedy of KAL 007. He also reminded the class about the expiration of the 1953 cease-fire accord between North and South Korea. He informed them that the accord was for only 50 years and was not renewed. He provided some details about KAL 007 that were not well publicized. While pointing out that there were many people on board of the aircraft including Congressman Larry McDonald from Georgia. He mentioned that many were speculating that McDonald himself was the Soviet's primary target.

Although a democrat, McDonald was well known for his unwavering anti-communist points of view which were believed to be second only to that of Senator Joseph McCarthy. He strongly believed in the Constitution and believed that there was a communist conspiracy. He used amendments to prevent government aid to homosexuals and supported the use of Laetrile, a non-approved drug, to treat cancer patients. He is perhaps best remembered for being the second president of the John Birch Society. Robert W. Welch Jr. was the first president who reigned from 1958 to 1983.

The JBS (based in Appleton, Wisconsin) was founded in Indianapolis, Indiana on Tuesday, 9 December 1958, with the purpose of fighting threats to the US Constitution and is known for its conservative stance against communism. It was founded by Robert W. Welch Jr. a retired candy manufacturer. The organization was named after Captain John Birch, an Army military intelligence officer and Baptist missionary, who was killed in Suchow, China, on Saturday 25 August 1945 (ten days after World War II had ended) by armed members of the Communist Party of China. Birch was immobilized by a gunshot wound to the leg and had his hands tied behind his back. He was then shot in the back of the head. The JBS considers Captain John Birch to be the first victim of the Cold War. Their vision is: Less Government, More Responsibility and—With God's Help—a Better World. Welch believed that both the US and Soviet governments were both the subject to infiltrations from conspiratorial internationalists, greedy bankers, and corrupt politicians. He felt that a New World Order or One World Government was a threat to the sovereignty of the United States. Welch opposed collectivism and saw it as the main threat to western civilization. He further believed that far left liberals were communist traitors.

Although Madison himself was not a member of the JBS, he certainly lived in a community that had vocal members. La Grange Parker High School had a lot of JBS members in their faculty and administration. As a country bumpkin school, they also had the FFA and the 4H Club, and rodeo was one of their sporting events just like football and basketball. For some reason they didn't have Boy Scouts.

"Okay, class, let's get started," Madison responded. "The theme of this edition seems to be about Korea so you might want to think about the Korean War. The writers apparently dedicated this particular game to Korea in response to what recently happened to the airliner. I noticed that they sent this express delivery. All right, for ten points, what is the most forward deployed military unit in the.... Rodney, I haven't even finished asking the question."

"I know the answer, Second of the Seventeenth Field Artillery Battalion."

"Well, you should listen to the entire question before answering. You did get it right, however. Ten points for Team One. Oh, there's a bonus question. Who is the commander of the Second of the Seventeenth Field Artillery Battalion?"

"That's easy, my brother, First Lieutenant Elwood Taquard."

"Wrong. Actually the commander is Lieutenant Colonel Elmer Ingel."

"No, it's not, it's my brother Elwood Taquard."

"Wait a minute. Are you trying to tell me that your brother is the commander of Second of the Seventeenth?"

"That's what I'm trying to tell you."

"No way. That would mean that he is controlling the border between North and South Korea. There's no way that they would let a lieutenant have that much authority."

"I am telling you that they did and that my information is much more current than what you have. If I'm lying I'm dying. Call them up if you don't believe me. I'll even give you the number."

"Just because your brother may be stationed in Korea doesn't make him the commander. No bonus points. Good try in trying to capture the lead."

Taquard's team lost by ten points. Current Event competitions were always close. Second period was Madison's free period. He went to the principal to talk about what Rodney mentioned.

"I'd like to make a few phone calls. Do you mind if I use your phones? I'll pay for the charges."

"You may, but you will have more privacy if you use the booth in the teacher's lounge."

"I don't want privacy. I'd like you to listen in. I need to call Korea."

"Korea? What the hell do you want to call them for? Those rice eating scum suckers. The way they bombed Pearl Harbor."

"That was Japan not Korea."

"Same thing, ain't it? Or was it Pearl Bailey. I always get those two mixed up."

"According to Rodney, Elwood is in command of Second of the Seventeenth."

"So?"

"If that's true, do you have any idea of how close to being in a war we actually are?"

"No. What does that have to do with Elwood?"

"Hostilities are building up. Second of the Seventeenth controls the border. Didn't you hear about the airliner that got shot down?"

"No."

"You are aware of the fact that there was a war in Korea back in the fifties."

"Yeah man, and we kicked their butts. We nuked them back into the fucking stone age."

"That was Japan. Korea didn't end. The cease-fire accord expired. Just let me use your phone so that I can at least sleep tonight."

"Okay, but if you're calling China you're gonna to pay for the charges."

"Korea, not China."

"Same difference, ain't it?"

"If Elwood is in charge he could get us in a war. And you know Elwood."

"Taquard? That snot-nosed punk. He didn't even cut his hair. He never spoke good English. All them Jews trying to start trouble."

"He's a war monger if there ever was one," Madison replied. "Did you know that he used to wear a bow tie to class on the days he had to dress up? Not the clip on mind you, I mean the kind that you tie yourself."

"Yeah, I remember that he was the only person in the school who knew how to tie one. Came in handy when we had that play. What the fuck was the name of that play? Henry, Harry, no wait it was Harvey. Harvey the Rabbit, or maybe it was Wally."

"It was Harvey. Did you know that he used to shave with a straight razor? I mean a straight razor, the kind that barbers used back in the forties and fifties. He even had a razor strap. He even knew how to sharpen it. I tell you, he was born about thirty years too late."

"Yeah, I heard about that after one of your overnight trips to one of your games. Did you say that he went into the Army?"

"Yes, and according to his brother he's a first lieutenant. I'm beginning to think that it runs in the family."

"Shit, I never would have guessed that he would go into the Army. I could have guessed a lot of other things but never the military."

"Like I said, maybe it runs in the family. His father was a general."

"I didn't know that. His father taught here last year. Who could ever forget that one?"

"Wait! A first lieutenant is an officer. And you have to go to college first before you can become an officer. How the hell did Taquard even manage get into college in the first place?"

"Maybe it was that scholarship that he received back when he was in the eleventh grade," Sours responded.

"Scholarship? I never knew about any scholarship."

"Yeah. It was only for one semester. He used it up in the summer between his junior and senior year. I thought everybody knew. He was the only student in the history of the school to have attended college full time before graduating from high school."

"And he passed?"

"That's the way I understood it. LeTourneau College I believe. Longview, Texas."

Madison made some preliminary phone calls through the Department of Defense to locate the unit that he was looking for.

"I got a number for Korea. Are you sure it's okay?" Madison asked.

"Go ahead and call it. We'll pay for it. I'd be interested in knowing how Elwood managed to get promoted in the Army."

"Second of the Seventeenth Field Artillery Battalion Headquarters, Sergeant Brand speaking, may I help you, sir? Be advised that this is an unsecured line."

"Excuse me, Sergeant Brand, can you tell me who the commander of Second of the Seventeenth is?" Madison asked.

"You mean now?"

"Yes."

"Right now it's Lieutenant Taquard."

"Elwood Taquard?"

"I don't know his first name. Nobody's allowed to call him by his first name."

"There is a lot of responsibility riding on his shoulders. If he's not careful he could get us in a war."

"Don't you know it?"

"I am surprised that the Army would give that much responsibility to a lieutenant."

"The Army didn't give it to him, Colonel Ingel did."

"Does that mean that he's in charge?"

"Head honcho, baby."

"Do you think that Lieutenant Taquard might get us involved in an actual war?"

"He's sure doing his best, that's for sure."

"Doesn't he realize how many people could be affected by his actions?"

"I don't think he cares."

"Maybe you could talk some sense into him."

"No can do."

"What if I were to talk some sense to him or maybe get someone else who could?"

"Better make it quick. You're probably one of the last people that I'll ever talk to."

"Well?" Principal Sours asked.

"It's worse than I thought."

"Is he the commander or ain't he?"

"He's the commander all right. He's about to get us all involved in a war."

"As a commander, that means he's in charge right?"

"Yes it does."

"Maybe we could talk to his boss."

"He doesn't have a boss. He is the boss. I'm telling you that there's nothing between him and starting a war. But we can call back. Maybe we can talk some sense into him. Maybe we could get someone else to talk some sense into him."

"Let's get his brother in here. Maybe he can talk some sense to him."

"You know, maybe we should be careful with this one. General Taquard proved to be no one to fool with. I mean about all that business with the basketball coach and yard sale last year."

"Oh, yeah. Let me tell you I was this close to knocking his block off myself."

"Yes, I heard about that incident that you had with him in the grocery store."

"Yeah, we got into a little argument."

"Little? They took you to the hospital in an ambulance."

"He got lucky, that's all."

"Look, all I'm saying is that we have to be careful with the way we handle Rodney. I don't want his father coming after me."

Rodney was called out of class and sent to the principal's office.

"Wait a minute, I didn't do it. Why are you always accusing me? I'm telling you, I had nothing to do with it," Rodney said to Principal Sours.

"No. It's nothing like that."

"We called your brother's unit in Korea. You were right, he is the commander of Second of the Seventeenth," Madison added.

"Then we get the bonus points. That means we won."

"Yes. We were both wondering if you could do us all a big favor."

"Actually, you'd be doing us all a favor," Sours added.

"As you already know, the cease fire accord between North and South Korea expired without renewal. And, now a Korean airliner has been shot down. Shooting down a passenger airliner is an act of war."

"How can I help?" Rodney asked.

"We want you to talk to your brother who is in charge up there. We want you to make sure that he doesn't start a war." Madison said with emphasis.

"You'd be saving a lot of lives," Sours added.

"Who will be paying for the call?"

"You damn Jew," Sours shouted. "All you guys ever think about is money."

"We'll pay for it and you can talk to him here and now. I even have the number."

"Okay, what do you want me to say?"

"Just tell him not to start any wars."

"You'd be saving a lot of lives," Sours added.

"Well, okay, I'll see what I can do."

The call was made and put on speakerphone.

"Second of the Seventeenth Field Artillery Battalion Headquarters, Sergeant Harper speaking, may I help you, sir? Be advised that this is an unsecured line."

"May I speak to Lieutenant Taquard?"

"He's not in at the moment. May I take a message?"

"Could you tell him that his brother called?"

"Yes."

"We want to make sure that he doesn't do anything drastic in this critical time of need," Madison added.

"I'm not in a position to tell him what to do or what not to do."

"When will he be back?" Sours asked.

"I don't know."

"Thank you for your time. We want to wish you the best of luck, you're in our prayers," Madison said in closing.

"Out here."

"Exactly how sensitive is the situation?" Sours asked Madison.

"Like a bull in boxing gloves riding on a unicycle juggling crystal balls."

"Thanks for coming in, Rodney. You can go back to class."

"Thanks," Rodney replied. "And, sir, don't forget to tell the class tomorrow that we won today's game."

"Okay, I tell them."

Considering the historical events that were taking place he began to wonder.

"Who knows what will happen next?"

"Don't worry, my brother will take care of everything," Rodney Taquard replied.

"How much of a difference can Taquard make anyhow?" Sours asked.

"All the difference in the world. If he wants to start a war he'll start one. It's all up to him."

"Shit, he may just be crazy enough to start one. He may just do it out of spite."

"There's not much else that we can do. Maybe we should've treated him better when he was young."

"Yeah, maybe so," Sours continued. "Hey, did you hear the one about the Jew lady who used inner tubes because she was? No, wait. It was the fat Italian woman who needed some inner tubes. Well do you know why she needed them? No, wait. How does it go again? Well anyway you get the idea."

# Chapter Thirteen
## *Internal Conflict*

The following morning Taquard ate his breakfast at the Camp Giant mess hall. They had a small but really good mess hall; in fact it was the best one that he had ever been at in Korea. He ate with the acting battery commander and requested six men for a special detail. The detail would be armed and provide personal security for Taquard. They would operate in overlapping eight hour shifts. That way Taquard had two guards with him at all times. A guard would begin his shift with one guard and finish up the second half of his eight hour shift with another. The guards were all young privates who were sworn in and took their duties very seriously. It was a good thing for Dingus and White that they departed Korea a couple of months earlier.

He also opened up the Officers Club for dinner meals only. A new lock was put on the entrance and there was a limited distribution of keys.

Taquard began his day with an opening meeting. He still longed for the time when he would be able to get a legitimate night's rest on the sergeant Major's couch.

"We're going to lay howitzers on North Korea. Two at Pelham, six at Giant. Giant will be our fall back position. We may have to engage in self firing in the event that we get overrun."

"Do you mean fire on ourselves?" one of the NCOs asked.

"Yes. We're going to need some foxholes."

"All the firing elements are out in the field, so are all the FDC," another added.

"That's where I come in."

"You're nothing but a fistie," Swackhammer stated. "The only people we have left behind are fisties."

"I learned how to operate a firing line and FDC at OBC. We'll be fine."

"Sir, if I may be so bold to say that you are putting us in a dangerous position that we don't need to be in. What you are doing is provoking the Koreans into a war," Swackhammer said to Taquard.

"If we don't prepare we're going to wish that we had. If we're lucky, we won't need any of this."

"Sir, it is rumored that we have two nuclear warheads somewhere on post," another NCO stated.

"If there are any we won't know about it until we get the order."

Taquard showed the layout model of Camps Pelham and Giant. Toy soldiers were assembled in certain areas. This was more refined and organized compared to the previous day.

"What are we going to do, play cowboys and Indians?" Swackhammer asked.

"Don't mess with those. They represent actual people. Take a look at your areas. Everyone is assigned certain parts of Camp Pelham except Charlie Battery, they have all of Giant. These toy soldiers represent the people in your batteries. The dark green soldiers represent HHB. Alpha, you've got the brown cowboys. Bravo, the light green soldiers are yours and Circus has the Indians. Charlie you have the white spacemen."

"What next, El Tee," an NCO asked, "Lincoln Logs?"

"Why not make Toy Land our logistical operating base?" another asked.

"And to think that I passed up the opportunity to buy a Barbie doll," another also added.

"In the name of establishing accountability we will use whatever method works. If you've got a better idea let's hear it. Otherwise shut your hole. These soldiers represent the actual people in your units. I need for you to validate this representation. This pile here represents the people who are unaccounted for. You'd better figure out how you're going to find them."

The sergeant major backed up Taquard and emphasized the importance of accountability and ensuring that everything was maintained. He also reminded the NCOs that the possible outbreak of war was not something to be ignored.

"We're not the nasty guard," he concluded.

"What about liberty?" one of the NCOs asked.

"No, not right now," Taquard answered. "However, we might be able to rotate groups to RC4. As commander I could let you guys decide what movie the theatre shows. And while I'm in command you won't have to pay admission. The only problem is that not everyone will get to go at the same time and the selection of movies is limited. No liberty at this time, but I am considering the RC4 rotation."

Taquard dismissed the group and pulled out some maps of North Korea. He studied the maps for a long time to determine the best way to point the howitzers. He had eight howitzers at his disposal but he wasn't sure about ammo, fuses, and powder. He did some investigating and discovered that there were several rounds from each of the firing batteries. They were staged by ARTEP preparation segments and for the actual ARTEP itself. There was plenty of ammo, fuses, and powder. The battalion would come back to base camp and recuperate and replenish their field stock as training took place. The only problem was that they would be out of ammo when the actual ARTEP was taking place. He decided to set up two fire direction centers instead of just one. He remembered the resources that they had at the education center on post. They had resources for teaching all aspects of gunnery and artillery operations. The S-3 shop had Tabular Firing Tables (TFT) and sticks. They even had clean grid sheets to be used on a firing board. All the instruments that were needed to set up three FDCs (Fire Direction Center) were available. He could listen to fire missions and double-check the data. The problem with gunnery is that it is easy to forget if you don't use it. Most artillery NCOs simply don't remember how to point howitzers in the specified direction. Most artillery officers forget gunnery as soon as they leave OBC. Many will never use it again throughout their careers. Many will never become battery fire direction officers. Of those who do, most rely on their NCO to do all the work. Taquard designated two vacant rooms in two separate buildings to house the FDCs. Fortunately, he found two NCOs who were trained on gunnery.

The remains of the battalion were unprepared, undermanned, untrained, undersupplied, and unmotivated. There was only one thing left to do, prepare for an attack. Most of the men lacked the simplest of rudimentary skills. In spite of what the unit statistics displayed, most of the soldiers were incapable of firing their weapons. Simple tasks such as challenge and password were beyond the grasp of unit members. Even with the abundance of on hand educational resources, soldiers were not in a position to take advantage of them because of their limited ability to read. The soldiers lacked the ability to comprehend what they could read. Most writers didn't know how to write. Simplicity in writing went out of fashion long before Taquard went into the Army. Taquard knew that he was going to have to simplify his explanations to be understood by the soldiers. He was going to have to explain things the way Wally explained things to the Beaver in "Leave it to Beaver." Even then he wouldn't be guaranteed of any success. He would have to convince his soldiers that the enemy could attack during the night while they were sleeping. The use of toy soldiers to illustrate a point in subject manner was a valid one.

Taquard's plan was explained in the simplest of terms. "You see these yellow goofs over here? They are the enemy and want to kill us. They will probably attack us. If they do we must fight back to survive. This up here is north. The will be coming in from the north. They may attack without warning, maybe at night. The only way to respond is to kill them. Kill as many of them as possible. When in doubt, kill. There are no rules for killing just like there are no rules in a street fight. We will not take prisoners. If these goofs get in too close we will have to back up. If they get in among us we are finished. If we begin to get overrun we will move back to these howitzers here. The howitzers will go from an indirect to a direct fire mode. Howitzer number two will prepare for self fire. Make sure to take cove during self fire missions. There are about 350 of us and about 4,000 of them that will be coming at us. Camp Giant is our final fall back position. Ammunition has been pre-positioned for our use. If they overrun us at the howitzers we will go to Camp Giant. The howitzers at Giant will conduct self fire missions. We will be fighting infantry style. After we run out of ammo it will be hand to hand fighting."

Second Division was the best division in the Army and brought out the best in their soldiers. They, in spite of their deficiencies, were second to none in the US Army. As bad as the situation and the soldiers appeared to be, they were the best that the Army had to offer.

Fortunately there were resources (manuals, library tapes, and publications) around that could rejuvenate Taquard's knowledge of pointing the howitzers in the desired direction into North Korea. Aiming circles backed up by safety circles were emplaced to ensure accuracy in laying the howitzers in the correct direction. In a very short period of time artillery skills were passed on and acquired by the other NCOs. The training and preparation for what seemed to be an imminent battle with the North Koreans included practice and testing. The NCOs who were well attuned to manual gunnery skills set up training workshops for others to attend. Passing on knowledge from one person to another was not a mere preparation for war, it meant survival. Other NCOs set of forward observation cells with practical courses of instruction. Another group established training in vehicle maintenance. The medics provided expert training in field first aid. Unlike similar blocks of instruction that were provided in OBC, these courses were interesting and were taught by legitimate instructors. OBC was more concerned with running herds of students through several classes where the instructor was required to spew out certain information in a limited amount of time. This was actually legitimate and worthwhile training for all to attend. Even though the training was interesting, it was no concession for the six day work week that was modified to seven.

The problem with fighting Orientals is the fact that they are hardheaded and persistent. Even when they are losing they continue fighting. Their tenacious will continues to drive them even when they are being beaten badly. They are slow to surrender. While they are an inferior foe in the technological arena they are nevertheless a worthy opponent worth considering. Viet Nam was a good example of success of a tenacious army standing up to a technologically superior foe. The ruthless

Japanese fought hard even after Emperor Hirohito sacrificed countless teenagers (most were between thirteen and fourteen) to attack Pearl Harbor. Not only did the Japanese continue to fight for their emperor, they worshipped him like a god. Americans were displeased with Jimmy Carter for even the slightest of errors. While Americans cannot fathom any form of logic that differs from their own, it pays to realize that other people in other parts of the world think differently. Also, they can kill you. Taquard had no choice but to be decisive and demanding. Surrender and the possibility of taking prisoners was not an option.

The Arabs had mixed allegiances towards their leaders and hated their neighbor more than they loved their families. Leaders spent their time ruthless controlling their subjects. The Arab nations could not muster enough cohesiveness among themselves to pursue a common goal. For over 5,000 years the Arabs shared the common goal of hating the Jews and wanting them eliminated from the face of the earth. Israel was a small nation surrounded by its enemies yet it had never lost a war. Taquard was hoping for another miracle. He had to pull the soldiers together and he didn't have a lot of time or options. And like the Jews, his group was surrounded by enemies: the North Koreans on one side and North Korean sympathizers on the other.

The unit was unprepared, under manned, untrained, under supplied, unmotivated, and unwilling. Most of them didn't even know how to fire their assigned weapons. Challenge and password was beyond their comprehension. Soldiers couldn't read or comprehend or understand what they read. Many of the resources and manuals were poorly written. The writers themselves didn't know how to write. Simplicity was a principle that, although it remained paramount, was often ignored. Taquard was going to have to simplify tasks and duties right down to the Wally explaining something to the Beaver level. He would have to begin with his NCOs. He got more toy soldiers to illustrate his points and provide a physical representation of how important accountability truly is. Taquard addressed his inner circle of NCOs who were either battery commanders or primary battalion staff members.

"You see these yellow goofs here? They are the enemy. They will be attacking from the north. North is in this direction. This map is not to scale. These guys could attack us at any time, even when we are asleep. They could even attack while we are at the bar. We have got to kill them or they will kill us. Somebody has to be awake at all times. There's a whole lot of the goofs running around so try to make your shots count."

## COMBATIVE CONFLICT RULE NUMBER 1: When in doubt, kill.

"As they get closer we have to kill them and pull back to our prepared fallback positions as their reinforcements continue to advance. Try not to get killed. Support the man next to you. Put your differences aside and help each other out. Don't be selfish. We have howitzers at the fallback positions. These howitzers will go from an indirect mode to a direct firing mode when the enemy breaches our perimeter; howitzer number two will be dedicated for self-fire missions. We will need self-fire if we get overrun. There are thousands of those bastards out there. Don't try to take prisoners, don't worry about the Geneva Convention, just kill these bastards and keep on killing them. Don't stop killing them. Our final fallback position is Camp Giant. There are howitzers and pre-positioned ammo waiting there. We will take this trail from Pelham to Giant. Stay together. They have six howitzers which will provide indirect fire north of Pelham and Pelham itself. When we fall back to Giant the odd numbered howitzers will provide direct fire at the enemy, the even numbered ones will conduct self-fire. The rest of us will resort to hand to hand infantry combat. After that we will use whatever ammo we can get our hands on. And after that we will use whatever we can for a weapon. They outnumber us at about fifteen to one, maybe more."

Directions were depicted on hand drawn maps. The NCOs copied information down as the produced maps of their own. Howitzers were numbered and preparations were made to accommodate pre-positioned ammunition. True and magnetic north points were painted on the road. Critical points information was painted on the buildings and signs were constructed and emplaced at specific locations to ensure that everyone knew what to do and where to do it when the time came.

Although self-fire missions were not taught at OBC, Taquard acquired the information and need for such a mission from a Viet Nam veteran. Point the tubes straight up, set the fuses on the lowest time setting possible, get in a foxhole, cover it up, and pull the lanyard.

Round robin training took place as the emphasis of the need to kill a lot of people was sinking in. While learning how to adjust fire only took a few hours, several hours were dedicated to gunnery. Video trainers were utilized after a decade of collecting dust. Training took place during the day while fortification reinforcement took place during the night. Both the clock and calendar lost its purpose.

After the evening meeting Swackhammer met with Finch.

"He's got everyone busting their asses, if they're not working, they're training. If they're not training, they're testing. That aiming circle ain't too bad once you get the hang of it, but those damn sticks. Site, quadrant, charge, that FDC is an impossibility in and of itself," Swackhammer claimed in disgust.

"Did you talk to the others?"

"Yeah, all of the other commanders are pretty much with me."

"We got to be sure."

"We don't need them all anyway. But, now he has a bodyguard detail assigned to him around the clock."

"Bodyguards? Wait! That's good. It shows that he's scared."

"How do we get to him? He doesn't have any consistency. His eating habits change constantly. He doesn't have a routine. He opened up the Officers Club, but he doesn't always eat there."

"Keep watching him. He's bound to establish a routine, even if it's by accident. Besides if a person doesn't establish a routine, then set up an ambush. Create an incident that will certainly require his presence."

"That's just it. Sometimes, he's at Alpha Battery, sometimes he goes to the motor pool, sometimes he's inspecting bunkers. He just gets up and goes. No schedule, no planning, he just gets up and goes. He has two command conferences a day, one in the morning and one in the evening. Other than those two conferences, he has no schedule."

"Maybe you ought to go with him to wherever it is that he goes after the meetings."

"He's got two sergeants who, in addition to his body guards, hang around him all the time day in and day out."

"You need to know where he goes."

"Sir, he doesn't trust me."

"You can't let that stop you. You have enough people on your side. You can take him out. You could get him at night when he's sleeping."

"What about the bodyguards?"

"Put them on a special detail. Tell Taquard you can't spare them."

"They don't belong to me. They don't belong to HHB. They don't belong to anybody."

"How many does he have?"

"Six, two per eight-hour shift."

"Okay, so poison is out. Wait a minute. Can you get a silencer?"

"Well, we could make one. Real easy, all we need is one of those plastic Coke bottles."

"Could you put it on an M-16?"

"Yeah, you can put them on anything. Only problem is that you only get one shot."

"Why?"

"Because either way you look at it, if you miss he will run away."

"Do you think that you could nail him in one shot?"

"I'm an expert when it comes to shooting. I'll get him. I will need a scope."

"Do you know where you can get a scope?"

"Yeah, I know just the place."

"Where's that?"

The HHB arms room. I'll even use someone else's weapon. Some of the rifles have night scopes already mounted on them."

"What about the sighting?"

"Taquard has had us on the range for qualifications. Most of the weapons have sights and back up sights. Zeroed in and adjusted. Not only that, but the weapons have had organizational maintenance pulled on them. Taquard has seen to that."

"Talk about poetic justice."

"I can't get a Coke bottle though. The PX doesn't carry drinks and all of the ajossie huts deal strictly with cans."

"I'll get one for you."

"Actually, a 7-Up bottle would be better. Their green color will reduce reflection. Could you make it a 7-Up bottle?"

Finch opened up his refrigerator and pulled out a large bottle of 7-Up.

"Sir, it's a good thing that you like 7-Up," Swackhammer remarked.

"I drink it all of the time. You want to know what else is funny?"

"What's that?"

"It's Taquard's favorite drink."

"That boy was meant to die."

They both shared a laugh together as Finch poured 7-Up into two large glasses.

"Thirsty?" Finch asked.

"Between the two of us, we'll polish off this bottle in no time at all."

"What about tracing the bullet? Does the arms room NCO have a way to account for ammo?"

"Yes. He has a very strict and exact accountability system in place. Something the division safety guys taught him. He has installed shadow boards all over the arms room. His area is dedicated for storage and accountability. Maintenance is done in another nearby area."

"That presents a problem. It has to look like nobody's been in the arms room."

"That's the good news. You see, I have some ammo that nobody knows anything about. It won't be my weapon in the first place and I'll have it back in place before anyone knows what happened. The weapons security and ammunition accountability will be the perfect alibi."

"How will you get the weapon in the first place?"

"The way I figure it, it has to be a one man job. I can break into the arms room from the back. There's a window there that's secured by a lock. I can cut the lock and replace it with another lock that looks just like it. Same make and model too."

"But if the arms room sergeant tries to open the lock," Finch inquired.

"I will replace the keys with the new ones. He'll never know that the lock has been changed."

"Good. Are you sure that the window lock keys are kept inside of the arms room?"

"Yes, I checked on it the other day. I asked the NCO to brief me on all of his security procedures. Remember, he works for me."

"Good. Good. Now let's just make sure that you turn all of the other NCOs against Taquard. I want lots of suspects when this thing goes down. Did he record the serial number of the locks?"

"No. He had an extra lock that he didn't even know about. That's the one I'm going to replace the other lock with."

"There are some bolt cutters in the motor pool if you need them."

"Yes, I was wondering about that. I'll see if I can redirect him into some type of routine."

"You still have the problem about the bodyguards."

"I won't hit them."

"But they'll respond."

"Let them respond. With Taquard out of the way I will more or less be running things the way I want to. Then you could intervene before the others get back. By the way I'm going to need a key to this building."

"Why is that?"

"Nobody will know where the shot came from. The roof of this building is perfect. I can get a clear shot at most places on this facility. And nobody else has access to this place. Not even Taquard."

"I'd better not be here when you shoot him. Remember I live here. Are you going to be okay with the key? You and only you will have access to this building while I'm gone."

"Yes, I got it covered. No one else will ever know. Just be gone when I shoot him."

"When will that be?"

"I'll give you a day's notice."

"Better make it two."

"It may be hard to pinpoint an exact date for an assassination."

"Give me an estimated date, a ball park figure. You don't have to do it now. Just tell me when you're ready and I'll leave. Here's your key. We were all issued extra keys. Only captains and above live here and there are none of those on this post. At least not now."

"But after I take out Taquard, I'll need you back the following day. How will we communicate?"

"Easy, I'll call the second floor hallway phone of this building at 2130 hours sharp."

"I'll answer it if I need to, otherwise I won't be in the building in the first place."

"No one else has a key to this building except you. By the way, what will you do if you can't get back to the arms room after you kill him?"

"That's easy. The HHB motor pool is in the opposite direction of the arms room. I can secure it in Taquard's APC. Just so happens, I made an extra key so that I could get into his vehicle. I did it when the NCOs were changed out."

As another night began Taquard and the MPs patrolled the ville. They were looking for missing soldiers. Sun Yu Ri was a town that had about forty clubs with brothels. That was a lot of clubs for a town that supported just one battalion. The policy of putting the town off-limits was devastating to their economy. The clubs counteracted with a few acts of their own. Not only did Taquard have to worry about his own people and the imminent situation at hand, he had the local Koreans to put up with. Businesses and clubs were still operating but not at nearly the usual volume. Taquard noticed that the ville was lit up as if everything were back to normal. Music was playing loudly, smoke poured out into the street when the door was opened, and the smell of alcohol filled the air. The clubs were entertaining soldiers as usual. They had an ace up their sleeve. So did Taquard.

Taquard walked into a club alone as his MPs were searching the rest of the ville. This was a service member's golden opportunity to mouth off to an officer. Clubs savored moments of insubordination and did everything that they could to promote it. This was Taquard's first club of the evening.

"Well, well, El Tee. I don't work for you. My unit says that I'm allowed to come in here. You got a problem with that?"

Taquard left with a mirage of heckling from the patrons and Koreans.

"And don't you come back, you chickenshit motherfucker," one of the soldiers shouted to Taquard.

Taquard returned back to Pelham. He ran into Swackhammer.

"How's everything going in the ville tonight?"

"Are those bunkers finished? Like I want them?"

"You know, sir, it seems a little unfair for you to go out to quote unquote inspect the ville while everyone else is restricted to post. Who's to say that you aren't getting a little on the side?"

"Are they ready? Twelve deep."

"Twelve, I thought you said six."

"Are they ready or not?"

"No, sir, not twelve."

"I take it that you have some people working on it now since they aren't ready."

"No, sir. It's night time."

"Can you get me twenty soldiers to meet me here in an hour?"

"Yes, sir. May I ask why?"

"While your men are busting their asses every day while being restricted to post there are a bunch of GIs partying it up in the ville as we speak."

"Yes, that's true."

"We are going to requisition some manual labor. Do you think they'll be interested?"

"I'm on my way. We'll be ready in fifteen minutes not an hour."

A few minutes later Swackhammer had assembled about 70 soldiers with ax handles and ready for trouble on the bridge where he ran into Taquard.

Taquard addressed the group. "The idea is to supervise the workers. We will release them tomorrow morning after breakfast. The more work that they do, the less work you will have to do. They all have overnight passes and the local commander, that would be me, has put the clubs off-limits to soldiers for reasons of security."

The arresting crowd departed with Taquard and Swackhammer. They arrived at the club where Taquard had an encounter earlier.

"Break up into smaller groups. I will give you a demonstration of what I want you to do. Then you will do likewise."

Drunken GIs who staggered the streets sobered up quickly when they saw the assembly outside of the club. Falling down staggering turned into sprinting in the opposite direction. For legal purposes, there is no such thing as anyone being drunk beyond comprehension. A person may drink until he passes out, but he is nevertheless accountable for his actions until he actually does.

Taquard entered the club with his soldiers.

"This club is off-limits to US military, all US military. You are all under arrest. You can come peacefully or you can fight. Either way, you will be coming with me," Taquard announced.

"Gee, sir, we were only kidding earlier. We didn't mean anything by it. We was only having fun."

"ID card, now."

He compliantly handed his ID card over.

"Turn off that music now. Listen up. You are all under arrest. You can thank this gentleman for that. Everybody, turn over your ID cards."

"Sir, we were just about to leave."

Taquard motioned over to one of his soldiers, "Give me a baton."

"Sir, we don't want any trouble," the soldier said as he handed his ID card over.

The detail collected all of the ID cards and put the people in a formation outside of the bar. They were marched into Pelham.

"Okay," Swackhammer ordered, "spilt up in your groups and start policing up the other bars. Check out the rooms for any short timers."

Taquard instructed another NCO to ensure that the names of arrested soldiers went on the blotter report. It didn't take long for the news to spread throughout the ville. The clubs were deserted. One bust and the place looked like a ghost town. One of the soldiers came running to Taquard.

"Sir, there's a civilian in one of the bars."

Taquard went into the bar and approached the civilian.

"Are you an American?"

"Yeah. I'm a tourist. I don't work for the military."

"I see. Well, we have a very sensitive situation here. Americans aren't allowed in the Western Corridor except on official duty. This place is off-limits to Americans. I'll give you a chance to leave."

Without another word the man departed.

The newly acquired work force went into action without delay.

"This is bullshit," one of the workers exclaimed.

"If you want your ID card back you will work," Swackhammer said. "Otherwise your commander can come here and pick it up for you. If any of you slack off everyone will be punished."

Swackhammer was just the person to supervise an all night detail. He got more work out of the work force through the use of force than anyone else could. The work of filling up sand bags and stacking them continued up until the moment it was time to serve breakfast. They left Camp Pelham sober and tired. They left with their ID cards, and more importantly, they left with a clean record even though their names were on the blotter. They left Camp Pelham with a desire never to return again. News about Camp Pelham traveled throughout the country. New arrivals heard about the atrocities of Camp Pelham. Korean civilian tour buses that ran through Sun Yu Ri with bus loads of tourists were turned around at gunpoint. Even the US media was run out of town. Buses loaded with new arrivals for Camp Pelham were allowed to pass through the ville. After dropping off the newbies, it departed empty.

Koreans lined the fences of Camp Pelham every day protesting Taquard and his restrictions. It was bad enough that Taquard wouldn't let his own people in the clubs, but he made sure that no one else went in either. Financially, the businesses couldn't hold out for long. Enduring the customer drought was taking its toll. Everyone was demanding to see Taquard. Many of the Koreans were surprised to see that the boss was just a twenty-four-year-old kid. Taquard walked the perimeter and looked at the Koreans. He couldn't afford to let the soldiers out on pass at this time. One of the KATUSAs came up to Taquard. He informed him that all of the bars and mamasans had unanimously agreed to cover all of the credit tabs of all of the soldiers in the unit. The soldier debts at the bars and businesses were null and void. Taquard informed him that he couldn't make any concessions.

Fortification details were in full swing. As things were coming to order new problems began to rise. NCOs began contemplating mutiny. Taquard viewed the situation as critical. When things settled down for the evening, Taquard took the first shower that he had had in three days. After that he took a three hour nap. Days were demanding, but so were the nights. The place never slept. After his mass at the bar, Sun Yu Ri never saw another soldier or tourist. Those who knew him as a Second Lieutenant were angered by his sudden and untimely surge of authority. The turtles were struck with awe at the sight of Taquard and the rank of First Lieutenant. He had more authority than any lieutenant in the entire army. Turtles who were riding the bus to Camp Pelham would talk about the stories that they had heard.

"I heard about lieutenants but from what I understand this one tops them all."

"Yeah, he has a Sergeant Major working for him."

"We heard about him back at Uijeon-bu."

"He works for the most powerful major in the Army."

"How did we ever manage to get stuck with this assignment?"

"You know what lies just past Camp Pelham? Heartbreak Ridge."

"The one year tour will be the longest year of your life."

Shortly after making First Lieutenant, he had his portrait made at a local studio. The shop owner made an addition and enlarged portrait. He displayed it in his front window and used additional copies for advertising. Coincidently, Taquard would become a model later on in life while serving in Japan as a captain. When the turtle buses passed through town on their way to Pelham they noticed the picture and began talking. Everyone knew it was him. They also knew his reputation, which was bad to say the least. Turtles were grabbed and immediately put to work. In spite of everything, turtles looked up to Taquard and demonstrated a great deal of respect.

A bus load of new arrivals came daily. NCOs from every battery were standing by scarfing up the newbies as they walked off the bus. Everyone was grabbing up as many as they could get.

"Hey, pogue," one of the NCOs would shout at a newcomer. "Get your ass over here."

"Yes, sir."

"All you guys follow me. Pick up your shit and start walking. This is your orientation, welcome to Camp Pelham. Everything that we do around here is done all day every day. As soon as we drop off you gear I'll be putting you to work. After you get done working tonight grab your gear and find a place in the barracks. Don't complain, what you get is what you will have for the next year. Yes you will have roommates, several of them. Eat breakfast tomorrow, report to the howitzers for training, then you'll go to the adjust fire station, then you'll be doing direct fire operations. After training you will eat lunch and go to work. You will have a break for dinner that will be followed by more backbreaking work. Your work schedule is the same every day, seven days a week. Eat, train, work. I want you guys in bed by 2330, you have a very long day ahead of you tomorrow."

He took them to the battery orderly room.

"All right you guys, drop your shit and come with me."

"But don't we have to in-process?" one of the new soldiers asked.

"Yeah, but you won't be doing any of that today. I hope you guys remember how to fire your weapons. All right you two go get them oil drums and clean them out, you guys will see the motor sergeant. We got a lot of work to be done on these vehicles. Oh you other guys, we need you to get some maddoxes and split up some rocks."

"Split up rocks? We're not prisoners."

"Just be glad you ain't."

"We just came from a long journey. We've been traveling for days. When do we get a break?"

"Dinner, then after that, back to work you go. If you were expecting a free ride, you came to the wrong place."

"Is it true that Camp Pelham is being run by a lieutenant?"

"That's right. Let me tell you something. Ain't nobody going to work you as hard as this lieutenant. And I mean nobody."

Camp Pelham was well fortified but there was still a lot of work to be done. Every vehicle was accounted for, many were completely maintained. All but one person in the battalion was accounted for.

At 2130, Swackhammer answered the phone.

"Yes."

"Well?"

"I'm going to try later tonight. We'd better change our call time from 2130 to 0700."

"Okay."

Swackhammer went to the HHB arms room. He went to the back of the building. It was pitch black back there. What little that there was on post never made it to the back of the dedicated arms room building. There was one thing that everyone agreed on when it came to Swackhammer. He never failed. He was an asshole, but a very capable one. He could do anything and he did everything with a professional style. He was prepared. He had everything that he needed, but nothing extra. He took his bolt cutters and cut the lock on the back window.

Specialist Four Hammond finally arrived in the late night hours and found himself in one of the battalion offices. He was the last unaccountable soldier in the battalion.

Swackhammer attempted to open the window. Even without a lock, the window just wouldn't open. The window housing was rusted onto the metal frame. He continued trying. Then it budged slightly.

"Sergeant Swackhammer!"

Swackhammer froze in fright while dropping his replacement lock and keys. He looked around.

"Sergeant Swackhammer!"

Swackhammer closed the window which took effort and went to the front of the building.

"What's going on here?" he asked.

"Yes, we were looking for you," a junior NCO replied. We got him. Our last and final missing soldier. We are now at 100%. You know what that means, don't you?"

"What?"

"Maybe Lieutenant will cut us a break."

"Oh, yeah, maybe. Where is he now?"

"In the orderly room."

Swackhammer went to the orderly room.

"Put on your uniform and report back here. Sergeant, make sure that he does it in a timely manner. I don't want him going AWOL again."

Swackhammer got a flashlight and went to the back of the arms room to retrieve the locks, keys, and bolt cutter. He replaced the window lock and disposed of the old lock that had been cut. Then he returned to the orderly room to an awaiting Hammond.

"CQ, get me Sergeant Higgins."

"What do you want me to do?" Hammond asked.

"Demonstrate to everyone why you shouldn't go AWOL."

"I had a pass, man."

"No you didn't, nigger."

"That's a racist remark. I'm going to report you."

Swackhammer came out from behind the desk and punched Hammond in the mouth.

"You can't do that!"

Swackhammer threw Hammond on the ground and kicked his broken arm that was in a cast. Hammond screamed.

"You're right, I can't do that."

Higgins reported to Swackhammer.

"Get that nigger a shovel. Put his sorry ass to work. Show him what we've been doing while he's been gone. Make sure he's supervised. I don't want him to put down that shovel for the next three days. He's officially on rehab."

"Let's move it, nigger."

"I'm going to report you for calling me that."

Higgins punched him in the face and threw additional punches to vital areas. Higgins affectionately referred to his belts as attention getters.

"Listen and listen good, nigger boy. You're going to dig or I'll break you in half. We got a lot of digging to do and a lot of sand bags to fill up. You will do it or I will make you wish that you did."

"You're going to get yours, mutherfucker."

Higgins kicked him in the back.

"No talking while you're on rehab."

Swackhammer went to Taquard.

"Sir, we may have to put Hammond in D cell."

"That cell is only designed for one person. We got two people in there already. One's there for attempted first degree murder, and the other is in there for desertion along with rape, black marketing, resisting arrest, and a bunch of other charges. He even put two MPs in the hospital. Did you get a look at that guy?"

"No."

"He's huge. He could play front line for the Pittsburgh Steelers."

"Nevertheless, we may have to put him in D cell."

"Well, if we have to we have to."

"I've got a better idea. We don't feed the prisoners and we let them know whose fault it is. That way if Hammond gets in there he'll wish that he hadn't."

"Feed them something. I don't want them starving to death on my watch. Maybe you could put them on the sand bag detail if you can control them. Let's just think it over for now."

At one in the morning, Taquard had lost track of the days, every one was demanding, long, and slow to end. Time dragged on slowly. It was time to hit the Sergeant Major's couch. He unlaced his boots and took them off. He laid down on the couch. It felt so good. It was comfortable, even without a pillow. He dreamt about sleeping and now he was about to go to sleep. He absorbed himself in peaceful bliss. His beeper went off. The people in the vault could hear him shouting and cussing from down the hall. Taquard barged in the vault.

"What the fuck happened?"

"Sir, one of our forward observers just spotted some North Koreans coming down Imjim Ri," one of the duty NCOs responded while clenching the radio handset.

"How many?"

"Eight. Two rafts, four in each."

"Can they confirm that they are North Koreans?"

"Positive," the sergeant said as he handed the handset to Taquard. Their call sign is Oscar 31, yours is Papa 6."

"Oscar 31, Papa 6, do you still have them in sight?"

"Yes, we're watching through our night observation devices."

"Are they armed?"

"Yes, heavy machine guns, AK-47s. RPGs, lots of ammo. They're armed to the teeth."

"Rock the house."

Without any hesitation the forward observers shot at the North Koreans with M-16s and M-60 machine guns on fully automatic mode. The North Koreans were sitting ducks.

Taquard instructed the duty NCO to alert the battalion. "Send reinforcements up to the observation site."

About seven minutes later another radio transmission came.

"Papa 6, Oscar 31, eight confirmed kills."

"Happiness is a confirmed kill."

The alerted battalion took up their positions at assigned posts. Another crew went to the observation post. Ammunition and weapons were distributed. Somehow the once sleepy Taquard wasn't tired in the least and was ready to go at full steam ahead.

Hammond continued to dig amongst the commotion.

"Hey man, if the Koreans come down here I'm a dead man," he protested.

"You know the rules," Higgins replied, "no weapons for you while you are on rehabilitation."

"But man, they'll kill me."

"And if you move from your place I'll kill you. Now get back to digging."

The battalion was on radio silence. All of the lights were turned off. Runners communicated between positions at Camp Pelham. Taquard posted himself in the vault. A runner came in.

"What is it?"

"Sir, the sarge was wondering how long we are going to keep on doing this."

"I don't know but we may be under attack, now get ready."

"Yes, sir."

The runner departed. Taquard waited attentively. The same runner returned.

"What now?"

"Sir, the sarge was wondering. Some of the men forgot their jackets and are getting cold, can we…"

"Rotate them to get their jackets for crying out loud. Nobody's by himself. Why do you think I wanted at least two people at each position in the first place?"

The runner departed.

"Okay, I'll be back, I need to go to the arms room and get my weapon," Taquard said to the staff duty NCOs.

"Actually, you don't have to," one of the NCOs said to him as he handed him an ivory handled gold plated Colt 45 in a holster attached to a gun belt.

"What's this?"

"It's stated in the protocol. The commander gets this in time of war. Afterwards, the Smithsonian gets it."

Taquard adjusted the belt and put it on. It looked like something out of a Hollywood western. The gun had engravings. It was accompanied with silver bullets. The shell casings were engraved. The holster was genuine cowhide covered with decorative markings. Even though the holster was reinforced and complicated it was constructed from one single piece of leather.

"Forget it," Taquard said as he took off the belt, "I'll get my own. This piece of shit has never been fired before. Americans want history to be glamorous and pretty. They want recognition without enduring the hardships."

After getting his own weapon, Taquard inspected the battalion positions. He spent about fifteen minutes at each position, talked to the soldiers. He found out what was going on through their minds and they found out what he was thinking as well. He provided words of encouragement. By 0500 he hadn't even visited half of the positions. He notified NCOs and informed to release the cooks for duty. He started winding down the positions, cancelled training for that day, and instituted a day of rest. Half of the battalion was off that day and the other half would be off the following day. The soldiers officially declared this day as "Sleep Day." The FDCs were configured in such a way that their sleep quarters and work place were one and the same. Taquard managed to take time off as well. One always had to be careful about taking a day off in the Army, even if it was approved and legitimate.

The prisoners sat in D cell complaining about not being fed. The prisoners had been on limited rations since their arrival. They were informed that their treatment was dependant on their behavior and how those on rehabilitation behaved. While using the bathroom the rapist made a snide remark towards his escort. Both prisoners lost their bathroom privileges for a week. They had to clean up the cell before they were allowed on escorted bathroom usage. After that they were put on a detail of cleaning porta potty holes. Coincidentally, the porta johns were located right smack next to the holes where they buried the kimchee for the six-month fermentation.

Hammond continued digging dirt and filling sand bags with his broken arm. He was given breaks and time off for meals. Sleeping was out of the question. To break up the monotony, the MPs put the prisoners in shackles and on detail with Hammond. There was an additional set of shackles connecting the two prisoners. This demonstrated to them that there really was a rehabilitation program. They also demonstrated to Hammond that idle threats were not so idle after all. Two of the guards grabbed the rapist and handcuffed him to a chain link perimeter fence. Then they pulled his pants down.

"Hey! What the hell do you think you're doing? I didn't do anything," the prisoner yelled.

One of the guards produced a whip. He instructed that every time that a rehab does or says anything wrong that they would pay the price for it. Then he whipped the rapist three times. He screamed.

"Understand?" the guard asked.

"Yes," the rapist responded.

"Not you, you stupid son of a bitch. I was talking to him," the guard said as he pointed to Hammond. He delivered three more lashes to the protesting rapist.

"Yes, sir. I understand," Hammond responded.

The rapist was released from the fence and the detail was back in full motion. Hammond did everything to ensure that the prisoners weren't punished any more. Just prior to dinner break, the rapist struck Hammond in the head with a shovel.

"Sergeant Swackhammer," Rosario said while handing him a file.

"What the fuck do you want?" Swackhammer asked.

"It's the CQ log."

"I can see that. What's the big deal?"

"It was misplaced. The form 31 was misfiled. Well, not exactly misfiled. The old clerk had a different filing system. He used it up until his departure."

"Like I could give a shit. What does this have to do with me?"

"You see, the school used to teach the Martindale-Watkins Filing Systems Method. It works great, but it is difficult to learn, apply, and transfer. Then they started teaching the Locklear-Resneck method which was replaced by the Laplace-Bridges method."

"Why are you telling me this?"

"Clerk Cochran used the Martindale-Watkins method up until the time he left."

"I know that you spick mutherfuckers have a problem speaking English. So start speaking English or shut the fuck up.

"Hammond's leave was approved. He was legit. We just didn't know about it because it was filed differently."

"Give me that file."

"Technically speaking, Hammond has been punished for a crime that he did not commit."

"You just let me handle this. Does anyone else know about this?"

"No, Sergeant Swackhammer."

"You just make sure that you keep it that way. I'll handle this. And for the record, Hammond's crime was insubordination not AWOL."

Swackhammer passed by a trash burn barrel. He lit the file on fire and disposed of it in the barrel in a prompt and unobserved manner.

After the dinner break, Higgins went to Swackhammer's office.

"What's everyone want with me?"

"Sergeant Swackhammer, we feel that Specialist Hammond is rehabilitated."

"Good. Then take him off of rehab and give him the next forty-eight hours off."

"Yes, Sergeant."

"After he cleans up, take him to the clinic to get his arm looked at."

A new cast was put on Hammond. Miraculously, in spite of his ordeal, his arm suffered no additional injuries.

Taquard managed to get rest during the day. His list of projects that he had to accomplish was lengthy. He contemplated another unscheduled alert drill for one of the batteries. The rehab program was completed and over. Hammond was more than glad to be off of it and he was determined to redeem himself in the eyes of the command. After dinner, the entire camp was at peace. Everyone was asleep. Guard mount was at a minimum and everyone got the night off. It was relaxing for everyone. The soldiers at Camp Pelham cherished their sleep time and didn't take it for granted.

Of all the times to wig out, one of the typical specialist fours had to do it on the one and only peaceful night that Camp Pelham had ever had since Taquard took command. This guy went completely bonkers while he was freaking out. This was a Freudian specimen textbook model if there ever was one. He went on about how he saw his mother's underwear hanging from the light and how he just couldn't take it anymore. It was too darn freaky to explain. He was having problems with his girlfriend from back home. It seemed that he picked her up at a strip club on Platte Avenue in Colorado Springs while he was stationed at Fort Carson. Apparently he married a stripper who was very adept at performing sexual acts of perversion on stage. He married her then she moved in with his brother when he got orders to go to Korea. This was done because Korea was an unaccompanied tour of duty. She evidently continued to work at the club in spite of his protests. He also suspected that his brother was having sex with his wife. The bar where she worked refused to accept collect calls from Korea. Whatever his problem was, no one had any time to put up with it. As soon as he mentioned his desire to carve designs into people he was tossed into D cell. The other two prisoners beat the living shit out of him. D cell was overcrowded with the attempted murder who apologized for cutting the wrong person's throat, though he did state that he would cut the correct one next time, along with a rapist who looked like he could play defensive line for the Pittsburgh Steelers, and a psycho who looked like he couldn't find his ass with both hands. The following evening, the psycho was released from D cell and automatically put on rehab. That meant additional punishment for the prisoners. The MPs informed the prisoners that life was going to get worse for them and continue to get worse until the psycho got out of rehab. Their fate depended on the psycho. No more free rides.

"Hammond," one of the NCOs yelled, "Wake up. I got a special detail for you."

"Wait a minute," Hammond protested, "I've been fully rehabilitated.

I've been given two days off. Even the doctor has assigned me to quarters. I don't have to—"

"You're right. You don't have to do it if you don't want to."

"What?"

"It's strictly voluntary. You don't have to do it."

"But I have quarters."

"Yes you do. But, Sergeant Swackhammer wanted to offer you a job to show you how much he appreciates you being part of the unit."

"What's the job?"

"Rehabilitation."

"No way. I'm not on that any more."

"Not you. Someone else is on rehab and we need a supervisor. Sergeant Swackhammer wanted to offer you the job just to let you know that you are part of this battalion."

"Shit, I'm ready, let's go."

Hammond was dressed in no time flat.

"As supervisor, your first order of business is to take away this guy's rank," the sergeant said as he was escorting Hammond to the psycho who was recently placed on rehabilitation.

"Give me that rank, you stupid mutherfucker," Hammond said to the psycho as he tore the spec four insignias off of his collar.

As far as supervisors went, Hammond was extremely diligent in the execution of his duties. He knew how to endure abuse, but he also knew how to deliver it as well. Sand bags were now being filled with gravel that was the result of detail workers smashing large stones with maddoxes. While transporting gravel from one point to another in a wheelbarrow, Hammond was observed jabbing the psycho in the back with a stick while shouting, "Move it, you mutherfucker!"

He also shouted racial slurs directed against whites while ensuring that his psycho didn't slack off for an instant. An occasional hit to the side of the head with the stick provided the motivation necessary to keep the subject working. The two prisoners were also put back to work in accordance with the policy that they were to accompany those who were on rehabilitation. They had two supervisors assigned to them who would, among other things, whip them when Hammond wasn't pleased with the psycho's performance, which was frequent. Hammond had more endurance that anyone had imagined. He never tired out and never stopped shouting. He could deliver blows with the stick constantly. At the end of his eight hour shift he informed his relief that he didn't need a relief. He worked about halfway into his second shift when he was relieved. Even though he insisted on remaining on shift he was ordered to take a break. The prisoners were returned to their cells at midnight. Camp Pelham began looking like Fort Knox with its fortifications and reinforcements.

Camp Pelham, more than anything else was ready for an imminent attack. Taquard, as well as most of the NCOs, were certain that they would die at Camp Pelham in a conflict with the North Koreans. They knew that it was only a matter of time before they would be fighting for their lives. The enlisted men on the other hand were more concerned about the whores in the ville.

The following morning the prisoners were put on supervised detail along with the psycho. Then the unimaginable happened, Camp Pelham ran out of sand bags. The solution was simple; they ordered more and put the detail on grass-cutting detail. The grass hadn't been cut since Taquard took command. He fired about 99% of the Koreans his first day on the job. Many jobs, such as grass cutting, were never performed. This created additional work for the prison detail. They also had to perform the duties the way the Koreans with the tools that the Koreans used. It was especially noteworthy to discover that the Koreans had not discovered power mowers; they were still using the old-fashioned *Leave It to Beaver* grass cutters that required pushing and a lot of effort. That is what the Koreans used and that is what the prisoners used. There was no way that they would run out of things for the prisoners to do. They worked into the late evening. After the prisoners went back to their cell Hammond was still supervising the psycho. It was dark outside but there was enough light provided by the street lamps to keep a detail going.

Swackhammer oiled the hinges on the window of the arms room. He tested it to ensure that it would open with ease. The window opened but it creaked loudly. Swackhammer was able to recover from the flaws of his earlier attempt to get in the arms room. Now all he had to do was get the keys to the new window lock into the arms room key custodian locker. Swackhammer was always one to cover his bases and then cover even more bases in case he might need them. He worked the hinges to the window. No matter how much he oiled them and worked them they continued to creak loudly. He would be a lot happier if they didn't squeak, but it was good enough. He positioned himself ready to go through the window.

"What the hell do you think you're doing, you crazy son of a bitch?"

Startled Swackhammer dropped the lock, keys, and oil. It was Hammond yelling at the psycho. He was just a few yards away but couldn't see Swackhammer who was in an unlighted area behind the arms room. The close proximity made it sound as if Hammond was addressing Swackhammer. Swackhammer closed the window and left. He returned later with a flashlight to retrieve the lock, keys, and oil that he left behind earlier. It was lucky for him that he was able to find them with no difficulty. He once again locked the window and once again he decided to postpone his mission. He changed his clothes since they had oil on them as a result of being startled. Killing Taquard wasn't easy, and no matter how careful he planned things out, something unexpected always occurred. Swackhammer had the right idea of going solo on this mission. Meanwhile, there was another group who was planning to assassinate Taquard as well. Their plans were boggled down during their discussions. They knew Swackhammer's feelings towards Taquard, but they also knew that Swackhammer always looked out for Swackhammer first and foremost. He could go either way on an issue including this one. As far as Swackhammer was concerned, he felt that a group would hinder his progress. Hammond reluctantly accepted another relief for supervising the psycho.

"It looks like you worked this guy to death," the relief said to Hammond.

"You'd better hope that he dies before he decides to carve designs in your back."

"Shit! Let me borrow your stick."

Swackhammer was not one to give up on a mission. He communicated with Finch and convinced him to remain off post. He had observed

Taquard and established a very slight method of predictability. It was all that he needed to eliminate him. He patiently waited until after the sun went down then waited some more for additional and continuous darkness. The rear of the arms room structure was a perfect hiding place at night. It was about 2300 hours when Swackhammer went to the back of the arms room and unlocked the window and climbed in unnoticed by anyone. He was always cautious and smart. One he was inside he picked an M16 rifle with a scope mounted to it. He knew his way around the arms room well enough to find the keys he needed to perform his mission. The records validated the zeroing and accuracy of the weapon. This particular weapon was positioned on a rack that wasn't conspicuous. It was the perfect weapon. Not only was it ready for accurate firing, its absence wouldn't be noticed immediately. He replaced the rear window lock keys with the previous set of keys. Normally, a lock was accompanied with two keys but in this case there were three. Swackhammer kept the third key while the key inventory appeared to be legitimate in every way. He carefully snuck back out of the window and secured it with the lock. He had everything figured out. He approached the officer's quarters between buildings in the Alpha Battery area to avoid being noticed. Then he used Finch's key to get into the building. It was easier than he imagined. He went upstairs and accessed the roof from a permanent ladder that was positioned for maintenance access. From the roof he could see the battalion headquarters building. He positioned himself with the use of pallets and other odds and ends, including a chair that was already on the roof. The barrel of the rifle did not extend beyond the roof. It was the perfect place for an assassin to be. He maintained stealth throughout every step of his mission. Slowly and quietly, he placed the silencer that was configured from a plastic 7-Up bottle on to the rifle. It fit just as expected. It was perfect. It did not interfere with the line of sight from the scope. Swackhammer knew the exact distance of his target and sighted accordingly. Then he loaded the weapon. He was all set. His arms rested on a makeshift bench that was, in spite of its composite of materials, sturdy. No one could have asked for a better arrangement. He aimed the rifle at the main entrance of the headquarters. There was an outdoor light in the vicinity that provided ample light for an assassin's mission. He waited. He didn't have to wait very long before Taquard stepped outside to take a smoke break without his bodyguards. Swackhammer put Taquard in his sights. It was the perfect opportunity. He aimed the rifle carefully and put his finger on the trigger. Taquard was in perfect alignment with the crosshairs on the scope that was set for that range. Taquard was still. Swackhammer took a deep breath and readied himself for the kill. He looked and aimed deliberately. He applied some pressure on the trigger. He kept Taquard in the crosshairs. He paused and took a deep breath. Sweat ran down his forehead. He watched Taquard but he didn't move. He just stood there smoking his cigarette. Swackhammer did everything that a person could think of to perform his mission. He positioned himself and the rifle again. Once again, Taquard was a perfect target. The finger was on the trigger and Taquard was in the crosshairs. Swackhammer was a man with nerves of steel as well as a determined man with a mission. He was an expert marksman when it came to shooting. He was an experienced hunter with countless numbers of trophies but he had never killed a human being before. He wasn't afraid to kill anybody, especially Taquard, but he was concerned about being discovered if he did kill him. After some more deep breaths he tried to shoot Taquard again. He took careful aim with his finger on the trigger. Taquard was aligned perfectly. The rifle was steady. Pull was applied to the trigger. He just couldn't pull the trigger all the way. He just couldn't do it. It became apparent to him that he could not kill Taquard even though he still wanted him dead. Although he himself couldn't kill Taquard, he wasn't beyond encouraging anyone else to do it. He made sure that everything was the way he found it before he arrived. He peered back at the headquarters and noticed that Taquard was still outside smoking. It was as if Taquard was daring him to shoot him. He was still a perfect target and there was time for another attempt. Although he was having second thoughts, Swackhammer decided to abort. He went back to the arms room without being noticed. He secured the weapon back on the rack where he found it. When he left through the back window he locked it and took a set of bolt cutters from the supply room and cut up the key into unrecognizable pieces.

During his next conversation with Finch he informed him that the hit was behind schedule but still in pursuit.

"What's the scoop, Sergeant?"

"I'm telling you, Taquard hasn't been that easy to kill. I've been trying every night."

"What's going on?"

"Well, last night was the first time that I have been able to do this thing without a sudden abort. Every night someone comes up to me with some type of emergency situation that requires my attention. I had to abort. It was too risky."

"What happened last night?"

"Everything was perfect. I was on the roof and everything. It was all set."

"Then what happened?"

"Taquard was a no-show. Some of the other guys said that he went to Giant."

"It's getting harder and harder for me to stay off post. When will you be able to take him out?"

"We can't rush these things. You know we all have to be careful. There'll be another chance. I would've taken him out last night but he just wasn't there. Just dumb luck I guess. But don't you worry, his luck is about to run out."

"Are you going to try again tonight?"

"Yes, I always do. I want him out of the way just as much as you do. Oh, there's other good news."

"What?"

"Others want him out of the way too. Word has it that someone else may be planning to do him in as well. I won't interfere with them one bit."

"Don't count on it. A lot of guys chicken out when it comes to doing something like that. They may talk about it but when it comes down to actually doing it you can forget it. I know you're not like that. I'm counting on you and so is everyone else. Remember that you are doing this for yourself as well. We all want to live. Keep me posted. Remember once Taquard is dead I'll be able to come in and make sure that you don't get caught. This has to be done soon. I need to get back before the colonel does. Time is running out."

The next command meeting was loaded with instructions. Shopping lists were consolidated to maximize the results of supply runs. Training and work schedules were coordinated and reflected the changes that were taking place. Defective items and individual equipment was turned for direct exchange. Unlike stateside units, Korea not only had a legitimate supply stock that was plentiful, you didn't have to make any trades to get the supplies that you needed. Paperwork was minimal and often not required. If you wanted it, you got it. Medics in the US couldn't get replacement bandages with out filling out requisition support forms and justifying why they wasted bandages on bleeding victims. Alert gear was prepared, inspected and emplaced at specified locations. Wooden boxes, crates, and other required necessities were built in the workshop. New equipment arrived and discarded equipment was sent back for orderly disposal. Buildings and things that needed painting were painted. While some were working, others were training. The pace was demanding but not compared the previous week's pace. Dry fire missions (artillery missions without ammo) were practiced.

During the afternoon command meeting Taquard instructed the battery commanders to construct sand tables depicting their local areas and other areas of responsibility. Taquard had made one of his own. Although it was constructed with dirt instead of sand it was extremely detailed. He gave bags of toy soldiers, or a suitable substitute such as cowboys and Indians, to each of the battery commanders. There was a toy soldier for each and every man in the entire battalion. Each commander could designate his own color/code configuration. There would be additional designators to depict the level of training that the individual soldier had achieved as well as his skill level. Other depicted information addressed how well supplied the individual and unit was. Even the medical status of the soldiers was depicted. Deficiencies and shortcomings would also be displayed on the sand tables. Each commander was given binders with tasks, record sheets, checklists, and directives to be implemented in the unit. Protests were not entertained. Taquard informed that he would inspect the areas in three days. The obstacles that had to be overcome were numerous, but it was necessary to accomplish the required tasks in a timely manner.

"We also need to be infantry combat ready," Taquard informed the commanders. "Rotate your men to the firing range and get them qualified on their weapons. We can spare about 500 rounds per man; if you can do it with less, even better. I have another ammo shipment coming in but I don't know exactly when it will arrive. Keep accurate records of your men and their progress. These binders that I gave you will help out. Identify and correct weak points and shortcomings. Continue rehearsing alert procedures. I want everyone to know what to do when the time comes. Tomorrow at 0900 hours I will be conducting a battalion formation. Have your units ready, I will also be inspecting them. The uniform is full combat gear with weapons. Account for those on detail."

"These binders are massive, how are we supposed to do all of this? There's an IG checklist in here. We have to do that too?" one of the commanders asked in protest.

"That's correct. Put your NCOs to work. Break up the tasks; divide them out, share the wealth. Do a little at a time. Start with the easy tasks. I don't care how you do it but make sure that you do it."

"We'll need a full time staff just to keep the records up."

"Let me tell you something. You need to know the status of every man and so do I. You are in a captain's position. That means that you are in an officer's slot. Officer has the word office in it for a reason. Get it?"

After the meeting Taquard went to the clinic.

"How's everything going, Doc?"

"Same as usual."

"How about my shot records? How am I doing?"

"You're all caught up."

"How about the rest of the battalion?"

"Believe it or not, they're all caught up too. Seems like a lot of soldiers came in here to update their shot record to get out of duty. I've been providing shots during sick call when necessary. Usually, it's not necessary. Remember that when soldiers in process they are required to go through the clinic. Most of the shots that we give are good for three years. Your entire battalion is combat ready, at least from where I'm sitting."

"How is sick call going?"

"We always have a crowd. I just send them back to duty."

"The work schedule is demanding. It's all my doing, but I don't see any other way around it."

"You're doing the right thing. The situation is bad to say the least. If we get through it, it will only be because you got everyone ready."

"Everyone is complaining, even the commanders."

"Look, your battalion supports the division. This is the closest unit in the military. We are closer to the enemy than anyone else. There are no options."

"There's one, Doc. Adrenaline."

"No way."

"Come on, Doc, you know how that stuff is."

"No, no way. Besides that stuff is so highly controlled it isn't even funny."

Months earlier Taquard broke out in hives for some unknown reason. Hives were all over his body. They were large and they were everywhere. Doc had the perfect remedy, adrenaline from a bull's back. Before the injection was completed, Elwood watched his hives shrink and go away. He physically watched the hives disappear in a matter of minutes. Taquard, like anyone else, had his security clearance suspended while he was on adrenaline. He was also exempt fro participating in Physical Training (PT), road marches, Staff Duty Officer (SDO), and anything that could possibly involve physical activity. He was further instructed not to engage in any physical activity whatsoever. He was to report to the Doc on a daily basis while he was on adrenaline, and had to be watched. Though there were no significant side effects, Taquard stayed wide awake for the next three days. He felt the uncontrollable urge to tie horseshoes into knots.

This was an unforgettable high. He also felt as if he could take on Arnold Schwarzenegger.

While Taquard was trying to figure out how to physically function throughout his ordeal Swackhammer was pursuing an alternate agenda. He held secret meetings to motivate the disposition of Taquard.

"The burial site is all set. It's a fortified bunked on the south east corner of the compound. No one ever goes there. It's remote and there are over 500 sandbags in place just waiting to be moved. They'll never find him," one of the NCOs said.

"Five hundred sandbags? That'll take all night," another retorted.

"No it won't. With eight of us it should take no more than a couple of hours. After the first thirty, we can get a detail to finish up. Heck, we can do our part in a couple of minutes. Put a detail to work and leave. By morning no one will ever know what happened to Taquard."

"The bottom line is that we have to get rid of Taquard. The sooner the better. With him out of the way, we can run things the way they should be run," Swackhammer emphasized.

"Exactly how do you propose to get rid of him? He's got bodyguards and there's always some NCO sucking up to him."

"Even if we ambush him or stage an incident, there'll still be people around him."

"We've got to get him alone."

"Or we could shoot him from outside of the perimeter. Everybody will think the Koreans did it. The way the Koreans feel about him it wouldn't be all that hard to believe."

"Even if we can't shoot him we could always use explosives. Explosives are hard to trace and Finch could come back and bury the investigation," Swackhammer added.

"Finch? That sorry mutherfucker. There's no telling what that stupid son of a bitch is likely to do."

"He's on our side. He wants Taquard out of the way just as much as we do."

"Then why doesn't he come in here and take over? After all he's a captain and Taquard is only a lieutenant."

"There's some glitch with this assignment and the colonel doesn't want Finch to interfere directly. Officer stuff. Who knows," Swackhammer responded.

"How in the hell could you not want a captain in charge at a time like this? Better still, why isn't the colonel here?"

"I don't know that Finch is the answer. I think I like Taquard better."

"Replacing Taquard with Finch is like keeping the weasel out of the chicken coop by killing all the chickens."

"Either you're in or you are out," Swackhammer directed bluntly.

"If you're going to give me an ultimatum then I'm out."

"Okay," Swackhammer interjected. "Maybe there's a way to keep Finch out of this one as well."

"How are you going to do that?"

"By telling him that Taquard is still alive."

"So, Finch is in on this too."

"No, he's just backing us up," Swackhammer responded.

"We don't need Finch or Taquard. And why in the hell didn't they make Finch the commander in the first place?"

"Maybe the colonel didn't want Finch to begin with."

Swackhammer stepped outside for a breath of fresh cool air when he noticed Hammond supervising the rehabilitation program for the psycho.

"Specialist Hammond," Swackhammer cried out, "a new shipment of sandbags just arrived."

"Good, now I can put this bastard back to some backbreaking work."

"It looks like he's had enough. It looks like someone chewed him up and spit him out. Nice job on the grass though."

"All it takes is a little effort," Hammond responded.

"Even when I was a kid, lawnmowers had motors. This one is even before my time. Well, maybe it's time to let him go."

"No way," Hammond protested. "He spoke about killing people and I'm going to break him if it takes the rest of my tour to do so."

"Hammond, go to bed and get some sleep. I'll take it from here."

"But, Sarge, you don't understand."

"I do understand and I'm releasing him before you work him to death."

Swackhammer ordered the psycho back to the barracks to take a shower, clean up, and report back.

While the NCOs were trying to get their act together Taquard was busy with other pending actions. After departing the clinic, one of the new NCOs approached him.

"Sir, can I have a word with you?"

"Is it important?"

"Yes, sir. I think it is."

"What?"

"Can we speak privately?"

"I'm going back to the office. We'll speak there. This better be important. I haven't unlaced my boots in two days."

Upon arriving to the office the NCO stated, "Sir, there's been talk. From what the other NCOs have been saying. I don't want my name to be mentioned."

"What is it? If it's another one of these puzzles that I have to figure out, I'm not going to figure it out."

"Sir, they're talking about a possible mutiny, sir."

"Mutiny?"

"Mutiny by assassination."

"One of Swackhammer's bright ideas I suppose," Taquard responded casually.

Taquard didn't express any shock or surprise whatsoever. He picked up the phone, told the MP Sergeant to come over to his office, and picked up a UCMJ (Uniform Code of Military Justice) manual which had a broken spine, dog eared pages, notes, and highlighted markings.

"When the MP Sergeant arrives, you are going to tell him the same thing that you told me."

"But, sir, I don't want my name to come up."

"This is the Army. We do things differently, oh here he is now."

"Sir, Sergeant Hostrop reporting, sir."

"Tell him the rumor about the mutiny by assassination."

"That's right. I overheard some of the other NCOs talking about it. They heard a rumor about it. No one knows how it got started or anything."

"Do you have any names?" Hostrop asked.

"Well, I'm brand-new to the outfit and—"

"That means no," Taquard interjected. "That's where you come in."

"You want me to provide you with bodyguards?"

"No. I already have some. There's a better way to handle this."

"How would that be?"

"Firing squad."

"Firing squad?" Hostrop and the new NCO questioned in unison.

"Yeah. A seven-man firing squad. The regulations say that it has to have seven members. Can you get me a firing squad?"

"No problem."

"Are you talking about a real firing squad?" the new NCO asked.

"Yes. A real firing squad. One that shoots real bullets at real people. Conspiracy to mutiny is punishable by death in times of war. Technically we are at war since neither side surrendered to the other. And let's not forget, the armistice has expired without being renewed. What's the matter? Don't you have the stomach to watch someone being executed?"

"But, sir, it's just a rumor."

"It's just a directive. Rumors qualify as conspiracies. Sergeant Hostrop, the firing point will be at Fiddler's Green just beyond the helicopter pad."

"Yes, sir, I'll get right on it."

"And I want you to attach a name to the next rumor that you hear."

"You're going to actually shoot them?"

"Yes. It's not like I have a lot of options here. Normally, we would offer them a choice between hanging, electrocution, or firing squad. We don't have an electric chair but I suppose we could hang them. Sergeant Hostrop, can you and your men construct a gallows for a hanging?"

"Yes, sir. There's a regulation on how to build one and a strict protocol for conducting a hanging. Do we have a chaplain?"

"Actually we do. How long until you can construct a gallows?"

"Two days should do it."

"Okay guys, it's time for me to get some sleep. I'll see you later. The sooner I start cutting notches in my holster the better."

The psycho private reported to Swackhammer as ordered. Swackhammer was unaware of Taquard's previous meeting about assembling a firing squad.

"How'd you like to go back to America?"

"Oh boy, would I ever."

"It can be arranged you know. There's a lot of people who will back you up. But in order for us to pull the strings to make your return trip possible, there is something that you gotta do first."

"What's that?"

"Kill the El Tee."

"No way. I ain't doing it."

"Didn't you say that you wanted to kill someone?"

"A lot of people have been laughing at me because my brother is screwing my girl friend."

"I'd be laughing too. So if you want to kill someone, why not kill the person who is keeping you here. If you kill him we all get to go home. You can go back and see your girl friend. Think about it. You could be with her next week."

"What do I have to do?"

"Just kill the lieutenant. It's really not that difficult," Swackhammer said while handing a large knife to the psycho.

"But what if someone sees me?"

"So what if they do? Everyone wants the lieutenant dead anyway. But try not to be seen."

The psycho left Swackhammer's office and wondered around the headquarters area with the large knife in his hand. He strolled around in the dark with a large unsheathed knife in the ready position.

"Psssst," Swackhammer said to the psycho. "He's not here. He's in the battalion area. You'll find him there."

Hammond observed the psycho at a distance in the dark as he was departing the clinic to have his arm looked at. Hammond did what came natural; he picked up a stick and approached the psycho. The psycho continued lurking around in the dark with the large knife in the ready position. He did not notice Hammond coming his way. Hammond was right behind him when he reached the battalion headquarters building. He didn't know whether to go in and kill the lieutenant or wait for him to come out of the building. While he was thinking about it Hammond poked him in the back with a stick and he dropped the knife. Before he could pick it up Hammond hit him across the head with the stick and began beating him. The commotion alerted others. The psycho was once again arrested and thrown into D cell with the two previous hosts.

The D cell Sergeant took out the attempted murderer and rapist and gave each of the thirty lashes. He made sure that the subjects were well aware that the lashes were compliments of their former and present guest.

The rehabilitation program was once again in effect. After their return to the cell they beat the living crap out of the psycho. By the next morning he was beaten so badly the Doc considered transferring him to a confinement facility that had an infirmary. Apparently he had multiple fractures to his arm. He also sustained head injuries as well.

The next morning at 0830, Taquard held a battalion formation. There were very shortcomings. It was amazing. The unit was in shape and continued to do everything that they could do to prepare for the upcoming threat. The one thing that the battalion didn't bother with was NBC (Nuclear, Biological, and Chemical) MOPP (Military Oriented Protective Posture) gear. Taquard never saw a need for it. He conducted an inventory and accountability assessment. There was one AWOL in the battalion. Taquard addressed the battalion.

"Men, our survivability depends on each and every one of you. While we may be undermanned, we are going to postpone our fate as long as possible. We have to prepare ourselves now to enable us to kill as many Koreans as possible. The only thing that's keeping us alive is our preparation."

The newcomers were the most motivated troops in the battalion. After a few weeks most of the detachment consisted of newcomers. They realized, unlike stateside units, that this was an actual situation that was brewing and that it could turn out bad if not fatal. Taquard lacked the bearing that he once had as a new Second Lieutenant. He now sported a five o'clock shadow by noon. His uniform was faded. His steel pot cover and LBE (Load Bearing Equipment) was worn and tattered. He hardly ever wore his hat while he was the garrison commander; it looked faded and worn too. He also wore sunglasses regularly. This was taboo back in the states. His boots were regulation but not shined like they once were. Instead of wearing jump boots that he was authorized to wear he wore green canvass jungle boots with 550 cord laces. Even with less black leather to shine, he simply used black dye on an occasional basis. With the option of wearing either BDUS (Battle Dress Uniform) or fatigues, he selected fatigues without starch. His gear and overall appearance showed a lot of mileage on a rough journey. It was hard to believe that this was the same Taquard who was the spit and polish role model several months earlier. He had a crew cut like Major Coldhammer and smoked Salem lights just like Major Coldhammer. And like Major Coldhammer, he wrote with a fountain pen utilizing blue/mars black colored ink. Coldhammer's rationale was that he wanted his signature to be readily recognizable and virtually impossible to forge. Taquard did the same. Coldhammer had a Zippo lighter with a gold oak leaf. So did Taquard. Most of the battalion who were mostly recruits by this time had never seen Coldhammer even though they heard of him. As Taquard's tenure as commander grew so did the resemblance of the battalion. Soldiers and NCOs throughout the battalion selected fatigues over BDUs and preferred jungle boots with 550 cord laces over the Hollywood jump boots. They sported crew cuts. Sunglasses were adopted throughout as were Salem lights and fountain pens. The gear was serviceable but not starched. And like Taquard, uniforms were washed but not ironed. Zippo lighters with gold oak leaves arrived in the mail as orders were submitted. Swackhammer sustained his spit and polish image and demanded the same from others. Taquard had reached the point where he was beyond proving himself. He proved himself to himself and that was all that mattered. In the past, his dedication to appearance was motivated by trying to gain the acceptance of others or another bout of fishing for compliments. It was here and now that Taquard achieved self-actualization. Unit members were achieving it as well.

In 1943 Abraham Maslow, a psychologist, proposed the concept of ranking needs. His theory is known as Maslow's Hierarchy of Needs. His theory has been described as a pyramid consisting of five levels implying that only a few people reach the pinnacle of self-actualization. According to this theory, one can only advance when all of the needs at lower levels are met. The lowest level is labeled as physiological needs consisting of the need to eat, drink, sleep, and other similar needs. Our behavior and priorities is determined by our needs. When the physiological needs are met, then the individual focuses on safety and well-being. He concentrates on job security as well as security from crime and accidents. When the safety needs are fulfilled the individual goes into the social acceptance arena of the pyramid. They focus on the acceptance of others and pursue belonging to a group such as a religious organization, school sports team, gang, club, fraternity, civic group, and more. In this realm of the pyramid the individual pursues sexual intimacy. People in this group become susceptible to peer pressure and standards of conformity. Most Americans are at this level of the pyramid. The forth level of the pyramid is the esteem level. Instead of seeking mere acceptance of a group, this individual wants the respect of others. People with low esteem need to be respected by others and they tend to seek fame, glory, and recognition. Self-actualization is the top of the pyramid. Self-actualized people embrace the facts of a person and situation, including themselves. They enjoy themselves and their lives. They tend to be very objective and creative, perhaps even artistic.

Taquard's battalion had a purpose and was in pursuit of their goals killing their enemy. This was unlike the dog and pony shows that the stateside units would participate in. Units were so busy putting on shows that they never had time to train. Dog and pony shows were more stressful than actual combat. In a real combat environment, individuals were allowed to take unscheduled breaks and cut themselves slack as much as possible. Sleeping during the middle of the day was acceptable. There was work to be done and it was getting accomplished without micro management. Sleeping was not allowed in the field with the stateside units and there was no shortage of dicking around with the soldiers. Soldiers didn't mind working as long as there was a purpose to it. Stateside units created work when it was unnecessary. It was apparent to the battalion that Lieutenant Taquard was concerned about the unit and the soldiers who were in it. Taquard had the luxury of being assigned to a unit that had a purpose and mission while the stateside units were pursuing political agendas. And in spite of direct enemy conflict, it was still superior to the stateside units. Combat readiness is a myth. There is no such thing. The only exception to the rule is the country that is about to start a war. Other than that, countries don't even worry about war. Taquard was in a war zone and had encountered the enemy already. Stateside units bragged about their levels of combat readiness, and while they had the charts to prove otherwise they were no match for Taquard's detachment and the soldiers in the battalion knew it. Those who had been in stateside units knew this to be true more than the others did.

By lunch time the news about an assembled firing squad had circulated throughout the battalion. As news circulated, stories were exaggerated. Someone even tied a hangman's noose on an elevated horizontal steel post and put wooden crates underneath it. Plotting NCOs started divorcing themselves from any conversations that had to do with assassinating Taquard. They ran for cover and solidified their finger pointing techniques.

Swackhammer went to the clinic to see the psycho who was being treated.

"Excuse me, Doc, do you mind remaining present while I question this prisoner?"

"Not at all."

"Well, well, well. I hear that you made an attempt on the lieutenant's life last night."

"You told me to do it."

"Doc, do you suppose that the damage to his head has affected his disillusioned mind as well?"

"He's hurt, but his mind is okay."

"It's true, the sarge said that if I killed the lieutenant then he would send me home," the psycho said.

"That is a fucking lie," Swackhammer responded in an authoritative manner.

"You promised, Sarge."

"I think he's gone plumb crazy, Doc. Nobody gets out of here, you stupid son of a bitch," Swackhammer yelled to the psycho. "Nobody is leaving to go home and especially not you. You are out of your mind, you stupid asshole. What do you think, Doc?"

"I think that Taquard would be interested in knowing why he thinks you had something to do with his attempted assassination."

Swackhammer escorted the psycho back to D cell. Under the orders of Swackhammer, the two other prisoners were given thirty lashes each. Afterwards when all three prisoners were back together Swackhammer addressed the two who were whipped.

"You two just don't get it, do you? Your fate depends on how well this other guy behaves. He's been bragging about how he was going to kill some people. That is not the behavior that I am willing to tolerate. You'll be getting thirty lashes tomorrow. Meanwhile you can just sit there and think about it."

Swackhammer mentioned to Taquard that there was an attempt on his life and suggested using the firing squad that he had heard about.

"That's very interesting," Taquard responded. "Somehow he is under the impression that you put him up to it."

"I would never do anything like that," Swackhammer answered.

"No, I'm sure you wouldn't dream of such a thing. But let's see what we can find out before we put him in front of a firing squad."

While Swackhammer was scheming of a way to cover his tracks and break as many links to the psycho as possible, the psycho was getting the living tar beaten out of him. The MPs had to take him from D cell straight to the clinic where the doc once again performed miraculously. He also ordered a MEDEVAC (Medical Evacuation) for the psycho with the stipulation that he be incarcerated. He was virtually no longer a problem for Swackhammer. While Swackhammer initially plotted to have Taquard assassinated, he was doing everything possible to distance himself from any such rumor. He wanted to ensure that any such conversation didn't have his name attached to it. The psycho was being carried out on a stretcher as a bus load of turtles arrived. They witnessed the MEDEVAC and were informed that this could be them if they didn't tow the line. This introduction was followed by unit assignments delivered in a very impersonal manner.

With the frequent arrival of turtles, Taquard wondered why he wasn't getting any officers. When new arrivals got off of the bus they fell in formation and were divided by grade and specialty. The Sergeant Major would usually assign numbers to the units unlike the previous snatch and grab. Last minute changes and swaps were made on the spot very much like choosing teams in a sandlot softball game. While most units accepted newbies in civilian attire or in any way they saw fit to appear, Camp Pelham required the new arrivals to arrive in full battle dress. Then the turtles were marched to their respective battery orderly for in processing. In processing was abbreviated and quick. Before the turtles knew it they were put to work. After the work day was finished, the unit worried about assigning bunks for the turtles. After a bunk was assigned the turtle had to figure out a way to acquire linen and bedding. Usually they just used their sleeping bags. Sometime over a period of time to include the middle of the night soldiers would acquire the logistical support that they were once promised. Midnight requisitions eventually resulted in accessing more than a soldier was promised or authorized. Although Korea was very supportive in providing for the logistical needs of their units, Camp Pelham was the last stop for the logistical supply line. Stops along the way had a tendency to unload a little more than they were supposed to. Stateside units operated their logistical operations like the Confederacy. If you didn't have something to trade you didn't get what you were authorized to or needed. That is why many soldiers resorted to midnight requisitions in order to get their entitlements. The stateside battalions were role models for Sun Records management techniques.

Newcomers would develop acquaintances without delay and quickly become familiar with Camp Pelham and the area of operations. Everyone was surprised at the egregious unorthodox manner in which Camp Pelham operated under the command and control of Lieutenant Taquard. It did not function in accordance with the typical clock that was based on daylight hours. It just went. Planning was informal and basic. Schedules were simple and coordination was minimal. Staff coordination meetings weren't established. If a unit wanted to qualify with practice grenades they simply picked up the grenades and went to the range. It was that simple and if others missed out on the training they could do the same. When a group decided to practice dry fire missions they simply did it at their own pace. Everything was spontaneous. Sometimes groups would conduct training from 2300 to 0400. Celestial surveying was one of several courses that had to be conducted at night. The job was more important than the presentation. Details weren't addressed too thoroughly and there was minimal paperwork. This was not your typical stateside dog and pony show. Everyone functioned at their own pace, and breaks became more and more frequent. Supplies came in by bus, helicopter, air drop, truck, coordinated delivery, spontaneous delivery, on demand pick up, or any other way imaginable. One could never tell when or how supplies would arrive but regardless when or how they arrived;

Camp Pelham was always ready to receive them. There was order to all of the confusion. Inspections and alerts were conducted without notice, but no special preparation was necessary. Taquard was looking for functionality rather a spit and shine appearance. It was like a legitimate *McHale's Navy*. Everyone was a member of a big family and didn't need to ask for permission to go into the refrigerator.

No person was assigned to a post by himself. Guards left their post to go to the bathroom or mess hall while their counterparts remained on duty. They were even allowed to sleep on duty as long as the other one was awake. Soldiers were even allowed to play cards on duty. Long and excessive periods of high intensity vigilance would wear out a soldier in a short period of time and basically screw him up psychologically. This was practiced in the stateside units and heavily practiced by those deployed in a war but were never near the action. These Rear Echelon Mutherfuckers, (REMFs) where not only screwed up psychologically, they tended to brag a lot. Self-induced prolonged high-intensity vigilance was goofy.

Everyone seemed to operate in accordance to their own schedule. The wrinkles were beginning to iron themselves out in the rear detachment. Though the supervision wasn't direct and constant, it was effective.

With only one person left unaccounted for in a rear detachment that was almost as big as the battalion main, Taquard decided to address the matter with the MP Sergeant.

"We've got only one person missing in the entire battalion. I want you and your men to go into the ville and look for him. I don't care how many doors you have to kick in or how many people you have to push out of the way to do it. I don't want you to kill him when you bring him in. I don't care if you have to beat him to bring him in but I want him alive when he gets in. I will give a hundred dollars and a two day pass to whoever brings him in. I don't care how you bring him in just as long as he's breathing."

The sergeant darted out of the office and gathered his men and went to work. Coincidentally, the detail consisted of the same people who were selected to serve on the firing squad. The force went out with a lot of energy and enthusiasm as they competed for the opportunity to be rewarded for beat the living snot out of someone. Not only that, but everyone could use two days off and a hundred dollars.

Twenty minutes hadn't passed until a specialist four ran into Taquard's office to turn himself in. Now the unit was at 100% and fully accounted for. No one collected the prize that was offered for his return.

Taquard once again lost track of how long he had been awake. He couldn't remember the last time since he unlaced his boots. Now he was ready for that special moment, approaching the Sergeant Major's couch. He sat down and savored the moment while he untied his boots. He took off his boots that seemed to have been molded around his feet. He laid down and started to go into a long awaited slumber. He drifted to sleep dreaming about sleeping.

Down the hall in the vault were two operators and a sergeant who were laughing. They didn't say a word to each other but they all shared an experience while they continued to laugh. Sergeant Schindler pressed the button. They couldn't hear the beeper going off but they could hear Taquard.

"What the fuck? Three fucking days. Three fucking days without a nap and now this. I can't even take a shit without some asshole screwing with my break time."

He barged into the vault.

"What?"

"Another lunatic is on the loose again."

"Don't tell me, another spec four."

"We don't know yet, but it's coming from headquarters battery."

The culprit in question, who happened to be a Specialist Four, was smashing up mirrors and windows in one of the HHB barracks bathrooms. This aroused the entire camp in a chain reaction. Taquard was paged while the entire camp was awakening to the incident. His hands were bloody as a result of his tirade. He just went berserk. He complained and informed Taquard that he was scheduled to leave the next morning. His bags were even packed.

"How in the hell did he ever get the idea that he was leaving tomorrow?" Taquard asked Swackhammer.

"My DEROS is up," exclaimed the culprit.

"The physician's assistant's report says that he is capable of returning to duty."

"That's right," Swackhammer answered. "The doc says that he's just fine. You should see what he did to the bathroom."

"First someone needs to figure out how to convince these asshole specialists that they need to learn how to behave. He will forfeit one month's pay and he in now busted to private. You decide what to do with him from here. You have the option of putting him in D cell if you wish."

"Yes, sir."

"You'd better figure out a way to convince these grease balls what involuntary extension means."

"Yes, sir. I will sir."

"The next spec four that causes any more trouble will be the preliminary action of all the spec fours getting busted."

"Yes, sir. I'm going to make and example out of this here douche bag right here and now. How in the hell do you think that you were going to go home tomorrow when you haven't even turned your stuff in?"

"I don't know, Sergeant."

"Get your shit. You're moving out."

Swackhammer selected a place between the barracks for Watt to stay.

"This is your new place. Take out your shelter halves and set up your new quarters."

"But Sarge—"

"Don't ever address me as Sarge again, you son of a bitch. Follow me. I have something that I need for you to do before you unpack."

Swackhammer took Watt to the black barracks. Oddly enough, they had managed to go back to sleep after being awakened from the incident. After a few minutes they were in a deep sleep. In spite of the loud snoring everyone apparently was very comfortable.

"Now go wake up Hammond."

"I don't know where his bunk is."

"That's easy. All you have to do is wake up everyone."

"I ain't going to do that Sarge, I mean Sergeant."

"The correct form of address is Sergeant Swackhammer, you stupid son of a bitch. Either you can wake them up or I will. And when I do it,

I'm making sure that they know who's responsible. All you have to do is go to the far wall and put your hand on it."

"Put my hand on the wall?"

"And say 'Nigger! Nigger! Nigger,' real loud three times."

"Ain't no way I'm going to do that."

"If you don't, you'll wish you did. If you do I'll make sure that you're out of here by tomorrow morning."

"What do you mean?"

"Look, asshole. I'll be right here. Here's a chance to pull off another one of your shenanigans. No one will touch you. I'll wait for you right here. If you were to do this, it would be worth it for me to get you to Camp Casey tomorrow morning so that you could go home. After doing something that outrageous, they sure as hell can't keep you here now can they? Sending you back home will be considered a legitimate option. Hell, it's the only option. I could get you out of here before Taquard even knew you were gone. It's almost impossible to get out of here, but you have the chance to get out of here, I don't. If you have any other ideas I'd like to hear them."

"I don't know if I should do that."

"If you hurry, you'll be out of there before anyone knows what happened. Think about what's going to happen to you if you don't do it."

"Are you sure that I'll get to go home tomorrow?"

"Guaranteed. Look, if you don't want to do it then don't do it. I'll let Lieutenant Taquard deal with you."

Private Watt quietly went to the other side of the room and put his hand on the wall. Swackhammer gave him the thumbs up signal. As Watt quickly and loudly shouted, "Nigger! Nigger! Nigger," Swackhammer turned on the lights and closed the door. There was a lock hasp mounted to the outside of the door and Swackhammer secured it with a lock that he just happened to have on him. It didn't take took long for even the most casual observer to surmise that Private Watt was getting the living hell beaten out of him. After several minutes as others from different barracks were being aroused from their sleep Swackhammer opened the door and broke up the beating.

"What's going on around here?" Swackhammer shouted.

"But Sarge," Watt answered, "you told me to do it."

"I did no such thing. This man is officially on rehabilitation." Swackhammer told the others. "I need a supervisor. Where's Hammond? And this piece of shit is the guy who tore up your barracks bathroom. You should take a look at what he did to it. He is under the false impression that he is going to fly out of here tomorrow. His bags are packed and just outside of this barracks on the north side. He will be sleeping outside. I need some volunteers to help him unpack."

Specialist Hammond approached Swackhammer.

"I'm ready to rehabilitate this mutherfucker."

"Good," Swackhammer stated. "Because so far you've been doing a lousy job of convincing people that your rehabilitation program is no fun."

"I'll be ready in a moment. Let me get dressed. I still have my stick."

"By the way, all of the bunkers are pretty much complete. The fortifications are in place and all of the grass has been cut. What are you going to do with him?"

"I was thinking that we could align the turtle traps with sand bags. Everybody keeps falling in them all the time."

"Good idea."

"We could run between them if the Koreans ever get inside the camp."

"Okay. Stack them twelve high and six deep on each side."

"We got more sand bags but where are you going to get the dirt?"

"Dirt? We got gravel."

"We don't have any gravel."

"Yes we do. We got a pick and a pile of rocks. That's all we need."

Hammond wasted no time in putting Watt to work. Hammond was determined and had a lot of energy that was heavily demonstrated for the entire eight hour shift. Meanwhile, the soldiers from the barracks dumped Watt's gear out between two barracks buildings and urinated on it.

Days passed slowly, each feeling weeks. Captain Finch returned to post but remained incognito. Swackhammer gave up any notions of a mutiny although Finch tried to persuade him otherwise. Camp Pelham settled into a routine. The work/training schedule was modified to a six-hour day. Six hours of work, training, or posted position. The rest of the day was at the soldier's discretion. Rest days were incorporated informally into each soldier's work week.

When there was contact with the battalion main it was strictly to relay priority information. They were having their problems too. Managing preliminary rehearsals for an ARTEP was no easy task. Unlike the stateside counterpart units, Second Division graded their units on their performance instead of political posture. And unlike the United States, results were not determined in advance.

Even with preparation and practice, night movements were difficult in Korea. Even Ingel himself found himself as a convoy escort leader from time to time. One of the problems throughout the Army was telling units were and when to go. Maps were scarce and usually inaccurate. And oddly enough, the map storage containers back in garrison were overflowing with maps. Commanders, Army wide, had a tendency of keeping information to themselves. They simply didn't trust their lieutenants. Convoys usually resulted in losses. Captains usually never saw the need to equip their vehicle drivers with radios or maps. It wasn't uncommon for a commander to lose nearly an entire convoy. This was an established tradition that the Army would continue to cherish. Commanders would lead the convoy by taking off like a bat out of hell and deliberately try to lose the vehicle behind them. This was a stateside idiosyncrasy that was widely practiced.

Fire missions were difficult as well. The truth was that as much as units trained in Korea, it wasn't quite enough. Stateside units trained a lot less. During the ARTEP rehearsals a round exploded over another firing battery. This was the result of a manufacturer's deficiency and the shipment of a faulty lot. The lot was designated for destruction but it was shipped to the Army instead. Once the incident occurred the units went into a witch hunt frenzy as they always do. Even after the issue was settled, the finger pointing, accusations, and run for cover continued. The Army believes that whenever an incident occurs, somebody must hang for it. There has to be a dead cat on the line. West Pointers are exempt from being blamed for something even if it was entirely their fault. Civilians, who were out of reach weren't hunted either. But no matter what the problem was or who was at fault, someone always had to pay.

Taquard arrived to the field to see the colonel. However, he didn't wear his web gear. When Ingel noticed him he addressed him. Unlike other commanders, Ingel didn't blow his top. Instead he gave a very subtle reprimand. Exploding commanders were often ridiculed behind their backs and were often the subject of impersonations.

"Sir, I have a message for you from higher headquarters, it's urgent."

"Elwood, where's your web gear?"

"No excuse, sir."

He took the note saying, "I trust a man to lead an entire battalion on my behalf and he forgets his web gear when he goes to the field. I don't know what I should think about that."

It was the worst reprimand that Taquard ever received in his life. It was also the most effective. Other commanders screamed and yelled to the point that everyone including the commander forgot what the reprimand was all about in the first place. It got to the point where Taquard became very adept to tuning people out.

Operations at Camp Pelham went into an adjust fire mode when the media came into the area to cover a story. As before Taquard's battalion went into action and forced them to leave. DMZ tour buses were turned around when they arrived in Sun Yu Ri. The ville was monitored to ensure that there were no Americans present. Bars and other businesses were financially drained while Taquard ensured that they wouldn't have any customers.

Engineers from all over the world came to camp Pelham to fix a forward observer simulator that nobody ever used. The simulator was like a large theater with a big screen featuring terrain and mock targets. The purpose of the simulator was to train forward observers without using artillery ammunition. It was also argued that it saved vast amounts of money incurred with artillery missions. It looked great on paper. The simulator was a far cry from reality. Even the people who never went to the field ever used it. It was a two dimensional screen replicating a three dimensional terrain feature. There was no way to provide quality substitution for actually observing live rounds. Besides, the firing batteries needed training as well and would have to fire rounds regardless what simulators were available. Not only that, but the fire direction center needed practice too. Live fire exercises could not take place without forward observers. The theater simulator was a joke on wheels. The intent of the simulator was to only train the forward observers. Mastery in the exercising the use of the simulator did not make one a better forward observer in the field. Being able to accurately adjust fire in a timely manner didn't help a person use the simulator. However, the Army figured that the simulator was a good idea. They built new buildings to support each and every simulator and installed them word wide. The installation and unforeseen costs incurred in operating the simulator quickly exceeded the price of a decades worth of assorted artillery ammunition. Repairs were needed before soldiers could even begin to use the simulator. Maintenance costs were beginning to pile up before it was even used. Programming costs were lots higher than expected. The mounting costs of this one simulator escalated to the level of exceeding that of what it would take to supply ten artillery battalions with ten years worth of ammunition. In spite of the money that was spent and the amount of technical experts who worked on the simulator, no one was ever able to use it. Even if it did work it would never be able to do the job that it was intended to do. Taquard inspected the simulator but didn't see any value in it. He had thousands of actual artillery rounds at his immediate disposal. He decided to choose live over Memorex. As engineers rotated through Camp Pelham, Taquard informed them to depart and to never return. No matter how the plead and protested Taquard had them escorted off post.

Pelham under Taquard was like a field exercise with buildings. Taquard was called away from camp more frequently as time passed. The camp seemed to be able to run itself. New things were always happening and Taquard did his best to establish a routine and ensure some stability. An escort team arrived and took the murderer from D cell and transported him to another unspecified location. That was good for Taquard, except for the fact that he was tasked by division to deliver the other prisoner to Camp Casey. This type of detail is known as a package delivery and the prisoner himself is referred to as the package. The protocol for delivering packages is very detailed and must be followed to the letter and be completed before a delivery can be accomplished. The details also incorporate time limits and several obstacles in addition to delivering the package. If there was one thing that the Judge Advocate General (JAG) did well, it was to screw up everyone's lives. Military trials can best be described as a stacked deck in a kangaroo court with Judge Roy Bean presiding. Instead of the accused being innocent until proven guilty, in the Army the accused is guilty until after being proven innocent. If you were a law student who couldn't amount to being a public pretender for the district attorney's office then JAG was the place for you. Your prime graduates from Harvard Law usually went to a renowned three name law firm that handled high profile cases before they went into private practice. Others who didn't fare as well ended up working as prosecutors for the district attorney. The trash haulers wound up working for the district attorney as a public defender, more appropriately referred to as a public pretender. The pool where JAG got their lawyers was from the bunch that weren't professional enough to become trash haulers.

The scale that Taquard tended to use for categorizing people and groups came from the Air Force. There are many types of pilots in the Air Force but they are not all the same. The best pilots who are at the top of the pyramid are the test pilots. They are the best. The next best are the instructor pilots. Fighter pilots are the third best, but they are still in an elite category. Bomber pilots are fourth, but they are still in a category that warrants respect in their own right. Following that are the cargo and personnel transport pilots who are affectionately known as trash haulers. Below them are the fuel transport pilots who either deliver fuel from place to place or conduct air refueling missions commonly referred to in the Air Force as passing gas.

It was often said that there were three ways to do something: the right way, the wrong way, and the Army way. Military justice was certainly done the Army way. The Army way is screwed up, but a lot of grown ups like it so it is considered right even when it is obviously wrong. No matter how goofy something is, if the majority of the people support it, it is considered to be a good idea. Not only did the Army embrace goofy ideas, they did it with a fever. Go Fever has been defined as the concept of rushing into something blindly at full speed ahead for long periods of time. The Army had Go Fever when it came to supporting goofy ideas.

What a normal person would consider to be utterly ridiculous, the Army embraced without considering an opposing option. The Army didn't have a monopoly on supporting goofy ideas and concepts. History was full of examples of conformity reaching levels beyond stupidity. The people directly involved couldn't see the problem any better than the people in the Army. People supported Hitler when they shouldn't've. Americans in private schools were once told not to make the same mistakes. Sun Record management techniques and bureaucracy was the fiber that held organizations together. Instead of Taquard determining how the rapist was to be delivered to Camp Casey, JAG imposed so many restrictions on him it became another impossible mission that had to be accomplished on time and without excuses.

The problem that JAG imposed on Taquard was that the rapist had to be escorted by an officer which meant that Taquard himself had to go on the mission. There was no one else. No substitutes were allowed. This was unlike the way prisoner escort duty was depicted in *The Package*, about a Sergeant, Gene Hackman, who loses his package during a transport, or *The Last Detail*, about a Petty Officer, Jack Nicholson, who decides to give the prisoner the time of his live before taking him to prison. As much as Taquard wanted to, he didn't have the option of delegating the detail to an NCO. This restriction was the beginning of many more to follow. The delivery date was nonnegotiable. Taquard didn't even think about renegotiating the details of the tasking, he wanted to get rid of the rapist as soon as possible. In his mind, questioning the terms and condition of the delivery could result in postponing the mission for an unspecified amount of time, perhaps several months. The escort detail was assembled and went to work. Taquard drew a Colt 45 along with three full magazines. The driver, as well as the other guard each had M-16s. The instructions were clear, if the prisoner attempted to escape he was to be shot and even killed if necessary. Killing, while usually not permissible, was fully authorized in this case. The only vehicle that they could get was a truck. The driver, the package, and Taquard rode in the cab while the other guard rode in the back.

"If you so much as flinch, I'm emptying this magazine into you," Taquard told the prisoner as he put a clip in to his 45.

The prisoner was handcuffed behind his back and the laces were removed from his shoes prior to the detail departure. Taquard referenced the protocol but his main concern was securing the package. The two-hour ride seemed more like four and although the package was big enough to play for the Pittsburgh Steelers and tough enough to put MPs in the hospital, trigger happy Taquard with itchy fingers made him nervous. Taquard securely gripped the gun and had it pointed the package for the duration of the ride. After arriving at Camp Casey Taquard noticed that the package must be accompanied by a full set of uniforms and accessories. Prison uniforms are identical to the Army ones with a few modifications. Fortunately, a shopping voucher along with a very detailed shopping list was included with the transport paperwork.

This detour meant going shopping. The package delivery service went to clothing sales to pick up what was required. Needless to say, the employees as well as the clientele at clothing sales were surprised to see a handcuffed prisoner with an armed escort come into the store. However, there was a requirement to fulfill and the party was perfectly within their realm of their mission in their arrival. The amounts of things that they had to provide for the package were tremendous. The list included four sets of uniforms and two sets of boots. Instead of fitting the uniform items on the package himself the detail simply guessed the sizes although the package did provide input. The list included accessories such as underwear, belts, socks, and a lot more. While they were looking at the list and the protocol requirements Taquard was wondering if it was even possible to accomplish the mission. The funny thing about Clothing sales was their inventory. They had plenty of extremely large and small uniform accessories on hand while lacking in the sizes to accommodate people who met the height and weight standards. Their stock was as bizarre as the employees. They had plenty of Lieutenant General insignia even though the highest ranking person in the division was only a Major General. Finding Captain tracks or Lieutenant bars was a real chore. Belts were difficult to find even though there were loads of Lieutenant General tie bars and mess dress accessories. Some items, like parachute bags, were in stock, but the clerks refused to sell them. When customers brought parachute bags or other items to the counter they ran to the back room and didn't come back out until the customer left. Dealing with them was an experience, not just because they could hardly speak English, but their ignorance and arrogance was so appalling. Their sorry attitude was reflected in their service. If you didn't see it, they didn't have it. Special orders were simply tossed in the trash can after the paperwork was filled out and as soon as the customer left. If Taquard performed for one day the way these people work every day he would have been fired. The military had standards for most its people, but tolerated egregious incompetence from its civilian workers. Not only that, but unlike the soldiers the civilians had job security. The military would be better off without them in most cases. In most cases, the civilians viewed themselves as independent contractors who worked for themselves. That is why Taquard fired approximately 500 ajossie civilians on the first day of the job as installation commander. In all fairness and honesty, civilian contractors didn't begin as sorry malcontents. Some installations began hiring local civilians to provide security. The local contractors were far more professional than the military police. They did a far greater job than the MPs, and they did it in less time. They also did it for less money and were more congenial in dealing with the military. Civilian contractors were brought in several arenas of the military and with the same results. In short, they did a better job than their military counterparts for less money in less time. However, over a period of time the civilian contractor performance would deteriorate and the price of the contract would go up. This deterioration would usually begin after the military successfully scrapped their own indigenous personnel resources to do the job. Replacing civilians became nearly impossible, the military would have to begin training their own people to do the job which took time and cost additional money. The fact of the matter was that the civilian contractors had a grip on the military and could raise their prices as they often did. This was the epitome of job security and they worked how they pleased. Factually, the civilians no longer worked for the military, they worked for themselves. They were usually diligent about showing up to work frequently and on time (usually very early) not because of their commitment to the job, but to protect their turf from the military. Contrary to this was the fact that a huge portion of the ajossie civilians didn't show up to work at all except for pay day. Taquard had proven that eliminating civilians and replacing them with soldiers was a lot easier than anticipated. A soldier who didn't know the job but tried was far greater than an experienced civilian who didn't give a crap. The few civilians that Taquard didn't fire [such as barbers, PX (Post Exchange) workers, and seamstresses] understood that they could be fired instantly. They worked as if their job depended on it. This was not the case at Camp Casey. Ajossie protested the arrival of Taquard's detail by saying that weapons weren't allowed in his store. Taquard moved his group in anyway.

"You get the fuck out of my store, you goddam Americans," ajossie shouted.

When screaming ajossie grabbed Taquard, the guard butt stroked him across in the face. When ajossie fell on the floor Taquard kicked him repeatedly. One thing that was accurately depicted in the movies was that people will attempt to compromise your package delivery.

**PACKAGE DETAIL RULE NUMBER 1: Treat all people who are not on the detail as if they are trying to get you to lose your package.**

**PACKAGE DETAIL RULE NUMBER 2: Keep the package under your grip at all times and when in doubt, shoot.**

**PACKAGE DETAIL RULE NUMBER 3: Bring an extra set of handcuffs and shackles.**

**PACKAGE DETAIL RULE NUMBER 4: Make damn sure that you get a receipt for the package when you transfer him to the next link in the chain of custody.**

**PACKAGE DETAIL RULE NUMBER 5: Do not get sidetracked, and do not let anyone allow you to get sidetracked.**

"Keep the package secured," Taquard yelled. "Don't you ever do that to me again you kimchee sweating son of a bitch. I will kill you the next time you touch me. And another thing kimchee breath, this is a United States store on a United States facility. It is not your store, it's our store."

"I call MPs on you, you mudderfucker."

Ajossie ran to the phone and called the MPs. The driver picked up a box and started filling it with items specified on the list. The MPs arrived at clothing sales to address ajossie's complaints. The MP team consisted of one sergeant and two specialist fours.

"Sarge," Taquard said, "show me a regulation that says that we can't bring weapons into clothing sales during a package delivery."

"No, sir, there is no such rule or policy. We do it all the time. Ajossie says that you beat him."

"And what is the normal course of action when some one commits assault and battery against the director of a package delivery while attempting to compromise the security of the package?"

"Ajossie attacked you, sir?"

"Yes."

"I'll let the installation command know so that they can replace the ajossie, I don't know why we insist on hiring these motherfuckers, they've been nothing but trouble since we hired them."

The detail completed the shopping at clothing sales and filled out the voucher while the MP sergeant was notifying the installation command element.

"Did we get everything that we needed?"

"No, sir," The driver responded to Taquard's question, "we're still a few items short. Maybe the PX will have them."

The detail went into the PX, which was next door to clothing sales, only to be greeted by a screaming ajossie who spit while he spoke and protested the bringing of weapons into his store. He shouted at the detail to get out of his store and as he approached Taquard the driver butt stroked him in the face.

"I call MPs on you, you mudderfucker."

They were able to find most of what they were looking for as the MPs arrived at the scene. It was the same detail as it was for clothing sales. The scenario was exactly the same.

"Looks like we have to go to the watch repair," Taquard said.

"Watch repair?" the guard asked inquisitively.

"Yeah, we need to get some name tags made. The protocol procedures state that the uniforms must be ready for used to include name tags and markings. Maybe we can get in a rush job."

"I hope that's it but that could take all day," the driver said.

"I got an idea," Taquard said. "We'll handcuff the prisoner to this pole while one of us does the shopping."

"Sounds good," the driver and guard agreed.

"Excuse me. I need to go to the bathroom," the package stated.

"Number one or two?" Taquard asked.

"Uh, number two."

The detail went to the bathroom and approached one of the stalls.

"Okay," Taquard said while he was looking at the paperwork addressing package protocol.

"Well, well, well, there are even instructions on how to take a shit in here. Secure the door, no one else comes in here until we are finished."

"Yes, sir," replied the driver.

"Okay, you will follow all of my directives as I give them to you. Sergeant, unhandcuff the prisoner. Prisoner, put your hands behind your head and interlace your fingers. Sergeant, make sure that he does it. Prisoner, keep your hands behind your head and your finger interlaced at all times. Prisoner, kick off your shoes. Prisoner, face the guard. Sergeant, stand back and point the weapon at the prisoner, make sure that he is not close enough to grab it. Prisoner, you have ten seconds to undo your pants and pull them down, do it now. Put your hands behind you head and interlace your fingers. Prisoner, sit on the toilet, the seat stays up. The door stays open."

Although the handcuffs were taken off for a brief time, he was closely watched at gunpoint.

"Man, I have to take a dump, couldn't I just close the door for a minute."

"No, the door stays open," the driver answered as he adjusted his deliberate aim of his rifle onto the prisoner.

"See anything you like?"

The driver shot the toilet that the prisoner was sitting on. One shot caused the toilet to fall apart and the prisoner to be on the floor with water spilling all over the place. The driver shot another well placed shot between the prisoner's legs.

"I dare you to shoot your mouth again, nigger."

The prisoner was ordered to another toilet to conduct his business with the toilet seat up. The protocol specified that prisoners who are defecating will do so with the seat up.

"Keep your hands up. You can shit with your hands up," the driver instructed. "And don't play with yourself."

"Hurry up, there's a time limit," Taquard reminded the prisoner. "You will have ten seconds to pull up your pants and secure them."

After the prisoner was finished with his business they handcuffed him behind his back.

"Throw his shoes away," Taquard ordered.

"Hey," the prisoner protested.

The guard butt-stroked him in the stomach with his M-16 rifle.

"The protocol is very specific about throwing away the shoes after the prisoner relieves himself. We have a few other things that we have to do."

The prisoner was handcuffed to a pole outside of the PX. Taquard took the uniforms to the cleaners to be washed and dried and went to the Watch Repair get some name tags made up. The list of requirements for preparing the prisoner for a transfer was exhaustive but the detail was meeting the requirements in spite of the hurdles. The uniforms had to be washed and dried before they could be altered or have name tags sewn on them.

"We may as well eat lunch. The protocol says that we have to feed him. It even says how."

One of the sergeants went to the Food Shack and ordered some hot dogs with French fries and grape drinks. There was a table and chairs next to the pole that the prisoner was secured to. A set of shackles were secured to his handcuffs and the pole. The prisoner leaned forward to eat his food while his hands were behind his back.

"After we finish up here we will wait for the clothes to come out of the cleaners and then take them to the alterations shop for modification. They will also have to sew on the name tags."

Waiting was difficult but the prisoner remained secured. Fortunately, everything was in the same proximity and the tasks could be accomplished on foot. The cleaners and watch repair were able to finish the orders in a timely manner. The four clean uniforms were taken to the alterations shop along with the name tags and instructions for modifying the uniforms. The letter P would be sewn on the back of the uniform and on the front left pocket. The P on the back would be very large and extremely visible. Alterations were able to meet their order in less than two hours. They were approaching the dead line which was 1500 hours. Before they could deliver the package, they had to clean him up and dispose of his property and put him in a uniform. They took the prisoner to an on post massage parlor called "The Steam and Cream." The detail had to pay for the use of the room. Normally, a customer would pay $6.00 for a bath and massage that would be provided by a Korean lady. For $20 extra a customer would get what was affectionately referred to as the Special. The curious thing was a female who was in the waiting area waiting to get serviced. While random numbers were drawn to see which available lady was to service a male, the female had her choice of which lady was to serve her.

"We need to mail some of his belongings back," Taquard said to the detail as he was looking at the transport paperwork.

"I'd better look for a box to put that stuff in."

"No, there are some envelopes included for that. His clothes don't go, just his wallet, effects, watch, and a few other items. Everything has to be cataloged, recorded, and documented."

The prisoner provided an address and surrendered his personal effects. The paperwork was filled out and the records were produced. Taquard sent the effects with the driver to the MP station.

"The MP desk has to log this stuff in and stamp this paperwork. Make sure that they stamp our receipt verifying that everything is correct. They will check the contents of the envelopes and they will seal them. They will also provide you with a voucher number. Here are the places that they need to sign, make sure that they print their name legibly beneath their signature. If you have any questions just call us at The Steam and Cream."

When it was the detail's turn to utilize one of the rooms the prisoner was unhandcuffed and ordered to strip. His clothes were placed in a plastic bag for disposal. Although the prisoner bathed himself, it was closely monitored at gunpoint.

"Prisoner, you have two minutes to wet your body. Do it now.

Prisoner, you have two minutes to lather your hair, use soap not shampoo. Do it now. Prisoner, you will now rinse your hair, you have two minutes."

Each interval took two minutes. After several minutes the prisoner was clean. This was followed by a two-minute drying session. A two-minutes time window for getting dressed was also provided in accordance with the instructions. The package was dressed in his new prison uniform and was handcuffed. The laces from his boots were removed before they let him slip on his boots. The detail walked over to the MP station and met the driver who was still in the process of ensuring that all of the documentation was complete and accurate.

"We need to have these burned," Taquard said while handing the plastic bag with the prisoner's clothes to one of the MP Sergeants. "The burning also has to be on record. I have the paperwork here."

"Okay, sir, the personal effects are in order. Everything's in place," the driver said to Taquard.

"Good enough. Thanks. I'll just double-check all of this before we go to the post office. Hey, Sergeant, we'll be back to get the documentation for the burning of the prisoner's clothes."

"Okay," the MP Sergeant answered.

The detail went to the post office and mailed the effects in accordance to strict procedures that were outlined in great detail in the transfer packet. Documentation was produced and information was recorded. After that the detail went back to the MP station to get documentation for the burned items.

"It would have been a lot easier if we just threw the clothes away," Taquard said.

"No," answered the MP Sergeant, "a lot of people have gone dumpster diving after realizing that they couldn't justify why they didn't have an MP validation stamp."

"Who's to say that we didn't bring him here already dressed?"

"And where did you get the uniforms? They are controlled items. Believe me others have already tried it only to wish that they hadn't. You're doing the right thing. As bad as it may seem, you are actually doing everything in the most efficient manner."

"Okay everything is complete and in order. Let's get over to the JAG before it closes. We don't have much time."

The detail arrived with the package at the JAG at 1459 hours.

"Hey. Chief," Taquard shouted at the Warrant Officer. "We got your package."

"You're late."

"No, we're not. We have a minute to spare."

"Sir," the guard said as he noticed a time clock. "Let me see that paper."

He put it in the time clock which produced a stamp that said 3 Oct 1983, 1459:07.

"Here's the proof that we need to validate our delivery time."

"Wait, that clock's here to establish and validate delivery times," Taquard said as he was frantically going through the paperwork.

Then he put in another piece of paper, in a certain way, in the clock to produce a stamp reading 3 Oct 1983, 1459:49.

**ARMY OPERATIONS RULE NUMBER 1: Trust no one.**

**ARMY OPERATIONS RULE NUMBER 2: Always get proof of your whereabouts when you are on a detail.**

**ARMY OPERATIONS RULE NUMBER 3: Always get additional proof of your whereabouts when you are on a detail.**

"We had to get this stamped on a certain sheet in a specified place to get credit for the delivery," Taquard said to the guard. "Okay Chief, we got it."

"I said that you're late," the Warrant Officer replied.

"We made it on time, we can prove it."

"No you can't, you're deadline is at 1455 not 1500. Read the paperwork, it says that you have to arrive five minutes early."

"It says 1500, look, here we are and everything's ready, we need to make a transfer."

"No. Since you're late we will not make the transfer. You will have to petition for another transfer date and time. Meanwhile you will be called in to state why you failed to conduct the transfer on time."

Taquard took the detail to Division Headquarters. Taquard had been to Division several times in the past and he had established a few connections. The detail was immediately noticed when they arrived. They were stopped by a captain who demanded to know what was going on. Taquard explained the situation to the captain and showed him the paperwork. This was quickly escalated up to a major who elevated it further to a lieutenant colonel. The lieutenant colonel escorted the detail to the JAG. He didn't want to elevate the issue any further and he didn't want the detail to continue hanging around the flag pole. A direct contact between this lieutenant colonel and the JAG lieutenant colonel and the matter was settled. A JAG major informed the detail that they would have to remain with the prisoner in a waiting area while the packet was processed.

"Where do we wait?"

"Right over there is fine," he answered while pointing to a table and chairs. "Uh, the prisoner is not allowed to sit on the furniture."

At 1600 the detail started to get anxious. When they inquired about the situation they were informed to continue waiting. They rotated to the bathroom and food pick up. At 1723 a JAG lieutenant approached Taquard and went over the paperwork. Additional protocol procedures were followed to the letter and documented. Instead of unhandcuffing the prisoner, the Jag lieutenant handed a pair of handcuffs and shackles to the guard and recorded the event in a specified portion of the paperwork. Then a validation voucher was handed over to Taquard. The package was credited as delivered and received and was put in the Warrant Officer's custody.

"Unless there's anything else that we need while we are here, let's get the fuck out of this damn place," Taquard ordered the driver.

"This has been an ordeal and a half," the driver added.

Returning back to Pelham was a relief for the detail. The ordeal of transferring a package was ridiculous. He knew that he was going to have to incorporate more soldiers into the civilian sector of the military. He also knew that he was going to have to develop ways to streamline the processes without compromising the mission. He was becoming more critical of those who sacrificed the military by tolerating civilian incompetence.

The following day, the PX received six soldiers who would be trained in its operations. The two ajossies protested but were quickly subdued when one of them was beaten and carried out of the gate. The remaining ajossie was informed that he would be next if he didn't cooperate. He and the other six soldiers were further informed that they were going to convert the PX into a dual purpose PX with a clothing sales annex. It was amazing how quickly things happened in Korea when people put their minds to it. Daily deliveries included supplies and more personnel. The battalion was nearly actual battalion size and accommodating all of the newcomers was accomplished without interfering with the property of those participating in the ARTEP. Taquard was now beginning to consider the possibility of implementing a DEROS for those who had been scheduled to leave. Command and staff meetings were reduced to once every other day. Inspections and alerts were reduced in their frequency as well. Taquard had a battalion that was well under control and proved that it was able to function by itself. Missions were being accomplished and training requirements were being met. Orders were being followed even though they weren't in writing. Taquard had determined that the battalion was fully trained. Subsequent training would be determined by applicable commanders. Newcomers would be trained as part of their in processing. The one thing that was never done under Taquard's command, work was never created to fill an empty void. When there was no work to be done, the soldiers were allowed to relax and do whatever they wanted.

The long-overdue DEROS schedule was addressed at a command and staff meeting. Since none of the commanders were eligible for DEROS, he informed them to come up with a recommendation which could include releasing everyone who had met his DEROS. It was decided with the support of the commanders and staff that all soldiers who had met their DEROS would be sent back to the states. This special request was approved telephonically in one day at the division level. The soldiers were given two days to out process and pack their gear. The first wave of DEROS departures under Taquard's command included over 200 people and took five busses to support. In spite of the arduous conditions and limited time frame, every soldier who was scheduled for DEROS was ready. The operation went smoothly and was completed without a hitch. People were generally motivated to leave Korea and did whatever it took to ensure that there were no possible obstacles that could interfere with their departure.

After the mass exodus, another DEROS departure was scheduled. Two days later another 100 soldiers left with the support of three buses. Two days after that, yet another 100 soldiers departed. The DEROS schedule continued to be implemented until every DEROS qualified soldier, including Watt who had been rehabilitated, had departed. While DEROS was taking place, the seven day work week was reduced to five. Pelham was virtually deserted. It was quiet and soldiers weren't obligated to show up to work when there wasn't any work to be done. The remaining soldiers cleaned up the areas of the soldiers who were participating in the ARTEP because their spaces were recently utilized by others. Newcomers who were using another soldier's (ARTEP) area were reassigned quarters that would not interfere with the battalion's return. Bedding was laundered and areas were cleaned up. While preparing for the return of the battalion they utilized IG inspection checklists so that they could simultaneously prepare for an unannounced IG inspection while getting the camp in order.

Soldiers voluntarily participated in MP village patrol to ensure that Americans weren't present while Sun Yu Ri still remained off-limits. The Koreans continued to protest Taquard's actions while offering concessions to the soldiers. The bars and businesses in town had been without a single customer for nearly three months. Village patrol was a chance to get off post, see other people, and relax a little. Taquard was known as "Number 10 GI" by the Koreans. This was an insult that Taquard took as a compliment. Soldiers who were on village patrol also had the opportunity to sneak in a sip of a drink or two on the house. Taquard periodically patrolled the ville himself to ensure that the enforcement detail was enforcing rules instead of violating them. Enforcement tours didn't last the whole night as they did previously, they only lasted a couple of hours. On a quiet night after everyone returned back to post the advanced element of the battalion returned back to Camp Pelham. LTC Ingel's return was a welcomed sight. The battalion passed their ARTEP and the rear detachment was in order. Taquard welcomed Ingel back more than anyone else. Although his brief command position may have been the envy of many captains, Taquard himself found it to be a burdening responsibility rather than a moment of glory. His command could be compared to that of playing in the Super Bowl. While it seems like a wonderful thing to experience it is pure tension for the players who are in the midst of playing the game. Super Bowl X would be an accurate comparison because neither side was guaranteed a victory until the very end. Taquard was successful in holding down the fort while Ingel was with the main element preparing for and taking the ARTEP, but his success wasn't guaranteed until the final hours of his tenure. There are easy Super Bowls that are enjoyable to play in just as there are easy commands, but this was not an easy assignment by a long shot. Taquard may have had the opportunity to bask in glory but didn't do so because he was overwhelmed with responsibility.

# Chapter Fourteen
*Battery Level*

In accordance with international agreements the Koreans who were fired under Taquard's hammer were rehired and given back pay. The post was no longer on restriction and Sun Yu Ri was no longer off-limits to anyone. All of the FIST teams were transferred to firing batteries. Assigning a FIST team to a firing battery was like putting a black and white TV next to a colored one. Taquard's team was assigned to Charlie Battery which was located at Camp Giant. Every member of the FIST team, with the exception of Taquard and the FIST NCO, moved to Camp Giant which was one mile from Camp Pelham if you took an off road short cut.

Moving to a new and smaller location was difficult. The office and barracks configurations could barely accommodate what they already had, let alone another team. A third lieutenant was an unwelcome addition to the office. The battery had difficulty physically fitting the team into the cramped spaces and no way of incorporating the team into the training schedule. Even though Taquard had successfully completed his tour as a rear detachment and installation commander, he was the most junior officer in time in grade and age. Lieutenant Darnell, the battery XO, was the best battery XO that Taquard would ever see in his career just as Major Coldhammer would be the best battalion XO that he would ever see.

Darnell laid out the reception in a straightforward manner. The candor was appreciated even though the content left a lot to be desired. Unlike typical company or battery level XOs, Darnell took responsibility for his actions and kept the unit functioning. Most XOs would hang around and be a thorn in everybody's side while the commander did all of the work. Being an XO was great; you had all of the authority and none of the responsibility. Darnell, was different, he actually ran the battery and made sure that missions were accomplished to standards.

"Elwood, this is my desk and this is my office. If I have to take all the ass chewings around here then I'm taking the desk and office. You are not my friend, Watson is not my friend. I have no friends. What I have is this job and nothing else," Darnell told Taquard. "Watson may have some space in his office for you. He doesn't get the ass chewings like I do and he doesn't do near the amount of work either."

Even though Darnell told Taquard that there was no friendship between them, they eventually became friends. Taquard respected Darnell's straightforwardness and honesty. Darnell was easy to understand and figure out; all you had to do was listen. His philosophy in life was expressed in simple terms from an opposing point of view. If you were willing to understand that people in other countries might do things differently that you would, he was easy to understand. It was fair to say that First Lieutenant Darnell was the most philosophical lieutenant that Taquard had ever met in his entire life.

"You know, Elwood, the military is a reflection of the country. Decadent country, decadent military. These codes of honor that everyone keeps talking about don't add up to dry dog shit if the people in the country don't add up to dry dog shit. The truth of the matter is that people in the United States don't subscribe to the virtues that honor codes should be founded on. Instead of behaving in a mature responsible manner, they behave like trash and talk about morals. Ant this is reflected in our military as well."

The new Charlie Battery Commander, Captain Burke, was all work and no play. He never entertained a joke or made light of a situation, never. He was extremely dedicated and competent and put in more working hours a day than anyone else. For no reason in particular, Burke and Darnell were always at each other's throats. They were constantly fighting. They were both intelligent and professional but seemed to dislike each other.

FIST teams were now incorporated into the firing batteries and just like Charlie battery, Alpha and Bravo Batteries weren't prepared or willing to accept another team into their unit. The new configuration, which was identical to the previous configuration prior to the FIST teams being moved from the firing batteries to the headquarters battery, was really creating havoc on the batteries who didn't want a bunch of fisties in their unit. Now instead of being known as bastard children, the fisties were known as excess baggage. Their status didn't change even their location did. The one advantage that the fisties did have was that they were able to keep their M113 tracked vehicles. This gave them a place to be during the work day. Taquard proposed doing PT with the headquarters command since he lived in their proximity. Burke declined the suggestion which meant that Taquard had to get up extra early in the morning and go from Camp Pelham to Camp Giant in the freezing cold. Luckily for him, there was a taxi that happened to be outside of the gate very early in the morning. For one dollar, he drove Taquard to Camp Giant. It was worth a dollar just to stay out of the cold. Unfortunately, after PT was finished, there were no taxis to take him back from Giant to Pelham. He would walk from Giant to Pelham after doing morning PT then take a shower and change into his uniform. Then he would walk back from Pelham to Giant because for some particular reason taxis were not available during that time of day. At the end of the day, Taquard found himself walking back to Pelham from Giant once again. This meant waking up earlier than usual every morning and coming back home later than everyone else. On days that he couldn't make it back by the midnight curfew he found a place at the battery location to rack out. If he and his FIST NCO left Camp Giant by 2340 they would make it back to Pelham before curfew. PT was conducted five days a week with a five-mile run on Fridays accompanied by a twelve-mile road march every month. Taquard didn't spend time with his team as he moved in to the Fire Direction Center (FDC). This wasn't a bad place for him to be in. He got along with the NCO and was with a unit instead of being isolated on a hill. During field exercises, he never even saw his team. Instead, he worked in the FDC.

Both Taquard and Darnell challenged Burke's authority based on legitimate convictions. Burke was legitimate in his demands, but nevertheless the challenges were justified. Nothing was clearly black or white, everything was a hazy gray. As long as Darnell and Taquard performed their duties above and beyond the call of duty then their methodologies were strictly their business.

One problem that Taquard faced was that of being a former commander himself. He viewed situations differently. While filing requisitions was necessary and provided a record of keeping higher organizations informed, the format itself wasn't important to Taquard if it compromised speed. Discarding reports or information simply because someone was able to question the format was seen as a dereliction of duty in Taquard's eyes. Links in the chain should process operations, not stop them. The intent of the format was to ensure that complete information was provided in a simple manner. When the format did not fulfill the needs of the initiator then it was acceptable to modify it so that it would. The original intent of the format and the purpose of requisitions were forgotten. What may have functioned perfectly well at the general Staff level may or may not have even been necessary at the battery level.

Burke was the battery commander, but Taquard had command experience at a higher level. While there was an understanding and command experience was not an issue with Taquard, others made note and comment about this situation. Taquard was forced on to Burke against his will. Being a battery commander was a real challenge. To make matters worse, the battalion staff consisted of members who needed their command time as well and would do everything possible to make sure that the present commander failed.

As the junior lieutenant in the battery, Taquard had no function other than to tag along with the FDO. Once again, he was at the bottom of the pit. He found out that rank doesn't always depend on what you wear on your right collar, but on the environment. What may have made him a general in the civil war meant nothing in the new army. Wearing a silver bar wasn't much better than wearing a gold one.

Taquard deployed to the field with the FDC, but without a definite function. The FIST team deployed separately so there was no contact between Taquard and his original team. Field duty in Korea in the wintertime is cold. The problem with a field exercise that follows an ARTEP is that there are usually no rounds to fire. This was no exception. While it is acceptable to send the infantry out into the field without artillery support, artillerymen hate going out to the field when there are no rounds to fire or adjust. Nevertheless, the firing battery went out and made movements in the cold frigid winter for about a week and a half without any ammunition. Other than the fact that the slicky boys were in full force as usual and the fact that everyone froze their asses off, it was a very unmemorable exercise. The reason that the exercise was so memorable to Taquard was not because of what happened during the exercise, besides getting his jacket stolen during the winter, but because of what followed. One of the problems that wasn't anticipated was returning Taquard home after an exercise. It was a problem because he lived on a different post than the firing battery. Fortunately for Taquard, the FDC agreed to go a few miles out of their way and swing by Camp Pelham to drop him off. Unlike the fisties who returned home from the field in the afternoon, if they went to the field at all, the firing batteries in Korea arrived back much later. It was three in the morning when Taquard got back from his first field exercise as an indigenous firing battery member. He was dirty, tired, and beat. He got to his room, dropped his gear on the floor, turned on his electric heater, and lay down on the bed. He was exhausted and ready to go to sleep even without taking a shower. He had lain down for less than five minutes when he heard a knock on his door. Even though he tried to ignore it, but the knocking was persistent even after ten minutes. Taquard checked to see who it was. There was a sergeant and a specialist at his door, neither of whom he recognized. Both were wearing full field battle gear and had M16 rifles.

"What is it?"

"Sir, there's a jeep waiting for you," the sergeant answered.

"What's going on?"

"We're supposed to drive you somewhere."

"I just got back from the field not five minutes ago, it's late, and I'm going to bed."

"Sir, we have orders."

"What orders?"

"We have to leave right now."

"Am I under arrest?"

"No, sir. You are not under arrest, but we have to leave right away."

"What kind of orders are you talking about? Who gave these orders?"

"Sir, we can't tell you. You better pack your gear; you're going to be gone for a few days. That is all that I can tell you."

"Are you sure about all this?"

"Yes, sir, very sure. It's important."

"How do you know you even have the right guy? It's the middle of the night and you can't see shit around here."

"Sir, you're the one we came to get. First Lieutenant Elwood Aaron Taquard, 919-14-"

"I got it," Taquard interrupted. "Let me get my stuff."

When they got out of the junior officer's quarters there was a jeep waiting for them right by the entrance.

"Normally, people park in the parking lot instead of on the grass," Taquard commented.

"This is not a normal situation," the sergeant replied.

"And where exactly where in the hell is it that we are going in the middle of the night?"

"I'm afraid I can't tell you."

"Do either one of you have any idea what time it is?"

"Yes, sir, we do."

They drove in the jeep for a little over two hours when the sergeant, who was also the driver, stopped the jeep in the middle of nowhere in the middle of the road.

"What's this?" Taquard asked.

"This is as far as we go. We're dropping you off here."

"There's nothing here."

"Just follow the road over the hill."

"Can't you just drive me to wherever it is I'm supposed to be going?"

"No, sir, orders are orders."

"Wait here until I give you the signal before it's time to leave."

"Yes, sir."

Taquard departed with all of his gear and rucksack full of his belongings. He walked up the hill not knowing what to think. When he got to the top of the hill he saw massive camp below that resembled a city. It was in the midst of nowhere between heavy forest vegetation. It was a temporary compound that was secured with countless strands of concertina wire. This place had "Do No Enter," or better still, "Go Away" written all over it. It was out of the way and was secured to the hilt to ensure that there were no unwanted visitors. The tent city surrounded by barriers and security resembled a well-fortified fortress. Taquard wasn't even sure that he was supposed to be there in the first place. He regretted telling his only mode of transportation to leave. He didn't even know how to get in the temporary facility let alone what to do once he got there. He finally approached the edge of the compound and found an entrance station. Only then did he realize that he hadn't shaved in the last couple of days. He was addressed by a guard.

"Sir, state your business here, sir."

"Uhhh, I was brought here, but they didn't say why."

"Please state your name sir, clearance level, and your social security number."

Taquard complied. Even though he was only a lieutenant, he had an SCI (Special Compartmentalized Information) security clearance which was above Top Secret. The guard used the information to reference a ledger.

"Sir, may I see your ID card?"

Taquard complied.

"Sir, you are cleared to enter. Upon entering, you will exit the door on your right."

When he entered the compound he saw more configured posts surrounded by more concertina wire. It was a conglomeration of areas each surrounded by concertina wire and dedicated security all surrounded by even more concertina wire and security. As he went from one security point to another he was given further directions. He arrived at yet another security point when he was asked to give his full name while the desk sergeant referred to another roster.

"Yes, sir. You're on the list. Please proceed this way," the sergeant said to Taquard as he pointed to an exit.

He was greeted by his FIST NCO who happened to have the clearance credentials to participate in this type of venture.

"Sir, it's good to see you."

"What is going on around here?"

"Let me introduce you to Captain Nakamura. He'll fill you in on everything that you need to know," Staff Sergeant Beaumont said as he led Taquard into a tent.

The tent was set up with a lot of chairs, tables, field desks, and briefing charts. Captain Nakamura noticed Taquard and Beaumont.

"You must be Lieutenant Taquard," he said while extending his hand in a friendly manner.

"Yes, sir."

"I've heard a lot about you. This is big. We got a lot of four star generals in on this one. Army, Air Force, and full admirals as well."

"What's going on sir?"

"I'll explain everything. First let me fill you in on what will take place. You look tired."

"Yes, sir. I've been up all night. I just got out of the field."

"Yes, I know. Your men have set up a place for you. We had to intercept them during your field duty without anybody knowing about it. I can't stress enough how important secrecy is around. You must not tell anyone anything. No one is to know about this."

"Yes, sir."

"Where are you?"

"I don't know, sir."

"You are at your unit, that's where you are. This place doesn't exist."

"Yes, sir. My captain—"

"Never mind about your captain. You are at your regular place of duty doing what you would normally be doing. Here's the deal. I need you to clean up and get some sleep. Take as much time as you need and sleep as long as you want."

Taquard went to another area that was set up for him by his men who all had top level security clearances as well. He was able to take a quick shower and get something to eat before going to sleep. He slept all day and all night into the next day. After waking up he was greeted by SSG Beaumont.

"Sir, I brought you some breakfast, thought you might be hungry."

"Thank you. I'm still in the dark here. Wait is that my uniform over there?"

"Yes, sir, it is. We swung by your room and picked it up for you, your houseboy let us in. I hope you don't mind."

"No, it's all right."

"Not many people have our level of security clearance. We are doing everything here. You name it, it's being done right here and now."

"What's being done?"

"Everything. The whole scenario. Command decisions are being made. That's what's going on."

"I thought that you were in the field with me."

"No, sir. We were diverted just after you left. We've been here the whole time."

"How did you manage to keep the APC (Armored personnel Carrier)? What's it doing here? I thought Captain Burke wanted to get rid of it."

"He does, but we've been hiding it in the scrap yard. He doesn't know we still have it. And another thing, he's not to know anything about what's going on here. He doesn't have the security clearance for it."

"But what do they want with us?"

"You'll find out. Captain Nakamura will get you up to speed on everything."

Captain Nakamura walked into the area.

"Well, Lieutenant, did you get enough sleep?"

"Yes, sir."

"Anything else you need? Something else to eat? How about some coffee?"

"Yes, sir, coffee would be great."

"Okay, first I am going to give you some briefings," he said to Taquard as he handed him a cup of coffee. "I'm going to give you some information that most people don't know anything about."

"Yes, sir."

"Let's talk about the attack on Pearl Harbor. Many people believe that Franklin D. Roosevelt knew about the attack in advance but decided not to react to it. This is false. The Japanese sent a cable to their ambassador to the US prior to the attack. The Japanese knew about the attack. We were able to intercept it during its transmission. However, we were not able to decode it in time. Historically speaking, the Japanese start wars before they declare war on a nation. It's part of their strategy. To them it makes sense. We were caught off guard. All of us including FDR himself."

"That's not really news."

"To some people it is. Some people prefer to believe a lie over the truth. Here's another one. This one's in print," Nakamura continued while showing Taquard some articles. "Here we have a suicide. This newspaper clipping says that this Russian defector committed suicide."

"Hey, I know that guy," Taquard announced. "I mean, I knew him."

"What? How did you know him?"

"I met him when I was a kid. I spoke to him and everything and you're right, it wasn't a suicide, it was an assassination."

"I didn't say that, but I was about to. Here is another article about the same incident, only this time, it says that he was killed as a result of an accident."

"He said that they would kill him and that it would be made to look like an accident, most likely suicide."

"That's what he told you?"

"Yes, about two months before it happened."

"Well, he was right. The point that I'm making here is that the media is full of misinformation and disinformation. Usually, this is deliberate. And in our case there will be no information. This too is a deliberate action. One thing that you will learn about people, including Americans, is that they can't handle the truth."

"You know there's a book about that guy. Maybe it's out of print now."

"Yes, I've read it, I assume you have too."

"Yes, sir I have, but it is no match compared to hearing him tell it in person."

"You're the only person here who has ever actually met him."

Taquard recalled his meeting with Sergei and thought about his life and the remarkable influence that he had in such a short period of time.

Sergei was born on 1 March 1951 and grew up as an orphan in the United Soviet Socialist Republic. His father was killed under Khrushchev's orders when he was only four years old. His mother died soon afterwards. He fled for his life from the orphan house when he was six. Remaining at the orphanage meant certain death. For the next ten days he lived at the Novosibirsk Central Train Station where he acquired survival skills that would benefit him later in life. From there he was taken to a children's home by the police. The children's home was not an orphanage; it was a place for children who had been forcibly taken away from their parents for the benefit of the state. Having unsavory political beliefs or believing in God was grounds for imprisonment. Sergei lost one of his front teeth while fighting for and getting the position of king at the children's home. He became king through fighting and brutal force where there was no room for conflicting beliefs. Engaging in crime was taught in the schools and was also a means of existence.

In school he grew up learning the values of the state and the importance of conformity. He was taught that the state was more important than the family or individual. As a teenager he was well indoctrinated in the communist manifesto and engaged in warfare against those who secretly worshiped God and practiced Christian beliefs. He worked with others to prevent the smuggling in of Bibles and other forms of prohibited literature.

He served his country with unwavering loyalty as he carried out missions to serve the interests of the state. He tortured and murdered many while believing in his country and its cause. To him, the cause was of greater importance than the individual. He discovered that he was wrong.

He often wondered why people were willing to endure unfathomable levels of pain, torture, suffering, and death for their beliefs in the Holy

Bible and Jesus Christ. Listening to him tell about the abuse that was delivered in the name of the state gave me a feeling that I cannot record in words. I will never forget it. He was able to speak of his actions and how victims endured a suffering that was worse than death. He was not able to describe it as well in writing.

In 1970, there was a surge of believers among the Russian youth. Sergei noted profound contradictions in what he was taught and what he observed. He kept handwritten pages of Bibles that belonged to his victims and began to read them. He was seeking the truth even if it was contrary to everything that he believed in. The truth was the instrument that he would use to climb out of the abyss. He decided to defect.

On 3 September 1971 he jumped ship off of the west coast of Canada in frigid waters. One of the most desperate moments that he recalled was remembering the saying: "I want to die with my boots on." Ironically, the boots were killing him. They filled with water and were pulling him down. Fortunately, he had enough foresight to bring a knife with him. He used his knife to cut through his trouser legs and rip the boots one at a time while desperately holding his breath and ducking under the water. After three hours of swimming in excruciating cold he found back at the ship again back where he started. He was faced with a dilemma. Should he go back to the warm ship with the inviting lights shining through the portholes? He made a second escape attempt by swimming for Canada once again. Eventually, he reached rocks at the bottom of a cliff. He climbed up 200 feet to the top of the cliff to avoid being washed back to sea. It was only then that he noticed that he had to swim an additional two miles to reach the village across more water. He swam through the darkness through the pouring rain thinking that he was so near death and so far away from home.

He successfully escaped and found freedom and refuge from Christian churches and believers in North America. He traveled to America and told people about his life, experiences, and his belief in Jesus Christ. The one thing that Christians repeated failed to do was to view strangers with skepticism. They were not cautious when it came to trusting people. They would have done well to have listened to the words of George Washington when he warned people to be intimate with just a few people but only after they were well tried before given confidence. Sergei became an individual in a land of conformists. Perhaps he wasn't the only one in that predicament.

In October of 1972 I had the pleasure of meeting Sergei. It was also the first Christian sermon that I had ever attended. It was the first time that had ever even been inside of a Christian church. His story was extremely interesting and his delivery was enthusiastic and sincere. No one could ever have said it better. His life story surpassed the foundation of thriller novels. I listened attentively even though I was a recent teenager who was prone to fidgeting. I still remember him to this day. I told others about him. Most people just didn't get it. I have even run into others who have read his book and/or heard of him. Even among that group some got it while others didn't. While he was telling his story he predicted his own death. He said that his execution would be carried out by the KGB and that it could happen even in the United States. He said that it would look like an accident, most likely a suicide. After hearing him tell his life story I spoke with him briefly and was inspired. Several weeks after I met him he was killed in Los Angeles. Later, I read the book about his life entitled *The Persecutor*. The book was no match to actually speaking to him personally. On January 1, 1973 he was found dead with a bullet through his head in Los Angeles, California. Initial official reports stated that his death was the result of an intentional suicide. Later, reports would be revised to reflect the cause of death as an accident. He was twenty-one.

"Here is a picture of the aftermath of..."

"The Kent State massacre. I did my graduate thesis on it. I did my oral presentation on May 4, 1980 on the ten year anniversary of the incident."

"As you may or may not know, this was no accident."

"I came to the same conclusion."

"Sticking all those jokers with weapons from the Nasty Guard with those crazy students together for four days straight and people are surprised that sparks flew. If you want to make sure that things get all fucked up, call the Nasty Guard."

"Yes, sir, as a matter of fact, I met two of them too."

"You met two people who were involved in Kent State?"

"Yes, sir. But I didn't ask them any questions. I ran into them accidentally while I working on my thesis. It was entirely coincidental."

"Well, four students were killed and nine others were wounded. One of the fatal shots to the neck came from 390 feet away. Another neck wound, although not fatal, came from 750 feet away. Those were no accidents. And let's not forget that one of the fatalities was an ROTC student who was killed at 382 feet away. They couldn't've been more flagrant if they tried. They got away with it and the country supported them."

"Who exactly did you meet from the Kent State massacre?"

"One from each side."

"Anyone who was shot?"

"Yes. He asked me for some help pushing his wheelchair up a hill. I did it in exchange for him holding my books. As it turned they were books about Kent State. He was one of the students who got shot. He told me when he saw my books. Talk about eerie coincidences. I didn't ask him any questions. I didn't even get his name, but it would be extremely easy to find out. And as far as the guardsman is concerned, it would be better to pretend like he never existed."

"Never mind then. Well, you are now going to participate in something else that never existed. I'm giving you some information and I will be giving you a lot more. I started out with trivia, but it is obvious that you are just the type of person that we are looking for. Besides, the general was really impressed with the way you handled Camp Pelham while you were in command."

"Thank you, sir. But that was really rough duty."

"Another thing, people are set on their beliefs even if they are wrong. They would rather continue their beliefs no matter how wrong they may be rather than seek the truth. Here's another thing that people never consider. The Bible in most cases is wrong. What I mean by that is that there are several types of Bibles on the market these days. They can't all be correct. They could all be wrong, but they can't all be correct. Not only does the verbiage vary, so does the doctrine. The only true word of God comes from the authorized King James Version; all of the others are imitations. Notice that I did not endorse the New King James Version. I know that this sounds like trivia, but it is important that you know the difference between fact and fiction. Then of course there is just plain bullshit. For example, it has been said that urine is good for a wound. Yeah, urine. I've actually heard people say that urinating on a wound is a good thing. Well, it's not."

Captain Nakamura spent the rest of the day briefing Taquard. It was a series of casual and informal briefings even though the level was above Top Secret. Hollywood depicts high level classified briefings as being stiff necked and highly formal, but the actual experience was quite the opposite. He introduced an action plan to Taquard and went over it with him in a thorough manner.

"Now comes the good part. Why you are here. I want you to go over this plan. Your purpose of being here is to go over this plan and to either approve, disapprove, or modify it. You're the only artillery officer here. And the code for access to the command module is that you are to inform them that the Boston Red Sox beat the New York Yankees in the World Series. This code will remain in effect after we leave here. It will determine who was with us in the future. There is another code that we will go by in the future as well. When we are introducing someone to someone else we may refer to him as a Red Sox fan or Yankees fan. A Red Sox fan is a friend, a Yankee is an enemy and is not to be trusted. If the subject is about baseball and a friend happens to be a Yankee fan then refer to Piper airplanes. A Piper Cub is a friend, a Piper Tomahawk is an enemy."

"This is an amazing action. So far I can't find any faults with it."

"When you have made your decisions concerning the plan you will be briefing the generals on it."

"When do I have to brief the generals?"

"Thirty minutes after you tell me that you're ready to brief them."

Taquard went over the plan. He studied every aspect very carefully. After a few hours of going over it he informed Nakamura that he was ready.

"I only have one slight modification. And I have a question as well. How can we possibly support such an operation?"

"We can't. But once this is approved, we will get all the resources that we need to make this work."

"But there's no time line."

"No. Remember that this is a contingency operation. Let's hope that we don't need it."

Nakamura noted the modification that Taquard mentioned and annotated it in the briefing. He escorted Taquard to a large tent that was filled with stars. Unlike the anal retentive stateside units that seek peak stress levels for fictitious or inconsequential information, this briefing was relaxed, informal, and had a purpose. There were even snacks and something to drink while the meeting took place. And unlike stateside briefings where the person giving the briefing gets his ass chewed for no legitimate reason, this was a legitimate meeting with no screaming or shouting. Not only does Hollywood have the wrong idea about the Army, the Army has the wrong idea about the Army. This was how the Army was supposed to be like; it was very professional and getting the job done was more important than how things looked. The meeting was informal and short. Decisions were made and set up for implementation. Subsequent actions to support the decisions were put into place.

After the meeting, Taquard was met by Nakamura.

"Okay, this concludes your portion of this operation. You guys can go back now. And remember, you were never here."

"Yes, sir."

The team packed up their gear and left the compound. Other modules were departing was well. The APC traveled by itself, something that is very unusual, for about two hours before arriving at Camp Giant. They went past Giant on to Pelham to drop off Taquard and his gear. He performed field recovery operations to maintain his stuff. The one thing that an individual learns in the Army is to conduct field recovery operations on the sly; otherwise you will never take care of either yourself or your gear. As far as the unit is concerned, a soldier needs to spend his time servicing unit equipment, vehicles, and common areas. Basically, Taquard took the rest of the day off to recover and take care of his equipment.

The following day Taquard reported to Ingel to provide him with an overview of what went on. He felt that Ingel was entitled to a little information and his security clearance was validated. Even though he wouldn't violate any classification protocols, he felt like he should at least talk to the colonel. As it turned out, the colonel wasn't interested in hearing about the operation and Taquard was told to report back to his unit.

"Where the fuck have you been?" Burke asked Taquard upon his reporting to the unit.

"I've been here," Taquard responded. "Just where I was supposed to be."

"No, you weren't."

"Lets talk to Colonel Ingel, he'll tell you the same thing."

"I need to know where you have been."

"I'll get Colonel Ingel to talk to you."

"My ass. And since you refuse to tell me where you were I am reporting this incident to Blunt."

"Go ahead, he'll tell you the same thing."

Just like he said that he would, Burke called Blunt.

"Yes, sir," Blunt responded. "What can I do for you?"

"I'm reporting Taquard absent for duty for the past few days, he won't tell me where he's been."

"He's been with you the whole time. That's his place of duty and that's where he's been."

"Is this some kind of joke or something? I'm telling you that he hasn't been here. I'm the commander and I know who's been here and who hasn't and I'm telling you that he hasn't been here. I know you two are friends. You two are always up to something. I'll talk to the colonel about this."

"Okay, he'll see both of you in one hour."

"What are you talking about?"

"He's expecting both of you in one hour."

"Wait, I didn't schedule an appointment."

"Yes, sir, you did. When you said that you wanted to talk to the colonel you made an appointment and your appointment is in one hour and I have to remind you not to be late."

"Blunt, you're an asshole!"

An hour later both Burke and Taquard were in the colonel's office to discuss Taquard's whereabouts. There were a lot of unanswered questions that Burke wanted resolved.

"Look, for the record, Taquard has been at his assigned duty area performing his duties in an impeccable manner," stated Lieutenant Colonel Ingel. "That's all there is to it and that is the end of the discussion."

After departing Ingel's office Burke pulled Taquard to the side and said, "What the fuck is going on around here and where have you been?"

"Sir, I would tell you if I could, but I can't. Besides, Colonel Ingel cleared up the matter."

"Well, I just want you to know that whatever it is, I don't like it one single bit."

"I understand, but there's nothing that can be done about it."

"Well, I'm going to get to the bottom of this. I'm going to find out where you've been and what you've been up to."

"No, sir, you won't. You don't even want to try. You're better off not knowing."

The day went on as usual with the APC field recovery operations. Even though the APC was protested by the battery commanders, Lieutenant Colonel Ingel insisted that they accept them. It wasn't like Ingel could simply toss all the APCs at a junk yard and forget about them. The NCOs found refuge at the battalion motor pool as they did previously to the unit reconfiguration. Although the FIST teams and APCs were officially part of the firing batteries, the fisties knew to stay out of sight. The rivalry between the batteries and FISTs continued. It was more accurately described as the FISTs wanting to belong to a club that didn't want them. As much as Ingel wanted to change this attitude within his battalion, he couldn't.

Captain Burke remained curious about what was going on with Taquard. In addition to being a forward observer, Taquard was a forward observer with a security clearance that was higher than Burke's. Taquard was rubbing people the wrong way on two fronts. Later that evening Taquard received a call from Ingel in the barracks.

"Elwood, I need to see you in my office first thing tomorrow morning."

"Yes, sir, is anything wrong?"

"I need to know something about what happened. Nothing that will violate and security protocols but something. The general is coming here tomorrow to talk to me about what happened."

Taquard saw Ingel the following morning and prepared him for the general's visit. Later that afternoon the general met with Ingel and the meeting went really well.

Additional field exercises with ammunition and Taquard's team's participation followed during the next several weeks without ant surprise subsequent operations. Field operations also meant counting the days down until the time of departure. Another assignment came up that would also help Taquard with his countdown.

"Taquard," Blunt shouted as he came into his room without knocking. "Pack your bags."

"What's going on this time?"

"You're leaving tomorrow. I got your orders."

"Tomorrow? I haven't even cleared yet."

"Not those kind of orders, TDY (temporary duty)."

"TDY?"

"Air Assault School."

"What?"

"There's a slot at the Air Assault School. The colonel selected you. You're leaving first thing tomorrow morning."

"Wow, when did this happen?"

"We were allocated to support the new Air Assault School."

"New?"

"Yes, they just opened one up in Hawaii."

"Hawaii? No kidding."

"Here's a packing list. You can buy whatever else you need when you get there."

# Chapter Fifteen
## *Air Assault*

The departure to Hawaii was a welcomed one. It was so good to leave South Korea, also known as the land of the morning calm. It was a long flight that went against the sun. Many people believe that traveling in this direction for long periods of time will drain a person of his energy. It didn't matter, Taquard was young. He landed in Honolulu, the state capital, on the island of Oahu. If Oahu means the gathering place, then it was appropriately named. There have been many challenges to the actual origin and meaning of the word.

He knew that he would be going there eventually but this was a welcomed detour. Hawaii wasn't without it problems. When he arrived at the airport there was no one there to meet him. He reported to the military desk and was put in contact with Schofield Barracks. They were unaware of his arrival but were able to verify his slot at the school. They sent another lieutenant to the airport to pick him up.

"I'm Lieutenant Ackworth, I was sent here to pick you up."

"Great. I'm ready to start school."

"Yeah, me too. We're in the same class."

"Do you have a schedule?"

"We'll take the PT test tomorrow afternoon. The day after tomorrow which is Friday, we will have a twelve-mile road march. Then we are free for the weekend. Where are you staying?"

"I thought you knew. I have no idea."

"Crap. Can you rent a car and find a place to stay?"

"I tried that already. No one will rent me a car on account of my age. They want older drivers."

"Shit! It's only for a couple of weeks. Maybe they have some place on post where you can stay. Do you have a full uniform?"

"Yes."

"Good, because you'll need it for the PT test. Many places are doing their PT tests in shorts and tennis shoes, but not Air Assault. They want you to do it in BDUs and boots. By the way, how many push-ups can you do?"

"Fifty or sixty."

"Good, because when they say that you have to do forty-five push-ups they really mean about fifty to sixty. They're brutal when it comes to grading push-ups."

"You mean like Airborne and Ranger?"

"Yes, I'd say so. This is a new school and they still have something to prove."

The population on Oahu was at 101% capacity. On post housing was maxed out. The Schofield Barracks Hotel had been demolished due to cockroach infestation. First, large tents were built around the hotel; then it was fumigated for two months. That didn't work. A lot of other things were tried in efforts to control the cockroaches. Finally, they decided to demolish the hotel and burn the site. Then they decided not to rebuild it. After several additional attempts at finding a place for Taquard to stay, Ackworth finally decided to put him up at his place. It was only a small inconvenience that would only last for a short time.

"Well, it's not much, but it's home."

The first day at Air Assault School consisted of taking a PT test. With the exception of the eight pull-ups that were required for both Airborne and Ranger the standards for the PT test were the same: forty-five push-ups, forty-five sit-ups, and a two-mile run in less than sixteen minutes. The PT test was performed in boots in either a BDU uniform or fatigues. There was a Brigadier General who was present at the PT test; he challenged students to do their best and encouraged them to make it through the course. He bet perspective students a case of beer that they wouldn't make it. He got a lot of acceptances. When he spoke to Taquard a counter challenge was offered. Instead of beer (Taquard was a non-drinker) Taquard challenged the general for one month's pay. Although the pay checks were of different value Taquard thought that it was a fair condition. The general didn't take Taquard up on his counteroffer. Ackworth and Taquard, who were both in shape, both passed the PT test without any difficulty.

"The next thing we have to do is get ready for the road march tomorrow. I'm telling you Elwood that last push-up of yours really had me going for a while. I thought you weren't going to make it."

"What do we have to do between now and then?"

"Swing by Clothing Sales and make sure that we have everything on the list. After the road march they're going to inventory out ALICE packs to make sure that we have everything that we're supposed to carry. If we're short we fail."

The second day of the school consisted of a twelve-mile road march with full gear that had to be completed in less than three hours. The packing list for the ruck sack had to be adhered to. The weight couldn't be any less than what the packing list prescribed. Most students packed a little extra just to ensure that the weight of their ruck sack was never in question. The rules of the road march were read to the students. Absolutely no assistance would be rendered.

"If someone is falling behind, God have mercy on that person, because you'd better not," one of the instructors informed the group.

The twelve-mile course included going up large hills and uneven terrain. There was no pace walker, although one was expected. The start and finish points were one and the same. The course was set up in such a way that attempting a shortcut would lengthen the course. There were cadre members along the course and at the halfway point where prospective Air Assault students had to check in. Each person was assigned a number that was attached to him for ready identification. The cadre noted the numbers at the halfway point. It was amazing how close the prospects cut their times. Ackworth and Taquard stepped out at a brisk pace and kept it up through the march. Running with a heavy back pack was impossible to do for a very long period of time. Ackworth and Taquard stayed together for most of the course. When the finish line was in sight, Ackworth left Taquard behind. Times were called out at the finish line. Ackworth had less than ten minutes to spare. In the distance Taquard struggled as he could hear the times being called out. He barely made it with less than three minutes to spare. After the road march was completed by everyone who made it within the time limit, the ruck sacks were inventoried. Most of the students made it. There was a National Guardsman who was dismissed from the course because he was caught catching a ride during the road march. The car, a bright yellow Buick Regal, was all too familiar to the cadre in the area for it to go unnoticed for a few hours.

Unlike Ranger, Air Assault left the weekends open to the students. Although Taquard tried his best to enjoy Hawaii, he was perturbed by the fact that he didn't have a vehicle. He relied on Ackworth and others to give him transportation. With the help of a new acquaintance Taquard decided to try our SCUBA (Self Contained Underwater Breathing Apparatus) diving during the free weekends.

Clay, another lieutenant, introduced Taquard to a SCUBA instructor, Ron, who was teaching an Open Water orienteering course. They needed another student for the class to make. For a price Taquard could rent gear and take a course. He would have to buy some of his own gear, like a mouthpiece for example. This was a welcomed opportunity for Taquard. He suffered from blisters on his feet from the road march as he always did. He had ten blisters on his left foot and fourteen on his right. Some were small but all were irritating, some were bloody, others were huge, but all were painful. He always popped his blisters. Salt water from the ocean would be good for treating his popped blisters.

The first day consisted of a pool dive, two day dives, and a night dive. The second day consisted of three dives (a knot test dive/regular dive, a salvage dive/test, and a regular fun dive). Prior to the pool dive, the students sat in a classroom and learned about the fundamentals of SCUBA diving. Since this abbreviated course included salvage diving, a lot of knots were taught. Knot tying was a big part of the course.

"Everything that I teach you in the classroom will be tested both here and in the water," the instructor emphasized. You will have time to practice your knots because the knot test is tomorrow. The knots have to be tied precisely and quickly. After the knot test tomorrow morning, you will take the test again under water. Again, you will be graded on both speed and accurately," Ron authoritatively addressed.

There are some things in SCUBA diving that you just don't rent or borrow. In addition to a mouthpiece a SCUBA mask is a personal item that is not designed for sharing. The best type of mask on the market at that time was a double seal silicon mask with side windows and a built in purge valve. Silicon provides a good seal without irritating the skin like rubber does. Some people prefer gum to silicon. Gum provides a better seal but it is less comfortable. The masks with optional purge valves should never be cut. Purge valves are a must but a mask that doesn't have a built in purge valve should never be modified to attempt making a purge valve. Another piece of equipment that Taquard bought was a silicon snorkel with the purge valve at the bottom.

"There are a lot of toys and accessories that you can buy for SCUBA diving. Don't get too carried away. At this point I do not recommend that you buy a knife or an underwater writing card. If you really have to have a knife like most people do, remember that a SCUBA knife is not a weapon. It is a tool for prying, but most of all it is an ornament that makes you look cool. Diving tables will be provided to you. Keep in mind that you are in Hawaii. Hawaiians steal. Watch your gear at all times," Ron stated.

"There's no Hawaiians in the class," one of the students noted.

"But the locals are on the beaches and they will steal."

"Hey, there are no colored black people in the class either," another student added.

"Actually I've never had a black student. Not really sure why."

"Hey," one of the students whispered to another.

"What?" another student responded.

"How come Hawaiians and blacks don't marry?"

"I don't know, why?"

"Because they're afraid that their children will grow up to be too lazy to steal."

"You two are going to have to pay attention and hold your jokes for later," Ron interrupted. "Besides, I've heard that joke before."

The classroom session was followed with hands-on activities and a practical exercise. Then the students went into the pool that was behind the shop which also served as a classroom. It was scary going under the water for the first time with a regulator. It wasn't natural. Heavy fast breathing consumed the air rapidly. The students used up their air in about fifteen minutes with a tank that should last for about an hour. It wasn't so bad once you got under the water but inexperience consumes air quickly. After a session in the pool the students came out of the pool and exchanged tanks.

"You're going in again and then it's off to the beach. If you swallow any water in the ocean don't spit out your regulator. You can vomit through the regulator."

The second pool dive went much better and the students managed to stay underwater for about half an hour. Pool diving was beneficial although most SCUBA schools don't bother with it.

"Everyone, remember that you will have a test tomorrow morning so don't forget to study and practice your knots. For you smokers, your underwater times will be reduced. I suggest that you quit. Also, no drinking tonight. Alcohol has an adverse effect on your body when it is under pressure. Stay in the group. I will pair you up. I'll choose your partner, not you."

Clay and Taquard were not selected as partners. Even though the instructor knew that they were friends he did not pair them up with each other.

"Reminder, your right hand is you and your left hand is your partner. Maintain contact with your partner."

The underwater hand signals were reviewed. Pointing with two hands with the right hand forward of the left means, "I'll lead, you follow." As simple and as self-explanatory as the signals were, confusion was still a possibility.

"Another thing that I need to tell you is that it is illegal to hunt for female lobster. The fine for catching a female lobster is one dollar an egg. A female lobster will hold about three to four thousand eggs at a time. If you accidentally catch a female lobster use your knife and perform a sex change before you come ashore. Hawaiian lobsters taste like crap. If you want a good lobster, Maine lobster is the best."

The class did two additional dives on the beach. Each dive lasted for about an hour. On the first dive the class came across some fishermen. They couldn't believe that the fishermen were using Snap-On tool accessories as fishing weights. The knives and mesh net bags came in handy. The class relieved the fishermen of their weights.

"I can't believe that anyone would use Snap-On tools for fishing weights. Well he won't have that problem anymore," one of the students said as he was holding up a bag of tools. The tools looked good even when wet.

The students exchanged their tanks and went back into the ocean. The fishermen were at it again. More Snap-On tools were ready for the taking. One of the fishermen hooked a nice fish which one of the students wanted. The student followed the reeling in of the fish with a mesh bag and took out his knife. He surfaced above the water lever just in time to cut the line and bag himself a fish at the expense of the fisherman. Experience comes quickly in the arena of SCUBA diving. Other students approached swimmers and scared the crap out of them by grabbing them. Others still went under a large boat that was giving people a glass bottom boat ride. Taquard accidentally came face to face with a moray eel. It was dark green and about four feet in length. The eel came right at him before Taquard saw anything. The eel hit Taquard's SCUBA mask with its nose. Contrary to popular belief that was depicted in the movie *The Deep*, morays are timid. Before Taquard could respond, the eel quickly swam away. In spite of his encounter and good fortune Taquard had no intention of pushing his luck with morays.

The day dives were followed by a break which included a great meal. Clay and Taquard went to a steak restaurant with an awesome salad bar. The steaks were great but the big rave was the salad bar. Nobody but nobody offers better salad bars than the places in Hawaii. The epitome of what a salad bar should be like is represented in several restaurants throughout Hawaii. Hawaii had an abundance of food. The food was fresh and delicious.

The night dive that was met with great anticipation went very well. This was the first night dive for the students. Ron issued out flashlights to each student. The underwater activities change at night as they do on land. Many animals are nocturnal. The students observed new animals as they swam around slowly. Getting caught up in the scenery was good to a point. A person still had to be cautious. Taquard swam with his beam of light pointed directly in front of him but when he pointed it down he noticed that he was only a couple of feet above a bed of moray eels. There were thousands of them. Fortunately, they were all asleep. The slept with their eyes opened and although they didn't make any noise doing it, they snored.

The following morning began with test taking. After the written exams were graded Ron tested the students in knot tying. The students sat far enough apart, while being under a time constraint, so that they couldn't refer to each other during the test. Ron would flip to a sign, with the name of a knot on it, on his flip chart and start his stop watch. The students, in addition to knowing how to tie a knot, had to know the name of the knots as well. Taquard recognized the names of the knots and knew how to tie them within the time limit. Most of the students passed. The standard for proceeding to the next phase of the class was to tie all knots correctly within the time limit.

Taquard's partner, Steve, said, "I barely made it through that knot test. A couple of those were just dumb luck. You were really flying through those knots. I just hope that I can pass the test again in the ocean."

"Don't worry, Steve, you'll make it."

When the class arrived at the beach Ron took them underwater and administered another knot test. He had an underwater stop watch. Taquard was able to pass the knot test again on his first try. He was adept with knots and performed it with ease. A retest was given to the students who failed the test the first time. Steve passed the retest.

After the test was completed, the class used the remainder of their initial tanks to go diving and hunting. The second dive consisted of an underwater land navigation test. There were buried anchors at designated locations under the water. Each anchor had a code painted on it. There was an anchor for each pair of students. The student pairs would find the buried anchor and uncover it, read and record the code, and return with the answer.

"Does everyone understand the rules of this test? Your time limit is before you run out of air," Ron instructed. "Oh, there is one more thing that I forgot to tell you. The anchors are all painted white. The anchor number and codes are painted in blue. But you can't read the codes under water. They have all been painted with a special paint that can't be seen under water even though it can be read while it is wet. Once you have brought your anchor to the surface verify the anchor number to make sure that it matches your team number. You don't want to come back with the wrong code."

"How heavy are the anchors?" a student asked.

"Too heavy for you to swim with."

"Then how do we get them to the surface?"

"With your nets and bags. Just like I taught you."

"Elwood," Steve whispered to Taquard, "what are we going to do? You tie these knots a lot better than I can."

"I'll tie the knots, you provide the air."

"Deal."

"If we get in a real jam, we'll abort and I will let you use my octopus."

The plastic cards were made for underwater writing. A regular pencil was all that was required. The problem with the card was that it couldn't be erased underwater. The students plotted their course before going in to the water. There were no landmarks to go by as there is for land navigation. The pace had to be carefully measured and kept track of while referring to the compass. Direction of travel had to be changed while searching for the anchor. Ron sure how to make a challenging test. To the team's surprise, the anchor was buried at the first site that they dug at. Four mesh net bags were tied to different places on the anchor with ropes. The application of the knots was utilized. Then, the secure mesh bags were lined with plastic bags. Steve then filled the bags with his air. Just like Ron said it would, the anchor surfaces once the bags were filled. And just like Ron said, the blue paint was invisible under water. Once the team and anchor surfaced they could read the team number and code.

"Hey look, that's our team number, A1. It's right here. Yeah, Ron was right you can't read the paint under water but you can read it up here, even when it's wet. Ron's always right."

"Elwood, can you see the code? I'm ready to write."

"You don't need to write it down."

"Why not?"

"I'll remember it. I won't forget."

Steve looked and read it: BITCHEYE.

"What does it mean?"

"It means that one of the Bitcheye Commandos made it to Hawaii before I did."

"What?"

"It's a long story. Not one worth telling. Let's bury the anchor and get back."

Air Assault turned out to be no joke. It was a hard course. Even a Ranger dropped out. Students who were Airborne or Rangers or both (there was a leg Ranger in the class) would scoff at the course and horse around. Their joking around didn't go unnoticed by the cadre. They responded by making the course even more difficult. The first day of the course itself was committed to eliminating students. The students had to hike up a large hill on a steep trail to the conditioning site. The PT was rigorous. Any student who fell behind in the repetitions of the conditioning drills was sent to the mud pit. Like Airborne, students wore white T-shirts. A trip to the mud pit converted white T-shirts into brown. The formation started turning brown. By the end of conditioning drill session all but three T-shirts were brown. Of the three that were remaining, two were Rangers, including Taquard, and the other one was Ackworth. They were rewarded by being sent to the mud pit. This was followed by an obstacle course. The obstacle course was grueling just by itself but the cadre had the students perform additional conditioning drills between stations while waiting for their turn to negotiate an obstacle. Some students were injured and dismissed from the course, others dropped out from their own choosing. Elimination Day successfully trimmed down the class size.

When muddy Ackworth and Taquard returned home a neighbor showered them off with a hose. It was amazing how dirty they were. All they could do was think about cleaning up and getting some sleep. After they showered they went to sleep and didn't wake up until the following morning when it was time to go back to school. The second day was dedicated to rappelling instruction. One thing that became apparent about the school was the professionalism of the cadre. Like Ranger, the TAC (Training Advising Counseling) Officer was an NCO. The Commandant of the school was also an NCO. The cadre consisted of Infantry Airborne Rangers who were also decorated Pathfinders. Even the Corporal was highly decorated. This was a new school that had a solid foundation. The cadre knew that they were competing with Airborne and Ranger. Sometimes it appeared that they were making things difficult just so that they could compete. Students didn't make fun of the cadre like in previous courses, they respected them.

Like Airborne and Ranger, the class was required to come up with a motto. The motto for this particular class was "Death on a Rope." Ackworth, who was also Airborne, jokingly referred to it as, "Pigs in a Blanket."

One interesting note about Air Assault School (AAS) is that the students are taught to break right when faced with oncoming traffic that is straight ahead. Like ships in the ocean, if they are headed straight for each other, they will both turn right. This advanced coordination saves lives. In Air assault, it prevents injuries. The annoyance of people running into each other accidentally is eliminated.

The Rappelling Phase of the course included lessons in knot tying and instruction which the students had to account for with written examinations. The amounts of knots that the students had to learn exceeded the amount required for Ranger. Students rappelled off of a tower with full gear repeatedly. The hardest part of rappelling off of the fifty-five-foot rappelling towers was climbing up them with full gear while you were tired. Instead of using stairs like with the 34 foot towers at Airborne, these towers utilized ladders; steep ladders that went from the ground to the top platform of the towers. Even though the ladders were permanent fixtures and part of the structure they were a pain to climb. They didn't do a lot to help those with acrophobia which Taquard had. The students were graded on their rappelling performance. Students were limited to two bounds on the tower. Taquard was always afraid of heights and had problems controlling his fear. On the Friday of the first week Taquard was not measuring up to the rappelling standards. He was given additional tries but there were limits. On the very last possible try Taquard concentrated on his rappelling form to the extent that he shortchanged his distances. He was still more than halfway up the tower when he completed his second bound. The only option, and not a very good one at that, was to land on the ground on the next bound. It would be the only way that he could stay in the course. That is exactly what he did. The problem was that he injured himself so badly that he could hardly walk. Although he passed the Rappelling Phase of the course he wasn't able to walk without assistance. He bruised his right heel severely. It would take more than ten years to recover. That weekend was dedicated to lying down and resting instead of SCUBA diving.

By the following Monday, Taquard had decided that there was no way that he was going to finish Air Assault. During the previous weeks he wore sanitized uniforms which had sew on rank, branch, unit patch, name, and Army tape. No awards were worn. The only clean uniform that he had left was a set of fatigues that had Airborne wings and a Ranger tab. A lot of people in Hawaii up to that time weren't aware of the fact that Taquard went to both Airborne and Ranger. He didn't really care since he made up his mind to quit anyway. At the assembly point Taquard informed the TAC officer that he was dropping out of AAS. The request of dropping out was denied. The mind set of returning back to a place to relax was interrupted by staying at school. Taquard had to struggle throughout the course. He fell out of the PT run which was done on a rigorous mountain trail. Students were allowed to fall out of a run and still remain in the class as long as they didn't have any other deficiencies.

The Sling Loading and Rigging Phase of the course was mentally challenging. It incorporated written and performance tests that the students had to pass. The students also learned how to establish landing zones and how to safely guide helicopters in for landings. This phase didn't have as much PT as the previous one.

The TAC officer addressed the students on many occasions; however, this particular announcement was voluntary.

"As you may or may not know Airborne and Ranger both offer church services. The services are not mandatory but they are available. Air Assault, in keeping with the other schools that award badges, offers a church service as well. There is a stipulation that a church service will be offered. I will be giving the service since we don't have a chaplain. Anyone who does not wish to attend the service may be excused."

None of the students selected the option of leaving. As it turned out, it was one of the most memorable sermons that Taquard had ever heard in his life; perhaps it was the most memorable.

"There are a lot of people mentioned in the Bible. Does anyone know who Judas Iscariot is? Do you remember what he did? Judas was a buddy fucker. Don't be a Judas. Don't be a buddy fucker. Your unit is only as good as the people who are in it. How well you operate as a group depends on how well you can trust one another. If you can't trust each other then your unit is worthless. No amount of rules and directives will ever change that. A good system needs good people in order for it to work. A good system with bad people is useless. Good people under a faulty system are rendered useless by the system. In order to have an ideal team, first of all you need good people. Second you need a good system. And extremely important, you need trust among each other. Trust begins with the small things. If you fuck somebody over something trivial, you will fuck them over something important. Another way of applying this pearl of wisdom is to say that you should not betray the trust of others, and don't give your trust to others easily. Insist that others earn your trust. Don't fuck your buddy."

The final phase consisted of skid side rappelling, rappelling out of helicopters, and STABO missions. It also included the Air Assault Mile where the students were broken down into small groups and had to carry another student for a mile through rough mountainous terrain, water, a cave, and extremely steep slopes.

This phase transformed the students in many ways. The skid side of the tower has no wall support for the student whatsoever. Once a person gets used to rappelling off of the skid side he never wants to waste his tower climb on the wall again. The skid side is more challenging and more difficult than rappelling down a wall, but it is also a lot more fun. AAS can be described as a place where the cadre forces you to do things that you don't want to do, but were glad that they did.

The instructors knew exactly how to get unwilling students out of the helicopters. They took them 300 feet off of the ground in helicopters. The positioned the students in the form that they were trained on. The students secured their ropes to their D rings and the instructor inspected the rigging. The students, who deployed four at a time, stepped out onto the helicopter skid. They were frightened their first time out. The instructor would motion to the students, two at a time, to back up in the L stance. His hand motions included flicking his fingers out. His fingers were within a couple of inches of the students eyes. The student's natural response was to back away. When the student backed away to the point of no return the instructor told him to hold. Then he signaled the deployment of two students who were positioned diagonally from each other simultaneously. Then the other two students got the signal. Other than Taquard, there wasn't a single injury in the class. Unlike most days where students were released by the end of the day, helicopter rappelling consisted of night rappelling as well. The amount of required rappels that a student had to perform was unknown. One thing that was for sure, they exceeded that amount by a lot. Repeated helicopter rappels were performed to the point where the students were on the verge of becoming experts.

The Air Assault Mile was another eliminator obstacle incorporated in the course. Taquard was selected as the stretcher man in his group. Being the stretcher man was the hardest position of all. Although the stretcher man was being carried, there were dues that he had to pay. In the other groups, the biggest man in the group was selected as the stretcher man. One might surmise that being the stretcher man consisted of lying in the stretcher and relaxing while everyone else carried you around. Nothing could be further from the truth. The students were inexperienced in carrying a stretcher with a person on it. They had a habit of dropping the stretcher man. The stretcher man got banged up along the way. Switching carriers sometimes resulted in dropping the stretcher man, even head first. The rocky terrain was not the ideal place for a person to be dropped on. The cave was about waist high in water. Smoke grenades were released by the cadre. The team had to find their way out of the cave through the smoke without getting injured or dropping the stretcher man. The one thing that Ackworth wasn't about to do was to drop Taquard. Once the students were out of the cave smoke was no longer an object. Prior to AAS, the students would freak out when confronted by smoke. No more. Towards the end of the Air Assault Mile (AAM) the stretcher man was released. The students engaged in rope crossings over a small area that was surrounded by waterfalls. It looked like every location for a paradise scene in a movie. Falling off of the ropes meant falling into the nice cool water and having a blast. Everyone, including the cadre, enjoyed themselves. The AAS was fortunate to own such a prime piece of real estate. They made good use of it too. The experience of living made AAS worthwhile. After the session of enjoying paradise, the students had to get back to the ordeal. Spoon, another student on Taquard's team who was a cook, ran to the stretcher before Taquard could get to it.

"That's not your stretcher," the instructor said. "Get in it anyway. You want it you can have it."

The other students rigged him onto the stretcher. After the rigging was completed the instructor told the students to flip the stretcher over. The new stretcher man was on his face and told to negotiate a muddy hill on his own. He had to use his arms to climb the hill while the rest of him was tired to a stretcher.

"That's your lesson for trying to buddy fuck somebody," the cadre instructor addressed.

"This man is injured; you know it and so does everyone else. If you don't make it up the hill on your own you don't get the wings. These wings are forged with honor."

Spoon made it, but it wasn't easy. The entire team made it.

The other challenge that the students did not want to face was the STABO mission. STABO was required of all students. The students were corralled into one mass group and tightly controlled. Students were dreaming up ways to get out of the STABO mission and made every effort to do so. On the other side of the Landing Zone (LZ) was another group of cadre who established another control point. The second control point was more secure than the first. Four students were removed from the first control point and configured on the LZ side by side. The four students were rigged together. Then the helicopter hovered above them and the students were attached to ropes that were deployed from the helicopter. Then the helicopter lifted them in the air and flew the students around to various terrain features as they hung. After the mission the students were returned to the LZ. Four other students were rigged and stand by. The students who completed their STABO mission were corralled into the second control point. Taquard decide that all he had to do was to keep his eyes closed. The ordeal required no effort or skill on the part of the student. Taquard was nervous and he and Ackworth were in the same four man group. There was no shame in being afraid, everyone was afraid. While the students were afraid they were also alert to the point of ensuring that their rigging was secured. Cadre members double-checked everything in a thorough and timely manner. They were professional in every way every step of the way. Taquard could feel his fear as the group was hooked up.

"Keep your eyes open for five seconds," the instructor said. "I'll be watching you. Five seconds."

The lift-off occurred with the sergeant standing in front of the students. He watched them closely. Five seconds hadn't passed when the feel of fear was replaced by a rush. STABO was fun. It was better than jumping out of an airplane. Everyone felt like Superman. It was a lot of fun as well as a great experience. It was apparent to everyone in the group that they were having fun. They sang, yelled, talked it up, and laughed with each other. There was nothing like it in the world. After they got back on the ground they were sent to the second control point. While the students at the first control point were trying to finagle their way out of a STABO, the students at the second control point were desperately trying to get another STABO mission. The course could only accommodate one STABO mission per student.

There was a lot of fun at AAS but it was hard-earned fun that had to be earned. It was worth it. Everything about AAS was worth it, even if it meant struggling through the last week with an injury.

The graduating ceremony went well. Each student rappelled down the tower to receive his diploma. The names were called out one at a time and each graduate received recognition. The familiar Brigadier General was in the bleachers observing the ceremony. He was there to congratulate the graduates and make good on his promises to deliver a case of beer to anyone who took his bet.

Taquard's Air Assault wings were pinned above his Airborne wings although normally the Airborne wings are placed above the Air Assault wings. All of the Airborne graduates had their Air Assault wings pinned above their Airborne wings. No one made an issue of it even though the Airborne wings still stood above the Air assault wings in the minds of applicable graduates. And for the graduates who didn't have Airborne; they wore their Air Assault wings just as proudly. The first set of wings was always the most special even when subsequent badges had a higher rating.

Unlike Airborne school the wings that were presented were subdued. Also unlike Airborne, Air Assault awarded their students with blood wings. One of the horror stories that was circulating about Airborne was the presentation of blood wings. Blood wings are wings without the pin clasps (AKA acorns). The badge pins poke a recipient in the chest causing the chest to bleed. The wings were awarded to the graduate without acorns and the instructor pounded the wings into the graduate's chest with his fist. This was the beginning of bleeding. The new graduate had to pick up his diploma. To do this he had to go between two files of cadre to the diploma pick up site. That meant that the new graduate was confronted by two cadre members at a time. One cadre member braced his hands on the graduate's back; the other instructor pounded the wings in the graduate's chest with his fist. Then the graduate was turned around and routine was repeated. Every cadre member pounded the wings into every graduate's chest. The only exception, for obvious reasons, was the one and only female graduate. Her wings were pinned on with acorns. As for the other graduates, the pain was endured to the point that the chest became numb after a few poundings. After that the poundings caused no additional pain. As cruel as it may have appeared, blood wings were not as big of a deal as one might expect. The first pounding was the worst and that was that bad because it came unexpectedly.

For all the hype that was made about Fort Campbell being the real

AAS, there was no doubt that Schofield Barracks offered a legitimate AAS that stood on its own. Graduates of the Schofield AAS could care less about the comparison to that of Fort Campbell. Their wings shined just as brightly.

Following the receiving of the diplomas, the cadre had a surprise party for the graduates. Usually, military parties included alcohol, but unlike Ranger school, alcohol wasn't offered. Taquard liked the cadre from the beginning and was proud of his accomplishment at AAS. He was still suffering from his injury, but he did manage to graduate just the same. He enjoyed visiting with the cadre in a casual setting as he knew he would.

During the party on of the TAC officers made the announcement that there were openings for Rappel Master School (RMS) that was beginning the following week. All the student had to do was volunteer and get permission from his unit to attend. The reason that the AAS had students to begin with was because the units within the division had prospect quotas that they had to fulfill. Each company sized element had to send a certain amount of people to the course. They weren't required to graduate so units usually sent people who they knew would fail early on. While the infantry units sent their soldiers to AAS willingly, other units protested the school and sent their people reluctantly. Without the support of the division the AAS was on the verge of collapse. The school was still in its infancy and it was still uncertain whether or not it would stay around. Since Ackworth was providing a place for Taquard to stay the unit got credit for sending two soldiers instead of one. Rappel Master had no such quota. RMS wasn't set up for nearly as many students and all perspective students had to be AAS graduates. This course trained graduated how to become AAS instructors.

"Hey, Lieutenant Taquard, congratulations on your Air Assault wings," Sergeant Urlacker said.

"Thank you, I appreciate it."

"Have you thought about attending Rappel Master?"

"I'd love to if I wasn't hurt."

"It's not a physical course. You can make it through easily. Your injury won't get any worse."

"I don't know how I can get permission from my unit to attend. It's such short notice."

"Sergeant Hill already called your unit. Major Coldhammer gave his blessings. All it comes down to is whether or not you would like to attend."

"In that case I will attend."

"I thought so," Urlacker said as he handed a set of amendments to Taquard. "I took the liberty of getting your orders published."

Although Taquard was excited about attending Rappel Master he still had a couple of obstacles to overcome. He didn't have a place to stay or any form of transportation.

"Hey, Mike," Taquard said to Ackworth, "I gotta problem that I need to iron out."

"What is it, Elwood?"

"I'm staying in Hawaii for another week. I got no transportation or a place to stay."

"You volunteered for Rappel Master?"

"Yes, I have the orders right here."

"I guess you'll have to stay with me. I guess a few more days won't matter."

"But what about transportation?"

"I'll have to drop you off and pick you up every day. It won't be easy, but I don't see any other way."

"Okay, but it sure seems inconvenient."

"Not as inconvenient as being at Air Assault School all over again."

"They said that it's easy."

"I'm sure they did. But the fact of the matter is that I don't want to be around to find out."

# Chapter Sixteen
## *Rappel Master*

By the time Taquard was to report to Rappel Master School he had made several arrangements to either find a place of his own or to possibly lift the burden off of Ackworth by staying with another acquaintance. In the process however, he managed to borrow a car. It wasn't much of a car but it did run. No one was sure what make the vehicle was and it had an appropriate bumper sticker on it that said "This is not an abandoned vehicle."

During his free weekend, he and his diving partner went scuba diving on the beaches of the north shore of Oahu. They also attracted the attention of Japanese ladies who were on vacation. The two of them along with Japanese tourists were a recipe for trouble.

During the weekend, Taquard and his diving partner were doing two long dives during the day and went out at night and stayed out all night long. They also tended to drink and smoke too much. While scuba diving is a fantastic remedy to smoking, hanging out with Japanese isn't. Smoking cuts down a diver's underwater time. The one thing that a diver wants while he is under water is air.

In addition to drinking and smoking they went dancing. When the weekend was over they continued going out. Partying all night long into the early hours of the next morning didn't do much to help either of them make it through the work day. Taquard and his friend were working while their Japanese female counterparts slept during the day.

Fortunately, Rappel Master didn't have any PT on the schedule. It also had a small student body of fourteen students. No females. Taquard, number thirteen, was the only student who was an officer. The commandant of the school was a Master Sergeant. Nevertheless, he knew that they weren't going to cut him any breaks. However, he did have the same instructors that he had for AAS. It was a gentleman's course but the material was harder and there were a lot more tests. Also, there was loads of rappelling. Even to the experienced rappeller this course had a lot to offer. This course made experts out of the students who were already experienced to begin with.

In addition to the tall fifty-five-foot towers that were used by the AAS as well as for many other courses, there were additional, although much shorter towers and platforms that were set up for the Rappel Master's Course. Some platforms were about fifteen feet long at an angled slope. The students practiced on short platforms instead of the tall towers. There they learned how to teach novices the art of rappelling. They learned new ways to rappel and practiced new techniques. The short platforms were fantastic for acclimating to and getting comfortable to new rappelling techniques and form. It would be impossible to introduce advanced techniques from a high platform. The problem with the short platforms was that they outlived their purpose within a very short period of time. Students, who were unafraid, practiced on them for a short period of time before they were eager to go to the towers. What worked well on the short platform worked well on the towers. The students loved it. Advanced rappelling was faster than the basic techniques and was a rush. Students, upon finishing a rappel, recovered and darted back up the tower for more. Instead of limiting the number of rappels that a student could the students could do as many as they wanted which was a lot. Unlike AAS, the students didn't have any extra gear to wear. Also, rappelling performance wasn't graded. The students already knew how to rappel and they were having fun doing it. Fun was not only allowed at Rappel Master, it was encouraged. Learning through fun made experts out of anyone. This course was fun.

The course was broken down into four basic rappelling phases. The course began by applying advanced techniques of the standard rappel.

This was followed by an informal rappelling session where students managed themselves and performed as many rappels as they could. Unlike the students in AAS who had to be motivated to climb up the tower in pursuit of their silver wings, the Rappel Masters climbed up the tower willingly because they didn't have to wait for other rappellers on the platform and because rappelling was a blast. The advanced technique began by aggressively throwing the, below the D ring portion, rope out as far as you could throw it. This was followed not by putting your hand behind your back, but by leaving the arm fully extended while slightly raising it at a higher elevation than the shoulder while maintaining a grip on the rope. This posture allows the speed of the rappel to be controlled by the simple and slight rotation of the wrist. In ROTC, cadets joked about extending the arm out completely during a rappel. At Rappel Master that was the only way a rappel was done as opposed to the ROTC six inch arm movement out before quickly putting the break hand back to the center of the lower part of the back. ROTC rappels consisted of sliding slowly and breaking.

Then the students applied advanced techniques to the Australian rappel. Rappelling with your back to the ground was standard, the opposite rigging where a person was looking at the ground while he was rappelling was known as the Australian rappel. It was named that way, not because of the way Australians rappel, but because everything in Australia is backwards. There were both basic and advanced techniques to the Australian rappel. Instead of holding the rope across your chest to break the rappel, the advanced technique posture consisted of extending the arm fully straight above the head (like the Statue of Liberty trying to reach higher). The rope is still gripped with the extended hand. With this position, the person can control his speed (including stopping) with a simple movement of the wrist. The students were taught the advanced way which, although much harder to learn and requires a solid foundation in rappelling, is a lot faster than the basic technique and a lot more fun. In spite of its reputation and the horror stories that are affiliated with it, the other fun thing about rappelling is the skid side. This renders the wall useless. The towers had two sides that were dedicated to rappelling, the wall and the skid side. This is where the person steps off of a helicopter skid and bounds onto nothing. While it looks terrifying, it's actually a lot of fun. Once a person begins performing skid side rappels he no longer wants to waste his tower climb on the wall. Advanced techniques were applied to the standard skid side rappel. Again, the speed of the rappels was enhanced and the students enjoyed it immensely. They enjoyed it even more than the wall. The enjoyment of the course was further enhanced when the instructors taught advanced rappelling techniques for Australian skid side rappelling. The best way to ensure that the students became proficient in rappelling was to let them go at their own pace which in this case was fast.

The students were graded on knot tying, rappelling rigging and inspection, instruction performance, and modifications. They had to be accountable for material that was presented to them.

The day before Taquard was to report to Rappel Master he and his friend stayed up late drinking, smoking, dancing, and hanging out with the same Japanese ladies that they met on the north shore. It was nine consecutive days of double dating. This was a rough schedule for any working man. Though Taquard had to report to work by 0830 hours he insisted on playing hard.

The women had a definite advantage over Taquard and his friend. The evenings began by Taquard and his friend returning home from work, cleaning up and changing into civilian clothes. As soon as they could get ready they drove from Mililani to Waikiki Beach to the Prince Kuhio Hotel to pick up the ladies. Clay always did the driving since he knew the roads better as well as being a faster driver. Then the foursome would go shopping. Since everything was in the immediate vicinity no additional driving was required. Everything was within walking distance. Then they would go a nice restaurant to have dinner. The ladies were partial to seafood. Cigarettes were a must. The ladies had fierce nicotine fits. In the beginning, Taquard and Clay were under the assumption that the ladies didn't smoke. That along with a serious language barrier prolonged their tobacco use. Although Taquard was a smoker himself, he stopped when he began scuba diving and didn't miss it. He started up again when the ladies found a convenience store that sold Japanese cigarettes. The popular brand was Mild Seven, and they were good. They were the best cigarettes that Taquard had ever had. In spite of his obligations to Rappel Master and SCUBA diving, Taquard and the ladies smoked heavily.

A lot of napkins and ink were used by the foursome in their many attempts to communicate. At dinner, the alcohol consumption began. Dinner was followed up by going to a bar, dancing, a movie, a comedy workshop, more shopping, and a variety of other local nightlife activities. This was topped off by going to a coffee bar and having ice coffee. The bar was open all night. After coffee, the ladies were returned back to their hotels. The duo drove back to Mililani to cop some zzz's before it was time to wake up and get ready to go back to work.

Honolulu is a spooky place at night. A person had to work to stay out of trouble. Honolulu was heavily populated with the wrong types of people. Every misfit gravitated to Honolulu. The place was loaded with homosexuals, everything from pairs of joy boys wearing collars with black bow ties without shirts to fat overweight Hawaiians with ponytails sporting very tight and revealing fluorescent lime g-strings. The local paired scene was something that Taquard didn't want to be a part of. With all the fudge packers that the island was crowded with the women went crazy seeking out straight men.

The local Hawaiian customs were very difficult for Taquard to get used to. First of all, you never go down to the Waikiki area at night without a weapon, preferably more than one. A concealed gun, always fully loaded with extra bullets on hand, and a sharp folding knife have been proven to be effective. Even though it is illegal to carry a gun in Hawaii, everyone, including Elwood and Clay, carried them anyway. The biggest selling items in Hawaii are prostitution and drugs. Hookers are not, contrary to popular belief, attractive. Although the hookers were considerably better than the trailer park whores of northeastern Georgia, they still weren't in the attractive "I want to ask her out on a date" category. On Kuhio Drive, Kawakawa Avenue, or other streets in the vicinity at night, a pedestrian couldn't walk for more than twenty seconds without being approached with an offer to either buy drugs or get asked out by a whore. They weren't shy. Even if a man was with a lady the hookers still continued to make blatant offers. Sometimes they would grab on to a guy's arm. They were aggressive to say the least.

**VISITOR TO HAWAII RULE NUMBER 1: Stay the hell away from Hotel Street. Don't ask why, just stay the hell away from there.**

From the parking lot to the hotel the duo was propositioned repeatedly. When a black hooker grabbed by Taquard on the arm for the first time, he was surprised and responded spontaneously.

"Holy shit! A colored lady just touched me. I need to wash up."

"What's wrong with you? Haven't you ever been with a black lady before?"

"No, I haven't."

"That was really rude. What's a matter? Don't you like black people?"

"Not as rude as trying to have sex with a total stranger. And just because I can get along with a black person doesn't mean that I want to go to bed with them. Just because I'm a nice guy doesn't mean you have to rub my face in it."

"Maybe you ought to give it a try, asshole."

"I already have a date."

"Is she as good as me?"

"Gee, now let me think, a nice beautiful Japanese lady who is not a street whore, or some ugly colored piece of shit who has sex with anybody and everybody for money. I think I'll keep my date. Besides, you have black skin."

Encounters with whores and drug dealers were part of the Hawaiian culture. You couldn't go for half of a minute without being bothered. The foursome was approached constantly. This was a problem during the day, but even more of a problem at night.

Sometimes the language barrier had its moments among the foursome. The ladies took them to a place when Clay stopped abruptly.

"What's wrong?" Taquard asked.

"That's Mahu's."

"So? What's Mahu's?"

"It's a fag bar."

"Eeewww. We sure as shit don't want to go in there."

"These ladies sure seem eager to go in there."

"Maybe they don't know what it is."

"Maybe we can find a translator. There's lots of Japanese around here. Hey, can you speak Japanese?" Clay said to a passerby.

"Yes."

"Can you explain to these young ladies what Mahu's is?"

"Sure."

He explained it to the ladies in Japanese. They answered back in Japanese. They still seemed like they wanted to go in. Clay had the translator translate again. The ladies still wanted to go.

"Look, Clay," Taquard said, "I'm not going in there. Dates or no dates, I'm not going in. If it means leaving the ladies behind then I'm leaving them behind."

"What's the matter," the translator interrupted. "Do you think that we're a bunch of freaks?"

"What? I didn't know that you were a…. Well, factually speaking that would make you a freak. A freak of nature."

"Tell the ladies we're not going in there," Clay further interrupted.

The ladies decided to stay with the duo and keep the foursome in tact.

"Wait," Taquard said.

"What is it?" Clay responded.

"You know all those female impersonators you pointed out to me."

"Yeah, they're all over the place, they're everywhere."

"And some of them are Oriental."

"Good point."

"And some of them are good, I mean really good."

"Another good point, well taken."

"Hey, fag boy! Get over here, we need you to do some more translating."

"What do you want now?"

"We need you to translate for us again."

"Why should I after you insulted me?"

"Tell her that I want to feel up her dress."

"Elwood," Clay interrupted. "You can't do that."

"Tell her. Clay, if this thing turns out to be a dude I'm kicking the living shit out of him and leaving it in the gutter."

The translator told Taquard's date what he wanted to do and why. She was offended and looked as if she was about to cry.

"Well, I guess that's the end of this date," Taquard said.

"Yeah, I guess so. Yours looks like she's about to lose it."

"Let's go. I need to get some sleep anyway."

"I guess it's better that we don't know. Good thing we didn't kiss them."

**VISITOR TO HAWAII RULE NUMBER 2: Beware of female impersonators.**

A lot of GIs have found themselves in embarrassing situations. Although homosexuality was not acceptable in the Army in those days, soldiers would find themselves in trouble with their commanders if they got word of the GI beating the hell out of an impersonator.

As the duo departed they were called back by their dates. Although they didn't speak English they managed to communicate their desire to continue the date without going into the gay bar.

"I'm not interested," Taquard said.

She made motions and demonstrated her approval of Taquard's proposal to confirm whether not she was a female. She leaned up against a car with her back towards Taquard and her legs spread. Taquard made the confirmation.

"She's definitely female. No doubt about that."

Clay's date responded in the same manner.

"This one's female too."

The date continued as the foursome enjoyed the evening. It was surprising how well the evening went. At the end of the date Taquard was concerned about the prior incident.

"Clay, do you think that they won't want to ever see us again?"

"Probably not. But they acted as if they did."

"That is surprising. I don't want to ask them out again."

"Me either, let's just say that we had fun and leave it at that."

As they dropped off the ladies at their hotel Clay's date managed to ask him, in very broken English, about the next evening. They both wanted to go out again. This was surprising but the duo agreed to come back although they were expecting to be stood up. It was true that the ladies were extremely convincing when it came to expressing their desire to continue seeing the Army duo. It was also true that Taquard questioned the sex of his date and successfully insulted the hell out of her. Clay didn't exactly approve of Taquard's methods but understood his point. They decided to go downtown again later that day with a back up plan of returning home to get some sleep.

**JAPANESE CUSTOM RULE NUMBER 1: The word "yes" actually means "maybe;" "maybe" means "no way." They rarely say "no" even if they want to and rarely do they admit that they don't know the answer to a question. That is why it is important to ask least two people for directions as it is considered polite to lie when asked a question when the answer is unknown.**

One of the main differences between AAS and Rappel Master is that there are no test retakes in Rappel Master. The AAS school taught the students many skills and had a variety of tests that followed. However, there were make up tests at the AAS. Rappel Master consisted of reviewing material that the student should have already and testing him with no retakes whatsoever. Advance rappelling techniques were also taught and performed.

This format presented a problem for Taquard who barely got any sleep after a night on the town. During the reviewing of knot tying Taquard was caught dozing off in class. He was called out by the instructor. Instead of taking his knot tying test the following day as scheduled he was tested right then and there. No review, no practice sessions, no preparation. He was tested on the spot. To complicate matters, the tests were timed. They had less time to correctly tie their knots than they did in AAS. The test format required each student to tie every knot of a prescribed series correctly within a specified amount of time. If one knot was tied incorrectly, he was dropped from the course right there and then. Taquard went into testing faced with sixteen knots on his horizon. The instructor was set on making an example out of Taquard in front of the entire class. Amazingly, Taquard performed flawlessly and passed the tests with time to spare. Factually speaking however, he had a lot of practice in Boy Scouts, ROTC Recondo, Ranger, and AAS. Even though he was fortunate enough to have passed the test, he made sure that he never slept in class again. He was lucky when it came to knots, he wouldn't be as lucky next time. No matter how hard it was for him to stay awake as a result of his night activities with his new lady friend.

Instead of getting stood up as the duo expected, the ladies arrived on time, nicely dressed, and ready to go. While the duo was able to square things with the ladies, the carousing was effecting their work days. Taquard was coping zzz's every chance he could. The problem with the rappelling was that it was so much fun that he jumped in and participated just like everyone else. He was enjoying himself and motivated by the fact that opportunities like this should not be taken for granted. Rappelling was enough to make him forget that he was tired and sleepy. After school, Taquard drove to Clay's place and went to meet the ladies. They continued dating as usual. The ladies took them to another place when Clay stopped abruptly.

"What's wrong?" Taquard asked.

"This is the American Veteran's Legion."

"So? Maybe they like the military."

"It's a dyke bar."

"Oh I can see the confusion. Maybe they were trying to be nice."

"Yeah, but dykes could really compromise our relationship with these ladies. Better to take them to a movie or something."

"Wait, I have an idea," Taquard said while trying to hail down a translator.

"If we went in we could look at the lesbians," Clay told Taquard. "The may not like guys, but they won't bother us either."

"How do lesbians look? They usually look like hell. I'm not talking about the ones in the movies or magazines; I mean the ones you meet in real life. Dykes are usually a bunch of fat slags. I seriously doubt that they could even compare to the ladies we are already with."

"No they won't."

Instead of going to the dyke bar they went to see the movie, *Sixteen Candles*. Even though they all knew that it was a sorry movie, they went anyway as the movie quality wasn't their main objective. The foursome engaged in a variety of activities and wandered throughout Honolulu oblivious to the perverted world around them. It was worth it for Taquard to indulge himself at the expense of sleep and rest.

The dating continued and while the men kept the ladies out of trouble and away from the undesirable places the ladies did their part as well.

Dating them was an experience that proved to be worthwhile in the long run. This was Taquard's introduction to sushi and other forms of Japanese food. The Japanese ladies knew the restaurants that served actual Japanese cuisine and taught the duo the difference between them and the imposter restaurants that served garbage.

**JAPANESE CUISINE RULE NUMBER 1: It is better to go to a Japanese restaurant with a Japanese chef as opposed to a Korean cook.**

Authentic Japanese restaurants had Japanese cooks and staff. It was not advisable to randomly try things on the menu if you were new to sushi. Taquard began with the standard maguro (tuna), tamago (cold scrambled eggs), tako (octopus), and a few starters under the guidance of his date. Gradually acclimating to Japanese food proved to pay big dividends as Taquard was elevated to enjoying more exotic dishes. One of the misconceptions about sushi is its meaning. Most Americans think that it means raw fish. It doesn't. It means rice. It is a special type of steamed rice that is prepared with vinegar and sugar and tastes much better than regular steamed rice. Rice is the only constant among the different types of sushi that is offered. Tamago doesn't contain any fish whatsoever. Sashimi means raw fish. It is fish that is served without the rice. Learning to eat Japanese food became a skill that came in handy later on. Taquard acclimated to Japanese food much faster than most people. Many people never become accustomed to it. The consumption of Japanese food includes the use of hashi (chopsticks) and the appropriate mixture of shoyu (soy sauce) and wasabi (green horse radish). The amount of wasabi that is mixed into the shoyu varies among personal preference. The sushi is generously dipped into the sauce and eaten whole. Sashimi is wrapped around sushi rice and then heavily dipped into the sauce for entire consumption. Each portion that is prepared and held with the hashi is that of one bite.

The ladies, even though they were tourists, knew many of the places to go and not go. When the group decided to go to a karaoke (pronounced Ka rah oh Kay, not carry oh key) bar the ladies steered them away. Instead, they went to a karaoke box. It was a lot better to sing karaoke in a private room as opposed to a bar. The private room which offered privacy had all the food, drinks, ashtrays, and all of the other amenities that a bar would offer. The songs that they all sang were a variety of both Japanese and English. The songs were presented in a video (music and otherwise) with the words of the song in the format of subtitles. You could be watching Sean Connery in 007 actions while singing Sakamoto Kyu's Ue O Muite Aruko. The Japanese ladies sang Japanese songs and even sang a few songs in English. The surprising thing about Japanese music was how upbeat it was. It wasn't anything that you would expect in a Chinese restaurant or a waiting room at the dentist's office. The music was actually good. Some Americans, Taquard included, were once familiar with Sakamoto Kyu; his song was a big hit in the 1963. Another band, A Taste of Honey, tried their rendition of his hit, popularly known as Sukiyaki. While most people would prefer the English version, it didn't even come close to comparing with the original. The song sounded much better in Japanese though most people would disagree. Taquard referred to hiragana and katakana charts when he attempted singing a Japanese song with the help of his date.

Later, Sakamoto Kyu, like previous rock stars, would be killed in an airplane crash. This would occur on Japan Airlines Flight 123 on 12 August 1985 and would be the biggest single airplane accident in history that also claimed the greatest number of fatalities.

There was another reason that the ladies kept the duo away from a Japanese Karaoke bar. Many of the Japanese, although they were in Hawaii, did not approve of gaijin. Gaijin is a derogatory derivative of the word "gaikokujin" which means not Japanese. Some people think that it means foreigner, but that is inaccurate. The hating of gaijin is a Japanese national past time. The word "gaijin" would be equivalent to calling a black person a fucking nigger, but without the level of respect. Although the dates didn't tell the duo about the word gaijin and why they shouldn't go to certain places that are frequented by Japanese, everything worked out smoothly. Everyone had had their fill of confrontation.

Dancing usually took place at a place called The Point After. The music and atmosphere was great. There were a lot of Japanese to intermingle with. The songs that everyone danced to were both in English and Japanese. Sakamoto Kyu was no longer the rave; all the young people wanted the contemporary artists. Their songs, although they were never popular in America, were really upbeat and good. Many Japanese artists were popular but the only two names that stood out in Taquard's mind were Seiko Matsuda and Kyoko Koizumi who was also known as Kyon Kyon.

While he was dating a Japanese lady, Taquard tried his best to pick up as much Japanese as possible but he realized that he had a long way to go. What little he learned he appreciated. He learned a lot on a very short period of time. Not so much Nihongo as he did in Japanese culture, Scuba diving, rappelling, and basically that there was a world beyond Korea, a world beyond the Army.

The coveted silver Air Assault wings were adorned with a star on top to signify the Rappel Master graduates. Only six graduated from that class. While the star looked good on Airborne wings, it didn't look that good on Air Assault wings. It was such a new award at the time that the only way that a person could get them was to graduate from the course and hang on to the set that was awarded to you. They had not made it to mass production and could no be purchased at Clothing Sales. Unlike AAS, the students were awarded their new wings in a casual manner. No blood wings. Taquard was awarded his new wings with a star on top in spite of his close call with the impromptu test and lack of sleep. He struggled throughout the entire course. The wings were a blessing to him. It not only meant that he had a star on his wings, it meant that he could catch up on some sleep over the weekend. The cadre congratulated the graduates with praise, handshakes, and words of encouragement. A major rushed toward the congregation with a set of amendments in his hand. He headed toward Taquard.

# Chapter Seventeen
## *The Trial*

While Taquard was attending Rappel Master training the results of an earlier urinalysis came in to the headquarters company. One of the instructors from the AAS came up hot. According to the results, the subject was guilty of consuming marijuana. Drug offenses were taken very seriously in the Army during that era, even in Hawaii.

The company commander, Captain Morales, decided to pursue charges. As the chief prosecutor, Morales also had the responsibility of appointing a defense counsel. He could choose any officer within his company. Naturally, it was in his best interest to choose the dumbest and most inexperienced lieutenant that he could find. This preparation would have to be made to offer the defendant a summary courts martial. If the defendant refused a summary then they would go directly to a formal courts martial. They had to play it by the book. This was the captain's first trial as a prosecutor. He would also have the responsibility of selecting a judge who would also act as a prosecutor. He would need another captain who was both competent and set on burning the defendant. At this stage of the proceedings he would have to settle for someone who was not a JAG officer.

"You know I don't have a lot of time to get this ready," Morales said to his executive officer (XO) Captain Campbell. "I'm sure he won't want a summary courts martial to begin with but we still have to offer it to him. Any ideas of who we can get to represent him?"

"Well, this may be a long shot, but we have a lieutenant who is visiting us from Korea."

"We can't use a visitor."

"Actually we can. He's here on orders."

"What?"

"He's a student at the Rappel Master's course. Technically, he belongs to us. He's a brand-new first lieutenant. He's probably been so tied up with all those field exercises that Korea is so notorious of that he wouldn't know a court proceeding from his asshole. Besides, this would hit him as such a complete surprise that he wouldn't even know how to prepare for such a thing. He doesn't know his way around and he has no connections. From what I hear, he likes to party hardy all the time and has trouble staying awake in class. I'm sure the defendant won't want him either, in which case JAG will handle everything from there. No way will he win with JAG."

"Good idea. When can you amend his orders?"

"We could amend them today and deliver them to him at the school. The class graduates today. All I have to do is talk to Captain Norris and the orders are amended. I can drive down to the school today and hand them to him before he graduates."

"Okay, see if you can do that. Meanwhile I will get everything set up with a judge. I spoke with the JAG and there's an engineer that we can use. Will these amendments interfere with him graduating from Rappel Master?"

"No. His extension would take place immediately but his new assignment as a defense counsel wouldn't be effective until Monday. With all the briefings and formalities that he'll have to go through next week he won't have time to work on the case. That is assuming that the defendant even wants him in the first place. When did you say that the hearings begin?"

"A week from Monday unless he decides to forgo a summary courts martial. If he doesn't accept a summary courts martial then it will begin at a later date. I don't know when that would be. However, we have to offer him a summary courts martial sometime next week."

As Taquard was walking out of the area where the Rappel Master he was approached by someone.

"Taquard, I'm Major Parker from division headquarters. I have a set of orders for you. You've been assigned as the defense counsel for Bayless in *The United States vs. Bayless.*"

"How did I get selected for that? I don't know anything about law."

"This is a good way to find out."

"I don't know where to begin."

"Don't worry. It's not like you have to win or anything. You'll get read in on Monday. Who knows, maybe there's a lawyer who may even help you out. Is that your car over there?"

"Yeah, I borrowed it from a friend."

"Good, now you can return it. This detail provides you with a place to stay and a vehicle. There were no rooms on Schofield barracks so we got you a room at the Hilton Hawaiian Village on Waikiki Beach."

"That sounds like a cool assignment."

"It is. Chances are that the defendant won't even accept a summary courts martial. But if he does, you'll be his counsel. And remember, you don't have to win this trial. Follow me, I'll show you how to get to division headquarters. You will report to the JAG Monday at 0900 hours. After that we will return your vehicle so that we can issue you a new one."

Taquard followed the major in his borrowed car and noted landmarks along the way. Once they got to building 580 the major got out of his car and provided Taquard with a map and further guidance.

"Second floor, take that entrance on the far right. Any questions?"

"What do I do between now and Monday?"

"Enjoy yourself, have a good time. Don't sweat it. If he turns down the summary courts martial we'll send you straight back to your unit. In the mean time, if I was you, I'd enjoy myself."

This worked out well with Taquard's plans because the Japanese ladies would still be in the area. Now he could catch up on his sleep and use his hotel room to entertain guests. As it turned out Taquard was given a double-room suite. The logic was that he would need a place to study and prepare for his case. The car that was provided was a brand new 1983 four-door BMW 325i.

After settling in his new quarters he invited Clay and the ladies over. The foursome picked up provisions including alcohol and went to the room. Room service was also available twenty-four hours a day. Room service was covered by the Army to cover Taquard's subsistence. Relaxing and watching TV was a great way to spend the weekend. The ladies crashed right there in the room. By Sunday evening the ladies had to go to their hotel and pack for their return trip to Japan. Clay went back to his place to prepare for another week of work. Taquard didn't have a lot to do to prepare for a trial that he wasn't likely to participate in.

The following Monday, he reported to the JAG office as he was instructed to do. He signed in and a warrant officer gave him folder that was inside a large envelope.

"Can you tell me anything about the case?"

"Read it yourself."

"I was told that there was somebody who may be able to help me out. Do you know who that would be?"

"No."

Just as the warrant officer concluded his pleasantries, Taquard was hailed by a major who emerged from a back room.

"Come in, come in," the major said, "I'm Major Woodward. I'll be directing the protocol of this case. Lieutenant Taquard, I want you to meet Staff Sergeant Bayless. He's the defendant."

"Sir, I have to tell you right now, I have never done anything like this before in my life. I've never been to law school. I haven't even attended a trial before."

"This is a good place to start. And from what you just told me, most people would think that would make you a better lawyer than most."

"I was told by Major Parker that there would be someone who could help me out."

"Yes, there is. Sergeant Bayless, you need to make a decision."

"I'll take the courts martial, I didn't do anything wrong."

"I understand, but I have to offer you a summary courts martial."

"I said I don't want it."

"I understand, but there is a formality that is involved here. You have been assigned a defense counsel. You will be given seventy-two hours to make a decision. You don't have to make a decision now."

"I know what I want and I don't need a summary court martial."

"You don't have to change your mind but I do have to offer you counsel and a reasonable amount of time to think it over. You aren't obligated to do anything between now and then."

"Who's supposed to help me out?"

"Yes, there's a Major Goldberger downstairs. He's a lawyer who doesn't handle cases. His job is to make the UCMJ (Uniform Code of Military Justice) and Geneva Convention readily available. In other words, he gives legal advice."

"Well, Sergeant Bayless, what do you say? Should we pay Major Goldberger a visit?"

"I guess it won't hurt anything."

The two departed the JAG office and went downstairs.

"I'm telling you, sir, these people are out to fuck me."

"That's what JAG does. This thing's already been decided."

"Then why the formalities?"

"So they can say that they gave you a fair chance so that you can't appeal it."

They entered Major Goldberger's office.

"Sir, I am Lieutenant Taquard and this is Sergeant Bayless. We have a case that—"

"Yes, come on in. Have a seat. You want some coffee? I got some coffee brewing."

"No, no thanks," Taquard responded.

Bayless didn't want any coffee either.

"Have you gone over the case?"

"No, I haven't."

"Well, you should."

"Sir, if I may be so bold to say, this is a stacked deck in a kangaroo court. I know it, he knows it, we all know it, everybody knows it. Besides, Sergeant Bayless doesn't want a summary courts martial."

"Maybe you ought to reconsider."

"Why? I didn't do anything wrong. They're just trying to burn me."

"Yes, I see your point. However, I happen to be familiar with your case. The judge is an engineer, not a lawyer."

"Shouldn't he be a lawyer?"

"No, you don't want an Army lawyer. Army lawyers are the worst kind. There not good enough to be public pretenders."

"But an engineer doesn't know anything about the law."

"But an engineer isn't tainted. Lawyers are."

"But sir, I can still get burned."

"At the summary level you will have grounds for an appeal. You are being represented by someone who is not a lawyer and being judged by someone who is not a lawyer. You lucked out. Besides if you win at the summary level you're off the hook. You're a free man. And if you are found guilty you will have some experience going into the next trial."

"So maybe it would be best to drive on as if we were going to have a summary courts martial trial," Taquard inferred.

"Yes, that's what I would do. First, you need to get read in on the case and then do some leg work and maybe make a few calls. Then you need to come back and see me tomorrow morning."

"Um, okay, but I was wondering if there was a place for me to work."

"Yes there is. I guess the JAG forgot to tell you about it."

"I thought I would be working out of my hotel room."

"Maybe that's what they wanted you to think. There are a whole bunch of rooms on the second floor on the far end. They're above the far left entrance. There's lots of privacy and they even have phones that you can use."

Taquard and Bayless went to a private office and perused over the case file.

"I can tell you exactly what happened."

"Okay."

"The tests say that I came up hot on the urinalysis. We took a test a few weeks ago."

"Okay, I have to read up on the procedures."

"I wasn't able to fill my jar up the first time. It took three attempts to get enough in it for a sample."

"I never had that problem, even after I went."

"I'm not kidding, but I'm telling you that I never did any drugs ever."

"The first thing that I have to do is find out whether or not they violated any procedures."

"They seemed to keep everything under control."

"Let's see how well they kept things under control. If you didn't do any drugs and if they say that you came up hot then there's a problem."

"Yes, sir, but I don't know what it is."

"I don't know either but we need to find out. Let's go to the Drug and Alcohol Control and see if we can get a copy of the procedures."

"That's a good idea."

"I was perusing over the trial procedures. Can you get me a list of character witnesses? We may need them."

"Sure, I got a lot of them including the Sergeant Major of the Army."

"That's a good one. I'll tell you what. Let's get some lunch and after that we can go to Drug and Alcohol. After that we'll see if we can get in touch with the sergeant major. He's a great reference but we're going to need more."

As far as Taquard could tell there were a lot of procedures to administering a urinalysis that had to be conducted in an environment that was constructed for a non-related function. The best source of information for procedures for administering a urinalysis testing would have to come from Drug and Alcohol Control who were the official experts, or so he thought. Their query was fielded by supervisory staff member named Ms. Tina Fletcher.

"Can I get a copy of the procedures for conducting a urinalysis?"

"Is your man guilty?"

"No, he's not," Taquard answered. "I came here to find out about the procedures."

"Can I see the case file?"

"No, but I can answer questions about it."

"The question is, is he guilty?"

"No, he's not."

"How do you know that?"

"Can I please get a copy of the procedures? What's the protocol for conducting a urinalysis?"

"And since you don't answer my questions, why should I help you out?"

"I assume he's innocent. A man is presumed innocent until he's proven guilty. That's in the Constitution."

"What does the Constitution have to do with anything? You are assuming that he is innocent which means he's guilty."

"What if he's not guilty?"

"If he came up hot on a urinalysis, he's guilty. He may say otherwise, but the fact is that he is guilty."

"Well, he is entitled to a fair trial. I'm here to see that he gets one. However, I do need to know the procedures involved in the urinalysis. He still has rights. That's in the Constitution."

"Actually, he doesn't have rights. He gave up his constitutional rights the day he joined the Army."

"What about a copy of the policies and regulations concerning a urinalysis?"

"You still haven't convinced me that I should help you out."

Taquard was staring to see how justice and fair trials were foreign to the Army. The more he thought about, the more convinced that Fletcher was right. The Army did take away a person's constitutional rights. His next step was to take Bayless back to the headquarters building and see if he could speak with the Sergeant Major of the Army. As an in processing instructor at the AAS, Bayless was able to generate loads of character witnesses. They were subjects of the same urinalysis.

To Taquard's surprise, with operator assistance, he was able to get in touch with the Sergeant Major of the Army. It was easy. He wasn't able to get any literature or written directives from Drug and Alcohol, but he was able to talk to the Sergeant Major of the Army. Not only that, but he knew Bayless, and furthermore, he was willing to take time out of his busy schedule to leave Washington, D.C., to come to Hawaii for a few weeks to testify on his behalf. Other people who were possible character references were also willing to travel all the way to Hawaii to help out. People were willing to travel to Hawaii even after Taquard warned them about the possibility of them having several days, maybe even weeks, of dead time. Congressmen and senators from all over the country traveled to Hawaii to conduct health and welfare visits and to see the soldiers from their districts and states. They were so proud of the soldiers that they even brought their families with them. There was an official that Taquard recognized from the news. He was on TV lambasting the military and criticizing them to no end. Apparently he had a change of heart and although Taquard ran into a lot of stateside politicians they always seemed in too much of a hurry to talk to him. Taquard never remembered seeing any politicians in Korea who were concerned about the soldier's health and welfare.

"What's up with all these politicians visiting the soldiers? I never saw it in Korea."

"They're all over the place," Bayless answered. "They come here all the time, especially during the holiday season. They'll poke their head into some unit on post to justify their visit, and then they'll spend the rest of their three week travel arrangement package on the beach with their families. They do it all the time."

"In other words, they are taking a vacation at the taxpayer's expense under the guise of taking care of soldiers."

"You got it."

"I have come to the conclusion that anyone who talks about taking care of soldiers does anything but. Kind of like sex, those who talk about it the most do it the least."

The first day was productive although he never got any written directives pertaining to how a urinalysis was supposed to be conducted. At about 1600 hours, he decided to call it a day. This gave him plenty of time to still enjoy himself. The one thing that Taquard didn't do was worry about the case while he was off duty. He enjoyed the night life and relaxed. He went to some Japanese shops and restaurants to reminisce about the Japanese lady that he was with earlier. He managed to learn even more about the Japanese after she left. His shopping sprees were followed up with trips to the Post Office since the souvenirs were too precious to take back with him to Korea. He mailed them to his parents' house.

Taquard and Bayless got together and went over the case again before they saw Goldberger. While they were walking down the hall they were stopped by a captain."Are you the guy who's been working on the urinalysis case?"

"Yes I am," Taquard answered.

"We just had the same problem with a unit that I was with. I'll get in touch with my former lieutenant and see if he can bring you a copy of the procedures."

"I wasn't able to get a copy for Drug and Alcohol."

"Who did you speak to, Burgess or Fletcher?"

"Fletcher."

"Neither one of them knows what they're doing. Why don't you swing by my office this afternoon and we'll see if we can get you a copy. I'm in room 310."

"These copies must be pretty hard to get."

"My lieutenant got his directly from Washington. Drug and Alcohol doesn't have any on hand."

"Aren't they responsible for doing the entire drug testing?"

"Yeah. You can tell what a great job they're doing. When I was a commander I had to throw the tests out. They weren't worth a damn."

"But this guy's being charged."

"Most commanders will prosecute without going over the procedures. JAG usually handles the case so the poor bastard doesn't stand a chance."

"But for some reason this case is not being handled by JAG."

"Count your blessings. JAG is there for one reason and one reason only. That is to prosecute the soldier. JAG is not there for the soldier, he's there for the commander. Anything that JAG does for the soldier is because it serves the commander's interest. Wills and Powers of Attorney make the soldier more accessible for a deployment. JAG is only there to screw the soldier."

"But, why isn't this case being handled by JAG?"

"They ran out of people. There are so many trials going on right now that it isn't even funny."

Bayless had to consider his options. He wasn't sure that he wanted to accept the summary courts martial. The one thing that he knew for sure was that he couldn't trust anyone. He could trust Taquard, but he didn't know for how long. There was still time for someone to get to him.

"How come no one has come to us about the case?" Bayless asked.

"Beats me. They probably figure that this visiting lieutenant here is incapable of presenting a good case. That's right, you were chosen for your incompetence," the captain said to Taquard.

"So they want me to lose this case?"

"Yes."

They went to see Goldberger who was impressed with the list of character references.

"There's one thing about being stationed in Hawaii. You never run short on character references. You'd better be careful with this one. A lot of people are willing to come to Hawaii but may not say what you want them to say once they get on the stand and are under oath. A lot of them fall apart when they are cross examined."

"I really do know the Sergeant Major of the Army."

"Yes, but you never really know someone until they take the stand to talk about you. How do you feel about taking a summary courts martial?"

"I think that it may be a good idea."

"The day after tomorrow, Lieutenant, you will have to enter a plea of 'not guilty,' present opening arguments, a list of people you intend to bring on as witnesses, and convince the JAG why the case should either be dismissed or why this man is entitled to a trial."

"I have to do all that?"

"Yes, unless of course he decides to go straight into a formal courts martial in which case he doesn't stand a chance in hell. Just because you're innocent doesn't mean that they won't find you guilty."

"The lady at the Drug and Alcohol said something about a soldier losing his constitutional rights once he goes into the Army. Is that true?"

"She's right. Technically a person has rights even when he goes into the Army, but factually speaking he doesn't have any rights at all. Remember in the civilian world a man is innocent until he's proven guilty, the burden of proof is on the prosecution. In the Army a man is guilty even after he's been proven innocent."

Taquard proceeded working on the case with Bayless by his side. The only thing that really mattered was the evidence against the defendant and how well the witnesses could support the evidence. Obtaining a copy of the policies and directives pertaining to administering a urinalysis was an enormous help to Taquard and his case. By the third day of preparation, Taquard had a case and was ready to go to court.

Major Gleason interrupted Taquard's preparation session.

"Lieutenant, there's been a formal complaint filed against you. Now just who in the hell do you think you are?"

"Excuse me, sir?"

"What the fuck do you mean going to going and bothering Ms. Fletcher? What the fuck is wrong with you?"

"I still don't get it. What are you talking about?"

"Why in the hell did you have to go and upset her for?"

"Upset her? I was just trying to work on this case."

"And now you think of yourself as a hotshot lawyer is that it?"

"Actually, I was thinking of myself as a lieutenant who doesn't have a clue on how to do this case. I admit that I don't know what I am doing and I am trying to find answers."

"Well, you can do it without upsetting people. I'd better not get any more reports about you or else you'll be the one who's up on charges."

Taquard was unable to find the answers that he was looking for, but he managed to upset people. Never mind that he was upset for trying to get information from a source that was the proclaimed authority in the area that he was seeking answers to. What he did manage to do was waste a lot of time, upset people, and get into trouble. He would have been better off if he just played ball and sunk the case. Pursuing legitimate justice in the Army was a sure recipe to getting in trouble. If you were faced with opposition you knew you were doing the right thing. One thing was for sure, they had to find another office to work out of.

He kept running to people who were interested in his predicament. Another captain told him about a roommate that he had while he was stationed in Korea. They called his roommate Maximum John because first of all, his name was John and second because he was a JAG lawyer who lost every single case that he was assigned to and every defendant received the maximum sentence.

"Just think, if you win this one you'll have a better record than most JAG lawyers," he said to Taquard.

On the morning of the forth day Bayless had to formally state his acceptance or denial of a summary courts martial. Bayless decided to accept the summary courts martial. After accepting the summary courts martial they were escorted to the court room where the trial was to take place. They were introduced to Captain Guttenberg who was the presiding judge. This was also his first trial and he had references at his immediate disposal to ensure that everything was copasetic. He read off the charges and announced the names of the prosecuting witnesses, many of whom were on the proposed character reference list. Up until this moment, neither Taquard nor Bayless knew that Fletcher was a prosecuting witness.

"Do you think that she decided to testify against me because of something you did?" Bayless quietly asked Taquard.

"No, she was a prosecuting witness all along, that's why she refused to help us. That's also why she got so upset."

"We could lose this one."

Taquard presented the judge with a list of witnesses that he intended to call to the stand. The judge looked it over.

"There's a lot of names on this list. A lot of these people are not in the immediate vicinity. You realize that you are subpoenaing most of the Air Assault cadre on this one."

"Yes, sir, I do."

"That means that the class that is going on now will be interrupted."

"I didn't know that there was a class going on. Does that mean that the class or trial will be postponed?"

"I'll have to find out. Trial begins on Monday at 0830 hours. That gives you all day today and tomorrow and this weekend for you to prepare for your case. I can use the witnesses in the immediate vicinity, but I'm not too sure about the others. And you'd better not be pulling my leg about the Sergeant Major of the Army."

The judge contacted the Pentagon to get an answer on his predicament. If the cadre attends the trial then the Air Assault students will be excused for that day. Either that or the cadre will not be available to attend the trial. As it happened, the day in question was Elimination Day, the day following the road march that was used to weed out prospective students. The Pentagon decided that the cadre will attend the trial and that the Air Assault students will be excused from class that day and any other days that the cadre is involved with the trial. It was also decided that the students would get full credit for effected blocks of instruction. This class got a free ride for one day which happened to be the day that was dedicated to reducing the class size.

While the judge was in contact with the Pentagon he also notified the Sergeant Major of the Army. To his surprise, he knew Bayless and acknowledged speaking to Taquard. Even though a lot of things were bizarre, it didn't make them any less true. Bizarre claims were backed up with proof.

Taquard spent the rest of his time trying to get in contact with prosecuting witnesses who he hadn't spoken with earlier. He established the chain of custody connecting Bayless to the dirty urine sample. He focused on each and every link of the chain and attempted to break every link. The way he saw it, the links consisted of the doctor who tested the samples, Ms. Fletcher who assigned control measures between Staff Sergeant Hess, the person who collected the samples, and the doctor. These were the three links that Taquard would have to break.

Monday morning fell like a sack of bricks on Bayless. The first witness was the doctor. Taquard objected to the doctor's testimony based on the fact that he was not able to get in touch with the doctor before the trial. His motion was denied.

The doctor explained the process of conducting the urinalysis testing. It was an education for everyone present. The urine sample is collected by the administrator (first link). He collects the samples and makes sure that complete samples are sealed. He records the names of the subjects and notes the control numbers on the samples. He knows who provided what sample. He forwards the samples to the manager (second link) who assigns control measures and additional control numbers to the samples. She knows who provided what sample. She maintains a control log. She then forwards the encoded samples to the doctor (the third and final link) who tests the samples. He does not know who provided which samples. He will test thirty-two samples at a time. The lot of thirty-two will include at least two previously confirmed dirty samples and at least two previously confirmed clean samples. The doctor does not know how many control samples will be in a batch nor does he have any idea which ones they are. The results of the doctors testing must correctly identify all the control samples. He must be perfect for the test to be legitimate. He will separate the samples into two groups: clean and dirty. He will identify these samples in a coded entry and forward them to the manager. She will extract the control samples after she validates the legitimacy of the test. Then she will focus on the dirty samples that are left over. She will refer to her records to determine who provided the dirty samples. The list of suspects is then forwarded to the local commanders and the prosecution begins.

The doctor explained that THC (tetrahydrocannabinol), which marijuana has, stays in a person's system for a very long time. It is extremely easy to ingest, but extremely hard to completely digest although it is found in feces and urine. A slight intake of THC will register a positive reading on the testing of the sample. For example, if a person were to smell burning marijuana within a month before he provided a urine sample, he would register hot. This would be a tainted sample. A level of tolerance is applied to the test to accommodate for accidental or minor ingestion of THC. The MPs smell burning marijuana all of the time during controlled burnings. Smoking one joint could register six months later depending on the sex, weight, and metabolism of the person in question. Eating poppy seed muffins will also register THC on a urinalysis. The level of tolerance accounts for such situations. Although there is a degree of tolerance applied to the test, smoking a joint a few weeks, or even a couple of months, before a test could register above the allowable tolerance level. The biggest factor in digesting THC to the acceptance tolerance level is time.

No matter how hard Taquard tried to corner the doctor, he couldn't. There was no beating the doctor. He qualified his tolerance level and defined a dirty sample as being at a notable and significant level. He used cocaine as another example to illustrate his point.

"If we were to charge every guilty person for possession of cocaine there wouldn't be anybody left on the outside. Everyone in this room is carrying cocaine on their person right now. Your money, which is made out of cloth, not paper, more than likely has cocaine in it. Not in a macroscopic amount mind you, but more than likely does have some cocaine in it. The sample for conviction must be of macroscopic value and enough to be beyond a reasonable doubt of intent."

There was no way to get to the doctor. No matter what he tried or how much he tried, he wasn't going to find anything wrong with the doctor. Taquard finally gave up and stopped asking questions. He was beat and he knew it. Bayless was nervous and it showed.

The judge warned the doctor, as well as all other witnesses, not to discuss the case with anyone other than the defense counsel while the case was still going on. The doctor was excused and wasn't called again.

The rest of the day was dedicated to the Air Assault cadre. Although they weren't as challenging as the doctor was, they couldn't give Taquard anything to support his case with even though he was reaching for anything.

"Sergeant Biletnikoff, were you surprised to find out that Sergeant Bayless came up hot on a urinalysis?"

"Yes."

"That is an inadmissible question is being struck from the record," the judge intervened. "Keep the questions in line with the facts as they pertain to this case. Do not solicit opinions."

The judge informed each Air Assault cadre member that he could may be recalled to testify again, but that he could return to duty. The second day of AAS went in accordance with the established original schedule.

It was a long day for Taquard and Bayless.

"You're getting torn up, sir. I'm telling my wife that I'm going to jail. I've got to get my affairs in order."

The second day of the trial was moved to another venue. The witnesses stood by as the judge set up the court.

"Sir, Your Honor, I must object to the testimony of Ms. Fletcher, when I interviewed her prior to the trial she did not identify herself as a prosecuting witness."

"Maybe she didn't know about the trial at the time."

"She filed a formal complaint against me."

"What complaint?"

"About me being rude to her. I was just trying to get a copy of the urinalysis procedures from her. I was preparing for my case. She never gave it to me."

"Who did she file the complaint with and what did it say?"

"Major Gleason, he's in building 580."

"Can you prove that?"

"Can you give me an hour?"

"Okay, you have one hour, then we will begin the trial."

Taquard rushed over to see Major Gleason.

"Sir, Lieutenant Taquard reporting, sir."

"I didn't call for you."

"Sir, I'd like to address the complaint that was filed by Ms. Fletcher."

"Okay, address it."

"I would like a copy of the formal complaint to give to the judge. He's as concerned about the conduct of the people involved with the trial as anyone else is."

"That's a good one. There's no way that you would tell the judge about your behavior. Maybe, you just want to make sure that I don't give it to him myself."

"Actually, all I would like is a copy. I don't need the original. You see, sir, Fletcher is a witness for the prosecution. Wouldn't it look better if I were to come clean with the judge before Fletcher takes the stand?"

"I see. Well, her complaint was verbal."

"For the record, could you make a written statement for the judge?"

"I can give you a hand written note saying that according to her you were rude to her while you were trying to get information from her. Obviously, you weren't entitled to that information or else she would have given it to you," Major Gleason said while he pulled out a purple felt tip marker and began writing.

> *Last week, Ms. Diana Fletcher called me to inform me about the unprofessional behavior of 1LT Taquard. He was persistent and rude in obtaining information that either Ms. Fletcher didn't have or that he wasn't entitled to. I disciplined Taquard on his unprofessional behavior and misconduct as an officer.*
>
> *Maj. Geo. Gleason*

Taquard delivered the note to the judge within the hour time limit.

"I also have his phone number, sir, if you need it."

The judge read the note and pondered it for a while.

"Okay, Lieutenant Taquard. She's dismissed. She should have identified herself as a prosecuting witness from the beginning. She did have that obligation to do so if she was aware of the fact that she would be called to testify, and it certainly appears that she was aware. It certainly appears as though she was withholding information that could help the defense counsel. She apparently attempted to interfere with you while you were preparing for the case.

"Thank you, Your Honor."

### Link Two: Eliminated

The only person left to testify was the administrator. Taquard knew the procedures backwards and forwards. He was able to corner the administrator with every question. It was no contest. While Taquard was beaten the day before, he was not going to be beaten this day. No matter how technical the questions were, Taquard was able to address the answers. Taquard was on a roll and the administrator was the one who was sweating. Although Taquard was confident, Bayless was still scared about his fate. The judge intervened and stopped the questioning.

"That's quite enough, Lieutenant Taquard," he said. "The witness is excused. You two go outside, we're taking a fifteen minute recess."

### Link Three: Broken

Taquard and Bayless waited outside on the lanai (the Hawaiian word for balcony) and waited during the short recess. Bayless was sweating the uncertainty of his fate. He didn't know what to think. Taquard, on the other hand was confident about the outcome of the trial.

After the recess the judge addressed both Taquard and Bayless. He informed them that the trial was over and that there would be no need to fly in several to act as character references.

"I am convinced that the urine sample in question is in fact dirty. However, there is a reasonable doubt as to whether or not this sample was produced by the accused. This trial is over. In accordance with the trial procedures for a summary courts martial the prosecution is obligated to keep the chain of custody from the crime to the defendant intact. The trial continues as long as the prosecution secures the chain of custody. Failure to do so will automatically end the trial. Judgment for the defense. You are found not guilty and are free to go."

This was the end of the trial. It was over on the second day and it wasn't even time for lunch. Bayless was relieved. He thanked both the judge and Taquard. It was a weight off of his shoulders to the point that a casual observer would notice it.

"Sir, I really appreciate everything that you've done for me. Thank you very much. Hey, I just had a thought. If you're going to be around here on Friday, we're going to have a Rappel Master Certification. We're taking some new students up in the chopper, you could certify."

"That's a thought, my orders have me departing this Saturday, but I have to let the JAG know about the outcome of this case and see if they will amend my orders and send me back to my unit early. If not, I'll be there."

On his way back to see the JAG he ran into a familiar captain who asked him how the trial went.

"Well, well, well. You have a better record than Maximum John."

Taquard met Major Woodward; he decided that it would be easier to just keep Taquard around for a while than to amend the orders once again.

"Cool, I'll just go back to my hotel and relax until it is time for me leave."

"Actually, you're not getting off that easily," the major said. "There's a 15-6 investigation pending that I need you to work on."

"Sir, I've never done anything like this in my life. I have no idea what a 15-6 investigation involves."

"Well, this is a good place to start."

"I understand that they take a long time to do. How much can I possibly do in a couple of days?"

"Not much. We don't expect you to finish it. All we want you to do is look at it. Getting a little work out of you beats getting nothing at all. You're being paid to be here. It's not like you won't be getting off by four."

"I'll see what I can do. Can you tell me anything about case? Anything at all?"

"Well, it has to do with some money that was stolen from one of the mess halls a couple of years ago."

"It's an old case."

"Yeah, nobody's even bothered to look at it. Finding the people that you need will be difficult."

"They could be anywhere by now."

"You will find them, and don't think that just because you are going back to your unit that you can sluff off. You're being watched and you will be productive."

"Yes, sir. One question."

"What is it?"

"How much support am I going to get on this one? You know how the Army always runs their lieutenants around in circles. I can't be accountable for performance and productivity if I have to rely on a bunch of people who are going to blow me off."

"You'll report to the installation command. They are interested in their cases, especially cases like this one. You'll find that they will support you beyond your expectations."

"Thank you, sir. I'm on my way there now."

"Lieutenant, I don't know what your impression of the 25th ID is, but not all organizations within this division operate like a bunch of blind faggots at a weenie roast."

# Chapter Eighteen
## *The 15-6 Investigation*

Taquard reported to the Installation Management Office and found his point of contact at the investigations division. He was greeted by his new supervisor, Xiling Woo, and a staff. Though of Chinese descent, Xiling was both born and rained in Hawaii and spoke English as her native language. By virtue of the fact that everyone was inexperienced, everything was run the way it was supposed to be.

"Here is the file on the case," Xiling said to Taquard. "I've never worked a case at this magnitude before."

"What's so significant about it?"

"Well, the regulations state that a case such as this has to be investigated by a field grade officer."

"I'm only company grade."

"We got an exception to policy. The backlog on these cases is so immense that we can't even begin to catch up. A lot of outsiders such as yourself have been called in."

"What makes this case so significant?"

"Some money was stolen. We have a preliminary report in the file. It should be enough to get you started."

"Where will I work?"

"You will work in this office. We have a couple desks that you can choose from. Jose will help you out in any way that you need."

Taquard settled in his new work area and acclimated himself to the case file. There was a lot to learn and do in a very short period of time. He knew that he didn't have the experience or the formal training for any type of investigation. All that he could do was to do his best. The investigation concerned the theft of money out of a mess hall. He wrote down the names of the people involved in the case on a legal pad. Though he had only a few days until it was time for him to leave he pursued the case diligently. Too diligently.

**Jumping in at high speed is amateurish and is a sign of immaturity.**

"Hey, Jose, there's a lot of people that were involved in this case. Many of them are probably gone."

"If you give me the names I will pull up their records and see if I can get in touch with them. We can fly them back to Hawaii if we need to."

"I guess the main thing for me to do is to determine who I need to speak to."

"We have a set of conference rooms down the hall table. There's a large room with a big conference table and private offices."

"Can I use them?"

"They're all yours."

"So let's say that we do get in touch with someone we need to talk to, then what?"

"That's easy. I coordinate with the airlines, hotels, and limousine companies and make arrangements for them to come over and see you. If you want them here tomorrow, I'll get them here."

"That's going to be impossible. You can't get anybody from the US to Hawaii overnight."

"Yes I can. Since this is a federal investigation of this category, I am allowed to dip into the congressional pool. That means that I can use hotel accommodations that have been set aside for congressmen and senators. That goes for planes and limos too."

"What about their commitments in the US?"

"So what? If they're employed we forward a voucher to the person who forwards it to their employer to submit through DoD channels and gets reimbursed for the temporary loss of the employee and the temporary hiring of the replacement."

"That's expensive."

"Don't forget, we still pay that person's salary, per diem, and mileage. The replacement gets time and a half."

"I guess there's no other way. Attempting to interview people will keep that Major off of my back."

"What time do you want to see them?"

"I don't know, the sooner the better. Can you get everybody?"

"No, you never will. But you can do as many as possible. You probably won't even get in touch with everybody."

"How about Thursday at ten in the morning?"

"We might get a few by then. At least you will have something to work with."

Taquard read the documents and copies of statements concerning the stolen money. There were about sixty pages of files to read and become familiar with. The one thing that Taquard didn't want was another amendment to his orders. To everyone's surprise, the staff was able to contact everyone on the legal pad.

"Actually, it wasn't as bad as I thought," Jose said. "I was able to make the coordination required to get everyone here by Thursday."

"What luck," Taquard answered.

"Turns out that of the sixteen names listed, ten of them are still in Hawaii and all sixteen of them still work for the federal government."

"I wonder how much money we've spent on this investigation so far."

"Let me see. I have itemized everything so far. I had to pay premium rates on such short notice. With the air fate, door to door transportation, per diem, hotels, replacement workers on short notice, and over time it comes to $23,698.17."

"Wow, that's a lot of money."

"That includes transporting everyone back to their points of origin. Are you planning on keeping anyone here for more than one day?"

"I'm not sure."

"If you think that you will just let me know. Of course that will cost more."

Formatting the investigation is just as important as the investigation itself. Preparing the format also helped in arranging the interviews and conducting the case in the most efficient manner. Taquard was constantly referring to the book on how to format his findings which also enhanced his performance.

Thursday morning was productive though uneventful. Taquard addressed the entire group at the beginning. This was followed by interviewing everyone individually in a private office. Unlike the typical investigator who interrupted subjects during an interrogation.

Taquard listened to the responses to his questions. He even listened to the trivial comments that were made. The private interviews were followed by another collective address where everyone was excused. There was nothing else to extract from any of the individuals involved or the group itself.

"Well, sir, you tried. You can't expect to crack a case in three days."

"No, but at least I have something for the next investigator to go by."

"You'll be leaving the day after tomorrow anyway so it really doesn't make a whole lot of difference."

"I'll put this together and send it over to JAG tomorrow morning."

The additional statements that were produced enhanced the quality of the investigation format and justified Taquard's existence on the island but did nothing at all to help solve the case. One of the tasks that he pursued was transcribing the documents into legible copies. Personal handwritten notes were typed with an official heading to address the document that it was transcribing. The same was done for journal entries and receipts. Numbers were important and were double-checked. The initiator of the investigation reported that money was stolen from the mess hall by an unknown thief. Preparation of the investigation revealed what the interviews could not. The mess financial log accounted for the collection of $674.50 after change was given. The change voucher was on hand and accounted for the return of the $2.00 that the mess hall was given in change to begin their working day. The deposit slip read $679.50. That meant what was once thought of as a theft was actually a credit of $5.00. Taquard surmised that someone may have thrown an extra $5.00 to cover a perceived shortage of funds or that maybe an officer paid for two meals as did the other officer that he was with. The possibilities of what went wrong were endless. The important thing was that the US government was not the victim of theft. The government came out $5.00 ahead. It took $23,698.17 to find that out. Previous documentation, outlying initial investigations, demonstrated that the commander insisted on the investigation while canceling any notions of forgoing it altogether. The difference was that Taquard's investigation was official. The government managed to turn a $5.00 credit into a $23,694.17 deficit.

Friday morning consisted of hanging around the office for a few hours before taking his case to JAG. Major Woodward read the findings and informed Taquard that they would have to conduct another investigation to determine whether or not his investigation was legitimate or not.

"Am I getting extended again?"

"No, you're leaving here tomorrow morning. You'll be picked up at your hotel room at nine. You'll give them your car keys and check out. Somebody will drive you to the airport."

"Does that mean that I am excused for the rest of the day?"

"No, I'm sure that I can find something for you to do."

"There's a Rappel Master Certification this afternoon, I could go to that."

"Yes, that's a good idea. You can do that."

"Do you want to see me after that?"

"No, you can go back to your room and pack. And, thanks for all of your help. I really appreciate it. We all do."

# Chapter Nineteen
*Rappel Master Certification*

The Rappel Master Certification was a one day course that began in the afternoon. Air Assault taught and trained students. They demonstrated their knowledge by passing tests and were awarded a set of silver wings. Rappel Master reviewed material and tested the students. They were awarded a star above their Air Assault wings. Rappel Master Certification tested the students on material which they were accountable for. There were no additions to the Air Assault wings, but it was a requirement to be an instructor. Instead of performing inspections on instructors, they would perform them on students who had never rappelled out of a helicopter before.

Taquard's class size was a grand total of three. Taquard was tested first. Remembering what he had learned in previous courses, he was able to pass his first test. The other two students didn't. The second series of tests included taking four Air Assault candidates up in a helicopter 300 feet off of the ground and safely rappelling them. The students were fully loaded with combat gear and nervous when the helicopter lifted them off of the ground.

Taquard put them in the L-shape position with his commands and flicking his fingers in their faces. Simple commands alone will not work for rookies. The automatic flinching caused the students to slide back on the rope. The slightest distance on the rope made a world of difference.

At first the students were focusing on staying in the helicopter, and then they knew there was no way they would be able to get back in. Then he held them there until they were ready to go on their own. The tired students were in the correct position caused by being far out on the skid and wanting to return back to the helicopter. He released two of the students who were diagonal from each other, waited and released the other two. There were no problems and the students landed safely. Taquard graduated top in his class by virtue of the fact that he was the only one left. He liked the experience and was certified to be an instructor at the AAS even though there were no cadre members who were officers. The only position for him to fill, assuming that they would hire him, was nothing other than that of the commandant billet. The possibility was remote, but Taquard was going for something far greater than recognition.

"Oh, there's something that just came in the other day. I'm not sure whether or not you are aware of it but the Rappel Master wings have been recalled," one of the cadre NCOs informed.

"What?"

"Yep. The Army changed its mind. Rappel Master wings are no longer authorized for wear. I know that sucks but that's the way things are. I thought I'd better let you know before you start wearing them. I see you have yet to get around to wearing your Air Assault wings."

Taquard departed the area after wishing the cadre farewell. Bayless was there to give an additional thank you. The trial was behind him and he was back to work. Everyone knew what had happened and appreciated the support that Taquard provided to them. Taquard went back to Honolulu without stopping by to see the JAG. It was a good TDY assignment in spite of the amendments. His new credentials were moderately impressive.

# Chapter Twenty
## *Back at the Battery*

While the success of the ARTEP was a great achievement for the battalion there were two other hurdles they were faced with. One was the IG inspection and the other was Team Stupid. Taquard wasn't planning on being around for either one of those fiascos. Instead, he was looking at his short timer's calendar and marking off each day as it went by. As Taquard's duty assignment approached the end of a full year, DEROS became a higher priority. All of the short timers were thinking about DEROS. There was a sign posted in the PAC (Personnel Administration Center) that said "Think DEROS" which was beside another sign that said, "Why take life seriously, you're not going to get out of it alive anyway?" Another posted sign in the PAC was, "Insanity is doing something over and over again and expecting different results," quoted from Albert Einstein. One thing that the PAC, under the command of Blunt, did do was display a sense of humor. They also provided short timer calendars and DEROS orders. Taquard made a lot of frequent visits to the PAC for some reason or another.

"Hey, how come Koreans never smile," Taquard overheard one PAC sergeant asking another.

"I don't know. Why?"

"Because they don't have a DEROS."

The big question in Taquard's mind was when and how he was to be notified about his DEROS. He knew that his time was approaching, but didn't know exactly when. He spoke to Blunt about it, but Blunt's nonchalant response about letting him know wasn't too comforting. It had been almost a week since Taquard had any contact with PAC. He called the PAC from the Charlie Battery orderly room just to stay in touch.

"Yes, Sergeant Diaz, this is Lieutenant Taquard. I haven't heard a word about my DEROS. It should be coming up any day now. What? Are you kidding me? How the hell do you expect me to clear in one day? Tomorrow morning? Shit! Okay."

Burke could only hear Taquard's side of the conversation, but he could piece the rest of it together and had come to the conclusion that he had just lost a lieutenant.

"Sir, I just spoke to—"

"Go ahead," Captain Burke said.

Taquard went into a frantic rush getting back to Camp Pelham to go to the PAC to pick up his clearing papers to begin the clearing process that had to be completed before 0600 hours the following morning. Fortunately, as an officer, he was able to clear a lot of the stations himself. The clearing usually takes about two weeks, but one week is enough. One day was unheard of. The two biggest challenges would be CIF (Central Issuing Facility) and hold Baggage. He went to the PAC, picked up his clearing papers, orders, and went to work. Clearing CIF would be one of the big challenges. Upon arriving, the Army issued every soldier enough field gear to overfill four duffle bags. The problem was that each and every item had to be returned in near mint condition. Many times, unused gear that was still in its original package was deemed to be too dirty to turn back in. All of Taquard's gear was brand-new when it was issued to him. However, a full year's worth of field use, abuse, neglect, and wear and tear made his tattered gear practically impossible to turn back in. He knew that he was going to have to pay for it. GIs ended up paying for gear that was damaged or unfit for returning. His steel pot was rusted all over, dirty, and dented. The cover was torn, rusted all over, moldy, and discolored. Putting it through the laundry eliminated the mold and rust, but didn't do a thing for the discoloration or tears. Throughout the year he also acquired and purchased a lot of other equipment. He didn't know whether a piece of gear was his or the Army's. Somehow he had acquired an OD medic wool blanket that he couldn't remember ever getting. It was a very nice blanket, but he had no idea where it came from or how he got it. The important thing was that it was his. To compound the problem with packing was that he lost his copy of the CIF sheet. The only thing that he could do was to take his gear to Camp Edwards and compare what he had with their records. He would have to pay for the difference and what wasn't acceptable for turn in. This is exactly what he did. Fortunately, he was able to hail a kimchee cab just outside of the gate. The first thing that he did when he got to CIF was to ask for a copy of his records.

"Are you sure that you drew your gear out of here, sir?" the corporal asked.

"Sure I'm sure. First I drew gear from the Turtle Farm and then I came here to draw even more gear. It was about a year ago."

"We don't have anything on file, you're not in our files."

"Do I turn in my stuff at Camp Casey?"

"No, you turn your stuff in here and we forward it to Casey."

"How about if I just leave this stuff with you?"

"We can't. We're not allowed to accept anything without a sheet."

"Can you clear me without a sheet?"

"Actually, your name appears on file, but no records. Since we didn't have any records on you we were going to ask you for a copy."

"I don't have a copy, I was hoping that you would have one. How about clearing me."

"No problem. Let me see your paperwork."

Within minutes Taquard had cleared CIF. This had to be some kind of record.

"What am I supposed to do with all of this gear?"

"Keep it. Hold Baggage is next door in the same building. Just give them a copy of your orders and they will ship it to your next unit."

This was Taquard's next stop anyway. He needed to make arrangements to have them come to his room and ship his stuff out.

"Look, I'm really in a jam. You see I have to leave here tomorrow and I just found out a few hours ago."

"Don't worry," answered Sergeant First Class Bigelow. "We get last minute requests all of the time."

"Thank you."

"Don't mention it. Did you clear CIF?"

"I did, here's the paperwork with their stamp on it."

"Good, that's the hardest one. Clearing CIF alone can take up to two weeks and hardly anybody can do it on their first try."

"They told me that you could ship some stuff from here in addition to going to my place to pick up some stuff."

"Yes, we do it all the time. Can I have a copy of your orders?"

"Yeah, sure. Here you go."

"All right. Okay, I will send a few guys over to your place this afternoon at about 1700 hours and they should be finished in about an hour or so. Oh, do you want to leave that gear with me I'll take care of it for you."

"Thank you."

Another soldier made some copies of orders and used one copy as a reference to cut some shipping stencils. A ready made crate was brought over where Taquard dumped in all of the stuff that he thought that he was going to have to turn in to CIF. The crates came in several sizes. This one seemed just about perfect. There wasn't a lot of dead space left in it after Taquard's gear was loaded in. Then the lid was put on and nailed shut. Then a stencil was put on the side and red spray paint was sprayed on. The crate was ready to go after a process that took less than ten minutes. Not only did they relieve him of all of the gear that he was carrying and have it sent forward, they scheduled their arrival to Taquard's room that very same afternoon. Hold baggage was fast, professional, and efficient.

Taquard returned to Pelham and cleared the rest of the stations, most of which he used his rank to clear himself, and returned back to his room to pack. Packing up wasn't too difficult since Taquard had very few possessions. But just to make the packing a little lighter and easier, he took a lot of stuff to the post office and mailed a lot of things home.

By five o'clock that afternoon, everything was ready to go. His bags were packed and all he had to do was wait for the movers to arrive. They arrived a few minutes late, but it was nothing to sweat. The moving party consisted of a three man team who brought in some ready made crates and lots of excelsior. They knew exactly what they were doing and how to do it. And like their counterparts at Camp Edwards, they were fast, professional, and efficient. Lids went on the crates and were nailed shut followed by the stencils being put into place for the red spray paint. They were finished in less than forty-five minutes.

Everything was gone except the packed bags that he was going to carry with him. All that he had left were some uniforms and a few essentials. He was cleared and ready to go to his next assignment in Hawaii. All that he had to do was wait until the next morning. He could hardly wait. As usual, Blunt came into his room without knocking.

"Hey, Elwood, let's go."

"Get out of here."

"Coldhammer wants to go on a fun run."

"At this hour? Hell, we did PT this morning."

"I'm not kidding, hurry up, get dressed, and let's go. The major's waiting."

"Well, I'm not going. Tell Coldhammer that he can just start the not so fun run without me."

"He wants us specifically. He mentioned you by name. Hey, what happened to your TV?"

"Look, dipshit. Take a good look around. What does it look like?"

"Looks like you moved or something. Why did you move all of your stuff out of here?"

"Because I'm leaving. This is it, John. My last night here at Camp Pelham."

"Why are you leaving Camp Pelham?"

"You know, for an S-1, you aren't very sharp are you? I'm leaving, here are my orders. Here are my clearing papers. They just picked up my stuff not fifteen minutes ago."

"Where did you get those orders?"

"Sergeant Diaz gave them to me."

"Oh, he wasn't supposed to give those orders to you."

"Then how else was I supposed to clear then?"

"Those orders have rescinded."

"What? When am I supposed to leave then?"

"A month, six weeks, we're not sure. You've been involuntarily extended. Sergeant Diaz didn't know. I thought I told Sergeant Garcia to get in touch with you. He must've forgotten. Anyway, get dressed the major's waiting."

"My stuff is being shipped off to Hawaii. How am I going to get my stuff back?"

"You'll be going to Hawaii later. They'll hold it for you until you get there. Anyway, get dressed, will you?"

# Chapter Twenty-One
## *Extension*

Like previous fun runs, this one was voluntary, but you had to volunteer. And as usual it was about five miles long through the ville and terrain that was not conducive to running. To ensure that the runners didn't take any shortcuts they were all loaded on to the back of a two-and-a-half-ton truck and taken to a location five miles away from Camp Pelham. Any attempted shortcuts would only lengthen the run. But, as usual, it was accomplished in record time. Taquard returned to his Spartan room after the run. He didn't have a lot to come back to after the movers had left. He did have enough essentials to get by and took a shower. He returned to his room when Lieutenant Schwartz came in.

"I came here to pick up your refrigerator, but if you want I'll let you keep the sodas."

"Get the fuck out of my room, you New York Jew."

"Since you're leaving, I thought that I'd take your refrigerator. Besides, the house boy said I could have it."

"It's not his to give. Now get your kike ass the fuck out of my room."

"Why do I have to wait? You're leaving soon, you don't need it, I do."

"I said get out."

Blunt came in as usual, unannounced.

"Dammit, Curtis, I already told you. That refrigerator goes to First

Lieutenant Davis once Elwood leaves, not you. Even if he leaves it to you, I'm taking it away and giving it to Davis."

"Davis just got here. I've been here for months. Why should he get it before me?"

"Because he outranks you, you stupid asshole."

"But 1 doesn't go by rank, it goes by DEROS."

"Bullshit! That's just some of that Jew shit that you kikes came up with."

Before he could respond Blunt threw him out of Taquard's room. Taquard didn't mind the slanderous remarks towards the New York Jews or kikes (which in the mind of many Jews meant New York Jew). Although he was sympathetic towards Jews he didn't like the New York Jews.

Taquard's extension meant that he was back preparing for the upcoming IG inspection. That meant that he was busy. Naturally, he would be in charge of Fire and Safety since he was also the Battalion Fire and Safety Officer. He was also assigned additional areas of responsibility for the upcoming inspection. Burke was more than happy to have him back Even though Burke didn't show it; Taquard knew that he appreciated him. In the past, Taquard hated Burke, but it was fair to say that Taquard and Burke were beginning to get along. In spite of all of the obstacles, they did develop a friendship.

The other concern that Taquard had was that of not knowing exactly when his departure would be. Since he sent all of his field gear forward, he would have to draw a new and complete issue if he had to participate in any field exercises. He was almost positive that he would be departing prior to the next field exercise, but anything less than 100% certain meant that he would have to visit CIF. The question was, how long could he hold off on such a visit.

The other area that Taquard was responsible for was NBC (Nuclear, Biological, and Chemical) readiness. This was more affectionately referred to as No Body Cares. As with the previous additional duties, Taquard consulted the experts when he was confronted with tasks that he knew absolutely nothing about. The biggest problem was finding out who the experts actually were. A lot of people, Swackhammer for example, claimed to be experts when in fact they weren't. Charlie Battery's NBC program was in sorry shape to say the very least. It seemed that Charlie Battery was always on its ass. No matter where a person went in the world, Charlie Battery was the worst outfit of any artillery battalion. Taquard did his part to ensure that his areas were up to standards. For the NBC arena, he consulted Lieutenant West, the battalion NBC Chief. West was the residential NBC guru who was a subject matter expert. He was the only person in the battalion who had attended the Chemical Corps Officer's basic Course. He also worked directly for Coldhammer. Burke himself, would occasionally work in the NBC room with Taquard, West, and some of the NBC NCOs in an effort to rectify the tremendous amount of shortcomings. West, although highly qualified for the position that he held, was as annoying as he was welcomed. He griped about anything and everything. While he perfected the deficiencies in the unit he had a nasty habit of picking up the phone to Call Coldhammer. After explaining the problem to Coldhammer, Coldhammer would insist on speaking to Burke. The led to a notorious Coldhammer ass chewing that no one wanted to be on the receiving of. Unfortunately for Burke, the NBC room had a phone. Whenever, West would pick up the phone, everyone in the room would listen attentively.

"Sir, this is Lieutenant West again. The unit doesn't have one single masked marked or labeled. There is no record of the masks, no accountability measures whatsoever. Not only that, but the entire filing system is so far outdated that it has be replaced completely. Even with what they have on hand there is no way that…. Uh, yes, sir. Yes, sir he is. Uh, sir, it's for you," West would say as he was handing the phone over to Captain Burke.

Though it wasn't clear to the others in the room, Coldhammer's ass chewings could be heard through the phone. It was obvious that Burke was shook up by the wrath of Coldhammer and understandably so. Everyone feared Coldhammer. Burke always responded with contrite answers while he was trying to gain information for solving problems without posing direct questions.

After he hung up, Burke asked Taquard, "Do you have any idea where we can get these tags that Coldhammer is talking about?"

"We have plenty in the battalion NBC room," West replied.

"Yes, good," Burke said to Taquard. "There's a special way that these tags have to be—"

"Stamped," interrupted West. "They have to be punched in a special way."

"Yes, that's right. We will make sure that everything is copasctic. Elwood, I need for you to go to the battalion NBC room tomorrow morning. See if you can get some tags. Also find out what the standards for marking them is. We don't want any mistakes."

"You just number them," West said.

"Check," Burke replied, "but there is a specific way of doing it."

"Yes, you need a special punch set and some tools to do it," West responded.

"Good. All right, Elwood. Find out if we can use their tools and punch set."

West picked up the phone.

"Sir, Lieutenant West speaking. Charlie Battery doesn't even have a punch set of their NBC tags. I'm afraid that it won't be as easy as just ordering another set with prescribed tools. They'll never get it in time for the IG inspection. While Burke can get a deficiency gig on this one, the battalion will be gigged on this one as well unless we do a statement of charges on Burke. Yes, sir, I'll prepare the paperwork on it first thing tomorrow morning. Uh, yes, sir. Yes, sir he is. Uh, sir, it's for you," West would say as he was handing the phone over to Captain Burke.

Taquard was wishing more and more that he hadn't've been involuntarily extended. He couldn't believe the amount of shit that he was enduring while there was an opportunity a few days earlier to leave this miserable place. He was ready to go. He thought about what Hawaii would be like.

Even at eleven PM, Coldhammer had a lot to say to Burke. He tore him apart some more. All that Burke could do was to respond with was, "Yes, sir, no excuse, sir."

Due to the curfew that was imposed, both Taquard and West were confined to Camp Giant. Since West had date of rank on Taquard, he slept on a foot locker while Taquard slept on the floor. Spending the nights at Camp Giant was becoming an institution. It seemed no matter how hard and how long Taquard worked, he just couldn't manage to get out of camp Giant in time to make it to Camp Pelham in tome to beat curfew.

"You know, sir," Taquard said, "we could get some of these orphans to clean out these insulators for us. Their hands are small and can fit in these things really well."

Even at 0122 hours in the cold dark morning, West managed to pick up the phone in response to Taquard's comment.

"West, put down the phone. Taquard was just kidding," Burke shouted. "You were kidding weren't you?"

"We'll see how funny the XO thinks it is," replied West.

He called the XO again.

"Sir, I'll be spending tomorrow evening at another battery location. The insulators at Charlie Battery are category Type A. They were supposed to have been exchanged over three months ago. Every one of these is expired. If division can't support a massive exchange on short notice..."

"Yeah, I know, it's for me."

When West wasn't around, Burke badmouthed him something awful. The next evening was another example.

"I wish that there was some way to keep that son of a bitch off of my back," Burke exclaimed.

"I hear you," Taquard said.

"How come you smoke so much?" Burke asked Taquard. "You smoke all of the time. It's a nasty habit. How do you do it? More importantly, why do you do it?"

"These are Salem Lights. They taste great and they're not that bad for you."

"What difference does it make? Cigarettes are cigarettes. They're all bad for you no matter if they're light or otherwise."

"I like to smoke. So does Major Coldhammer. Besides, these are his favorite brand."

"So, if Major Coldhammer does something, does that mean that you have to do it too?"

"We all do what Coldhammer tells us what to do. Besides, these happen to be West's favorite brand too."

"Coldhammer never told you to smoke."

"No, but I just happen to like smoking."

"Both of you are a little hyper if you ask me. Actually all three of you are hyper. And it strikes me as a little odd that all three of you smoke the same cigarettes."

"Odd? Coldhammer's my idol."

"Some idol."

"West likes him too."

"Great, just what I need. To be surrounded by sons of a bitches who smoke Salem Lights and don't see a problem with it."

"What's worse is that son of a bitch predecessor of yours who left you all of this shit. He ran the battery like a trailer park whore house. The only thing worse than his management was his dog-ass ugly face."

"He happens to be my best friend."

"He's a stupid motherfucker. That's what he is. And because of him, you are faced with all of this shit that you have to clean up."

"I happen to think that he did a good job."

"Yeah, sure, that's why we are in the NBC room every night past midnight working our asses off while everyone else is beating their meat."

"It's a damn good thing that you're PCSing before I can rate you. Get another extension and I don't give a damn what happens, I'll show you what I can do to you and your OER. And don't think that Coldhammer will be able to bail you out of this one this time. I still can't believe that you got an early promotion out of that one. Finch tries to fuck you and Coldhammer gives you an early promotion."

"That's just great. I am helping you and you are threatening me."

"It's not a threat, it's a promise."

"Fine, since you won't be rating me, then there is no point in me being here."

"Get back to work, El Tee."

"You know, you've got three Ds in this battery. Three lieutenants, each one is a D."

"And which D are you?"

"I'm the dumb one. I'm doing all of this shit and sucking on it to no end and the worst thing about it is that I can get out of it. I know better, but the simple fact of the matter is that I am supporting you for no other reason besides being dumb. Darnell's the defiant one. He stands up to you and fights you to your face and goes to bed at night. Now Newhouse, he's the deceitful one. Boy, there's deception if I ever saw it. He supports you to your face, but the second you turn your back, wham! He's putting a knife in it. But he sleeps at night too. For the past four days and nights I have been here not sleeping like everyone else. I'm sure that if I talk to Coldhammer, he'll figure out a way to utilize me at the battalion Fire and Safety level."

"I guess it wouldn't hurt for all of us to get some sleep for a change." Burke said. "You're free to leave."

"Thank you, sir."

"Oh, just a second."

"Sir?"

"You don't have to come in tomorrow, but I would appreciate it if you did. Look, I'm sure that I said some things that I shouldn't've said. Poindexter was a very good friend of mine. In spite of the way things are, he and I were good friends. If you get extended again, I'll support you on your OER. Not because you and Coldhammer get along, but because you deserve it. I'm not Captain Finch."

"I'll see you tomorrow, sir."

"Lieutenant Taquard, you're wrong about the D. You're dedicated."

Captain Burke was an example of an asshole who redeemed himself. There were confrontations, but in the end Burke turned out to be a good man. This was a deceptive lesson that was learned because by and large, people do not redeem them selves. Burke was the exception to the rule. Taquard came to admire Burke and supported him not because he had to.

Taquard would learn that it paid to follow some simple rules and assume that people were not the exception.

**INTERPERSONAL SKILL RULE NUMBER 1: People do not redeem themselves.**

## INTERPERSONAL SKILL RULE NUMBER 2: Once you make an enemy, that person remains your enemy for life.

Taquard's schedule was beating him down and it was starting to show. If it wasn't busting his ass at Giant, he was doing something for the man at Pelham. Either way, he was getting beaten down. A full year had gone by and Taquard had only six days off. Burke was on his second year and hadn't had any. No matter how things went, it was one pain in the ass after another. While there were always some soldiers who managed to get out of work like greased pigs, most of them were constantly pressed for time. Even though he didn't go to Camp Giant right away, Taquard was still required to do PT at Camp Pelham. You could never skip PT. The captains always stormed the lieutenant barracks in the morning to make sure that they went to PT. They didn't do it every day, but they did it most of the time. After PT at Pelham, Taquard took a nice hot shower, followed by a one-hour nap. He decided to take a long needed nap and rest in total bliss. It was 0756 and he lay down in his bed with the heater on and began to slumber. One hour of blissful sleep would be so wonderful. After a year, he deserved it. Taquard closed his eyes in great anticipation. The calm and serenity began to overtake his body. He didn't even worry about the possibility of oversleeping.

"Elwood, there you are," Blunt said as he barged into Taquard's room as usual. Blunt never knocked or announced his entrance. "Let's go, you're going to be late."

"What difference does it make? Burke said that I could come in late today."

"Work? I'm talking about the bridge crossing. You're up."

"What?"

"It's your turn to catch the cane. You got to be there at eight."

The local tradition at Camp Pelham was to conduct a bridge crossing ceremony to departing officers. This ceremony was a prelude to the last time that the officer would cross the bridge that would take him off post and off of Camp Pelham forever. Prior to crossing the bridge, the officer would throw the cane to the next officer who will cross the bridge. After that, he fires a blank round from a 105 howitzer and says, "On guard, sir."

In the history of Camp Pelham, nobody ever caught the cane. The departing officer wore a Class A uniform for his departure instead of fatigues or the new Battle Dress Uniform (BDU) that was being phased in. Before the throwing of the cane, the departing officer would walk down a long olive drab line of officers, from longest to shortest in time to tour completion, and shake their hands.

It was Canerra's turn to cross the bridge. Like most people who completed a tour in Korea, he did not get a promotion or medal. The most that a Second Lieutenant could possibly hope for was a promotion to First Lieutenant and an Army Commendation Medal (ARCOM). Canerra's self-serving attributes never ceased to amaze anyone. His arrogance was demonstrated by the fact that he had silver bars in his pocket along with First Lieutenant shoulder boards. A lot of Second Lieutenants would change their rank to First Lieutenant while they were traveling. This gave them bragging rights to strangers. After shaking hands with Taquard, both Canerra and Taquard took their positions. Canerra threw the cane short. Taquard picked up the cane and was officially the shortest officer in the battalion. He was a short timer and began to see light at the end of the tunnel.

"You're leaving in five days," Blunt told Taquard.

"Five days? That's the day of the inspection."

"We'll have the bridge crossing before the inspection. You will report to Camp Casey with all of your luggage the day after tomorrow. You'll come back here and spend the night. Then you will do your bridge crossing and go back to Casey."

"Well, I guess it's official then."

"West and Donahue will be going with you."

"How come they didn't catch the cane?"

"West is Chemical Corps. Artillery trumps all other branches in the event of a tie. You outrank Donahue. You will be the group leader."

Burke, who was also in attendance at the bridge crossing, approached Taquard.

"Congratulations on the cane Elwood. Listen, I..."

"We'll go to work together, sir."

"Thank you, Elwood."

"Elwood," Blunt added, "you don't have to go to work, you're officially on clearing status."

"That's okay, John. I already cleared. I don't even have hold baggage to worry about."

"You still don't have to work."

"I'd be more than grateful if he did," Burke interjected.

"It's okay, John, I don't mind."

"Well, if you change your mind you can come back here and chill out. You can tell Burke to take a hike. No offense, sir," Blunt said to Burke.

Even West continued working in the Charlie Battery NBC room as well, even though he didn't have to either. Work was diligent and continuous. The only difference was that this time West was able to rectify deficiencies without the use of a telephone call to Coldhammer.

"Hey what's this box here?"

"That looks like the punch set that we were looking for," West replied. "It looks like a punch set box all right."

"It looks old."

"Open it up and check what's inside."

Taquard opened the box.

"Are all the tools that we need here?"

"Yes," West answered.

"The tools look brand new, like they've never been used. Is everything here?"

"Yes, everything's there. The reason that it's never been used is because no one knew what it was for."

"Sir, maybe we should call the XO and tell him that we found the punch set," Taquard said to Burke.

"No, forget it," Burke answered.

"But, sir, with the statement of charges that West initiated..."

"Forget it. I would rather pay the charges than talk to Coldhammer."

"Sir, I could talk to him. We could clear your record. This could hurt your OER. I don't mind and besides, we're on speaking terms."

"Okay, I would appreciate that."

"After I talk to Coldhammer, I'll punch out these brass tags for the masks. We'll finish this up today. We're almost there."

A short phone call to Coldhammer and the statement of charges action was stopped.

"Okay sir, you're all set. No statement of charges on you. You're clear. The action was still at battalion level. It hadn't been forwarded yet."

"Thank you."

"You still haven't fixed the problem with exchanging the insulators." West added.

"Oh yeah," Taquard answered. "Sergeant Beaumont took the track to Casey for an annual organizational servicing."

"He still has that thing?" Burke asked.

"Yes, sir."

"I thought I told you to get rid of that thing once and for all."

"The BMO (Battalion Maintenance Officer) said that we have to keep it. But, the point is that while Sergeant Beaumont was taking the track in for maintenance and servicing, he also took the insulators to Casey for a direct exchange. If you don't believe me see for yourself. They're in these crates here."

In spite of the work taking place in the NBC room, the new crates went unnoticed.

"Jose," Burke said to West, "are these the insulators that we need for the inspection? Are these the right ones?"

"Yes, they're the ones we need all right. They're the latest model. Everyone else still has the S Series models. These are S Series Type P. How did you manage to get these? They're brand new."

"Sergeant Beaumont has a friend at division who works at the chemical school. He's also on the IG inspection team. Oh, and he also provided us with the binders that we will need for the inspection. Let me see if I can remember where I put those things. Oh yeah, they're in this box under the cabinet."

"Shit! This is everything that we need," West said while inspecting the binders. "All of the batteries should have these. They gave you a new TAMMS (The Army Maintenance Management System) file card holder too? This is exactly what we need. Every battery should have one."

"Yes, according to Beaumont, the previous ones are obsolete."

"Okay, sir," West said to Burke, "just post this paperwork and finishing punching the tags and you should be all set."

"Thank you, Elwood, I really appreciate it."

"Beaumont is the one who really deserves the thanks."

"Yes, he does."

"Beaumont is misunderstood, but he's a good man through and through."

"About the APC."

"It's at Camp Pelham in the battalion motor pool. The BMO wants them there for the inspection. And our APC has been assessed with a no faults noted rating by the IG team."

"The IG team hasn't inspected anything yet."

"The IG team from Camp Casey includes a composite of experts who are dual slotted. The guy at the Division Motor Pool happens to also be on the IG team. Sergeant Beaumont asked for an advanced inspection. He inspected the track and put locks and seals on the track, that is everything except the driver's hatch. Beaumont took it directly to the Battalion Motor Pool."

With just three days to go before the inspection, the battalion was frantic about getting both the unit and camp in inspection order. Every commander was aiming for a "no faults noted" rating in each of his areas. In addition, they also focused on enhancing the appearance of areas as well. The logic was that if something looked good then it was good, even if it wasn't, and if something didn't appear good then it wasn't good even if it was. Appearance mattered more than substance. Commanders had to be diligent in their preparations because they knew that there wasn't a single Korean on the IG team. Results couldn't be secured with money under the table. On the other side of the same coin, these sticklers to detail were overwhelmingly cooperative in preparing someone for an inspection if he requested it. The truth of the matter was that extremely few people ever approached the IG team prior to an inspection.

"Sir, all of your tags are set and ready. Everything is ready. I suggest that we lock up the NBC room and not let anyone touch it until the IG team gets here."

"I agree. Look, Elwood, I don't know how to thank you and Sergeant Beaumont for everything that you've done," Burke replied.

"By the way, I realize why I was so willing to work for you."

"Why is that?"

"Because you set the example."

"You take care, Elwood."

Taquard went to see Staff Sergeant Beaumont before departing Camp Giant.

"Sergeant Beaumont, this is it. I'm leaving."

"I'm sure going to miss you sir. It's not every day that an NCO feels that way about an officer."

"I'll let you in on a little secret. Most officers are trash."

"So are most of the NCOs. If you ever want to get any dirt on an NCO all you have to do is ask another NCO."

"Looks like they're moving people out of the ghetto."

"Yeah, see those new buildings up on the hill over there?"

"Yes."

"Those are the new barracks."

"Wow, I didn't know that."

"Nobody did. They're the results of a project that began about ten years ago. They just finished them up a couple of weeks ago."

"So you are moving in today I see."

"Yes, the IG team was here yesterday to do the inspection."

"But the IG inspection isn't due for a few more days."

"That's right. But before we could move in here it had to be inspected. The Sergeant Major thought that it would be a good idea to do the building inspection and IG inspection simultaneously. The inspection team and IG team both agreed. I was on the building preparation team."

"How did we do?"

"We got a favorable rating on the building inspection and a no faults noted on the IG inspection."

"But with all these GIs moving in the rating won't be any good anymore. There's no way that they can maintain those standards."

"The IG team has granted us a waiver to accommodate the move."

"If anyone deserves better quarters, those guys do."

"Three to a room, showers, clean toilets, washing machines and dryers, and they even have Coke machines."

"Wow, somebody finally got a break."

Taquard departed Giant at 1000 hours that morning. He never saw Beaumont again. Before the afternoon was over, he had cleared Pelham completely. He was able to keep his room until the bridge crossing. He decided to go to Camp Casey to get a head start on clearing the Turtle Farm. Upon arriving at the Turtle Farm he was quartered in the same billets that he was in when he was in when he arrived. Everything was exactly the same way it was a year ago. The only difference was that he out processed in the administrative building that was located next to the in processing one. He was the only one, other than staff, who was there. It didn't take very much time to clear each station.

"Excuse me, Sergeant Hayes," Taquard addressed. "What's the schedule for my final clearing?"

"You're all set, sir. You can do anything you want. The next formation is tomorrow at 1400 hours."

"Can I go back to my unit?"

"Yes you can if you want to, but you don't have to. Most people prefer not to go back to their units. Maybe you consider going to the post office and lightening your load or do some last minute souvenir shopping."

"Actually, I wanted to say goodbye."

"Understood, but you will need to be back here tomorrow by 1400 hours for a formation and a pre-pack inspection. You must be in your Class A uniform with all of your luggage. You are only authorized one carry on bag. Everything else will be considered checked baggage. You are only authorized two pieces of checked baggage. Everything else has to be shipped at your expense. According to your clearing packet, you have already cleared hold baggage."

"Okay, I got it. Is there anything else that I need to know?"

"Will you have any problem meeting the baggage limitations?"

"No, I'm down to two bags and one carry on."

"See you tomorrow."

The efficiency of Camp Casey's Turtle Farm was a role model that functioned just like clockwork. Everything that was required was immediately accessible and on hand. There was little excess. Everything operated strictly by the book. They processed nearly 1,000 people a week without a hitch. Operating smoothly was their routine. No one was ever rushed and there was no panic. Although they had to undergo IG inspections just like everyone else, they never prepared for them. Even though they never prepared for their inspections, they never failed any. In fact, they operated business as usual during inspections and came out of it with commendable ratings. Second Division's motto was "Second to None." They more than lived up to their motto.

Pelham was like its own world, the kind of world that people avoided. As far as Taquard was concerned, it was the best world to be in. He decided to return to Pelham to spend the night in preparation for his bridge crossing.

When he arrived back at Pelham, he was still part of the unit, but not part of the work force. After eating at the Officers Club, which still didn't have a television, he went back to his room to update his short timer's calendar. It was now broken up into hours as opposed to days.

"Hey, Taquard," Blunt shouted while barging in to his room unannounced with a large envelope in his hand. "This is classified."

"So?"

"It's from the boys in the vault."

"So give it back to the boys in the vault."

"It was generated by you."

"So get rid of it then."

"We can't. Only you can do that."

"Shit, I'll just take it back to the vault and destroy it."

"You can't. You've already out processed. You can't go in there anymore."

"Then how am I supposed to get rid of it then?"

"That's where you come in. You have to get rid of it and you have to figure out how to do it."

"How about if I sign it over to you and you take it to the incinerator and burn it?"

"No way. They just polished the incinerator for tomorrow's inspection. We're not supposed to touch it until after the inspection."

"How am I supposed to get rid of it then?"

"Find a way."

"Any ideas?"

"No, but I don't want to know how you do it."

There was no doubt about it; Taquard had to destroy the envelope and all of its contents. He emptied his trash can and poured the contents and envelope inside. Then he set fire to it. The flames got a lot bigger than anticipated. The flames began discoloring the desk that the trash can was next to. The desk was smoking. A piece of burning paper rose out of the can and headed towards the ceiling. Other pieces of burning paper did the same. Taquard ran out in the hall to get a fire extinguisher. It was gone. He returned back to his room to a burning fire. The burning papers that rose out of the trash can landed on the curtains that were burning when Taquard got back. He pulled down the curtains and threw them in the middle of the room and stomped on them. The carpet caught on fire. Taquard opened his portable refrigerator and started opening cans of grape juice. He used grape juice, ice, and his blankets to put out the fire. He used his mattress to smother the fire in the middle of the room. He also used a desk drawer to put on top of the trash can to smother the fire. When the drawer gave in to the flames while failing to extinguish the fire, Taquard replaced the drawer with another drawer. Then he grabbed a towel and ran to the bathroom and soaked it with water. He ran back with the wet towel and grabbed the trash can and took it to the shower. He flushed the remains of the papers down the toilet. Then he filled the trash can with water and went back to his room. He extinguished the burning desk and carpet. Eventually he was able to put everything out. By that time the room and all of its contents were either burned or severely scorched. However, the classified documents no longer existed. Luckily for him, his uniform and paperwork along with everything else in the closet remained in tact. He flipped the mattress over so that he would have something to sleep on. Also he had an extra blanket in the closet. He decided to take a shower and clean up. On his way back he ran in to Blunt and Schwartz.

"You smell anything burning?" Schwartz said.

"Yeah," answered Blunt, "it's those damn Koreans cooking that chicken in motor oil again."

"You know that the fire extinguisher is missing," Taquard said.

"It's under my bed," Blunt responded.

"What's it doing there?" Taquard asked.

"What do you mean what's it doing there? Where else would I put it?"

"How about where it belongs. We have an inspection tomorrow."

"Shit. I don't want one of these dumb ass lieutenants touching it before the inspection. That's why I hid it."

"I tell you I smell something burning," Schwartz added.

"And I'm telling you to go fuck yourself," Blunt answered. "By the way, did you still want Taquard's refrigerator?"

"Hell yes I want it."

"Well, you're going to have to move in his room to get it."

"How come?"

"That refrigerator is assigned to the room, we aren't in the business of moving refrigerators or furniture."

"I'll take it."

"Just wait," Taquard interjected.

"You'll move in tomorrow. Elwood still needs a place to sleep. I'll be assigning your room to a new turtle who's arriving tomorrow."

"Schwartz, maybe you're making a big deal out of this refrigerator. Who needs a refrigerator in December? Besides, new ones are on their way," Taquard said.

"No they aren't," Blunt answered. "Hey, where's that classified envelope I gave you?"

"I thought you told me to destroy it."

"I changed my mind."

"What do you want with it now?"

"Sergeant Diaz just informed me that a new paper shredder just arrived. You can use that to get rid of it."

"I'll take care of it myself," Taquard responded. "Hey, I noticed that my name is still on the placard where the fire extinguisher is supposed to be."

"The inspectors know you. Seeing your name on there will help us out."

The following morning Taquard did not do any PT and decided to swing by Camp Giant before his bridge crossing. When he looked at Charlie Battery he saw the closest thing to a mutiny that he had ever seen. The soldiers sabotaged every effort to pass the inspection. Vehicle cables were cut, the new barracks was trashed, fire extinguishers were emptied, and the place was utter chaos. With only a few hours to go, it was impossible to prepare for the inspection. No matter what his feelings may have been previously, Taquard would have never wished this on Burke ever.

"Captain Burke," Taquard shouted as he came into his office.

"He's not here," Darnell answered.

"Somebody sabotaged the whole place."

"Yeah, I know. Captain Burke is with the colonel discussing it now."

"What are we going to do?"

"Nothing. The MPs will do an investigation and make a report. It's not the first time that someone's tried to fuck up an inspection."

"So how will we pass?"

"We won't. I warned him about being such an asshole."

"I checked the NBC room. It hasn't been touched."

"That's because it was secured."

"Captain Burke worked his tail off just like everyone else. He never asked anyone to do anything that he himself didn't do."

"It was self-serving, don't kid yourself about that."

"He's a good man."

"He's an asshole and I hope he goes down."

Taquard returned to Camp Pelham for his bridge crossing ceremony.

"Where's your Class As?" Blunt asked.

"Camp Casey," Taquard answered.

"Bridge crossings require that you be in Class As."

"No kidding."

West and Donahue were dress in their Class A uniforms while Taquard was wearing BDUs.

"Maybe I shouldn't go," Taquard offered.

"Don't be crazy. You've got to go. Even if it's in BDUs."

"Hasn't anyone ever crossed the bridge crossing in BDUs before?"

"Nope, you'll be the first."

All of the battalion officers, with the exception of Darnell and House, were all lined up single file from the newest to the most veteran member. West led the trio as they went down the line. Taquard was the last in the group that went down the line shaking hands with every officer. Personal farewells were briefly exchanged. It was a special moment. Nobody cared about Taquard wearing BDUs. Burke thanked him for all of his efforts. Coldhammer gave him additional words of encouragement. It felt like Taquard was leaving his family behind. This would be the last time that he would see any of these men again. In Taquard's mind they were the best people on earth.

Following the farewells, Taquard and Case took their positions. In keeping with the tradition, Taquard threw the cane at Case in an uncatchable manner. It was thrown at high speed in a rapid reverse spinning motion. Case had to move out of the way to avoid getting hurt.

After the cane toss, Lieutenants West, Donahue, and Taquard were assembled. Taquard and Donahue each received ARCOMs. Taquard couldn't believe it. He accomplished his tour with a promotion and an ARCOM. That was the best that any Second Lieutenant could ever hope for.

During the ceremony the IG team arrived in a bus and stood by. While they disembarked, they remained quiet in honor of the ceremony.

Following the awards portion of the ceremony, Lieutenant West added two additions. This was the first time that a departing artillery officer wore BDUs to a bridge crossing. It was also the first time that a departing officer offered awards to the unit. It was a unique and special ceremony on many levels. The two awards that Lieutenant West offered to the officers of 2/17th were two small red capes with yellow letters. One cape said "Aw Shucks II" and the other said "Aw Shit II." The tradition that the officers had during Hail and Farewell ceremonies, besides getting drunk, was to present awards for screwing up. An officer would be the recipient of the "Aw Shucks" award (a small red cape with yellow letters) for a minor screw up. The "Aw Shit" award was the designator for a bigger screw up. The rule was that the award would be retired to the person who earned it three consecutive times. West managed to earn both awards (it was possible to earn more than one award at a time) three consecutive times. The "Drip of the Month" award was also recently retired. That award went to the commanding officer who had the most cases of VD in his battery. The stipulation was that the award would be retired if all units had less than 10% VD cases within the battery in a month. This award was retired during the ARTEP preparation and testing. The soldiers in the rear were restricted to post. This left the "Ditch Monster" award for the biggest accident in a month as the only award to be presented at officer club ceremonies. It also made for a much duller ceremony. The Hail and Farewell functions consisted of the announcing of one award followed by everyone leaving. With the introduction of "Aw Shucks II" and "Aw Shit II," West was hoping to rejuvenate the spirit of the club festivities.

This was also the longest bridge crossing on record. Each departing lieutenant took his turn in firing a blank round and saluting the remaining officers. West went first. His salute was accompanied with an enthusiastic, "On guard, sir." Then he ran across the bridge.

To add to the uniqueness of the ceremony, an NCO ran up to Blunt and whispered in his ear. Taquard was wondering when he was going to leave. Donahue loaded the cartridge into the breach of the howitzer. He stood by the cannon and gripped the lanyard firmly. He pulled the lanyard and said "On guard, sir." After that, he ran across the bridge.

After Donahue departed Blunt signaled a halt to the ceremony as he ran up to the lieutenant. He whispered in the colonel's ear.

"Sir, I just got word from the IG team," he said to the colonel.

"What happened?"

"One of the inspectors was wondering if you could provide him with transportation back to Casey. He decided not to inspect the battalion."

"Why not?"

"Because he determined that it wouldn't be necessary. He gave the entire battalion a no faults noted rating in both Fire and Safety. He's decided that an inspection isn't necessary."

"This isn't another one of your jokes is it?"

"No, sir, he's standing over there. You can ask him yourself. He saw

Taquard standing here and decided that he didn't need to do another inspection. He was certain that he wouldn't find any mistakes."

"Okay, I'll double-check this one out myself. Meanwhile, alert the Sergeant Major. My driver can take him back."

Taquard loaded the howitzer and fired it.

"On guard, sir," he said loudly.

He ran across the bridge departing the best unit that anyone could ever be a part of. It was an unforgettable experience that was second to none. It was the type of unit that you couldn't wait to get away from but didn't want to leave.

As Taquard was crossing the bridge he realized that although the Bitcheyes were never established as an institution, it didn't matter. After all, the Bitcheye concept steamed from individuality. And while it was never recognized on a large scale, it still had merit. It was never about the recognition or the publicity. It wasn't limited to a select few though very few would be worthy of the distinction. It meant holding the moral ground when no one else was looking. It consisted of standing against the majority when the majority was wrong. It meant keeping a promise even though you weren't forced to. It was a gift that an individual would give to himself though few would ever want to. Bitcheye Commando was a forgotten concept worth remembering. The inspiration came from elsewhere, but Taquard decided to pursue it for the simple reason that it would keep him on the right track when compromise was considered the logical choice.

# Epilogue

May 2003, a dead captain was found with a suicide note. It was a tragic case but not all together unexpected. No one seemed surprised. The Military Police (MP) assessed the crime scene and confirmed the cause of death to be suicide. They picked up the note and provided a preliminary report to the colonel who was on the scene. Then they cleaned up the scene with a vacuum cleaner and other cleaning supplies. Normally, black and white photographs would be taken at the scene but in this case none were taken. An investigation would normally follow, but in this case it didn't. The Judge Advocate General (JAG) confirmed that the soldier committed suicide. What would normally take weeks with the support of a formal Serious Incident Report (SIR) only took a few minutes and was founded on telephonic information provided by the colonel at the scene. There was very little written documentation. It was an open and shut case Army style. The case was closed within an hour. The ambulance arrived and picked up the body.

"I've never been ordered to do that before," the ambulance driver said to the paramedic.

"Do you ever remember ever being told to take a body from the scene directly to a crematorium?"

"No, but that's what the colonel told us to do."

"Have you taken the Master Paramedic Course?"

"No not yet I haven't. Why do you ask?"

"Because we were taught that when we are ordered to take a body to any place other than the hospital that we are to take the body to a civilian hospital or in the case where the subject happens to already be dead, a civilian authority such as the county coroner."

"Maybe we should call it in."

"No, we are not to call it in. Whenever we are told to do something that is obviously out of the ordinary we are to take the subject to a civilian authority without calling it in. And since when do colonels get directly involved with suicides? I mean to be on site and all. This is a textbook case scenario and I smell a rat."

Before the body could be cremated it was delivered to the hospital and subsequently delivered to the county coroner's office in an unmarked vehicle. The coroner and his assistant were able to receive the body and began examining it without delay. During the preliminary overview examination the coroner found a note hidden on the subject's body. It was obviously much more than just a simple note.

lsu bmu qnv wud nvg aei ueu igu dhq nfe vfu egv qhs lqh vbq nux dht ttu lix vaq vlq eug ubi vaw lgv abq vjg vbu xwl xvs uel pht thv biv ttl ew

666 420 200

768 773 776

832 075 375

MX The Gold Bug

Play the lottery. 9 15 22 35 37.18

"This man knew his assailant," the coroner said to his assistant.

"Looks like an encrypted message or something."

"This wasn't suicide."

"What about the suicide note?"

"It was planted. Notice how fast the Army came up with the suicide conclusion. They take forever just to do a simple fender bender report. Most accidents in the Army are intentional, I'd say at least three quarters of them. And that's a conservative estimate. Likewise, most suicides in the Army aren't suicides at all. And I don't have to mention that all of the documents that normally accompany a body have either obviously been fabricated or are conveniently missing."

"Yeah, this does seem kind of odd. I mean, that was fast. They're never that fast, ever. Everything was just perfect. Nothing is ever that perfect, ever."

"Another thing that we are forgetting is the fact that suicides should initially be investigated as homicides. After that it may be determined that a suicide actually took place."

"Yes, you're right, and an investigation would've taken some time. A lot more time than this. This report is only two paragraphs long, it's barely over half a page. If there's one thing I know about reports, they're never short. Usually they are several pages long and are accompanied by several files. Nothing's that perfect or that short. But how do we find out who killed him? The note's in code."

"All we have to do is break the code."

"How do we break it?"

"The note tells us how to break the code. He provided us with a reference. His style is obvious and tells us where to go."

"Yeah, but what does it mean? What is the reference?"

"Bitcheye Commando."

"Bitch.... What?"

"Bitcheye Commando."

"What's that?"

"Some group of Army ROTC cadets that never amounted to anything. They called themselves called Bitcheye Commandos."

"That's a funny name."

"Yes it is. No one really knows exactly where it came from."

"So how does that help us to break the code?"

"All we need to do is find a Bitcheye Commando handbook."

"They have a handbook?"

"Had, yes, I remember seeing one a long time ago in a secondhand bookstore. The cadets self published an inferior grade handbook for themselves. I guess they had a few left over or somebody didn't want theirs."

"Did you buy it?"

"No, but the title caught my eye. I remember glancing at it and wondering what it was about. It was only a buck but I decided not to waste my money. I remember flipping through the pages though. It looked kinda interesting."

"What was it about?"

"Military skills, survival techniques, wilderness survival, semaphore, map reading skills, knot tying, a lot of nice to know stuff. And there was a code sheet in it as well. This was a specific code that was produced by the Bitcheye Commandos for their exclusive use only. I guess they tried to establish themselves as a formal group but didn't succeed."

"So this guy was a Bitcheye?"

"No, they disbanded a long time before any of them ever went into the Army. They disbanded even before the handbook was even written. It said so on the inside cover. Not all of the cadets in the unit were in favor of the Bitcheye Commandos in the first place. Those that were interested lost interest and the group died off."

"Maybe he was a Bitcheye before they dissolved."

"No, former Bitcheyes would be a lot older."

"Then how did he get the code?"

"Easy, he got a copy of the handbook and decided to use it."

"I guess the Bitcheyes didn't die after all."

Printed in the United States
148150LV00002B/157/P